# AMOS JACKMAN

AMOS JACKMAN *by Daniel Doan*

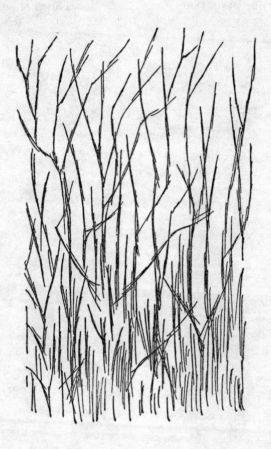

BEACON PRESS  *Beacon Hill*  Boston

*To*
*E. E. D.*

# PART I

*Chapter 1*

It was an eastern-facing farm. Amos Jackman stood in the door of the barn while the sun came over the ridge between Quartz Mountain and the long hump of Cobblestone. The mountains lay on the eastern horizon with the mists of dawn still upon the budding forest which covered their slopes. It was a wide view, and lonely. No house or plume of smoke appeared. There were only the fading shadows of the valley and the mountains. The farm was at the end of the road.

Carrying the milk pail, Amos walked to the house and paused by the granite doorstep. The sun was up and the warm rays came through the cool air of the May dawn. He felt reluctant to go inside, but he was hungry. After breakfast he would start for his camp back in the woods. He had done his share on the farm for a time. Now he wanted to return to the woods.

He pushed open the door into the kitchen. There was a spicy odor of frying doughnuts mixed with woodsmoke and closed-in winterness. His grandmother, small and quick, stood by the stove tending the doughnuts. A lamp burned in a bracket on the wall. Amos took the pail to the pantry and strained the milk into setting pans. Back in the kitchen, he filled a basin with hot water from the teakettle and added cold water from the barrel by the sink where a lead pipe trickled steadily. He washed his hands.

His grandmother looked up from the stove. "Going to be a good day?"

"Well, probably, for a while. Cloud up later, I guess."

Enclosed by the four walls, he felt a disturbing pressure about him. He wiped his hands on the roller towel by the sink and stared out the window at the mountains. He heard his father come in the back door. His older sister was moving about upstairs. Across the field, he saw Mort walking slowly from the little cemetery down the road. Whicher came in with an armful of wood from the shed. The family was ready for breakfast. Amos sat down in his place at the big table in the middle of the room. His grandmother put a plate of doughnuts on the table and returned to the skillet of frying eggs. His father sat down. Rose came in from the hall and began helping her grandmother at the stove. Amos took the platter of fried eggs which his father handed across the table to him.

His father asked, "Where's Mort?"

"Coming. I see him crossing the field just now."

His father grunted. A thin little man, with a gray moustache, he ate without enthusiasm.

Mort opened the door slowly and said in his deep voice, "Good morning." He moved with deliberation and formality as he sat down. Before he served himself, he bowed his head for a moment.

"Godfrey," Whicher said, "I could eat a horse."

Mort looked at him in disapproval but with a gentle smile on his face.

Amos ate hurriedly, for he could still feel the spell of the spring mountains, and he wanted to be outside. The kitchen was stifling, warm and close. He finished before his sister and grandmother sat down.

"I'm going out to the camp," he said.

Whicher cried, "Can I go? Let me go, Amos. I want to go trouting, too."

"No, and I ain't going trouting. I got some work to do on the camp." He felt he had to justify his escape with work, although he knew he'd catch trout before the day was over.

Whicher understood, too, and made a face. "Yah, that's an excuse."

His father put down his coffee cup. "Amos, you get the barn door fixed?"

"It's better than before the storm." Amos stood up. "I'll be back in a day or two."

While the others were still eating, he went down cellar. In the damp shadows, he picked out a few potatoes from the bin and dropped them in a burlap bag. He came back up the stairs. His grandmother held out a paper bag which he slid into the sack.

She said, "There's a slab of pork and doughnuts and bread."

"Well, I got some stuff in the camp from last winter when I was trapping." He added, "Thanks, Gram."

He took his denim jacket from a hook on the wall and went out the door.

The sun was well above the ridge now. His eyes roved over the varied greens of the budded trees. Here and there in the valley he noticed the pink of wild apple blossoms and the dark red of swamp maple flowers against the green. He felt free of the winter at last as he crossed the lower field and entered the woods. For a time he walked rapidly through the spruces along a little stream, but gradually the need to hurry left him and he paused by a shallow pool, no wider than a deer could leap, and

watched the running water. It was clear and fluid and almost alive—
different from the ice of the past months, different from the roily freshet
of early spring. He saw a school of fingerling trout poised in the current
above a little sand bar. The leaves of the trees, small as squirrels' ears,
were pale green over the water. They cast lazy shadows on the stones of
the brook bed. Grass and fiddlehead ferns had started growing along
the bank, and little flowers rose from the moss. A shadbush dropped petals like snow into the water. Singing birds were everywhere. He moved
slowly on.

Leaving the brook he climbed a low ridge and came out in a slash
where he had cut pulpwood the previous summer. The ridge slanted
northward into the valley. He could look back toward the farm. The
buildings, small now, appeared almost crouching in their fields while
the woods pressed in all around. To the west lay the ridge dividing the
valley from the rolling country and small hills—the tops of them visible—
which stretched to the river and the fertile river farms. Northward, along
Carr Brook, he could see the old pastures and fields grown up to hardhack and young pines and poplars. The roof of the Lovejoy place sagged
toward its broken chimney. In the bowl of the valley, the old schoolhouse
was deserted. Further along Carr Brook where the ledges of Quartz
Mountain formed an eastern wall, he could locate the shrunken clearing
around the Grimes place and could imagine the brook plunging over
the ruins of the milldam behind it.

At first he thought there was no sign of life at all, but watching steadily, he saw a wisp of smoke begin to rise from the chimney of the elaborate
log "camp" above the Derby Fields. He paused, curious because the
Tarltons usually never came up from the city until late June, and left
late in the fall. The big house had been built in the shelter of a ledge
just off the Ridge Road. He could almost see the tan walls of peeled
spruce where the sun shone through the surrounding trees.

The Tarltons lived in a different world and he knew them only as
visitors to Whichertown. Gregory Tarlton, stout, with the face of a
hawk grown fleshy, came in the fall to hunt. The year before, Amos had
taken him to a deer run on Quartz Mountain, and circling up the slope
of the mountain, had driven a deer past him. Gregory Tarlton had shot
the deer accurately in the neck with his imported rifle. Amos remembered
the return to the house, dragging the deer. There were expensive cars in
the yard and men and women gathering around while he stood silently
at one side. Tarlton had given him a five dollar bill for the day's hunt.

He turned eastward toward the mountains, passing through the last
of the old farm land, where at intervals lay cellar holes like abandoned

tombs in the floor of the young forest. He angled into the sun until he reached the logging road above the Grimes place. Pushing through the bushes on the opposite side, he came out on the open ledge above the ravine on Carr Brook. He dropped his bag of food and sat down in the sun to look at the foaming water.

On the far side of the ravine a bird was building a nest beneath an overhang of rock. He watched it as it darted out from the rock to the woods and back with a twist of moss in its bill, while its mate perched on a twig and called plaintively and twitched its tail, or fluttered into the air after insects.

He became aware of motion down the brook. A boy was fishing in the pool at the bottom of the gorge. Amos sat without moving and watched the awkward casts of the boy and his unsuccessful attempts to hook a trout which kept rising to the bait. And then the figure turned and he saw that it was a girl, dressed in boots and an old fishing jacket too large for her.

He watched her as she climbed over the rocks toward him and tossed the baited hook into the rock channel above the pool. In the swift water, the line tightened and bore up through the current; the girl yanked and a trout came clear of the water. Amos saw it was a good one. The trout fell from the hook back into the water. A look of anguished disappointment passed over the face of the girl. She clumsily reached for the hook and fumbled with the bait box at her belt. Amos could almost feel her dislike of touching the worms, and saw that she hesitated as she baited the hook, taking her hands from the worm once it was impaled and then forcing herself to thread it on further.

She did not notice him sitting quietly in the sunlight beside the spruce tree, but cast again into the water. Again the line drew tight. This time the girl raised the rod with a sweeping motion that pulled the trout clear of the current and landed it on the ledge in front of Amos. Dropping her rod, the girl scrambled up the rocks and knelt by the fish. It flopped on the narrow ledge, each thrust of its tail pushing it nearer the water.

Amos wondered why the girl didn't snatch it up and break its neck. She seemed afraid to touch it, and he could almost feel the effort with which she made herself reach out and grasp the struggling fish, while her mouth turned downward. Then she dropped it and he thought he saw tears in her eyes.

Without realizing what he was doing, he leaped forward and grabbed the fish, while the girl gave a startled gasp and backed away. He put

[ 4 ]

his thumb in the trout's mouth and pressed back, breaking the neck. The girl looked abruptly away and then toward him as he unhooked the fish and held it out to her. The spotted sides and the orange red of the fins and belly were water-bright.

"Where'd you come from?" she asked, and he remembered her. Remembered her coming out of the lodge last fall as her father paid him, standing on the big porch to look at the deer they'd hung outside. Remembered her a few summers back, skinny then and hair in pigtails, driving a beach wagon along the rough road to the farm, not knowing it ended there, lost and turning around in the dooryard.

She repeated, "Where'd you come from?"

He motioned over his shoulder toward the farm.

She took the fish gingerly by the gills and put it in the fish basket slung over her shoulder. "Thanks. You must be one of the Jackmans."

"That's right. I'm Amos."

"You took Dad hunting last fall."

He nodded. "Well," he said, "I'll be going along."

He felt more ill at ease than he could ever remember, as though it wasn't right to be alone in the woods with the girl. And yet he hesitated, while she said, "You couldn't stay till I catch another and show me how to take it off? I want to learn and Dad was going to take me, but he had to stay home and I made up my mind to go alone, it's such a lovely day."

"All right."

She tried to smile. "I don't like to touch them, but I'm going to learn." She was starting to bait the hook.

"Here," he said, "like this . . . I mean if you want me to show you."

"Yes, go ahead."

Unable to explain just what he meant, Amos took the hook and she dropped the worm in his hand. He slid the hook through the worm and again twice, finally burying the point.

"Doesn't that bother you? I hate to hurt them."

"Doubt if they feel much. Throw out in there." He pointed to a long riffle above the falls.

She cast out with an awkward overhand motion and the bait dropped short of the riffle. He wanted to take the rod from her; it seemed so simple to him and she was so clumsy. He wondered why she wanted to learn to catch trout. It didn't seem like anything a girl needed to know. His sister had never been interested in fishing.

She held out the rod. "You try."

He took the rod and let out a little more line from the reel. He swung the worm out toward the riffle and lowered the tip of the rod to drop the worm gently in the froth at the head of the riffle. The bait disappeared and the line settled a moment before it started to run out. He pulled back and as the trout swung clear of the water he brought it flopping through the air and clutched it against his shirt.

"Not much to it," he said as he held out the fish to her.

"You make it look easy. Please keep the fish."

"Take it. I'll get more."

"You going fishing?"

"Not right off," he answered shortly.

He felt that she had invaded his privacy. She didn't need to know where he was going or what he was doing—her an outsider. He gave the rod back, and bent to pick up his sack. Not knowing quite how to leave, he paused while she began to bait the hook again. By her concentration, he realized how much she wanted to do it right, yet he couldn't understand why it was so important. Curious, he waited.

This time when she caught the fish, she brought it in as he had done and held it for a moment against her jacket, before her face twisted and she took her hand away. The trout flopped off the hook to the ledge. She knelt and reached for it. Pressing it with both hands, her lips tight, she tried to break its neck, almost succeeded, and then dropped it. She stared down at the quivering tail.

"Damn it, I'm going to!"

She held the fish on the rock and bent its head back until the spine snapped. She got to her feet. Amos saw that her face was pale, but she tried to smile.

"That's the way, isn't it? I mean, I did it messy, but I'll be better at it the next time."

Amos nodded. "Still and all, you don't look as though you enjoyed it."

"No, but I'm going to get used to it." The color was coming back in her face. "I've got to stay here all summer. We're going to live here and I've got to learn different things. I won't sit at home every day." She looked at him quickly and then at the brook before she went on. "I used to read about the woods and about the old days of Indians and all. Did you ever read *Leatherstocking Tales*?"

"No."

"They're wonderful. And stories about the West and the covered wagons and the scouts hunting buffalo. All the roughness bothered me, but that's silly and I'm going to make myself live like them and stop reading about it."

"Well, I guess Whichertown ain't like the books."

Her eyes were bright. "No, but you could have gotten along in the old days, couldn't you?"

"The hunting and fishing part, probably."

"That's what I mean. But I'm so helpless. I could sit in the house and read novels and eat chocolates, but I'll be damned if I will! I'm going to be different, learn to be different."

Something about her fervor bothered him. It wasn't so acutely important: the woods and mountains were here and you lived in them and it wasn't difficult, or mixed up with books or the way other people lived. Yet she seemed so earnest about it that he told her, "I guess you'll get along all right."

As an afterthought that didn't fit in, he added, "Your pa hunts and fishes, don't he?"

"Yes, but that's different. He doesn't do it except with the right equipment and in a certain way—like—like other men play golf." She frowned a little. "He doesn't belong here. He's a city man going fishing and hunting. See?"

"Well, kind of." He lifted his sack to his shoulder. "I guess you'll be all right now."

She looked at the sack. "How can you go fishing if you don't have a rod?"

It wasn't any of her business, but somehow he couldn't tell her so or just go off and leave her. He said, "I got one up at the camp."

"You have a cabin off in the woods?"

"Well, a shack, sort of. Built it out of logs and old boards from a lumber camp." He felt that he was getting involved and he said, "Got some work to do there after the winter."

Abruptly he turned and strode off through the woods, in a direction away from the camp. Not that he cared if anyone knew where it was. His brothers knew, and Pa, but he didn't want everyone to know about it for it was almost secret, and personal, and he didn't want the Tarltons coming in there or finding the good pools above the pond. He walked fast and after a time, circled back until he was heading into the mountains again.

[ 7 ]

## Chapter 2

Climbing steadily up the valley of the brook, along the old logging road, Amos came to the wide swamp beyond the first steep ridge. The old road vanished here in a thicket of young spruce and he turned north through the woods to avoid the open bog.

There were no signs now of men, and the forest surrounded him. A thick tangle of bushes grew shoulder high and above them rose the big trees, yellow and white birches, maples, basswoods, and a scattering of pine and spruce. He moved slowly along the way he had always taken. Although there was no trail, he noticed here and there a tree or rock that he had passed before and the conformation of the land fitted into the pattern in his mind.

He was not lonely. Instead, he felt a slow timelessness surround him, until he was free of the necessities of ordinary life. There were no chores to be done at a certain time, no particular hours to waken or sleep or eat. Even the seasons held no urgency: spring did not mean fence mending, plowing or planting. The forest grew and blossomed now. Summer would come and fall and winter, but the future was dim and without requirements.

When he wanted to stop and watch a squirrel, or a bird, or study the tracks of a deer, he paused with unhurried patience.

He was climbing another ridge and returning to the brook. The slope became gradual. When he reached the stream again, it did not pour down over the rocks as it had, but flowed swiftly in deep reaches between its banks, dropping at intervals over short rapids. The rocks were dark and the water appeared black. Moss clung to the rocks above the water.

He followed the brook until he could see the glint of sunlight on the pond ahead. Moving slower, he passed among the tree trunks until he saw the cove at the outlet, with its jammed logs and rocks. Beyond in the open water, two black ducks swam in little zigzags, turning their heads to look toward Amos. Then they took wing, seeming to spring into flight straight up, quacking in alarm as he stepped out in the open. Wishing he had a shotgun, he watched them bank at the end of the pond and circle north against the spruces on the eastern slopes of Quartz Mountain. Although he thought they'd make good eating, he found something pleasing about the way they flew. He wondered if the girl who wanted to learn about fishing and the woods might have taken pleasure from their flight also.

He walked on around the pond.

At the far end, the inlet brook tumbled over a ledge into a cove. He climbed up the little path which he had made getting water, and saw the cabin.

He paused on the edge of the small clearing in the spruces to look at the door and the windows and the log walls. The door was still closed and held with a wooden pin. The glass remained unbroken in the two front windows. A piece of tar paper had been blown from the roof. Otherwise the camp hadn't changed since he left it in February. He remembered putting on his snowshoes and shouldering the pack with the blanket and the skins he'd trapped—a bobcat, two mink, and four foxes. The bobcat had been worth twenty dollars in bounty as well as what he got for the fur. All in three weeks' trapping.

The cabin then had looked as though the snow would never melt, for it reached to the eaves. Now there was grass by the door where the big drift had been and flowers under the trees and birds flitting among the spruces.

He went on and opened the door and dropped his sack in one corner. The floor was covered with chips and splinters from the woodpile by the stove, shredded cloth and torn paper from a mouse nest in a box under the table. Over it all was a sprinkling of balsam needles, dry brown, from the bunks. He looked at the toothmarks and droppings of a porcupine on the doorsill. He looked around the wall. The canned goods still rested on the shelf. The flour and sugar in cans would be safe. A bag of beans had been gnawed through and spread over the table. He moved to the table and picked up a jar of matches and set it beside an old coffee can that held candles.

He began picking up the refuse from the floor and used it to start a fire in the cook stove. The camp felt more like home when the fire crackled in the stove. He opened a can of beans and emptied it into a blackened frying pan which he took from a nail on the wall. He added wood to the stove and sat down on a log stool at the table.

While the beans heated, he sat and looked out the door. Then remembering the coffee, he took a pail and went to the brook. Returning, he filled the coffee pot and measured out coffee and set it to brew on the stove. He sat down on the bench again and looked out at the pond and the woods, found his pipe and lighted it while time passed and he hardly noticed.

When his meal was hot, he took the frying pan from the stove and set it on the table with the pot of coffee. He ate the beans from the pan, and drank his coffee from a mug to which he added a scant spoonful of sugar. The coffee smelled good and the beans filled his stomach and he was contented.

Idly, he thought of the girl and tried to picture her here in the cabin. She seemed so out of place that he could scarcely imagine the old fishing jacket and the boots and the anxious face with its high cheekbones and soft but angular jawline. She didn't belong at all.

He took his jointed steel fishing rod from the rafters and looked over the line on the reel, and the hook. He had more hooks in a tobacco can on the shelf. Going outside, he dug around in the moist earth behind the camp with a pointed stick until he found a few worms, which he put in the can with the hooks.

He began to fish at the inlet of the pond and followed the brook back into the woods where it ran deep and narrow in pools between the spruces. He walked slowly along the bank, trying not to shake the ground, but now and then a trout would dart away across a pool and he would have to go on to the next turn of the stream. He caught five before he had used up the worms, and two more on a belly fin which he cut from one of the trout on his string.

They seemed enough, but he fished on until he had caught four more. Then because he had worn the edge from his urge to fish, and he realized there were plenty more he could catch any time and the summer was long, he squatted by a pool and watched the water spiders skating across the dark surface. Under the shadowy spruces, the sun struck the water only in irregular splashes. He wondered why a trout never took the water spiders. Must be they stunk bad or tasted bad. A woodpecker was digging a hole in a stub over his head. He watched the bird until his neck ached. Getting to his feet he started back toward camp.

He left the brook and pushed slowly through the spruces on a little knoll and into a swamp where deer had yarded the winter before. He picked up an antler that had been half chewed up by porcupines. The brook made a wide curve which he cut across and came to the camp from the woods side. A red squirrel popped out of a hole under the eaves with a piece of doughnut in its mouth, and skittered over the roof and jumped into a tree. Amos tossed a chunk of wood at him.

The afternoon was well along and the sun shone across the pond into the little clearing. Birches and spruce were reflected in the still water. Amos sat down on the chopping block to light his pipe. He looked at the torn roofing paper on the cabin. He had part of a roll under the bunk and he could patch it. The sky was streaked with clouds and the wind came from the east. He took his trout down to the brook and began cleaning them with his jackknife. There was something different about the camp and the farm; that torn roofing would have bothered him at home. He'd have felt he ought to fix it. Of course probably Pa would have told him to fix it, right off after the storm. But still, he thought he'd fix it himself if he didn't have the old man prodding him. That was the difference between here and the farm. Like the guts of the trout—he could toss them over on the bank and forget them. A mink or some other critter would come along and eat them. He wiped the knife on a patch of moss and went back to the shack for a tin plate to hold the trout.

When he had finished with the fish, he noticed a dead spruce that had fallen beyond the brook. With the axe he cut it loose from its stump and limbed out the trunk which he dragged to the sawbuck at the cabin. A few black flies had come out in the sun that warmed the clearing. He was used to them and they didn't bother him as he sawed the spruce into stove lengths and split it on the chopping block. He sweat a little and when he finished his work, found that the air was chilly. He went inside and built up the fire and cooked the trout with salt pork slabs and some potatoes.

He ate his food and drank coffee and then smoked in the doorway until the sun went down, and twilight came. The air was cold. He went to the bunk and took off his shoes. Rolling up in the quilts on the bunk, he listened to the mice that started running across the floor as soon as he was quiet. The fire gleamed through a crack in the stove, making a flickering red light on the wall. He fell asleep.

He awoke in complete darkness. Even the windows were dark. He felt cold, with the quilt partly thrown off, restless and thinking of the girl, with half-awake surprise that he should be thinking of her that way, for wanting girls had never bothered him much. He got up and went to the door where the cold east wind struck him and he stood for a time looking out at the night. Then he went back to the bunk and pulled up the quilt and fell asleep.

## Chapter 3

The rain had not started when he awoke in the morning, but he could feel it in the air as he opened his eyes and looked out the windows at the gray sky beyond the spruce tops. There was a damp cold in the cabin. He didn't get up right off. Lying in the bunk, he considered the hole in the roofing paper. It was over the corner where the wood was piled and rain wouldn't do any harm. He began to think about fishing.

Sometimes on a rise of the brook, he could catch trout down in the bog below the pond, whereas ordinarily the open pools, almost without current in the wide meadows, were impossible to fish without scaring the trout. In clear weather the quaking bog disturbed the water and a line fell with a splash in the still reaches, no matter how easy you sneaked up or threw out. But in the rain. . . .

Scratching his stubble beard as he rested on one elbow, he tried to calculate when the rain would come. Maybe an hour, maybe a little longer—say the middle of the morning. He guessed now it was an hour or so after daylight.

On his feet, he padded to the door and opened it. Then he started a fire in the stove, and put on his shoes. He ate doughnuts and fried pork and two trout he saved from the night before, and drank coffee. Afterward, he split some kindling and stove wood and chopped himself a little flattened shovel to dig up worms in the soft earth behind the camp.

When he was ready to start, he put on his denim jacket and an old felt hat. A light drizzle had begun to fall. It changed to a steady rain as he reached the end of the pond. He saw it splashing on the surface of the water. In the thick woods below, he didn't notice it so much although the bushes were soon wet and his pants wet and then his boots. He stopped for a time when he reached the lower bog, under a thick pine, and lighted his pipe. He could watch the brook at his feet and the pine boughs kept off most of the rain.

After his second pipe, he noticed that the water of the brook had risen a trifle and was cloudy dark. He started out into the bog. Making his way through the alders, he pushed on into the shoulder-high bushes that grew among the hummocks. There were pitcher plants growing from the wet sphagnum moss about his feet. Overhead, a flock of cedar birds flew into the shelter of spruces beyond the bog and a red-winged blackbird swung on an alder branch. He was walking across the quaking bog itself, the half-floating mass of roots and vegetation bordering the channel of the brook. He moved slowly between the openings that went down into the muck. Although he stepped gently, the whole surface of the bog moved up and down.

He reached the edge of the channel, as near the water as he dared go, and for a time stood there while the rain soaked his shoulders and dripped from his hat. The rain dappled the surface of the brook. He baited the hook and tossed out his line, playing it so the drift of the slow current would carry it down beyond him. He didn't expect to catch many fish, but he knew there were some good ones in the channel. Maybe he'd get two or three. He lost track of the time he waited, for he wasn't thinking or worrying about the rain, just fishing with the patience of a heron hunched on the shore.

When the line began to move, he didn't jerk it right away. He let it out and let it out and then pulled back hard while the trout dove for the bottom and darted up and down the brook. He shortened the line and at last hoisted out the fish and grabbed it. The trout was big, maybe eleven or twelve inches long. He stopped a minute to look at it before he dropped it in his canvas bag, slung over one shoulder.

He was about to rebait and cast again, when he saw the girl. She pushed through the edge of the woods downstream and stopped to look out across the bog. He was surprised and yet he wasn't. She had been somewhere in the back of his thoughts. He watched her step out into the bog, as though she planned to fish the first bend of the channel. She carried her rod and had the fish basket on a strap over her shoulder. She wore the same old jacket and hat. He thought that it wasn't much of a place for a girl to go fishing, not unless she knew about the bog.

He raised his hand and called out, "Watch your step!"

She looked up quickly and then waved to him, shouting back, "I will!"

He saw her move nearer the brook, where the footing was most treacherous. For a moment she wavered on a hummock before she jumped awkwardly and went out of sight.

It was a long way across to her and he had to go around an arm of the brook. He couldn't run in the bog. With great steps, he lunged through the low bushes and waded across the puddles. At last he saw her wallowing shoulder deep in a hole between two hummocks. The

[ 13 ]

fish basket floated near her. She was struggling to pull herself up, like a person who has fallen through the ice. She grasped a bush which broke off in her hand. She saw him but didn't cry out or stop trying to lift herself. She didn't seem panicky. Her hand reached another bush and she pulled and wriggled partway out. She was covered with brown ooze. Amos seized her hands and pulled her out of the hole. She lay for a moment, holding herself tense while he took her shoulders and sat her up. She got to her feet.

"It was these damn boots," she gasped when she caught her breath. "Filled up and weighed a ton. God, look at the muck!"

"Sloppy, all right," he said. "Stinks, don't it?"

"Ugh, yes." She scraped her finger down her thigh and made a face.

He picked up her rod. "You better go down below to the brook and wash it off."

"I'm wet—I suppose I can't get any wetter and I might get cleaner." She took the rod from him and started off. He followed, forgetting his own rod which he dropped where he'd been fishing.

The bog was held back by a ridge of ground from which trees grew: Amos wondered if it might have been a beaver dam in the old days. He showed the girl a pool below the bog.

"I'll build you a fire. Tain't very warm to be swimming."

She went to the pool and sat down on a rock and took off her boots and her jacket, which she washed in the running water. Then she waded out and splashed water on her pants and scrubbed until the muck was gone. She took off her plaid shirt and washed that and came back ashore, her white arms and shoulders looking cold above the rounded silk-covered breasts. She wrung out the shirt and came to the little fire he'd started with spruce twigs and birch bark.

Not looking at her, after the first glance, he added bigger sticks to the fire, and dragged up a fallen green spruce to break the wind. He kicked apart a stump whose shell was still resinous and sound. Farther away he found a tangle of dead spruces. The fire blazed up and the girl stood in the shelter of the spruce and shivered while she held her shirt out to the blaze.

He said, "You better put your shirt back on. It'll warm you some and dry on you if the rain don't come down any harder."

He took the trout from his fish bag and cleaned it at the brook. Cutting a three-forked stick, he pushed the prongs through the split fish and went back to roast it at the fire.

After a time, he asked, "What were you doing way up here?"

"Exploring, I guess. I wanted to see if I could get where nobody'd fished before."

"You came pretty close. Not many folks bother to walk up this far."

"After you pulled me out, I thought maybe we were close to your camp and I could dry out there."

He shook his head. "Mile or so above the bog." He pointed with his thumb over his shoulder. "I'd have taken you there if it wa'n't so far. Besides, you'd get soaked afterwards going back through the woods. No trails beyond this pool."

He was aware now that she had become his responsibility. Having acted almost without thought, he could see it better, now he had time. He realized he'd have to show her how to get home the quickest way. She seemed kind of a nuisance. If she hadn't gone prowling up the brook and wading into the bog and falling in, he could have fished through the rise of water and might have caught half a dozen good trout—well, maybe three anyway.

The fire crackled and hissed in the rain. He pulled out some coals with a stick and arranged the trout away from the intense heat. Squatting on his heels and tending the fish, he said nothing, but sucked on his wet pipe. With a strange uneasiness, he considered the fact of a girl who took to fishing and the woods. She upset all his established attitudes about such things. She had even affected his own life in the woods. He could see that it was different having a girl with him now. Supposing he'd stopped to cook the trout alone. It would have been all right. He wouldn't have had to worry about drying her off with a big fire, or about getting her home. But there she was and he knew he'd be sorry to see her go, if she should take a notion to start back down the brook.

He turned the trout, then looked up at the girl, surprised to see that she had been watching him. There was a look about her eyes that made him stop as he was about to speak. She must have been watching him for some time. She must have been thinking of him as he had been thinking of her. In the cold rain that fell between them, he could not quite understand the vision that came to him of his warm camp and the girl drying herself in front of the stove, and looking at him. It was not something he should think about. In a moment it was gone. The rain continued to fall and the woods, wet and cold, surrounded them. He stood up and held out the trout.

"You hungry?"

"Yes," she said. "Yes, I'm hungry, all right." She came toward him

[ 15 ]

He took out his jackknife and began to cut up the trout on a stone near the fire. The fish was charred and the flesh crumbled from the bones. He wouldn't have minded it, but he thought it was a poor feed to offer a girl. He said apologetically, "It could stand a mite of salt."

"Wait." She picked up her fish basket and took out a waxed paper package. She knelt beside him and spread the paper out. It contained a small sandwich and a hard-boiled egg and a little packet of salt, all of them wet. "Probably tastes of swamp water," she said. "And it looks small and sissy."

"Be all right."

The rain formed in little drops on the waxed paper. She offered him half the sandwich. "Put the trout on the paper. We'll use it for a plate."

He reached for the half sandwich, then noticed his dirty hands and wiped them on his pants.

"That doesn't bother me," she said, sprinkling salt on the trout.

He chewed the sandwich and waited while she divided the trout and the egg. Her hands were small but strong. The nails were longer than he thought sensible and one of them was broken. She ought to trim them; probably she would when she kept breaking them, fishing and all.

They ate from the paper until the last shred was gone and only the ribs and backbone remained.

She reached in her shirt pocket as she saw him loading his pipe. Bringing out a pack of soggy cigarettes, she looked at them, shrugged, and threw them toward the fire. They fell short and he reached for them, opening the package and spreading them in a row on a log near the fire.

"No need to waste them," he said.

"They won't be much good."

"Maybe not." He stood up and dragged more branches on the fire, and squatted down again.

"I feel better," she said. "If I weren't so warm here and almost dry, I'd go out and see if I could catch some fish." She got to her feet and stretched. "I haven't thanked you for pulling me out of the swamp. I'm glad you were there."

"You'd have got out all right, I guess."

"Maybe, but I'd have had to walk home wet and muddy and probably caught pneumonia. I couldn't have started a fire." She showed him a wad of paper matches from her jacket pocket.

"They ain't much good," he said, reaching in his own pocket. He took out a flat tobacco tin that plug slice came in, and opened it to show her the wooden matches. He lit his pipe, watching her over the bowl. "That'll stand quite a ducking."

She smiled at him. "I see I've got a lot to learn."

"You'll learn all right." He tried to think of some way to tell her that he admired her. "You didn't go all to pieces and start for home on a dead run."

"I might have if you hadn't been there." She hesitated. "I was scared, but it makes a difference not being alone. I mean—well, you seemed to belong here in the woods and weren't bothered by the rain and the swamp. I guess that's what I was thinking while you were cooking the trout."

He didn't answer. He knew she'd been thinking more than that and he wondered why, seeing himself as he must look, dirty and stubble-bearded in wet jacket and pants smelling of smoke and the barn and the woods. He had sense enough to realize how he looked, and what he was. No need for anyone to tell him.

In the silence, he reached to the log where the cigarettes steamed in the heat, and taking the driest, offered it to her. He didn't get up. She took it and rolled it between her fingers. It was stained and shredded on the ends. She plucked loose the end tobacco and put the cigarette between her lips. She waited. Waiting for what, he wondered.

Finally she said, "Match, please."

He motioned to the fire.

"You could light it for me," she said.

He felt suddenly overcome by doing things for her and by her intrusion on his day's fishing and by the things he didn't understand between them. He said abruptly, "You ain't helpless."

He saw her eyes widen and flash as though she might hit him or swear at him, but she turned and picked up a twig from the fire. He watched her try again and again to light the cigarette from the twig; it kept going out before she could bring it from the fire.

He reached for a heavier stick, blew on the end to make it glow and held it up to her. She leaned over him and steadied the ember with her hand on his.

"Thanks." She puffed and let go of his hand. "Sorry to bother you. I'll know how, the next time." She sat down and began pulling on her boots. Then she dismantled her rod and slipped into the strap of her fish basket. "I've got to be going."

"You know the way?"

"I'm going to follow the brook."

"That's no good." He came to his feet slowly and with his heavy boots scattered the fire into the pool. "I'll show you the logging road."

## Chapter 4

When he got back to the camp, he was hungry and wet and put out because he'd been unable to catch any more trout, although he found his rod where he'd dropped it in the bog and had fished back toward camp. The brook had risen to a roily brown and the fish wouldn't bite. He had counted on eating trout and now, thanks to the girl, he had none.

He shut the door of the camp and felt, for a moment, alone or almost lonesome. The single room was cold and shadowy. Rain fell steadily on the roof and dripped off the eaves past the windows and trickled into the corner where the roof leaked. While he'd been gone the mice and squirrels had raided the shelves. The chunk of salt pork lay in the middle of the floor with a corner chewed off and paper shredded around it. He picked it up and put it on the table. As he bent over, his wet shirt stretched tight against his back and made him shiver.

He started a fire and put coffee on to boil. Standing with his hands held out over the stove, he let the heat steam the water from his pants and shirt. Gradually the cabin became warmer. He took off his jacket, hanging it on the wall behind the stove. He sat down and stirred his coffee while the heat dried his back.

He remembered one rainy night when he had been building the camp. Trying to sleep under a piece of tar paper on a pile of boughs, he couldn't keep dry. He'd found the paper at an abandoned logging camp far down the brook. It leaked and he soon felt so cold he had to get up and sit by the fire all night, shivering like a hound to keep warm. Yet that hadn't given him the empty feeling he had now. It wasn't being cold and wet and hungry and alone. It was the girl. He made up his mind to it, for that was the only different thing.

Restlessly, he set about cooking a meal. He peeled poatoes and made a hash from pork scraps, and ate it slowly, thinking what he would do. The rain still came down. He wondered if the girl had made it down the logging road all right. Though rough and washed out, the track had been plain enough where he left her in the big hardwoods. But now he remembered that it ended above the Grimes place in a tangle of young poplars and blackberry bushes. He told himself he needn't worry. She would know where she was when she reached the end of the logging road. She could hear the brook.

He thought of her walking down the old road beyond the Grimes place to the four corners in Whichertown, and turning right, up the Ridge Road. Of course she had made it. But the more he thought about her, the more he wished he'd taken her right down to the corners. People could get lost in foolish ways.

It bothered him. She was a plain nuisance. And yet that didn't make sense: on the one hand he was disturbed about her breaking into his fishing and making him feel responsible for her, while on the other hand he wanted to know she was all right—yes, almost wanted to see her now.

He got up and went to the door. There would be light for an hour. He wiped out the frying pan and dumped the coffee grounds in the fire. He laid his rod across the rafters and hung the quilts on a wire out of the way of mice. There was nothing more to do. He went out and shut the door, dropping the wooden pin in the hasp.

Almost his second step into the bushes soaked him through, sudden and cold. Then as he walked, he became used to the wet again and strode along without stopping.

The afternoon was gone as he approached the Grimes place. He had been watching her tracks on the logging road. He'd passed through the thicket where her feet had bent over the new grass, and now he saw her boot marks on the narrow dirt road.

They weren't enough. He had come this far and he wanted to be sure. Cutting across the old fields, with the sagging ridge of the barn on his left against the dark sky, he crossed the brook and climbed up the slope toward the Derby Fields and the Tarlton lodge. The woods were shadowy. He climbed fast until he came to the trail that led over the shoulder of Quartz Mountain. Turning west, he followed the trail more slowly until he reached the open fields and saw lights up the hill. He circled through the young pines in the field and came to the rock at one side of the lodge. The living room lights shone through the glass doors which led to the porch. Inside, Joan Tarlton was talking to her folks. She stood in front of the fireplace. He could see that she had changed to a dress. Nothing suggested the old fishing jacket and the felt hat and the boots covered with bog muck. It wasn't the same shivering girl who had stood before the fire he'd built.

Feeling let down and cheated and alone, he plunged down the hill and made his way back to the farm in the darkness of the deserted roads.

[ 19 ]

*Chapter 5*

Amos was aware in the deeper recesses of his mind that the Jackmans had been in Houghton since the early days when the town was first granted by the crown of England. They had settled in the mountains east of the river, the locality that became known as Whichertown. Probably there had been a reason for settling in the mountains. Whatever it was, nobody now remembered. Amos had never been told why. He knew that the farm had belonged to his family for generations. Although he remembered his grandfather only as a big man who told him stories of the Civil War, he realized that the farm had passed from Gramp to Pa as it had always been handed down. He knew that before Whichertown, the Jackmans had come to New Hampshire from Massachusetts and, still earlier, from England. But thoughts about these things never entered his mind unless Gram started talking about the old days.

Yet he had a feeling he belonged where he lived; the old house was more than home. He felt it that May night as he came up from Carr Brook and walked along the road leading to the farm. Dark clouds hid the eastern mountains, although the rain seemed to be letting up. On a starry night, the outlines of the mountains were clear on the horizon. Now there was only darkness and the sound of the stream on his left rushing down to join Carr Brook. He felt he was coming home and he wondered why he was content to travel with his back to the Tarlton lodge. He had wanted so much to reach it when he left the woods. Now he was glad of the lights ahead from his own place.

He belonged to the farm and to the cabin in the woods, while neither had anything to do with the Tarlton lodge. Sometimes he became tired of the farm, but after he had been away, and especially tonight, he was glad to be returning.

As he approached the lights at the end of the road and turned into the dooryard, his foxhound began to bay from the kennel by the barn. He walked over and scratched the dog's long ears.

"Shut up, Drum, it's just me."

The dog lifted his head and bayed, rattling his chain. The kitchen door opened and Amos' father stood in the lamplight.

"You, Amos?"

"Yeah."

"Still raining?"

"Some, Pa."

He went into the kitchen. His father stood aside and shut the door after him before returning to the rocker by the stove.

Whicher came from his place by the table lamp where he'd been carving a whistle.

"Lemme see the trout, Amos."

"There ain't any trout."

Amos took off his wet jacket and hat and hung them behind the stove.

"Now, Amos," Gram said, "I'd been counting on a mess of trout."

"Well, the brook come up so from the rain, I stopped fishing and hit for home. Trout won't bite for two days."

Gram was sitting across the table from Whicher, braiding a rug. Summer and winter, her hands were busy, wrinkled fingers moving surely with needles and yarn or braided strips of cloth or a rug hook.

"I'd counted on them," she said. "Can't recall a May passing but what one of the men brought home a mess of trout. You eaten, Amos?"

"Yes," he answered. "I'll catch you some trout when the brooks go down, Gram."

Morton turned from the window through which he'd been staring. "Wet night," he said.

Gram smiled teasingly at Rose. "No courting tonight. The boy don't care enough to wade through the mud. Road's bad, ain't it, Amos?"

"Well, it'd be poor wheeling. He could drive a horse."

"Maybe he will," Rose said. Turning back to the sink where she was washing butter, she glanced at her oval face in the mirror. "If he don't drive, he'll walk."

Amos stood in front of the stove loading his pipe. For the third time that day his clothes were drying. He saw his grandmother looking at his feet. She began to scold him.

"Amos Jackman, how many times must I tell you to keep off my floor with your muddy boots? You're worse'n Whicher. Get out now and take them off in the woodshed."

He moved gingerly across the floor, taking big steps. Safe in the woodshed, he sat down on the chopping block. In the darkness, he took off his boots and socks. There was always something to watch out for in a house, although he knew Gram didn't mean much by her tongue. He remembered his feeling as he came up the road and puzzled over the different ways a man could be hauled by different feelings, glad to be home and then annoyed by restrictions on muddy boots in the kitchen.

Barefoot and stepping carefully over the chips and bark, he moved back along the planks toward the crack of light around the door. He walked across the kitchen and put his boots and socks behind the stove. The scrubbed floor felt smooth under his bare feet.

Whicher was blowing into the whistle he had made, without a sound but the hissing air.

"You got the slit wrong," his father told him. "Show him how, Amos."

Amos laid his pipe on the oilcloth of the table, where it tipped over and spilled ashes. Quickly he picked it up and brushed the ashes off, glancing over at Gram.

"I see you," she said.

He grinned at her and scuffed the ashes with his foot. Little things like that, you could put over on Gram for a joke, but not muddy boots. He picked up the stick of willow and began to show Whicher how to carve a whistle.

Rose shaped the pat of butter with her hands, put it in a covered dish and went with it into the pantry. Then she washed her hands at the sink and took off her apron.

"That's done again," she said. "Someday I'm going to the store and buy my butter. I've had about enough of this working for every last little thing."

She walked quickly across the room, the heels of her best shoes tapping, and slammed the door into the hall.

Her father looked up. "What ails her?"

"She's afraid he won't come," Gram answered.

"More'n that."

"Our ways ain't good enough, since she worked down to the village last summer for the Marsleys. She'll fly the coop one of these days."

Warren Jackman sighed. "Sometimes I don't blame her. Ain't much of a life out here, but it suited me when I had my strength. Suited Ma, too."

Mort looked up when his father spoke of his mother. Amos watched them both. No telling about Mort, but his deep-set eyes shifted back to the window near his chair, and his hands twisted in his lap and then were still.

Amos said to his father, "You got your strength still, what you talking about?"

"Well, it's different. Lost my courage some."

And it did seem so, Amos thought. Of course Pa was small and light, but he could work along with anyone and he could lay out work for his boys. Alone though, he didn't seem to be able to do much, as if he needed help and the knowledge that he didn't have to do it all alone. He could talk about work which ought to be done, like the new sills for the barn, or seasonal things like getting out the manure on the land. Amos knew that mention of this work was almost an order and he'd start; then Pa would join in. But he remembered when it was different, when Pa used to set out at daylight for the woodlot or have the team harnessed before dawn to yard out the logs cut every winter on the side of Cobblestone Mountain. Maybe he was getting old. He'd worked hard all his life. And yet he'd begun to change after their mother's death.

Pa and Mort were both changed in their different ways by the accident. Mort felt he was responsible for it because he'd been working on the front end of the Ford before the wishbone broke and sent him and Ma over the ledges on Carr Brook.

Amos thought of his mother. She had been a little taller than Pa and very straight in the back. She walked straight. Her prominently boned face was stern under the tight-drawn hair parted in the middle, her face usually so emotionless but changing at times slowly to a smile and brightening eyes. He realized the farm had been different then, although now he was used to the idea of her death.

He didn't blame Mort. He didn't think it had anything to do with Mort's tinkering on the Ford, and had told him so, but anyone could see it was always at the back of Mort's mind because he made his daily trip down the road to the little cemetery where the Jackmans were buried, along with most of the other Whichertown people.

The cemetery dated back beyond the days Gram talked about, when the fields and pastures reached up the sides of the mountains, when on a winter's day you could count a dozen smokes rising in the still morning air and the school was full of kids, and men plowed the fields which were now forest and pastured cows where Amos had been cutting pulp last summer. Gram remembered when the ridge behind the house was a wheat field. Of course a lot of the people had gone away and many had died. Only the Jackmans were left to keep the forest out of the fields.

In a way he liked the valley as it was now; it was better country for hunting and trapping and fishing. It had become wilder, and nobody bothered a man. Why, it must be something like when the first Jackmans had settled here, after ten or fifteen years—mostly woods, with their clearing the only break in the wilderness until you traveled over the wagon track to the river valley.

Again though, he would be pulled toward the idea of the farm. Sometimes when he had enough of hunting and fishing, he thought he'd like to build up the farm and clear some more fields, really farm it, and enlarge the sugar orchard, raise some beef cattle, maybe some sheep if he could keep the bears and stray dogs away from them. And yet he wasn't sure of himself. His life had been divided between the woods and the farm ever since he could remember. There were times when he wanted nothing more than his shack in the woods, when the baying of his hound along a fox track on the side of Cobblestone would take him from yarding wood in the fall, and he'd leave the team in the barn and grab his shotgun and be gone for several days, following the hunt over the mountain where he'd shoot the fox and hunt again the next morning, sleeping in his shack nights. He'd known men who needed drink and men who needed women, even among the few people that lived between the farm and the village, but their compulsions didn't seem any stronger than his need for the woods.

Amos made the final cut on the whistle and slipped the bark back over the white wood. He handed it to Whicher.

"Try it."

Whicher put it to his lips and blew a blast. A grin crept up his thin face. "It works!"

"Sure it works. You didn't make the cut right."

Amos turned toward the door. The hound was baying again. He heard boots on the old iron scraper set in the granite doorstep. He opened the door. Pete Appledee stood there in the lamplight from the kitchen, his long frame bent down as he unbuckled his rubber overshoes.

"Evening, Amos."

"How are you, Pete?"

"Leg-weary." Pete slipped a flashlight into his coat pocket. "Tough walking for a guy who ain't used to nothing more rugged than pushing a steering wheel all day."

As he kicked off his overshoes and stepped into the kitchen, Pete seemed to bring with him something from the outside world. He drove a bread truck out of Manchester. Amos shut the door and noticed that everyone in the room appeared to wake up. His father smiled, showing his worn teeth. Gram said, "Hello, Pete," and Whicher stood expectantly waiting for the package of chewing gum Pete handed him, while Mort nodded slowly.

Pete took off his coat and hat. His suit coat didn't hide the square bones of his shoulders, and he seemed to stoop a little as though his sandy hair might touch the ceiling. The plain face, that Gram called steady, flushed as he reached in his coat pocket and handed Warren Jackman a newspaper.

"Much obliged, Pete." Pa moved toward the hall door. "Rose is around somewhere." He opened the door and called, "Rose!"

"I'm coming." Her voice was muffled from upstairs.

When she came in there was an expression of shy triumph in her eyes as she looked toward her grandmother.

"Hello, Pete."

Amos thought that nobody'd ever guess those two had gone to school together a few years back before Pete left the little shack over on the Ridge Road where his folks had lived. Rose and Pete might be strangers. But Amos had passed them in Pete's parked car down the road one night last fall when he was coming back from a coon hunt, and he knew you couldn't call them strangers. He sat down at the table and smoked his pipe. The room was silent while Rose busied herself with the coffee pot at the stove. She set out a plate of doughnuts. In her print dress, with her hair twisted up on her head, she looked pretty. Pete's eyes followed her about the room. She poured his coffee.

"Anyone else?"

Her father nodded and moved from his rocker by the stove to the table. She took another cup from the center of the table and filled it. Pete stirred his coffee and drank it slowly, holding the spoon in place in the cup with his thumb.

"I've got me a new job," he said finally.

Rose stopped as she approached the table, and then came on and sat down beside him. "Where?"

"Down to Somerville," he said, and added, "Massachusetts."

"Same kind of work?"

"Yeah. The business here ain't so good. Don't know if they can hold out till times get better, so I've been looking around."

"Well, that's nice, Pete." Rose spoke low.

"Pay's pretty good." Pete was looking at Warren Jackman. "I thought maybe Rose and me'd get married before I swap jobs. I'll have a couple of weeks off."

Rose was on her feet. "You might ask me first, Pete Appledee! What gives you the idea I'd marry you?"

Pete laughed in the silent way he had. "Never was one to beat around the bush. Your pa has the say so, don't he?"

"No!"

Warren Jackman had left the table and was fumbling with things on the shelf behind the stove. He found his cob pipe and began to shave tobacco from a plug with his jackknife. At last he said, "Reckon she's settled that end of it."

Rose, her face bright red, took Pete by the arm. "You come into the parlor with me. The idea! Busting out with something like that before you said a word to me."

Pete got to his feet. "Well, you will, won't you?"

"I don't know. I ain't made up my mind."

Still laughing, Pete let Rose lead him from the room.

The kitchen was silent until Whicher blew on the whistle.

Warren Jackman burst out, "Godfrey mighty, you get outside with that! Go on, git!"

Whicher looked startled. Amos motioned to the door with his eyes. He watched his father slump in the rocker as the door closed behind Whicher. Pa's cob pipe had gone out and he stared at the stove before he spoke.

"Seems kind of sudden."

Gram moved irritably in her chair. "Sudden nothing, Warren. What you think they been working up to the last six months? You got eyes. He's been gone on her since they was kids." She stood up. "I'm going to make myself a cup of tea. I think it's real nice. He's a good boy."

"Probably you're right. I just ain't got used to the idea yet." Pa's eyes strayed toward the hall door. "Won't be the same with her gone. Maybe Pete would stay and help work the place."

Gram sniffed. "Even if he was inclined to it, Rose wouldn't let him. She's bound to get away from the farm. Likely she stirred Pete into bettering himself. Besides, you was saying not an hour ago you don't blame her yourself."

"I know. If I had a trade, I might give up the place myself. But then again, I'd hate to see the old farm go back to woods. I don't know."

Amos said nothing, yet he thought he knew what little chance his father would have at a job, even if he had a trade, with the depression keeping men out of work so's the papers and valley men's talk were full of it. He didn't see a paper more than once a week, and read one less often than that, but sometimes he heard talk down to the store or at the creamery. He'd never been farther away than Fallsburg and he had no urge to go, but he thought he knew better than his father about the chances of a man from Whichertown. And yet Pete had made it, and all those people who once lived here—those that hadn't died. He wondered why they had wanted to leave.

His father said again, "Well, it won't be the same here."

Gram put down her cup. "Far's the work goes, I'm the one to complain. I'll have to do for all of you alone."

"The boys will have to help."

Through all the talk, Amos realized, Mort hadn't said a word. Now he spoke. "I can wash the floor, Gram."

"Sure you can, Mort. We'll get along."

As though asking himself, Mort said, "They'll be happy, won't they? Away off there?"

"I believe they will," Gram told him.

"It might help if I spoke to Him about them."

" 'Twouldn't hurt."

"Then I will."

Mort got up and went outside.

They didn't talk. Whicher came back in, hesitating at the door and then, as his father took no notice of him, returned to the chair at the table opposite Amos. Mort passed through the room, took up a lamp and, with a quiet "Good night," went into the hall. The light in the kitchen was dim. Amos got to his feet and turned up the lamp.

Thinking about Rose, he felt that she had always been destined to go away. She didn't belong on the farm. She had always found opportunities to go into the village, or to Fallsburg where she could look at the stores and people. She liked people and parties and dances. She had joined the Grange. She had been smart in school and, if there'd been any money, she might have gone to the University. She was clever with her hands, sewing and fixing dresses which always looked pretty on her.

Well, this was the natural end of it and Pete was just right for her. He wouldn't feel ashamed about her coming from Whichertown when they lived downcountry. Probably he'd get ahead and make money and Rose could have things she always wanted, and raise nice kids.

Yet, somehow, Amos couldn't quite picture Rose married and sleeping with a man. She had been his older sister, grown up before him when they were in their teens, but he never thought much about her marrying. Of course she needed a man and would be a good wife but he couldn't quite adjust himself to the idea, in spite of the parked car last fall and the other times there must have been since then. It was an idea to get used to slowly.

He went outside to look at the sky. The rain had stopped and the earth was fresh, smelling of woods and grass and wet ferns. The air was cool. A wind blowing high up seemed to be breaking the clouds in the west where the sky was not so dark. Clear tomorrow and now it was time to go to bed.

He went back toward the house, his bare feet cold and wet against the ground. He stopped at the outhouse off the woodshed before he went on into the kitchen. His father sat by the stove, but his grandmother and Whicher had gone to their rooms. He washed at the sink and drank water from the dipper. His father said nothing. The room was cool. He put a stick of wood in the stove.

"Getting late, Pa."

"I know."

He went into the cold hall. There was a faint light under the door into the parlor but he heard no voices. Going along the hall to the room he shared with Mort, he found that Mort had turned the lamp down low and was kneeling by the bed, in his underwear, his head sunk on his folded arms.

Amos shook him gently. "Get to bed, Mort."

Mort stirred and rose stiffly to his feet. "I shouldn't have fallen asleep. It wa'n't right and proper. I was tired and I had a lot to say to Him. You think He'll mind I fell asleep?"

"No."

"You don't?"

"No, I don't think He will." Amos felt that he had no right to say, but he was sure he had a right to comfort Mort. "Go to sleep."

He went to his own bed and undressed quickly and slid between the covers. He blew out the lamp. Mort was breathing evenly. Amos lay on his back and stared into the darkness. From beyond the wall at the far side of the room came the low voices of Rose and Pete. Amos shut his eyes. In the parlor the old sofa creaked and there was Rose's muffled laugh and hushed words. Rose needed a man and she'd make him a good wife. And perhaps be happy. Happy now, seemed like. He turned over and pulled up the quilt, trying not to think of the girl in the fishing jacket, but it was impossible and he felt warm all over. Then being tired, he was asleep.

## Chapter 6

The next morning after chores and breakfast, Amos hitched the horse Dick to the buggy and covered and roped two cans of milk to the back for the trip to the creamery. The sun was up and birds were singing and the air felt like spring, cool and clear with a softness suggesting warmer weather. The sound of high water came from the valley stream. The road was too deep in mud for the Ford.

Amos kept Dick at a steady walk along the flat stretch of road leading from the farm, past the woods at the end of the north field, past the little cemetery and down the hill into Whichertown. The second-growth trees opened into ragged fields bounded by stone walls and sagging barbed wire fences as he came down the hill past the Lovejoy place where empty windows stared out on the muddy road.

The small stream from the Jackman valley was high on its banks and the pool opposite the deserted schoolhouse looked dark. Across the flat of Whichertown the road was level. He approached the four corners where the Ridge Road continued straight up toward the Tarlton lodge. The right hand road led to the Grimes place while the road to the left wound down out of the hills toward the highway and the village. The wheels of the buggy rattled over the plank bridge across Carr Brook.

In the lodge up on the hill ahead of him, near the top of the Ridge Road, Joan Tarlton was probably just getting up, or maybe having breakfast. No need for her to get up before daylight and start the morning's work like Gram and Rose. He wondered where she slept and whether she took a bath before she dressed, the way Rose said Mrs. Marsley did. Or maybe Joan Tarlton didn't dress until later, eating breakfast in a lace wrapper. It seemed a strange way to live. What did she do all day? What did they do, her mother and father and Joan, the three of them and only the house to look after? He wondered how they got along during the mud season. Likely they hadn't been able to drive the car to the village for two weeks and another week would pass before the mud dried in the Ridge Road, even the north end out to the highway, which was better wheeling than from here up.

He stopped Dick beyond the bridge. Wanting to see Joan, and yet not wanting to be troubled by the way he felt about her, his thought came hesitantly that the neighborly thing would be to drive up there and see if they had errands at the village. It was a steep, unnecessary haul for Dick. Maybe the Knapps, over on the far end of the Ridge Road, were doing errands for them, getting their mail and groceries up to them by team. He'd look foolish if he offered to help when they were all right—driving into the yard and knocking on the door, maybe Joan in her lace wrapper coming to the door and looking at him as though she had never seen him before—or, almost as bad, Mr. and Mrs. Tarlton thanking him but wondering why he had come, and shutting the door. The heck with it.

He sucked a tooth at Dick and turned him left, but he felt tied up inside and his heart beat rapidly as though he had been running. He pulled Dick off the road, and felt better as he jumped down and started to unhitch.

He left the buggy by the side of the road and climbed on Dick's back, with the long reins doubled and knotted at the horse's withers. Dick didn't know what to make of it, thinking maybe they were going back to the farm, for he headed toward the bridge and Amos had to turn him sharply up the Ridge Road.

It went up steep from the corners, between brush-grown stone walls with alders and pines on either side in old pastures. Amos could feel Dick's muscles thrust and his hoofs sink into the mud as the horse climbed the hill. Dick was a close-knit chunky gelding and he liked to work. He kept at the hill until they came to a level place where Amos stopped to breathe him.

On his right, through the feathery young leaves, he could see the expanse of the Derby Fields, brown from the unmowed grass but with the new green shoots coming through and tinting the brown blades which lay flat among the young pines and poplars. There was a pile of rocks in the middle of the fields, cleared from the land years ago, and beyond it an apple tree budded pink at the cellar hole marking the spot where the Derby house had stood. Amos could barely remember when the place burned; he recalled being taken into the yard at home in the dark night with the older folks to see the red flames across the valley. He remembered Pa hitching up the team and throwing shovels and pails into the wagon. There had been another man, probably his Uncle Mort, who drove off with Pa. And that had been the end of another farm in Whichertown.

He started Dick up the hill. Shortly they came to the bare ridge and went toward the long shoulder of spruces stretching down from

Quartz Mountain. On the edge of the spruces, the Tarlton lodge looked out over the valley.

At the gate in the wall where the drive left the road, he hesitated, half a mind to keep going, but if he did that he'd have to come back and would look foolish. Or he could turn around now—yet that wouldn't do, for they'd probably seen him. He put Dick through the gate and noticed hoof tracks and wheel marks; the Knapps had been seeing to the Tarlton's needs and he shouldn't have come. But he kept on. The house of logs looked strange to him, as it always did.

He felt a tight breathless ache across his chest and suddenly he didn't care about why he'd come to the lodge, or about what anyone would think—Joan or her folks. He just wanted to see her and it didn't matter whether he could help them or how he looked, riding up in his old clothes and unshaven, on a shaggy work horse, or who the Tarltons were or who he was or the time of day or what excuse he had. He felt a strange wild careless happy sensation as when he was trailing a deer close, or waiting for a fox while Drum bayed toward him, or stepping out of the barn on a fall night as the moon came up over Cobblestone, orange as the hardwoods, with the wild smell of fall on the frosty air.

Birds rose from the bushes as he turned Dick toward the house and the air was filled with their singing while he hitched Dick to a tree and stepped up the porch stairs.

He didn't have to knock. A shadow passed quickly across the two big windows and Joan opened the door. She was smiling, a little flush on her cheeks, and her eyes not anxious but pleased and surprised. She had on a white blouse and a yellow skirt. Her brown hair was brushed back but the curls seemed to overflow the yellow ribbon. Her bare feet were tucked into lambskin moccasins.

"Hello, Amos," she said and he wondered that she remembered his name. "Come on in."

He looked down at his muddy boots. "Maybe I better not. I just stopped by to see if you—see if you got back all right." It was a small lie but he couldn't very well tell her he'd been at the house last night.

"Oh, I made it. I'm sort of lame this morning." She stretched and laughed. "Come on in and never mind about your boots. We're in and out all day."

"Well, all right."

After stamping his boots and scraping them on the door mat, he walked gingerly on the varnished floor. He could see no signs of mud and doubted if they tracked in and out this way. He had never been inside the house. That day last fall when he took Mr. Tarlton hunting, he had stayed outside. He looked about him at the log walls and the broad windows and at the big fireplace and chimney reaching clear to the roof at the gable end of the living room. It would be a poor place to try and heat, he thought, but they used it for summer and fall so maybe that didn't matter. He realized Joan was watching him.

She asked, "Do you like it?"

"Why yes, sure. Lot of good axe work went into them logs."

"It was built by some men from up north that Dad hired."

"I remember watching them work. I was about ten. They were from Maine, I think."

"Probably. Dad used to go hunting there."

He had been pleased to see her, but now it was getting difficult. He wished he could talk better and think of things to say. He couldn't just stand there and look at her.

"Let's go into the kitchen," she said. "I'm cleaning up the breakfast dishes and Mom's trying to bake some bread."

He knew that would be easier, although he didn't know what he'd say to her folks. He was glad not to find her in a lace wrapper, being served breakfast by a hired girl. He had almost expected it, but she was awake and busy and dressed. He followed her across the hall and into the dining room. As he passed the mahogany table and the coffee service on the sideboard, he could feel his muddy boots leaving tracks behind him. Watching her firm back and slim hips in the yellow skirt ahead of him, he didn't really care about his boots. The little brown curls above the nape of her neck danced as she walked.

"Mom and Dad," she said, "this is Amos Jackman. He pulled me out of the bog yesterday."

Mrs. Tarlton, wiping the flour from her fingers, came forward and shook hands with him. "Hello, Amos," she said, as though she had known him all her life. "Joan told us about falling into the bog. We're awfully glad you were there to help her."

"I guess she'd have wriggled out some way."

"Still, we're grateful," said Gregory Tarlton, looking up from the wood range and holding out his hand. He smiled with a wide grin that destroyed the fleshy hawk's features and made him look almost jovial. Joan resembled him in the high cheekbones and brown hair, while she had her mother's slimness and grace. Tarlton was a big man, maybe lean in other years. He stood taller than Amos, almost as broad but without the big bones and muscles. He looked at Amos and nodded. "Knew you were a good man last fall. Did you get a deer yourself?"

"Yes, I got one and so did Pa. We had deer meat enough."

"Amos," said Alice Tarlton, "do you know anything about wood stoves? I've got four pans of bread to bake and we can't get any heat in the oven."

Amos looked at the white electric stove. Mrs. Tarlton noticed, and explained. "The power isn't on yet. There's some trouble with our power plant and the man can't get in until the roads dry up. I never used the range except for warmth." She made a little helpless gesture. "Another year we won't come so early. It was a kind of experiment, like my baking bread."

Amos went to the wood stove and lifted the lids. A fire of split birch flamed brightly in the firebox. It was a big stove, in good condition. He tried the dampers and drafts, moved two of them with the short lever under the flange of the stove top.

"The heat wasn't going around the oven," he said. "Going right out of the firebox."

"What's that?" Tarlton moved closer.

Amos touched the little handle. "Down, it lets the heat go around the oven. Up, it shoots it into the chimney."

"Well, I'll be damned. There you are, Alice. Nothing to it." He squatted down to study the heat indicator. He came slowly to his feet and looked at his watch. He went to the window, stared at the sun, and without another word opened the cupboard over the sink. He took out a bottle of whiskey and two glasses.

"Amos, the sun is over the yardarm and the occasion demands a drink. Will you have yours neat or with water?"

Disconcerted, almost wondering if Tarlton were joking, Amos said, "Well, I don't know. I'm not much of a hand to drink. Guess I won't, thanks."

He realized it wasn't surprising Tarlton had whiskey. From Pete's talk, he knew there was a liquor store down to Fallsburg, and probably Tarlton had brought in a supply; still, it was something beyond his experience. Once he'd had a little of the beer which Pete brought Pa, and he'd take a glass of cider now and then, but this was new. He felt embarrassed refusing, although he really didn't want any.

Mrs. Tarlton came to his rescue. "What in the world are you thinking of, Greg, offering the boy a drink at this hour of the morning?"

"Hospitable thing to do." With apparent reluctance, Tarlton set down

[ 33 ]

the bottle and turned from the sink. "Well, we are grateful to you, Amos, for rescuing Joan and for fixing our stove."

"Don't amount to much, I guess," Amos said. And he added hurriedly, "I'm on my way to the village and thought maybe you'd have some errands or need something, what with the mud keeping you in, and all."

He could see Joan brighten. "May I go, Amos? I would so like to get to a store and see something different. I haven't been off the hill for two weeks."

"Glad to have you, but maybe you won't want to ride in a buggy."

"Why, I thought you were going on horseback and he could carry us both."

Amos smiled. "No, I just rode him up here. Left the buggy at the four corners." There seemed to be about her the same tenseness he had first noticed when she was catching trout at the gorge behind the Grimes place.

"Then there's nothing to stop us," she said. "Wait just a minute while I change my clothes."

Amos glanced at Tarlton. He was looking at his daughter with narrow eyes and smiling, yet Amos couldn't tell what he was thinking as he said, "The Knapps have brought us everything we really need."

"And Joan," her mother added, "we were going to clean the upstairs rooms."

"The heck with them. I've had my twenty-first birthday, you know." She wasn't quite joking and she must have realized it for she went on impetuously, "I'll clean the whole house tomorrow if Mrs. Knapp is still sick. But today I'll be darned if I'll stay cooped up here."

Tarlton said, "I wouldn't call yesterday being cooped up. Or the day before."

"Well, I mean, here I've got a chance to go to town—oh, why all the talk?" And she ran from the room, calling over her shoulder, "I'll be ready in a jiffy, Amos."

There was a sudden silence after she had gone.

Mrs. Tarlton said, "I'll make out a list. There are a few things we need."

Amos looked at the linoleum and thought maybe he'd better go, maybe things were getting too complicated just because he'd offered to run some errands. Just—that hadn't been it at all. And he didn't move. He'd come to see Joan and now he was going to see her alone and he wouldn't leave unless they ran him out. There didn't seem to be any likelihood of that. He heard glasses clink and looked up.

"Change your mind, Amos?" Tarlton asked, holding the bottle. "You may need it."

Amos shook his head. The way he felt now, he was dizzy enough without whiskey.

"Then you won't mind if I do? Alice?"

"No, thanks."

Amos watched him pour a drink and cut it with soda water from a siphon. Mrs. Tarlton was busy at the stove. Soon Joan came back, dressed in jodhpurs and short boots, leather jacket, and a little felt hat with a feather in it. She picked up a market basket from the corner. Amos thought it was an odd get-up and wondered what folks would say but he didn't suppose that mattered.

"I'm all set," she said. "Come on."

He followed her to the front door. Her folks came after him. At the door, Joan said, "I'll be back—when, Amos?"

"Be noon or after, depending on how long you want to stay."

"All right," her mother said.

Her father put his hand in his pocket and took out his wallet. "Well, Amos, we want to thank you again, for all the trouble." He had a bill in his hand. "Here's a little something. . . ."

Joan stepped between them. "Thanks so much, Dad," she said, taking the bill. "I'll see that Amos gets a present to remind him he pulled me out of the bog."

Her father seemed about to say something, but did not, smiling instead and nodding. Her mother asked quickly, "Are you both going to ride the horse?"

"Why, of course," said Joan.

"I guess not," Amos answered, going from the porch to unhitch Dick and lead him up to the steps. "Get on," he said.

"You can't walk through all that mud."

He smiled at her. "I'll manage."

She grasped Dick's mane and swung onto his back.

Amos turned Dick and led him out to the road. He was silent and for a time Joan stared ahead at the trees.

Then she said abruptly, "I'm awfully sorry about Dad offering you money."

"Don't bother me none."

"He sometimes forgets he can't buy or pay for everything."

"Sure. He's all right."

"Would you have taken the money?"

"Nope."

[ 35 ]

"Well then, aren't you mad that he thought you would?"

"Nope."

"Haven't you any pride?"

"Got enough, I guess. Not so much it bothers me." The mud was getting deep and he tossed her the reins and walked aside to the edge of the road. "Your pa and I look at things a little different, that's all. No sense talking about it."

She was silent again before she remarked, "I don't suppose you'd get on this horse with me?"

"No, I don't suppose I would."

"You'd rather slop along in the mud."

"I guess so."

"I'd say that was enough pride to bother you."

He had to smile at her. "Maybe it is, at that."

"I'll get off and walk."

" 'Twouldn't make me ride."

"What would?"

"Why, nothing I can think of."

"Oh, you're impossible. You make me feel like a helpless little girl and I don't like that."

"Never mind, we're almost to the corners and you can ride in the buggy."

She stared over his head. "I think you're afraid to sit that close to a girl."

"Might be. Here we are."

He took the reins and turned Dick down the road and held him still while Joan slid off. She did it easily, throwing one leg over Dick's back and sliding lightly to the ground.

He hitched up and stepped into the buggy. He thought he might offer his hand to her when she got in but before he could make up his mind, she had climbed beside him on the seat.

## Chapter 7

The buggy had no top, so the trees curving over the road from Whichertown were like a green tunnel. Amos drove Dick downgrade at a walk, saying nothing. Joan seemed absorbed by the brook at the left of the road, her eyes fixed on the rushing water and the boulder-lined pools.

After a time the road curved nearer the brook and they came to the ledge where nothing but a thin screen of bushes stood between the rutted mud and a drop of ten feet to the rocky stream bed. He had often thought before, as he passed the spot, and he realized again, that a single stone no bigger than a bushel basket would have stopped the Ford, and nobody hurt, just maybe a bent axle.

Instead the Ford had plunged over the ledge and crashed against the boulders and nobody ever knew whether Ma had been hurt bad in the fall or had bled to death from the glass cuts; she died while two men from a logging truck, which came along right after the accident, were trying to get her out. The men said Mort had been almost crazy trying to help, his arm broken and his face cut. Amos remembered getting out of the car which Doc Parsons had sent to the farm for him and Pa. He remembered lowering himself down the rocks while he stared at the battered car and at the blanket-covered body of his mother on the smooth stone darkened with blood. Beyond them the brook had flowed bright in the sun.

It was a hard thing to think, and he would never form it in words, but Mort might as well have been killed, too. The older brother who could tinker any piece of machinery on the farm was gone. He wouldn't pick up a wrench now, even to hand you. Nothing anyone said would prove to him that he hadn't been guilty of his mother's death. The wishbone connections had been so smashed you couldn't convince him he had put them back together right.

Amos remembered the showery June day Mort had been working on the Ford, before haying. He'd stopped at the wagon shed while Mort finished his work and stood up to look at the Ford. Rain dripped from the eaves. Mort had been proud of the job. "She'll steer good now."

But after the accident Mort wouldn't believe he'd done his work right. "I don't know," he'd say, "that bolt . . ." and his voice would fade as he turned away. After he took to brooding about it so much, Gram had the minister come out and talk to him two or three times, until Mort seemed to feel better. Amos considered the accident one of those senseless, inexplicable things that happened. There was nothing you could do about them except endure them in whatever way you could. He didn't see there was much in the Bible to help, but it comforted Mort.

He supposed that none of them were the same after Ma had gone. He could see her now, a strong quiet woman, large boned and slow, with an even disposition. Amos had always known what she would expect of him. If there was work to do, she held him to it. Even when he was young and sneaked off to go hunting or fishing, he knew there would be a penalty afterward. A boy had duties, the same as a man or a woman or a girl. School and work, and church when they could get out. Play and hunting and fishing came after. He thought now that he would have run completely wild if she hadn't been so firm. And with her gone, the discipline she had enforced still guided him through an ingrained sense of duty.

He had never been afraid of her and remembered her not for the times she had switched him but for the times she had nursed him when he was sick and helped him with school work, the times she had shown him spring flowers in the woods below the house. He thought of her as pretty and yet he knew she had a plain face, squarish-long and immobile under the gray hair. Her hands were large and fleshy, always working, and she had heavy arms and a straight figure in her plain cotton dress and apron.

It was strange to be thinking of her now as he drove down the old road with Joan Tarlton beside him, for she probably wouldn't approve of his being with Joan. She'd think Joan wasn't the right kind of a girl for him. She'd say, "You'll get into trouble if you aren't careful, her upbringing and money and all. You're being a fool, Amos."

And yet he wondered if she wouldn't understand how he was beginning to feel. She should know. She'd been the schoolteacher down to the village years ago and her father had a good business at the livery stable. She could have married almost any of the young fellows with more prospects than Warren Jackman. Pa used to plague her about it after they'd been to the village and she'd been talking with Cy Tillman, who ran the general store, or Doc Parsons. As far as Amos knew she never regretted marrying Pa. For her, he supposed, it hadn't been much of a life, yet she never suggested she might have married someone else rather than spend all her years with Pa on a hill farm. She must have felt pretty strong about Pa, so perhaps she'd understand.

Amos brought his mind back to the road. They had been driving for over a mile. They were about halfway to the highway and Joan hadn't said a word, just sitting there beside him watching the brook and looking at the trees and the birds and the sun and blue sky.

At last she turned to him and said, "It's downhill all the way. You don't notice it so much in a car."

"Pretty high, up to Whichertown." He leaned forward and pulled Dick back to the center of the road as the off wheel grated over a rock and lurched into a mudhole. "Don't seem to dry up much."

He watched the wheel turn and grind through the mud, bringing up muddy water which dripped from the rim. Dick held back in the breeching as they went down a steep pitch.

"Frost struck in deep this year," he said. "There wa'n't an awful lot of snow."

"I wish I could see what winter's like here. I've never been at the lodge after November. Maybe this year we'll stay later. Dad's talking about retiring." She reached up and pulled a leaf from a branch. "He might as well. His partner runs their real estate business."

"I see." Amos couldn't quite visualize a real estate business down-country, although he knew it wouldn't be like Cy Tillman selling farms as a sideline to his store.

"Dad's restless. Doesn't know just what to do with himself. Like me, I suppose. I've been out of school a year and haven't accomplished a thing."

"School?"

"Well, college. I graduated last June. I wanted to be different, so I waited on table in the Adirondacks during the summer." She laughed. "College seemed so silly when there were lots of things I wanted to do, like being a district nurse in Kentucky and a newspaper reporter and a lot of important things. Last winter I was a hostess at a dude ranch in Arizona. I don't know what I want but I love it here at the lodge and I'm going to lead the simple life for a while."

"Don't know's I'd call the lodge simple."

"Well, you see what I mean—Whichertown and so on."

"Whichertown's simple all right."

The road leveled out and the mud became deeper. Amos looked up at the fields on the bare ridge ahead of them and beyond to Bass Hill. He thought about Joan going to college and the jobs she spoke of. They were things he couldn't understand, but he realized they gave her a wider experience of the world than he had. And now she wanted to live in Whichertown. It was peculiar, with her education. Schooling through the eighth grade was all he'd ever concerned himself about; he hadn't taken to books like Rose. But Joan had gone to college and had worked in those far places, yet now she liked Whichertown, a place he knew more about than she ever could. It was strange.

She asked, "We're almost down to the main road, aren't we?"

"Pretty near."

The woods retreated beyond fields. As they passed a tar paper shack, a dog came out barking and Mrs. Winklet peered from a small window at them.

"The whole town'll know about us driving by," Amos said, "soon's she can get across the road to the Hostetters' telephone." He nodded toward the white cottage down the road.

"Maybe I should sit closer," Joan said, "so they'll have more to talk about."

"Have enough without that, I guess. Gittup, Dick."

They reached the gravel road which led to the village. Amos let Dick trot down the level stretch after they crossed the iron bridge over Carr Brook. The wheels rattled on the gravel, and clods of mud from Dick's hoofs struck the dashboard. The little valley opened up and the fields fell away to pastures on the hills, and woods beyond them. The big hills were to the east and the brook wound through meadows in wide oxbows while the road cut straight down the valley. They passed small farmhouses painted white, and unpainted barns, a sawmill, and a cluster of tar paper shacks. There were cows in the barnyards moving slowly with unaccustomed legs after the long winter in barns, toward the pastures along lanes leading through the fields to the bare ridges beyond the farm buildings. Ahead of them a stone wall extended up a pasture like a surveyor's line, to another wall against the sky. They passed a wooden dam in the brook where there had been a mill. After a time, the valley narrowed and the road followed the brook again where pine woods rose steep beside the ditches.

Dick walked down a hill with his hind legs slanted under his belly as he held back, past sand banks and out into a wide vista of the river valley. They saw the broad water flowing slowly between them and the Vermont shore beyond the long fields of the valley farms. There were big barns and barbed wire fences—no stones for walls here—and sometimes the tangled roots of a stump fence made from pines which had been cut years before. Dick trotted again, along a tarred road, and Amos turned him on the gravel shoulder to save his hoofs. Two wheels of the buggy were on the tar, two on the gravel, as they passed under the green elms. They trotted by houses of clapboards and of brick, not quite town homes because there were barns attached and fields stretching to the river. And then they came to the big white houses with barns separated by a lawn or drive—barns which had been built for driving horses and were now used for cars. As they passed the church and the brick town hall, Amos slowed the horse to a walk. The common, behind the white board fence on granite posts, looked new green.

"I've got to go across to the creamery," Amos said. "You want to get out at the store?"

"No, I'll go with you. I've never crossed the bridge in a buggy."

Amos lifted his hand to Ned Staver on the porch of the store and turned Dick at the garage and drove past Doc Parsons' house and the blacksmith shop, slowing Dick to a walk as they entered the long covered bridge. The buggy rolled past the brightly colored circus posters as Dick's hoofs thumped on the planks. Far ahead was a square of light like the end of a tunnel. Between the heavy timbers of the sides were windows which opened on the river and brought the air of spring into the old wood and dry horse-manure smell of the bridge.

Joan began reading the old patent medicine posters on the beams.

"Kemp's Natural Herb Rejuvenator, Hansdale's Bitters, Dr. Warner's Astringent Spavin Cure, Kickapoo Snake Oil, Dr. Bartlet's Guaranteed Liver Elixir." She stopped for breath. "My gosh, I never knew there were so many. I never had a chance to read them going through in a car."

"Some of them are old," Amos told her, "real old. I remember my Uncle Mort used to take Dr. Bartlet's Elixir. Powerful stuff, it was. Said it made him see double and feel single. My aunt was temperance and he didn't say that in front of her. Complained of his liver." Amos looked down at Joan and saw her smiling. "Said the Elixir was good for anything ailed a man. Made me try some once when I had a cough. Just about like swallowing a lighted kerosene lantern." He slapped the reins as Dick pulled up the hill on the far side of the bridge. "Pretty near there. Long ride, ain't it?"

"I liked it. I like it in the hills but I'm glad to see something different."

They crossed the railroad tracks and drove past the grimy station and beyond it to the grain store and creamery. There was a store across the street, and two houses; a hall where movies were shown once a week. That was all in the expanse of fields between the river bank and the hills except for a farm down the road.

"I'll go over to the store," Joan said, jumping down from the buggy.

Amos backed up to the loading platform of the creamery. He could smell the sweet steamy air from the open door and could hear the hum and clank of machinery inside. Arnold Partridge came to the door as he was loosening the rope around the milk cans. Arnold, in his knee-length rubber boots and hickory stripe overalls and undershirt, watched and rubbed his chin.

"Stepping out a little, ain't you, Amos?"

"Wouldn't say so. Tarltons been kept in by the mud."

"I thought the Knapps was sort of helping them out."

"Are, I guess. There was some special errand or other for today."

"Well, well."

"You going to get my two empties?"

"Give me time."

Amos waited for his cans and roped them on and took his slip. Arnold winked at him as he climbed into the buggy.

"That horse don't take much driving, does he, Amos?"

"Takes enough. Gittup."

He turned the buggy and stopped for a bag of feed at the grain store, and then drove across the road to wait for Joan. He lit his pipe and watched the cars go by and the teams come to the creamery, and the mud-splashed trucks. He looked at the store window. The display included drugs and patent medicines as well as groceries. Beyond the window he saw Joan standing by the counter where they sold fishing tackle and guns.

In a little while she came out with her market basket full of groceries and packages. In the other hand she carried a green cloth rod case. She tucked the basket in front and handed him the rod.

"That's from Dad. I told him I'd get you something."

For a minute he looked at it without believing she meant it for him. Then he said, "Now see here, I ain't going to take this. I got a fish pole. I can't take this. You better go back with it and tell them you made a mistake." He tried to force it into her hands.

Without paying the least attention to him, she climbed in beside him and sat looking straight ahead. "Of course you can take it. It's not like money. It's a present."

"I ain't going to take a present from a girl."

"It's from Dad. Don't be a damn fool."

"Then I'll take it back myself."

"For goodness' sake, stop making such a fuss about it. Can't you do anything gracefully? You could thank me and shut up."

"I'm going to take it back." He started to move over the wheel, pausing to wrap the reins around the whip.

"You are not!"

She grabbed his arm with a strong hand and leaned forward to slap Dick's rump.

"Here, what you think you're doing?"

The startled horse gave a jump and Amos was occupied with the reins for several minutes.

After he'd slowed Dick to a walk, he was almost of a mind to turn back, but decided maybe she was right. It wasn't proper to act like he had about a present that didn't matter to them, the cost of which was nothing to them. If they wanted to do something to show they appreciated the business about the bog, likely that was their way and he'd best let it pass. But he was still mad at the way she had gotten around him.

"You ain't to be trusted in a buggy," he said. "If Dick wa'n't good-natured we'd be in the ditch now, milk cans, groceries, fish pole and all."

"You didn't need to be so pigheaded."

"Pigheaded, now." He looked at her. "I should have left you in the bog."

"I'd have gotten out all right."

"I should have pushed you under."

They were driving down the hill into the bridge and he felt irritated by the way she talked, so he talked back, but he didn't want to fight with her. Arguing with girls was no good. You couldn't win and you couldn't shake sense into them. This was like the lighting of her cigarette in the woods, something that riled him because he hadn't acted right—didn't know how or didn't want to, he wasn't sure which. It was all tangled up in his head and he wanted things to be simple. The horse's hoofs went tunk-tunk, tunk-tunk on the planks of the bridge and the wheels rattled and the milk cans banged against the seat while Joan sat stiff beside him and it wasn't fun to be together any more.

They were out in the sun again and trotting up the road to the corner, back the way they had come. He almost forgot to turn in at the store. He stopped Dick at the rail.

Joan asked, "Will you see if there's any mail for us, please?"

The familiar store seemed different today as he walked across the porch and nodded at Ned Staver, loafing still on an empty egg crate. The big room had counters the length of it and along all the sides, counters for drygoods and shelves of hardware and counters for meat and groceries. You could buy 'most anything here. He liked to look over the axes and rifle cartridges. Sometimes Cy would pass out a sliver of cheese when he was cutting off a wedge for somebody, and there were rounded oval crackers in a glass-topped bin by the cookie boxes. He could listen to the men talking. Of course, coming from Whichertown, he didn't know many of the customers well, but he liked to hear the talk for a while. And sometimes he met his cousin, Jake Whicher, who had moved from Whichertown to a farm up the river valley. He and Jake would talk about the things they did when they were boys, like putting the hedgehog in the girls' backhouse at school, and rabbit hunting with Old Snarl who always smiled but looked as though he was snarling, and could run a rabbit in the deepest snow because of his long spindly legs.

But today Amos was in a hurry to mail Rose's order to Sears and to buy his tobacco and flour and coffee.

Cy glanced at him, and beyond him to the open door, while he was making out the slip for the groceries. His eyes twinkled in the round face but he didn't say anything until later when he walked behind the rack of pigeonholes and grille that formed the post office.

He handed Amos a circular. "You want the Tarltons'? I see you got the girl with you."

"All right."

Cy handed a paper and two letters through the grille. "How the trout biting out on the brook?"

"Water's too high now. Got a few the other day."

"Early anyhow. They don't really start to take hold till the flies get bad."

"That's about it."

Amos went out to the buggy and put the paper bag in back with the milk cans and set the bag of flour beside it.

He thought a minute and then went back into the store.

"I'll take a half pound of cheese and a box of soda crackers," he told Cy. "And I guess a nickel's worth of them chocolate creams."

Cy got the cheese and crackers and then weighed out the creams, grinning. "You'll need more than a nickel's worth of chocolates, Amos."

"You can go to hell."

He hurried out to the buggy and climbed in, handing Joan her mail and tucking the small paper bag under the seat.

Dick stepped out as they started down the road, knowing he was headed home.

Joan asked, "Mind if I read this letter?"

"No," he said, surprised. "Why should I?"

She looked up at him quickly. "No reason."

He turned Dick toward the hills and watched his ears cock forward as they passed the field where Pete Tucker was spreading manure with a heavy team and a big spreader. That rig would mire down at this time of year in the Jackman hill fields. Amos thought of the easy land here; it dried out quicker and you could get out earlier in the spring and with one of them spreader rigs you could set and drive while it sprayed out back, with the team doing all the work, instead of forking it out by main strength and ignorance. But when he looked about him at the rolling valley he didn't feel at home and he was satisfied with the hill farm surrounded by mountains. He was glad the road had begun to climb, slowing Dick to a walk, glad to hear the noise of Carr Brook and the water from the mountains of Whichertown.

Joan folded the letter and tucked it back in its envelope.

"Things are looking up," she said gaily. "My brother's coming for the weekend and he's bringing his roommate. He's an awful lot of fun," she went on. "Ronnie, I mean, the roommate. You should have seen him at the Country Club dance last New Year's. He'd been to Florida for the vacation—what a tan he had—and he brought back this rum. He got positively tight. He tried to teach me to tango." She laughed. "We had an awful lot of fun. He wants to marry me."

Amos slapped the reins. "You going to?"

"I wonder. Sometimes I think, who wants to be married to a tired businessman—he and Jack are at business school. I want to do more with my life than live in a suburb and raise kids and join women's clubs. Picture me in a women's club. Play golf and train maids you have to keep firing because your husband tries to corner them in the pantry. And dance close up to the guys at the Country Club and slip out on the terrace with them before moving on to their car and bottle under the seat."

"Don't sound right."

She threw up her hands in a dramatic gesture and laughed at herself. "But I have an inclination for it, a definite inclination for it. Damn it all, why shouldn't I have? I was brought up in Braemuir. And then again I turn inside out and want to be a social worker or a nurse in the Kentucky mountains and make something of myself and do great things and, oh God, where would Ronnie fit into that? Or any man for that matter." She sighed. "I get all mixed up."

Not knowing what to say, Amos didn't make any comment but clucked to Dick as the road leveled out. They rolled on in silence until they came to another grade and Dick settled into a walk again.

Joan asked, "Have you always lived in Whichertown?"

"Yes."

"I've always lived near Boston. For, let's see, fifteen years, since I was seven, in Braemuir. We've got a house on a hill that still has woods on it. Dad sold all the lots around or built houses and sold them and built some and rented them, but he kept the hill for us. It's not what you would call a hill, just a little knoll with the drive winding up the side of it and oak trees around the house, but it seems like a hill to us and quite woodsy. Maybe that's why I feel at home on the Ridge Road. I've never really lived in the city since I was little, but sometimes I like to visit it and shop and see the shows and all the people. I think it's exciting but not for all the time. Do you like Boston?"

"Never been there."

"You haven't?"

"Why should I? Got everything I need here in Houghton."

"Don't you want to get out and see the world?"

"Not particularly." He realized she thought he was some kind of strange creature and he added defensively, "I've been to Fallsburg."

She burst out laughing and laughed all the way past the Cushman farm. Nate Cushman stopped in the dooryard with an armful of wood and stared after them. Amos wished she'd shut up. At last she did and straightened her hat and put her boots on the dashboard and hugged her knees, looking sideway at him.

He said, "Nothing funny about that. Fallsburg's a place, ain't it? A city, ain't it?"

"Yes," she said. "Yes, I suppose it is. I was just laughing at the way you came out with the name, as though it were Boston and New York and London all rolled into one."

"I never hankered to travel," he said, "or I might have gone to them places."

"All right, I won't tease you about it." Impulsively, she laid her hand on his arm. "Houghton's all right and so's Whichertown."

"Suits me," he said.

But all the talk of cities and her home and her brother's roommate had put her away from him and Whichertown. He was acutely aware that she was an outsider with a different life behind her. Riding like this to town in an old buggy, with a hill farmer beside her, was a joke or, as you might say, a kind of spree or lark. He was silent as they pulled to the top of the hill where Carr Brook flowed in oxbows through the meadows. He didn't walk Dick for long to breathe him, but touched him up and trotted him fast toward the hills. They didn't speak until they came to the turn toward Whichertown. They passed the little farm and the tar paper shack and were in the woods again while Dick pulled steadily at a walk through the mud.

Amos stopped him at the waterbox where the road widened and a split log carried water from a spring in the hill to a wooden box. He let Dick drink, then turned him away and tucked the reins around the whip.

"He can do with a little rest."

Getting out of the buggy, he took the paper bag of cheese and crackers from the floor and unwrapped the cheese, offering her the chunk with the paper under it.

"Crackers in the bag," he said, pointing to the bag he laid on the seat.

She broke off a corner of the cheese and took one of the crackers. "You aren't mad?"

"No."

"You didn't talk for so long, I wondered."

"Wa'n't nothing to say." He bit into the tangy cheese and munched a cracker. It was a dry mouthful and after he'd chewed a minute he bent and drank from the waterbox.

Joan burst out, "For gosh sakes, the horse just drank there!"

"Sure," Amos said. "Don't hurt nothing."

She looked at him as though she couldn't believe her eyes or ears and he added, "Water's running and I drank up where it comes in."

He thought that she might want a drink herself, if there was something to drink out of, and he looked among the bushes beside the trough. Often there was a tumbler hanging on a twig. He found it and handed it to her.

She looked at the glass doubtfully but took it and climbed down from the buggy. She rinsed the glass under the flow from the hewed log, filled it, looked at it for a moment and then drank rapidly.

"Cold," she said.

"It's the same way in the middle of summer. Don't freeze either in the winter."

"It's good," she said and looked at the cheese and crackers on the seat of the buggy.

"Help yourself," he said.

He felt better now. He must have been hungry. Eating the crackers and cheese, he felt it was better up here than the river valley. He was more comfortable with the woods around him and the mountains not far ahead in Whichertown. The sun came into the little clearing, warm and bright. Joan unsnapped her leather jacket so it hung loose over her white blouse.

"This is nice," she said, looking at him squarely in the direct way she had. There was color in her cheeks, just a touch where the high cheekbones drew the soft skin tight. Her brown eyes were clear. "I like this."

She glanced about her at the trees. "The woods are full of birds. Just hear them singing all over the place. Do you know any of them?"

"Well, not by name. Seen 'em around a lot. There's always plenty in the spring."

"I used to know some of them when I was a Girl Scout." She pointed to a plump brownish bird on a twig near the waterbox. "That's a song sparrow. I've seen them around the house in Braemuir. I made up quite a bird list one year for a merit badge. Some of the girls and the leader used to come and we'd study the birds. The girls thought I was high-hat and I guess some of them were jealous of the list and the place I lived and Dad's business and what not. It always made me feel bad."

She turned to look at the sunny bank above the waterbox. "Those leaves look like mayflowers."

In a second she had scrambled up the bank and was kneeling on the ground. She began picking the flowers and then turned to him.

"Don't you want to pick some to take home?"

"No, I guess not."

"They smell awfully sweet." She pressed her nose into the bunch in her hand. "Men are so silly about flowers. They think it's sissy. Come on." She looked up. "Or are you in a hurry to get home?"

"No, got all day."

The bank where she knelt did look warm and sunny, and he wanted to be near her, so he stepped over the rocks to the soft hummock. Bending over he pulled a flower tentatively and stood looking down at her.

"Don't they smell nice?" She held up her bouquet. "Sweet and fresh like a spring morning."

He leaned over and she pushed the flowers against his face. He couldn't help smelling the spring scent of them, but the thought came to him what a fool he'd look if someone should come down the road. He straightened up, knowing nobody would come, but feeling ill at ease anyhow. She went back to picking. Her little hands darted among the green leaves that grew close to the ground and hid the pink and white buds.

At last, watching her, he squatted down and picked a few, but he didn't pay attention to what he was doing and he felt so queer and hot there, maybe from the sun, that he went back to the road and laid the flowers on the buggy seat while he filled his pipe. He took plenty of time about opening the flat tin and rolling the plug slice in the palm of his hand. He struck a match to the tobacco and smoked, staring at the brook.

Finally he heard her come down the bank and she was beside him.

"Here, you take some of these."

"No, they're yours. You picked them."

"Here." She split the bunch in half and held them out to him. "They'll look nice in the house. Smell nice, too."

"No, I wouldn't know what to do with them."

"Your mother would like them." She smiled, teasing. "You can tell her your girl picked them for you."

He didn't say anything, hoping she would stop.

"Wouldn't she?"

"Well," he said shortly, "I could give them to Mort. He sees to the flowers on her grave."

"Oh."

He saw that he had hurt her and when the words were out it was plain how they sounded.

"I didn't know," she said. "I'm awfully sorry. I'm always saying the damnedest things. I didn't know."

"Why should you? It's all right. Here," he said. "I'll take them home to Gram. She'll like them—Rose, too."

He tucked the flowers under the seat where they made a little green and white and pink mat on the burlap sack.

She was looking at him as he straightened up and he didn't know just what she was going to do, so he said quickly, "I guess we better be going."

He climbed in first and slid across the seat, making room for her. They were driving up the road before she spoke.

"I'm awfully sorry. I must have spoiled your day."

He wished she'd stop talking about it. Talk wasn't any good sometimes, but he knew she meant all right. He forced himself to explain to her.

"No, you didn't. I'm used to the idea. She was killed in an accident up the road here, around this bend." He pointed with the whip. "She and Mort went over the ledge there."

He didn't want to think about it after that. Before she could say anything more, he added, "Two years ago, and more. No use talking about it."

There was a silence that bothered him, and searching in his mind for some way to break the awkwardness, he remembered the chocolate creams on the floor in the little bag. He reached under the seat. The bag was mashed and the brown paper stained.

He opened it and held it out to her. "Here."

She reached into the bag and then because the bag was so small and the chocolates so few, she couldn't reach them. Finally she held his hand and reached deeper into the bag.

"My," she exclaimed, "chocolate creams. I love them. Thanks."

"Take another."

She did and he saw her lift it to her lips, with the chocolate staining her fingers as she bit into it and exposed the white cream filling. She raised her eyebrows and crinkled her eyes at him.

"Mmm—good, aren't they? Don't you want one?"

"Well," he said, realizing how few there were, "one maybe. I ain't much on candy."

"You mean you got them for me?"

He was fumbling with the bag, reins in the other hand. "Well, sort of. We had a tiff about the rod, and all. For you."

[ 49 ]

"That was sweet of you. Here, let me help." She took a chocolate from the bag and put it in his mouth. The simple gesture bothered him but she didn't seem to think anything of it, for she rattled on, "I don't know when I've had better chocolate creams. They're wonderful."

He knew she must have had more candy than he'd ever see in his life, and more chocolate creams than Cy sold in a year. He could picture big boxes of fancy chocolates on her birthday from her brother's roommate. He thought of his nickel bag and he thought of the nickel —a fourth part of the bounty on a hedgehog when he took the noses to the selectman—a nickel from the money he had earned selling the pulpwood that Pa had let him cut last summer. What did it amount to for her? A nickel wasn't a drop in the bucket to her and there wasn't any need of her running on about the little bag of creams. But looking down at her, he made up his mind that she meant what she said. She was sorry about his mother and she was trying to be nice and she meant every bit of it. She sat back with a chocolate cream in her mouth and smiled at him and looked around. "This is a lovely day."

He wished then that the road went on forever, but he could see the way growing steeper as they pulled up Footstep Hill, the last steep pitch approaching the four corners. Before he could think of anything to say, before he could really enjoy this new pleasure of being with her, they had come over the top of Footstep Hill and the corners lay ahead.

"I'll drive you home," he said.

"No, you won't. You've done enough for me today. Thanks an awful lot."

He stopped Dick and she jumped out, letters and paper in one hand and flowers in the other. She put them in the basket with the groceries and lifted it out. He didn't know how to say goodby. Dick was pulling on the bit.

"Well," he said, "thanks for the flowers and the rod."

She smiled at him. "Goodby. See you on the brook someday."

He eased up on the reins and Dick started for home. He glanced back. She waved.

## Chapter 8

In the next day or two, Amos began to realize that the simple thing of Rose getting married, which in a way they had been expecting, would change the family. It would be smaller, and Gram would be left with the work. He knew this bothered Rose, for she talked it over with Gram. Rose felt she shouldn't leave, but Gram told her to go ahead and live her own life; they'd manage without her. And they would, but Amos felt the diminishing of the family. He had seen other people leave Whichertown, yet this was the first time it had happened in his family, except for Ma, which was different.

Amos was thinking about these things while he and Mort mended the back pasture fence. It ran along the ridge southwest of the farm, through scattered pines and hemlocks. Of all the work on the farm, Amos sometimes thought he liked this best. It took him out into the woods. He could look about him at the green trees and feel that here he belonged.

The lower part of the fence was stone wall, the upper part two strands of barbed wire stapled to posts wedged between the rocks of the wall. Someone years ago had set out to build a good double wall with fill of smaller stones between the laid up rocks. But the work never had been finished. Probably the rough land here on the ridge had not been cleared enough to provide all the rocks. Farther along, where the wall turned left down into the valley, it was higher than a man's belt, and still among trees, so there the land must have been all cleared by some past Jackman, although the trees had come back in.

Amos thought of Joan and the time at the waterbox. He could feel again the warm sun and smell the mayflowers and there came back to him the memory of her.

He tried not to think of her. He worked beside Mort and tried not to remember.

They were opening the center of the wall with a crowbar and wedging in new leverwood posts which Amos cut. He pointed them on a stump, holding the axe in one hand and the post in the other. He sliced down the post to form a four-sided point.

Mort worked ahead, laying up the stones where the frost of past winters had rolled them. His motions were strong and methodical. With his broad back bent, and heavy arms and hands, he could pick up any of the stones along the wall.

When Amos had set in the posts, Mort stretched the wire with a claw hammer against the post. He'd still use a hammer because he didn't consider it a mechanical tool. Amos drove staples over the tightened wire. It was an old wire. In some places it had rusted for years on top of the stones until pine needles covered it. Sometimes it broke. Here and there along the wall there was no wire and they patched the gaps with poles and brush.

Amos was careful to trim out the brush along the wall. A cow wouldn't go through a fence if the brush was cut along it, but would follow the open space beside it. If the brush grew up and the fence was poor too, then you'd be hunting cows in August when the pasture dried up and feed got scarce, though what the critters expected to find in the woods beyond the fence, Amos could never understand.

Now in places this fence, to look at it, wouldn't keep in cows any better than a thick fog, yet they hadn't gone through it since Amos could remember. Pa thought it needed mending. He'd had a burst of ambition and started working on it yesterday, but his energy petered out and now Amos and Mort were finishing. Of course Mort had been restless and maybe Pa noticed he wanted to get away from the farm so had sent them up here.

Not that it needed mending really, since cows were such peculiar creatures. Take down there on the lower side where the fence was tight and the wall higher, cows would try to get over every time the apples were ripe in the old orchard. They never seemed to think of busting through up here and going around to the apples.

Mort was sitting on a ledge by the wall as Amos walked up after filling in a last gap with brush.

"Amos, I don't feel just right. I think maybe I'd like to go for a little jaunt down toward the brook."

"You better stay with me. No need to work. I can finish from here to the corner."

"It ain't the work. I mean it ain't the lifting and all, but it is the work, because it don't seem right to be keeping up the farm. Don't seem like I want to keep the fences up and the woods back. I just don't feel good here any more, I guess."

"Sure, things get to pushing a man sometimes. Especially in the spring. Maybe we can go brook trouting tomorrow." Amos didn't think Mort would go but there was no harm in suggesting it.

[ 52 ]

"I'd like to, Amos, but I can't bring myself to kill the trout no more. Funny, I used to take pleasure in brook trouting, before—well, a while back."

"I know." Amos looked at Mort's haggard face, and at the twisting hands. "Well, maybe we can go together to the creamery next time. Or to the pictures some night."

"I'd like that, but it don't help now." Mort stared off through the trees. "I guess He's the only one can help me much. I'd like to pray, Amos. I know you don't believe in it like I do, but if we both prayed, it might help me."

Amos bowed his head and Mort sank to his knees. He spoke aloud the Lord's Prayer and the Twenty-third Psalm.

"The Lord is my shepherd, I shall not want. . . ."

His voice was firm and deep. It seemed to fill the little clearing by the wall. After Mort said, "Amen," Amos could hear a bird singing in the woods. Mort got up and his face looked less tortured and he went back to work.

It was almost noon when they reached the corner of the wall. They hadn't spoken any more except about the work.

"I could eat something," Amos said, driving the axe into a stump and resting the crowbar against the wall. "We'd better hit for home. Finish the south side here easy, this afternoon."

"All right." Mort looked at him with calm eyes. "I'm hungry, so I know I'm all right. I'm not hungry sometimes. You see, if you put your trust in Him, He'll look after you."

"That's right, Mort."

They started walking down across the pasture. It sloped gradually toward the house and barn in the distance. It was a ledgy stretch of sparse grass and hardhack bushes with cow paths winding about among the rocks. Spruces bordered the north side and reached out little Christmas trees on the pasture side of the fence. Over some of the ledges, hemlocks spread their low branches. Thorn apple bushes and wild apple trees grew here and there. Amos liked to walk through it, past the old birch tree where a fox would pass sometimes. The pasture was cut by a ravine. In the fall partridges fed on the thorn apples there. Beyond the ravine the land dropped steeper and the weathered farm buildings grew larger all the time.

Amos could remember coming back this way from a fox hunt late in the afternoon of a cold winter day. The sun was gone behind him and the purple darkness crept over the valley. The lights of the house looked warm. He could feel the cold on his cheeks and the fox carcass over his shoulder, gun in his other hand. Snow crunched under his boots as he swung down the hill. Drum padded on ahead, not anxious to find a track but tired-curious and just poking about as he made for home.

When Amos was a kid he used to get the cows from the pasture here and, if Pa wasn't in sight, sometimes rode one until he became scared as the cow ran or he neared the barn.

There was a little brook trickling out of the ravine. One summer before he was old enough to venture far from the house, he had built a dam across the brook. Mort made him a toy boat out of an old shingle. The dam was gone but it had formed a pool where the cows still drank. And one day he had found that the brook went across the lower field to the stream in the valley. The brook in the ravine had looked small then, after he'd seen the larger one. Later when he'd been to Carr Brook, the stream in the valley seemed small.

He thought of Joan laughing because he had not traveled. You could travel quite a lot in a small territory.

They came to the barway into the upper field where Pa intended to plant the potatoes this spring. They left behind the short pasture grass and the budded hardhack and the young spruces that had begun to show pale green tips on their branches. They were in an old hayfield where the turf felt thick underfoot. Amos noticed that it had dried out a good deal. Soon he'd be able to get on it with the team. The sod hadn't been turned for years and it ought to grow a good crop of potatoes.

They came down to the house, walked past the barn and went into the woodshed.

Rose was serving dinner when they came into the kitchen. Except for the times she thought of leaving Gram, she had been wild as a hawk ever since she and Pete decided to get married. She rushed around the house, singing and teasing and fooling. Amos thought she acted sixteen instead of twenty-four, a year and a half older than he was. Now she waved the spoon at him as she dished boiled potatoes from the big kettle on the stove.

"Next Wednesday's the day," she said. "Pete was here while you've been gone. He drove almost to the corners and walked the rest of the way. The new man who's learning the route took the truck around the loop. Glad to get me married off?"

"Be a relief, Rose."

Pa was sitting in his chair by the stove. He got to his feet now and took his place at the table. Gram set before him the veal and potatoes. He began to fill his plate. Whicher came in, carrying the single-barreled shotgun.

"I almost got that old woodchuck down in the lower field. I sneaked up on him like an Injun, on my belly, and every time he rose up to look around I'd flatten out and when he went to feeding again I'd crawl up on him some more." Whicher stopped for breath. "If there'd been some long grass I'd have got him for sure but he seen me before I got close enough and ducked down his hole."

Amos wiped his face and hands on the roller towel. "Yes, and if there'd been more grass you couldn't have seen him. You unload that gun?"

"Course I did."

"Better break it open."

"There, see?" Whicher leaned it in a corner. "Shucks, I know enough to do that."

Warren Jackman looked up. "You mind what Amos said. And open it up when you come in the house. I don't aim to have any more accidents around here. Godalmighty, I got enough to think about without worrying about you and guns."

Amos watched Mort when Pa mentioned accidents. Sometimes Pa didn't think what he was saying, but Mort's face had been over the wash basin and likely he didn't hear. Amos sat down and began to eat while he continued to think of Mort. It was difficult not to say something that would bother Mort, feeling as he did about Ma's death. Amos wondered if he would ever get over that. Didn't seem Mort could keep brooding about it forever. Seemed as though it would just naturally fade in his mind until it became less and less painful, but it was two and a half years and Mort couldn't forget it. Religion seemed to help him resign himself to Ma's death, yet maybe religion was taking too much of a hold on him. Amos had never been much on praying; he wasn't sure he understood the sort of God he learned about in church. But he was aware of the mysteries of the earth, simple things like planting a row of corn or beans, and that was nearer faith than some folks came. Probably He appeared different to different people.

Amos continued eating his stewed veal and boiled potatoes.

Gram said, "I wish one of you boys would go out and get me some cowslips. Seems though every spring I get a hankering to eat boiled cowslips and brook trout."

"Water's still pretty high, Gram," Amos said. "Maybe tomorrow I can get you both. Whicher and I'll go."

"Now hold on," his father told him. "There's going to be some work done around here. You boys finished that fence?"

"Well, the upper end," Amos told him.

"All right, you finish the rest of it today. Whicher and I'll get out the manure on the potato piece. Tomorrow you, Amos, can turn it over and Mort and Whicher can pull some of the rocks with the steers. I don't aim to be planting potatoes in July, like I was last year on account of you boys helling around in the woods and fishing and what all."

Amos said nothing. When Pa got to organizing the farm work, or anything for that matter, you'd best hold your tongue and let him rave. Nothing ever turned out like he planned, but the work got done some way or another. Amos promised himself that he'd be the one dressing the potato piece and not plowing tomorrow. He had known his father long enough to make allowances for the difference between his planning and his accomplishment. And as for pulling rocks with the steers—they hadn't been worked since he yarded the logs with them in the winter. They'd be all over the field.

But Gram didn't hesitate to speak. "That's all right, Warren, you see to the work but I'm counting on my greens."

"Time enough Sunday."

And that was all he'd say. The men ate in silence. Rose began talking to Gram about her clothes.

"I'm awful afraid my dresses won't come in time, Gram. Can you help me with that green jersey, just in case? You could help me let it down."

"Why, yes, but I wouldn't worry about your dresses. Been my experience that what you wear ain't so awful important on a honeymoon."

"But, Gram, I'm going to Boston."

"Well, Boston. Honeymoon's a honeymoon whether it's in Boston or Whichertown. Now, let's get these dishes out of the way and that dress onto you. Probably we can fix it if there's enough hem. And you got them two dresses Mrs. Marsley give you." Gram stood up. "You men folk get outside if you're so all-fired anxious to go to work."

Amos pushed back his chair. "Come on, Mort."

They left the house and crossed the yard past the open door of the barn. The warm sun seemed to have penetrated the earth. Amos could almost feel it as they crossed the garden piece and slipped through the bars into the small pasture they called the calf pasture, where the five cows and the two heifers and the steers had been turned out. The cattle followed them up the slope to the next barway.

"We might as well let them into the big pasture," Amos said. He looked down at the barway in the lower wall to make sure it was closed;

[ 56 ]

then he slid back the poles in front of him and stepped into the big pasture. "I don't think they'll follow us up to the fence."

The cattle paused at the barway to sniff the poles that angled from the ground to the double posts still supporting them at one side. A black and white heifer went through the barway with a little leap. The others followed and started to graze on the new grass.

Amos moved away from them and caught up with Mort on the hill.

Near the upper corner where they had left the tools, there was a ledge overlooking the valley. Amos stood on the highest point of rock. He could see the roof of the Tarlton lodge. He remembered that Joan had said her brother and his roommate were coming for the weekend. This was Thursday. Probably they'd arrive tomorrow afternoon. The thought bothered him. He knew it shouldn't, but it did. He realized he had begun to think of Joan in a sort of possessive way, as though she was his girl. It was a new sensation. He had never felt that way about a girl in all his twenty-two and a half years. And it was foolish. Most likely she had forgotten all about him after they parted at the corners. He was afraid she had, but he couldn't really believe she'd not thought of him at least once or twice.

He understood that he was foolish to think of her and he also saw the difference between them. He was a Jackman of Whichertown and she was a Tarlton of Braemuir, Massachusetts. That made all the difference in the world. He could stand off and see that, all right. Ronnie was more her type—vacationing in Florida, taking her to country club dances, drinking rum and wearing good clothes and, later, making money. Although he understood all this, it didn't settle anything, and he made up his mind to see her before Ronnie arrived.

He felt better when he had decided this, although the idea scared him a little. He'd never gone to call on a girl and although he wasn't exactly in awe of the Tarltons, he wasn't easy with them. Yet he knew he'd go.

He left the ledge and went up the hill to the tools.

Mort was cutting brush along the wall. It didn't need much mending, a stone here or there fallen from the top row, a length of brush laid up on two crossed posts driven in on either side of the fence. They worked in silence almost halfway down to the lower wall.

At last Mort stopped and said, "Seems as though Gram ought to have her cowslips."

"She'll get them, Mort. You heard what Pa said."

"I know, but it ain't right she should wait. Gram's old and works hard and don't ask for much. I'm going down to the brook and get her some."

"You stay with me, Mort, till we finish the wall. Then we'll see."

"I've got to get them, Amos."

"Pa'll throw a fit. He'll think you just wanted to get out of the work."

"That ain't it at all." Mort frowned as though searching for the real reason. "I think Ma'd want me to do it for Gram."

"Maybe you're right, but wait till we're through here and I'll go along with you."

"No, I've got to do it now. Seems like Ma's telling me to do it now so Gram can have them for supper."

"Godfrey, Mort, it ain't the middle of the afternoon yet. There's plenty of time."

"I'm going now." Mort didn't look at him.

Amos tried to think of a way to stop him, and then gave up. "Where you figure on going, Mort?"

"Why, just down to the lower field, where the brook floods over the corner there."

Amos looked across the pasture. He could see the lower field. Maybe it would be all right. He could work along the wall and still keep an eye on Mort, part of the time. "That's as far as you'll go?"

"Yes, I'll find all the greens Gram will want right there."

"Go ahead then. I'll finish mending the wall."

Mort walked away and disappeared beyond the hemlocks. Amos stepped out into the open and watched him striding down through the pasture, a lonely man against whom Amos could not feel angry.

Over at the barn, he saw the team and dump cart backed up to the cellar. Pa and Whicher, forking manure from the pile under the barn into the cart, wouldn't notice Mort. The cattle were still grazing quietly not far from the calf pasture.

Amos went back to the wall. He worked fast, not bothering about all the rocks that had fallen, concerned only that the wall would keep in the cows. He stopped to look down into the lower field. Mort was sitting on a knoll above the low spot where the cowslips grew. Amos wondered why Mort hadn't started picking, but probably it was all right—he'd started thinking about Ma's accident, or about God.

Yet Amos worried and wanted to be with Mort. He reached the end of the wall and moved along the fence that closed in one section. A fallen tree had broken two strands of the barbed wire. With quick strokes of the axe he chopped away the trunk and split out a post. He drove the post into the ground and stapled the broken wire to it.

He couldn't see into the lower field because a clump of spruces and poplars grew where the land had been too rocky to clear. When he had repaired the fence, he walked quickly out into the pasture. Mort wasn't in sight. He left the tools by the fence, and walked toward the barway into the lower field.

Then he noticed that the cattle were not in the pasture. Farther along he learned why: the bars were down. He hurried through the opening. The cows were in the field, about halfway to the woods.

If they stayed there, they'd be all right. Amos thought of the hellebore which grew along the brook, green and lush but poisonous to cows. He'd better get Whicher to help him drive them back. Mort must have gone off into the woods.

Amos didn't stop to wonder why Mort had left the bars down. He ran toward the barn. The team was gone. Thinking that Mort perhaps had returned to the house, he crossed the dooryard and went into the kitchen.

Gram and Rose were fitting the green dress.

"Has Mort been here?"

"No," Rose told him.

Amos turned and went out. He found Pa and Whicher in the back field.

"Hey," he called, before he reached the wagon, "the cows got into the lower field. I need some help."

"Get Mort," Pa said. "We're busy."

Amos could see now that the rear wheels had sunk through the sod. "Mort's gone into the woods somewhere."

Pa stood by the team, reins in his hand. The horses had dug themselves fetlock-deep into the soft earth. Pa's face grew red. "Goddamn the mud!" He doubled back the slack of the reins and flailed them across Dick's back. "Gittup there!"

The team lurched ahead. The near tug broke and Dick went down on the pole. Pal began to kick and lunge.

Amos stepped forward and seized his bridle. Dick struggled to his feet and stood trembling and blowing.

Pa still held the reins, apparently unable to speak or move. The red flush left his face and he said at last, hoarsely, "Unhitch them, Whicher."

He dropped the reins and walked away.

Whicher quickly loosened the traces. One of them caught the splintered pole.

"Watch out," Amos warned. "Wait." He stepped Pal to one side and released the harness. "Now you run down and head them cattle away from the hellebore. I'll be along."

Whicher was gone at a run, his tow head bobbing and his heels flying.

Amos trotted to the barn beside the horses. Pa met him at the door and took the bridles. He didn't look at his son.

Amos waited a moment until Pa had led the horses across the barn floor to their stalls. Then he ran for the lower field.

Whicher was far down across the short grass near the cows, running to get between them and the brook where the hellebore grew. As Amos came near he saw that the black and white heifer was missing. He turned toward the woods. The stream flowed at the very edge of the field. He saw her then, standing in the shallow water. She reached her neck across the deeper water to a hellebore plant that grew on the bank.

He shouted at her and stooped to pick up a rock which he threw as he ran toward her. The cow rolled her eyes in his direction and reached again for the lush green leaves. Her tongue curled around the plant. He ran up, splashing knee-deep in the water. The cow lurched away from him. The poisonous leaves trailed from her mouth as she wheeled back into the field. He kept after her. Part of the plant dropped to the ground but the rest she had swallowed.

Amos picked up the broken leaves and threw them down into the water. He was out of breath. Resting, he saw that between the hummocks of swamp grass there were plenty of cowslips. Mort could have picked all he wanted.

Whicher called to him, "Look here."

Amos climbed up the little knoll where he had last seen Mort. Whicher pointed to the boots and socks on the ground.

Amos nodded. "Mort came down here to get some cowslips for Gram. God knows where he's gone now." He looked at the woods and shrugged. "Well, we've got to put the cows back in the pasture. Start them up toward the corner and I'll head 'em through the barway."

"Will that weed kill the heifer?"

"Don't know."

Amos walked slowly through the field, picking up a handful of stones as he went. He waited at the barway as Whicher drove the cows along the wall. At the last moment one of the heifers broke away into the open field again.

They tried it several times but it wasn't until Pa came up and helped drive them that the cows at last stepped through the barway as though they never intended doing anything else.

Then Pa asked, "Where'd you say Mort went?"

"In the woods somewhere. Went picking cowslips for Gram."

"Did he leave the bars down?"

Amos nodded.

Pa leaned against the wall, looking old and tired. "I can't figure him out. He knows that hellebore grows down there. Did the cows get into it?"

"Only the black and white heifer."

"I don't suppose there's much we can do for her. You ever hear of any way to doctor them?"

"No."

"Well, you and Whicher go after Mort. I don't feel up to it."

Amos led the way back to the knoll and picked up the shoes and socks.

"He'll need these. Whicher, you go around to the corner and look for tracks. I'll cross the brook. We'll meet up by them spruces."

Amos waded through the shallow water, passing the broken hellebore plant, and stepped across the channel of the brook. He walked along the bank through the trees, and came to a muddy spot where Mort's tracks showed in the wet earth. Amos could see that he had picked some cowslips here. Farther along he lost the tracks under the spruces. He heard Whicher pushing toward him through the bushes.

"See anything, Whicher?"

"No."

"I found where he picked the cowslips." Amos turned into the woods and Whicher followed.

The brook bubbled toward them down a little valley of hardwood trees. Amos watched ahead through the open woods. They passed through a growth of pines and came to a shallow pool. It was quiet and secluded. Amos saw Mort sitting on a log at the far end of the pool. He seemed to be absorbed in watching the little falls where the brook dropped into the pool. After a time he looked up.

Whicher kept close to Amos as he moved slowly around the pool. Amos thought it was almost like finding a stranger in the woods. Mort didn't seem to recognize them.

Amos asked quietly, "You get any cowslips, Mort?"

Mort let his eyes pass over the bundle made by his denim jacket at his feet. Amos saw that it was filled with the greens. Mort had taken it off and buttoned the front and tied the sleeves to form a crude bag for gathering the cowslips. Mort sat in his shirt sleeves, a big man, incongruous because of his bare feet and rolled pants and underwear. He looked to Amos like a boy who had been out wading in the spring.

Mort said to Amos, "I ain't going back."

"No?"

"I like it here."

"What do you like about it?"

"It's quiet and away from everything."

"So it is." Amos took out his pipe. "No harm in staying a while."

He squatted down and let his hands make a long business of rolling the plug slice in his palm and carefully loading the pipe. Whicher dabbled a stick in the water. Amos smoked slow and didn't look at Mort. His thoughts moved toward his own inclination to retreat into the woods. As Mort said, it was quiet and away from everything. He could understand that. If Mort had suggested they go out to the camp, he wouldn't have thought it strange. This hiding of Mort's was different.

He considered the two ways of acting and they appeared to be two sides of the same coin. He had never thought much about his own jaunts into the woods. It was just something he'd always done. When he got ready, he came back. It was part of the way he lived. The day would never come when he wouldn't want to come back at all.

His pipe burned out. Whicher had moved around the pool and now stood looking at him. Amos nodded toward the house.

"Go along, Whicher, if you have a mind to."

Whicher vanished into the woods.

Amos lit his pipe again. He'd wait a little longer. He thought of the wagon tongue he'd have to fix. He could shape up one of the leverwood poles in the shed, if one was long enough. He'd rather be walking down toward Carr Brook with the new fish rod. Maybe Joan would be there below the Derby Fields. Fish rod and wagon pole. Something you had to do and something you wanted to do.

Finally he said, "Well, Mort, the afternoon don't last forever." He pointed at the cowslips. "I'll take them along to Gram. She'll want to be picking them over for supper."

He got to his feet and laid Mort's shoes on the log beside him. Mort didn't move as Amos gathered up the coat.

Amos turned and took a few steps. He asked over his shoulder, "You want me to tend to the grave?"

Mort looked at him for a moment, then shook his head. He began putting on his socks and shoes. He asked, "You know about the barway?"

Amos nodded.

"Cows get out?"

"They did, but they're back." Amos didn't mention the heifer.

Mort frowned. "I don't know what made me do it. Seemed like I didn't want them to stay in the pasture. Didn't want our fence to hold them in, even after we'd been working on it." He stared at the pool. "I just couldn't go back and put up the bars. I sat down to think about it and then I wanted to pick the cowslips for Gram, so I did, and then I began to feel bad and I came over here."

Mort got to his feet and looked at the ground with a puzzled and guilty twist to his face. Finally he shrugged and looked at Amos with something near a smile. "Don't know how I could have forgot them bars. Pa's fit to be tied, I suppose."

"He'll get over it." Amos almost went on to say that the heifer might not. Instead, he silently led the way back to the field.

The sun was slanting toward the western ridge as they climbed up through the field. Amos handed Mort the cowslips. Let him take them into the house. Probably nobody would say much, but just then he didn't care particularly. He found that being with Mort had left him all on edge. He didn't want to think for Mort or try to understand his actions. He didn't want to be required to talk just so and act just so. He turned off toward the shed.

He could see Pa and Whicher in the tie-up with the heifer. Going to the door, he called, "She all right?"

"I guess she'll live. Couldn't have got much. I fed her a mess of bran and linseed oil." Pa leaned in the doorway. "What ailed Mort?"

"Just acting peculiar."

"I don't know what'll become of him. Times, I don't know what'll become of us all."

Amos was suddenly angry. "Don't talk like an old woman, Pa."

He turned back to the shed and carried one of the leverwood poles to the field where the wagon was stuck in the mud. He'd have to unbolt the old pole and fit and drill the new one, rig the irons. Then before he could move the wagon he'd have to fork out the manure and dig around the wheels. He looked at the sun. There was time to get a wrench and take off the old pole. Pa and Whicher and Mort could do the chores. After supper he might wash up and go over to the Tarltons'. A week ago he wouldn't have thought he might go calling on a girl. But going over there wasn't that. Joan wasn't his girl. Besides, they might have some errands for him when he went to the creamery tomorrow.

## Chapter 9

It was dark when Amos started out. There'd been some talk before he left, while he was washing at the sink, stripped to the waist and splashing water on his face and shoulders.

"Well," Gram remarked, "he never bothers to wash like that for us. Not on Thursday night. Hot water and white soap. Humph."

His father asked, "Going to get the line for that fish pole?"

Amos didn't answer. He had not told them where he was going, but they knew all right. And they knew why, although he'd said almost nothing about the rod or about pulling Joan Tarlton from the bog, or about the mayflowers she picked for him.

Rose was the only one with advice that amounted to anything.

"When you get there, don't stand and gawk. They're no different from anybody." She picked up a brush and comb from the shelf over the sink. "Let me straighten the part in your hair. My land, it's like trying to comb baled straw."

In his room, he put on his second-best pants and a clean blue shirt. Because of the mud he slipped into his laced rubbers. He found the red and black jacket he hadn't worn much in the barn.

As he was about to leave, Rose came and sniffed him. "If you don't get too close to her she won't know you ever cleaned out the cows."

"I don't aim to get too close to her."

Whicher snickered and Amos just looked at him. He left the lamplit kitchen.

It was good to be outside walking along the dark road. The air was cool and fresh. The mud didn't bother him much. It was drying fast. When his eyes got used to the dark he could walk along the road and see where to put his feet. Down in the wet places by the stream, the peepers were calling.

As he began climbing up the Ridge Road, he had to make his feet keep going. It was nonsense, because all he had to do was ask if there were any errands for tomorrow. Probably Mr. Tarlton would open the door, and he could ask about the errands and then it would be yes or no while he stood on the porch, and he'd go home, with maybe a hello from Joan. There wasn't anything to it. But he didn't feel easy about it and when he

[ 64 ]

thought that he might not see Joan at all, his heart sort of sagged—that was the only way he could think about the feeling—sagged, and he lost all his courage. He knew he wasn't coming over here to be neighborly about errands in the village. He'd known it all along.

He turned in the gate and what he saw didn't make him feel any better. There was a Model A roadster in front of the porch. At first he couldn't believe it, because of the mud, but there it was, plain in the light from the windows. They must have come a day early, somehow driving in from the other end of the Ridge Road.

He almost turned around. He stopped and thought about it. At last he continued walking toward the lodge. He'd come this far and he'd go the rest of the way.

He paused by the steps to wipe his feet in the grass. He went slowly up the steps and across the porch. Through the big windows he could see people in the living room. Joan looked toward the porch. He knocked hurriedly so she wouldn't think he had been standing there peering in.

The porch light came on and Joan opened the door. He said nothing while his heart beat in his chest. He remembered to take off his hat.

She smiled. "Why, Amos, how nice! Come on in."

"No, I just stopped over to see if you folks had anything you wanted in the village tomorrow."

"I don't know. I'll ask Mother. Come in." She stepped aside and held open the door.

Gregory Tarlton appeared behind Joan. "By God, Amos Jackman. Come in, come in." He shook hands. "I'll go make you a drink right off. Joan, take him in and introduce him."

Her eyes were bright. "I'm awfully glad you came." She put his hat on a table by the door and took him by the arm as she led him into the living room. "This is Amos," she announced.

He looked at two young men on the floor and at the girl sitting in a chair and Mrs. Tarlton sitting near the fireplace.

"Hello, Amos," said Mrs. Tarlton. "It's good to see you again." She looked at the others. "Amos pulled Joan out of a swamp several days ago. We're not sure she was worth the trouble."

"Shut up, Mother. He'd do it again, wouldn't you, Amos?" She moved with him into the middle of the room. "Anita, Amos Jackman. Anita Winship. And Ronnie Parkwood. Old brother Dave."

Amos nodded at the girl and stepped forward awkwardly to shake hands with Ronnie who got up from the floor with a lithe untangling of long legs. Dave lifted his hand in greeting and said something about deer hunting.

Ronnie pretended that his hand was hurt. "You're just our man," he said. "Can you lift that chair?" He pointed to a heavy chair.

Amos glanced at Ronnie to see what the joke was.

"We have a problem," Dave explained. "Got to lift that chair. Reputation and prestige of the younger generation at stake. Ronnie can't and I can't. Dad says he could twenty years ago and probably can now. Figures I should, not to mention Ronnie. Won't demonstrate till we do it."

They were silent, looking at Amos. He could feel himself getting red all the way down to his collar. Finally he said, "Looks like it could be done."

"Oh, it can be done," Ronnie told him, and lifted the chair by the back. "But, and this is the big but, you've got to lift it by one leg."

Ronnie lay down on the floor on his belly and carefully moved aside a highball glass. Amos watched, puzzled and bewildered. Ronnie gripped the chair by the leg and tried to lift it.

"See, it can't be done. I can't do it, anyhow. I doubt if it can be done. Try it. With a grip like yours maybe you can." He again pretended his hand had been hurt shaking with Amos.

"Yes, try it," they all said.

Only Mrs. Tarlton protested. "For goodness' sake, leave him alone. He walks in on a wild bunch like this and you ask him to lie on his stomach and lift a chair. What nonsense. Sit down, Amos."

"Well, I just stopped over—" Amos had the feeling of repeating himself. "Thought you might have some errands for tomorrow."

"Thanks an awful lot," Mrs. Tarlton said, "but I think we're all fixed."

Amos nodded and turned away, ready to retreat. He almost bumped into Mr. Tarlton with a glass in his hand.

"Before you go," said Tarlton, "and before you lift the chair—which I don't believe any member of this puny generation can do—drink this."

With his retreat cut off, Amos moved aside and came close to Joan. She took his arm again.

"You can't run off, Amos. Not without one drink."

"Of course not," her father said. "We haven't many neighbors and when one of them walks over these goddamn roads to see if he can help us out, he isn't going to leave without a drink."

The easiest thing for Amos seemed to be to take the glass.

"Drink it up," Joan urged. "You're way behind."

"Isn't he, though?" Dave Tarlton sat on the floor and waved his glass. "There's nothing worse than coming into a party cold sober. Drink up!"

"Go ahead," Tarlton said, "because the only good thing Roosevelt has done is repeal the Eighteenth."

Amos stared at the glass and then looked about him. There seemed to be only one thing to do. He tipped up the glass and drained it in three gulps. There appeared to be a little fire in it and he choked back a cough. He knew it was some stronger than cider.

A cheer went up from all but Mrs. Tarlton. She sank back in her chair and at last had to laugh. She took her glass and laughingly put it down again. "I think it's a shame to get the boy in here with this crazy crowd and make him drink if he doesn't want to."

"Now, Mother," said Joan. "We're just having a little fun, aren't we, Amos? Get him another, Dad. Now Amos will lift the chair."

Amos couldn't quite picture himself flat on his belly on the floor of the Tarlton lodge. He said, "I'm interrupting you folks. I'll just go along."

"No you won't," Joan told him.

"Got to uphold the prestige of modern youth," Dave said. "Gird up your loins and slay the giant of parental disapproval. Besides, I want to see Dad flop at it. Said he'd try if anyone of us could. Goes for you, too."

"Maybe you can't," said Ronnie.

"Well, I don't know." He turned toward Joan and saw her nod. "Try anything once, I guess."

Not quite sure what a fool they took him for and yet surprised that he could bring himself to do it at all, he lay down on the floor.

"Take off your jacket," Dave said. "Roll up your sleeves and gird up your loins. Take off your jacket."

"Never mind the jacket," Amos told him. He took hold of the chair leg.

"Wait a minute," Ronnie cautioned. "Got to be right down by the rug. You can't roll on your side. Arm off the floor."

Amos moved his grip against the deep pile of the rug. He made sure of his hold and lifted. The chair came off the floor. Almost easy, he thought, wondering why they made such a fuss about it.

"Yowie," shouted Dave. "He did it!"

"Did what?" asked Mr. Tarlton, coming into the room with another highball for Amos.

"Oh, Dad, you missed it," cried Joan. "He'll never do it again."

Amos lifted the chair once more.

They all began talking at the same time. An increasing sensation of confusion came over Amos. Dave jumped to his feet and pounded him on the back. Ronnie was trying to get Mr. Tarlton to lie down on the floor. Joan held his arm as he slowly stood up. He thought she was going to kiss him. She kept jumping up and down beside him. Anita took the glass from Mr. Tarlton and offered it to Amos with a bow of mock humility while Joan cried out, "Get away from him, you vixen. I found him and he's mine. He rescued me from the bog and our lives are inextricably entwined."

Amos took the glass and stood there holding it, all the while feeling stupid and bewildered, but pleased. They seemed to be having a good time and they weren't laughing at him. He felt warm inside and he couldn't make up his mind whether it was the whiskey or Joan.

They were trying to get Mr. Tarlton to do the chair stunt. At last he lay down on the floor and after many gestures of preparation failed completely, although he strained until his face turned red, while Ronnie and Dave jeered. Amos thought they shouldn't plague him so, but Mr. Tarlton didn't seem bothered by it. Amos wondered why they made so much of strength, but he guessed it was sort of a joke. There were more important things. Strength didn't matter so much. Yet he was pleased he had lifted the chair.

Mrs. Tarlton said, "Now take off your jacket, Amos. You've got to stay a while."

Amos let them take his jacket and he sat down in a chair. He drank from his glass carefully, a little afraid of what it would do to him. Everyone seemed to be talking at once. The conversation turned more and more to things he didn't know about, college and people in Braemuir. Mr. Tarlton kept busy on trips to and from the kitchen. Cheered on by Dave, Ronnie began to do imitations of the professors at the business school. Joan left Amos to join Ronnie, and Anita moved over beside Amos and sat down on the arm of his chair.

"Where do you live?" she asked.

"Over across the valley." He nodded his head toward Whichertown.

"Do you have a farm?"

"Well, I help out on ours."

"It must be wonderful. I think it's wonderful to be doing something like that. I mean when everything is going to hell in a handbasket. Don't you?"

"I couldn't say. Never did anything else."

"That's what I mean. I think it's wonderful the way Joan and her folks are going back to the land. Of course, Dave wants to forge ahead and get to be a big businessman and all that, but I don't know." She turned her large eyes on him. "It's more than you might expect to look at him, isn't it? I admire him for it, don't you?"

"Yes, sure."

"But I admire someone who lives a fundamental life, if you see what I mean, because it's basic, like sex. What do you think about sex, Mr. Jackman? I think it's wonderful, but what do you think about it?"

Amos stammered and finally came out with, "Golly, I couldn't say."

"I know, you're one of those strong fundamental men who doesn't have to think about it because it's just a natural part of living to him. I think that's the perfect way to be."

Amos drained his highball and looked around helplessly. If he could just get up and move about a little perhaps Anita would stop talking to him. But she sat close on the arm of his chair. Besides, his legs seemed a different part of him, for he was floating quietly in the chair and the people in the room were an animated show which he watched as he might watch a moving picture. He didn't think it strange that Dave was walking on his hands across the floor or that Joan was pretending to lead a band in which there was only one instrument, the piano that Ronnie was pounding.

Joan for the first time noticed Anita sitting in the chair beside Amos. She came toward them and stood with her hands on her hips.

"Behind my back, eh?" She took Anita by the hand. "You go dance with Dave. I'll tend to Amos."

"Don't bother us. We're talking about sex and the fundamentals of life." Anita stood up, laughing. "Ronnie, play us 'St. Louis Blues.' Come here, Dave."

Joan pulled Amos to his feet. "You've got to dance with me, Amos."

He smiled at her, the idea of his dancing was so funny. He didn't feel embarrassed that he couldn't. He said, "I don't know how."

"I'll show you." She placed his arm around her waist and took his hand. "All you have to do is walk to the music."

He didn't move. "I don't think I'd do very good at it." He watched Dave swing Anita around slow and easy. "Looks simple, but I wouldn't know where to put my feet."

Joan tried to lead him, but he stepped on her toe and she gave up. "Never mind. I'll have to give you some private lessons. We'll sing." She pulled him toward the piano.

He found that he could walk all right. His legs had become part of him again.

"Sing," Joan commanded.

He couldn't sing and he couldn't read the music where her finger pointed at the sheet on the rack, but he tried to hum along with the tune and it was nice to be near Joan. He had no feeling of being ill at ease as he had when Anita was with him. He watched Anita dancing

[ 69 ]

with Dave. Like they were glued together, he thought. Joan flipped the music sheets and they sang another song while Ronnie banged on the keys. Joan stood close to him and held his arm.

Mrs. Tarlton came into the room carrying a tray of sandwiches, and crackers with sardines on them and little cubes of cheese. Mr. Tarlton brought in a tray of highballs. Everybody gathered around the table near the piano. Amos tried to refuse a glass, but Mr. Tarlton insisted and Amos took it. If he ate some sandwiches they might sop up the whiskey, but he was worried about how he'd act if he drank more than he could handle. After he finished the highball and had some crackers and sardines, he said, "I guess I better go along. I get up pretty early, you know."

"Heck, stay a while," Joan said.

"Sure," Mr. Tarlton told him. "The night's young."

"Thanks, I better go." He nodded at Ronnie and Dave and Anita and said to Mr. and Mrs. Tarlton, "I had a good time."

"Come again, come again," Mr. Tarlton said, following him to the door with Mrs. Tarlton.

Joan brought his jacket. "Good night, Amos."

"Good night."

He went out on the porch and the door closed behind him.

He had almost reached the road when he heard footsteps behind him and turned to see Joan running toward him. He started back and met her. She held out his hat.

"I forgot to give it to you. I thought of keeping it," she said, "so you'd have to come back, but that didn't seem fair. Here it is."

He took the old felt hat, holding it and not understanding what was expected of him, but feeling that something was incomplete, he didn't know just what. Joan was looking at him. He couldn't see her face clearly in the darkness, only its outline and the shape of her body in the lights from the house.

"I'll walk with you to the gate," she said.

"You'll get all mud."

"I don't care. Parties are silly things. You get people tight and all mixed up and then you can't sort them out the way they're supposed to be." She was moving beside him. "I wish I didn't have to go back. Let's walk down the road a little."

"You better go back."

She slipped in a rut and he took her hand and she turned toward him. They stopped close and she put her arms around his neck. He kissed her clumsily on the cheek. She was warm and smelled sweet

[ 70 ]

and her face was soft while her breasts and thighs were firm against him. He put his arms around her.

The door at the lodge slammed and he heard feet on the porch. Joan turned her head.

"As you might expect," she said. "Ronnie. I suppose I better go back." She touched his hand.

He watched her go, bewildered and stirred to follow her, but unable to because, as she said, people got all mixed up and you couldn't sort them out the way they were supposed to be.

"Joan," Ronnie called. "You all right?"

"Of course." She stopped and waved. "Good night, Amos."

He saw Ronnie beside Joan on the porch under the light. They went into the house.

He started down the road. Longing for her came over him stronger than anything he had known. It didn't fade as he walked away. He could still feel her against him, her arms and her cheek soft and her body so firm and warm. He was sure he'd never be the same again, but his mind rejected his uncontrollable thoughts and he told himself that likely he'd get over it. But he didn't believe it, and he was glad. He walked down the muddy road feeling happy and strong as a bull.

## Chapter 10

Often when he finished a day's plowing, Amos would look at the stones he had turned out of the earth and think of the others below the surface which had caught the plow; he ought to roll them out and haul them to the wall, but there was enough work loading the loose ones on the stone boat and dragging them away. Some of the times when the plow jolted in his hands he knew it was not caused by rocks which could be moved but by the solid ledge of the state of New Hampshire. He could tell by the scraping roughness. Movable stones were smooth and suggested by their impact with the plow that they could be dug out and rolled over. But that grating solidness was ledge which went down to bedrock.

Thinking about the stones and the ledge as he walked the team back to the barn, he noticed the bushes growing along the walls, and the young trees seeding in from the woods. They combined with the rocks to keep a man working. He had to scratch up the ground and he had to hold back the trees. And he had to contend with the seasons and the weather. Sometimes it hardly seemed worth the work.

In a way, the woods were contending with him for the land. The bushes in the pasture, the wildflowers and weeds in the hay fields, the expanse of green hills around the farm—tree-growing hills—made him feel that he could never hold back the greenery. When he had studied geography in school the teacher had talked about jungles and there were pictures in the book. He thought that the geography fellow should see things grow in New Hampshire in June, a month from now. If it kept up all year there'd be nothing but greenery. It would choke you in your sleep.

He thought of Pa and he could understand why Pa was tired and discouraged.

Sometimes he pictured a bear roaming the woods, eating, growing fat, sleeping away the winter. That seemed like a good life. Times were, he didn't care if the woods swallowed the farm, for then he'd have nothing to do but hunt and fish and hire out at wages when he needed a little money. On days when he felt like that he could hardly drive himself to work the land or lay a shingle over a hole in the barn roof. Usually it ended with his taking off for the camp on the pond.

Other days, he could work around the sun and plan what he'd do to build up the farm the next day.

It seemed that there were two parts of him which fought over him. He'd be pulled one way and then the other.

Like today, he'd been working toward the last furrow since morning, and now, with the sun half down the sky, he was done and he knew he couldn't work any more for a time.

A reaction had set in after his visit to the Tarltons. When he thought of it the next day in the cold dawn of the cow tie-up, the evening took on an unreal quality like a dream. Although it warmed him and made his blood run faster to think of Joan, the actual circumstances had become remote. The Tarltons' living room was far removed from the barn where the cows at the tie-up ate their grain with long tongues, standing while he and Whicher milked. The evening had nothing to do with the manure smell and the hay smell and the cow smell, nor with the sound of milk pinging into an empty pail. The light of the sunrise on the narrow windows faded the lantern.

He knew it had been a single experience that would not be repeated. Joan would marry Ronnie. Probably today she was laughing with Ronnie about kissing the farmer. Perhaps she had done it just to get Ronnie mad, just because she had been drinking. Of course she had come out alone and she had no reason to think that Ronnie would follow her. But still probably she had planned it that way. He didn't know about women. He guessed he didn't understand anything about them. Likely, Joan Tarlton had let him kiss her just for the hell of it.

He thought about it and around it until he had worn it out and there was nothing left but the husk of the experience and this he took to be all there'd ever been. He decided to go to work and forget it.

So he had worked for two days and here Saturday afternoon had rolled around and he was ready to quit.

He put the horses in the barn and went to the house to get his new fishing rod.

"Gram, I'm going fishing."

"You be back tonight?"

"I expect so."

"Bring me some trout."

"All right."

He didn't stop to dig bait because he was so anxious to get away. He struck into the woods beyond the lower field, but he didn't head across the valley toward the upper reaches of Carr Brook. He found that his feet were leading him almost parallel to the road into Whichertown. He was thinking of Joan more than of fishing.

The sun was down toward setting. He came to Carr Brook below the Tarlton lodge, having crossed the old road that led to the Grimes place. A faint trail opened through the woods toward the hill.

He saw Ronnie and Joan coming down the path. He didn't want to meet them both and he felt that they wouldn't want to see him. The fishing rods they carried were just an excuse to get away from the house and be alone together. He moved up the brook, hoping to get out of sight before they noticed him.

He had not gone far when he heard Joan's voice above the sound of the water. She was calling his name. He wanted to keep going, but he wanted to see her, and he turned around. She waved to him and he raised his hand in return.

"Are they biting?" she shouted.

"I don't know. Haven't tried them."

She smiled. He watched her unreel the line and bait the hook. He saw that Ronnie was new at trout fishing and didn't seem to like it, for he walked awkwardly over the rocks and watched Joan get her line ready. He had none of the equipment of the city fisherman, and he baited the hook and tossed out the line in an unskilled way. Amos thought he had come with Joan just to be with her. Although Amos could understand that, he felt a pang of jealousy. He wished he were Ronnie.

Joan had come closer. "Are you going to fish here?"

"No, I'm going farther up."

Ronnie said, "Come on, Joan, we can fish downstream."

"No, the best fishing is up. Amos won't catch them all."

"I'm going to walk up a way," Amos said.

He turned into the woods. He didn't wave or look back, but strode rapidly beside the brook until he came into the fields by the Grimes place. He felt better as he walked. He was almost ready to walk up to the camp, but he couldn't go farther from Joan. When he came to the woods again, he cut down to the brook and stopped at a rotten log which he kicked open to find a few grubs.

He fished several pools and caught two trout. Then he sat on a smooth slab of rock and watched the water and thought of Joan. He couldn't think what to do about her.

He didn't know how long he sat there all mixed up between wanting her and knowing he'd never have her, when she came along the brook. She didn't appear to be fishing much, just climbing from pool to pool and dropping her line in here and there. She kept looking ahead and when she saw him she smiled.

"Hello," she said, as though she had been expecting to find him. "We always seem to be running into each other along here."

"Seems though."

Ronnie wasn't with her. She couldn't have done much fishing to get here so quickly, or maybe he'd been sitting on the rock a lot longer than he realized. She sat down beside him, her boots in the water, and idly trailed her baited hook in the riffle.

He said nothing.

"They aren't biting," she remarked. "Ronnie doesn't think much of trout fishing."

"Where is he?"

"Down the brook or gone home. We don't seem to hit it off like we did at Braemuir. Funny how people are different in different places." She looked at him soberly. "Ronnie always thought of me as a suburban girl in a dance dress or tennis clothes. Funny how well you can get to know someone and not know him at all. I honestly think I know you better."

"We seem to get along, most of the time."

[ 74 ]

She went on, "Last night he asked me again to marry him. I wish I knew what to do. What would you do?"

Amos had become preoccupied with having her near him and he wasn't following closely what she said. He had to think a minute to get straight what she meant.

"Well," he said at last. "I guess he's your kind, all right."

"Yes—yes, I suppose he is, but then I don't know. Sometimes I scare myself." She stopped speaking and then asked abruptly, "Did you like kissing me the other night?"

"What's that? Well, yes."

"So did I, and I don't generally. Funny thing." She stared at him as though he were in a glass case. "You aren't much to look at and we're altogether different. It isn't right that I should like you. Funny thing."

They sat without speaking a while, looking at the brook, until a voice said, "Well, well."

Ronnie had come up the brook and was standing below them watching. His pants were wet to the knees, the khaki cloth dark brown from the water.

"God's sake, Joan, I thought you'd gotten lost in the woods or fallen into one of these damn pools."

"Oh, Ronnie, don't be so dramatic."

"Well, I was worried."

"You were so slow."

"So I see. I think we better go back. The fish aren't biting."

"They'll start." She pointed to the two trout on a twig beside Amos.

"Let him catch them," Ronnie said. "It's a silly pastime."

"I like it."

Ronnie frowned at the brook. "Splashing around after six-inch fish."

"You can go back."

Ronnie sat down on a rock and lit a cigarette. He looked at his watch. "We're due at the cocktail party in an hour or so."

"Oh, that," Joan said. "I'd forgotten that." She smiled cheerfully. "Maybe we can't get out the road. I don't feel like going to the Marsleys' tonight."

"Of course we can get out the road." He disregarded Amos as he talked to her. "It'll do you good. You've been stuck here in the backwoods too long."

"I like it."

"Sure, of course you do. But let's have a change. It'll do you good. Come on."

She got slowly to her feet. Amos thought that she didn't want to go.

He hadn't said a word since Ronnie arrived. There didn't seem to be much he could say, although he wanted her to remain with him. For a moment he wished with all his heart that he wasn't a Whichertown farmer, that he had been born down to Fallsburg and had a father who owned a business, and himself working at a good job. Perhaps if he got out of Whichertown—no, if he had left a few years back . . . Well, it was a stupid wish, because it couldn't be. The bitterness of feeling that Joan was beyond reach stayed with him as he watched her reel in her line and prepare to leave. Although she had said she liked him, perhaps it didn't mean much.

Ronnie said to her, "Come on, Joan, we don't want to miss the party, or the dance at the town hall. We'll have fun."

Joan looked at Amos without smiling. "See you around, maybe," she said.

He found himself speaking at last. The words seemed unlikely afterward, but he did say, "I might be in the village myself."

They were gone down the brook, Ronnie picking his way carefully while Joan moved easily from rock to rock.

Amos started fishing. He had to catch the trout for Gram. He had to get them so he could go home and change his clothes to drive to the village.

He caught them after sunset, fifteen trout in all. He had climbed fast between the stretches of poor water, fishing only the deep pools. He was almost at the bog when he turned back.

On the way home in the twilight, he thought about giving up the trip to the village. It wouldn't accomplish anything. Joan was going to the Marsleys' with Ronnie and then to the dance at the town hall. He couldn't dance, he knew he'd never go inside the hall, and yet he had to be near her.

After supper, he went out to the shed to start the Ford. It hadn't been used since before the mud season and the battery was low. He had to crank a long time before it coughed into life. He let it run while he got a lantern and pumped up the tires with a hand pump.

Back in the kitchen he washed at the sink. Rose spoke to him.

"I'd just as soon go to the village with you, Amos."

"What makes you think I'm going?"

"You can't drive up to the Tarltons' yet. You are going down, ain't you?"

"Going to try it."

"Gram and I want to visit Mrs. Hardy and Whicher wants to go to the movies."

"Well, all right." Somehow he wished he were going alone, without the family. He wasn't usually bothered by any of them, and he wasn't ashamed of them. He just wanted to be alone, but he said nothing.

It was full dark when they started out. Amos drove slowly down the road until he got the feel of the muddy surface. Gram sat beside him, Rose and Whicher in back. Mort hadn't wanted to go, and Pa hadn't seemed interested. Perhaps Pa felt he ought to stay at the farm with Mort, but Amos suspected that Pa hadn't the energy and the trip to the village no longer appealed to him; he used to like to sit on the porch of the store and talk and watch the cars and teams and the people coming in for their Saturday night trading. But tonight Pa just sat listlessly in the kitchen and said, "No, don't believe I'll go."

Amos gave up wondering what was the matter with him and kept his mind on the driving. Mud didn't trouble him as much as he had expected. There were two bad spots, one at the bottom of Footstep Hill and one near the main road, where he had to tread down on the low pedal while the car lurched through the mud holes. And then they were on the gravel road, rolling down through the interval along Carr Brook, down the last slopes into the river valley.

There were lights shining on the asphalt of the village street, and lights in the houses under the elms and maples. Amos drove slowly past the cars parked in front of the Marsleys'. He saw the mud-splashed Ford roadster. He looked across the lawn at the lighted windows and wondered what Joan was doing.

"Step on it, Amos," Whicher said. "I don't want to be late to the pictures."

"Plenty of time."

"I need a quarter."

Gram opened her pocketbook and handed the money to Whicher in the back seat.

Amos turned at the gas pumps in front of Cy Tillman's store, and drove toward the bridge. He remembered going through the bridge with Joan, while she read the posters. The Model T ground up the hill beyond the bridge. There was a red warning light blinking at the railroad crossing.

Gram asked, "You see that light, Amos?"

"I see it."

He waited while the train roared by. Whicher leaned over his shoulder to watch.

"Godfrey," Whicher cried, "don't it go! I wish I lived down here. I'd come over every day to watch it. Maybe I'll be an engineer when I grow up."

[ 77 ]

"They might let you shovel the coal," Amos said.

"Heck, I'd do that even."

Amos thought, *Yes, you probably would*, although to him the idea of being shut up in the cab with the noise and the heat from the red door held none of the romantic appeal it seemed to have for Whicher. The speed and rush of the engine and cars was something to endure as they went past, not something of which you longed to be a part.

At the store where Joan had bought the rod, he waited while Gram and Rose went inside. Whicher jumped out of the car and joined the group at the lighted front of the hall. From a poster on the wall of the building, Amos could see that the picture was to be a Western.

When Gram and Rose came out of the store with their packages, he drove them back across the bridge and down the village street to the little cottage where Mrs. Hardy lived, beyond and opposite the Marsleys. Gram had known Mrs. Hardy for years and she'd been sort of an aunt to Rose. They'd have a long talk about the wedding and the news of the village.

Amos was alone in the Ford, at a loss what to do. Finally he drove toward the town hall and parked in the shadows by the common. He felt that he was outside the activity of the town and he wondered what had made him come.

Cars slowed down and parked in the field beside the hall. Men with fiddles and cornets in cases went inside and after a time Amos heard the tuning-up notes of the instruments. He rested his foot on the side of the Ford where there wasn't any door, and watched and listened.

Down the street at the Marsleys' he saw the lights of the house through the trees, and shadows passing inside. He didn't know which was Joan; he couldn't tell.

Dance music came from the hall. Men and women and boys and girls went up the granite steps. He could see them dancing inside. Jim Sheridan, the constable, stood at the door with his star on his checkered shirt, his bald head gleaming in the light.

Spring smelled different down here in the valley—more of field and farms than of woods, of ferns and mud from the river banks perhaps, and of gasoline. There was a certain heaviness in the air. A horse and buggy came clopping down the street, with a lantern swinging under the axletree.

At last he heard voices and laughter from the Marsleys' house. Looking down the street, he could see Joan in the group. They came toward the hall and went up the steps. For a moment Joan looked toward him, toward the Ford parked under the maples.

He raised his hand to wave, but she didn't see him, or she didn't want to see him. He continued the motion as though he weren't going to wave, and held to the roof frame of the car, pretending to stretch. He shifted in the seat. It didn't seem possible that she hadn't recognized him, for the lights of a passing car had flared across him as she stood on the steps. He was overwhelmed by the feeling that she didn't want to recognize him when she was with the Marsleys and their friends. But perhaps the lights had blinded her and she couldn't see him. He stared straight ahead through the windshield and when he looked back they had gone inside.

It was not like being with her on the brook this afternoon. Suddenly he hated all the people and the cars and the music and the dancers passing the lighted windows. He felt so out of place that he longed for Whichertown and its familiar surroundings. But he could not take his eyes from the windows. He wanted to see Joan and when she did not appear he got out of the car and approached the hall. He was quite close to one of the windows when he saw her dancing in Ronnie's arms. The way she looked up at Ronnie and clung to him made Amos' heart ache. He walked away and sat on the board fence around the common. Although he could see the windows over the tops of the parked cars, for a time he didn't try to find Joan among the dancers, but stared at the ground. And then he had to look. She was still dancing with Ronnie.

He wished that he had stayed in Whichertown. This wasn't his place. He wondered why he had felt that he must come to the village. It had seemed necessary to see her again. He had wanted to be near her. It seemed foolish now.

Finally, he lowered himself from the fence and walked slowly back to the Ford. He'd go to the Hardys' and wait until Whicher came from the pictures. There was nothing here for him.

And then he saw Joan and Ronnie coming out of the hall. She held Ronnie's arm and they were laughing about something. She looked toward him and at once called out, "There's Amos!" She left Ronnie and ran to him.

"Amos, I'm so glad I saw you. I want to say goodby. We're leaving early in the morning for Braemuir—Ronnie and Dave and Anita and I." She talked rapidly. "I wouldn't want you to think I'd left without saying goodby."

"You won't be coming back?"

"No, I'm going to get a job in Boston."

"Well," he said slowly. "I see."

"I made up my mind to it tonight. I think it's a good idea, don't you?"

"No," he said.

"It is. It will be. I'm sure it's the right thing. And so is Ronnie."

Ronnie had been waiting. "Let's go, darling."

"In a minute. Please don't rush me. I'm fond of Amos and I want to say goodby to him."

Anita and Dave passed them. "Coming, you two?" Dave asked. "A terrible drought has set in. I see an oasis ahead. Hi there, Amos."

"Come on, Joan." Ronnie moved forward and took her arm.

Joan pulled away. "Let go of me. I'm going to say goodby to Amos. You beat it."

"Not without you. Come on, Joan. Don't make a spectacle of yourself right here on the street."

Joan was beside Amos. "Ronnie's worried about my making a spectacle. Worries about things like that. Appearances are everything. Good boy, Ronnie. Leave me alone for a while and then I'll watch appearances all the rest of my life."

"Oh, for God's sake, Joan."

Amos moved toward the car. "I expect I better be going along."

"Yes," Ronnie said. "Why don't you, Amos? Then perhaps I can talk some sense into Joan." He took Joan's arm again and led her away.

Amos reached into the car and turned on the ignition and adjusted the spark and gas levers. He stepped around to the front and cranked the engine.

Goodbys were not worth saying if they didn't mean what was in his heart. He could see that she had decided where she belonged, but he felt that she was torn between what she thought was right and what she wanted to do. He didn't know how to tell her that she belonged with him in Whichertown.

He got in the car and drove down the street to the Hardys', past the Marsley house. He stopped outside but didn't go in. He sat in the car and felt drained of all his strength.

He was aroused by the sound of footsteps down the street. He turned and saw Joan walking fast toward him. Her high heels rapped on the asphalt.

She stood beside the car. "There," she said. "They didn't want me to say goodby to you but I sneaked out the back way. I saw you stop here. Were you waiting for me? You were, weren't you?"

He said slowly, "I would have if I'd known." He nodded toward the house. "Gram and Rose are in there."

"Isn't that lucky? But you would have stopped if you'd known I could sneak out?"

[ 80 ]

"I'd have waited all night, I guess."

Although the light behind her was faint, he could see that she was smiling at him and he felt again the warm exchange between them. It had nothing to do with what they were talking about or with what was happening, but seemed to flow from their being together.

He stepped over the side of the Ford and stood beside her. "Why are you going back to Braemuir?"

"Oh, I've got to." She took his arm, and they walked slowly across the street. "It's the only thing. I don't belong here and I got so mixed up. I felt better when I made up my mind what I should do. I thought about it after I'd left you on the brook." She spoke earnestly and kept her eyes on his face. "I'm no good for you and if I stayed I couldn't stop seeing you and it would be a mess and I hate messes. See what I mean?"

"I see what you think you mean."

She hesitated, as though unable to say anything more about it, and then added, "I promised Ronnie."

"You going to marry him?"

"Maybe. I just promised him to try the city again—that is, down home where we both belong."

They were standing under a big maple by the drive that led into the Marsley yard. Beyond them was a patch of light from a lamp on the gate.

"So," she said, "you see how it is."

"Yes. Seems kind of foolish."

"It's the right thing. I know it is."

"You do?"

"Yes, it is. I know it. Amos, don't look at me like that. Oh, Amos."

He stepped forward and took her in his arms. It was awkward to find her lips but he and Joan were meant to be like this and he felt her arms go around his neck.

At last she pushed back from him. "That's not goodby, Amos. It was supposed to be."

"No need to be." He could feel her still close against him, her waist small and supple against his hand.

"It's got to be. I made up my mind. Amos, don't hold me so close. I can't be yours—it isn't right. I want you so and yet I don't. . . ."

He said, "We could get married."

"No. It would never work. Oh God, I just wanted to say goodby and now I'm all mixed up again. Let me go, Amos."

She was crying as she turned abruptly. "Goodby, Amos."

[ 81 ]

She ran toward the drive and he didn't try to follow. He saw her go into the house.

He leaned against the old maple and felt the bark rough through his shirt. He looked at the house, the big house of the Marsleys, and saw, dim through the young leaves before the windows, the fine paneling and woodwork and the figures of people standing around a table with silver dishes behind it in a cabinet. He seemed to be looking into a strange world and he couldn't see Joan, for she had disappeared into it. He closed his eyes to shut it out.

That was the way Whicher found him, and said, "Amos, wake up. Why you sleeping there against that tree?"

"I ain't sleeping," Amos told him. "Go into the Hardys' and get Gram and Rose. It's time we were heading home."

## Chapter 11

The following week, on Decoration Day, Rose was married.

All week Amos had driven himself at the farm work. He had been aware of the preparations at the house in a vague way that did not touch him.

The weather was cold for the end of May, with no hint of the warmer days which must be only a short time off in June. There was a cold east wind blowing across the valley from Quartz Mountain and Cobblestone. It rippled the green grass about the plowed piece where Amos planted potatoes. Although the earth spoke of warmth and summer, with its green leaves and growth, wild strawberry flowers in the grass and peas sprouting in the garden, birds swooping after insects in the air or singing in the trees, and the sun hot in sheltered places, yet the sky and winds seemed to war against the advance of the season. The wind thrashed the purple lilacs that grew by the back door and stripped the tender leaves from the maples, scattering them across the field. It showered apple petals in a miniature snowstorm.

Amos furrowed the potato rows with Whicher riding Dick. The wind blew out the horse's mane and tail and flattened Whicher's hair and billowed Amos' shirt cold on his back. Mort sat by the back door of the house, cutting seed potatoes. With the approach of Decoration Day, he sometimes spoke of the flowers he planned to take to the cemetery.

Amos worked with a single-mindedness which almost kept him from thinking of Joan. For minutes at a time he might forget and then it would come to him that she was gone. He would work harder—hoeing at the furrows to cover the potatoes, lifting the rocks in the cornfield he plowed. And he stayed out of the house except for meals and sleep. He was saddened by the happy intimacy of Gram and Rose as they worked over dresses or talked about furniture and sheets and dishes for the place Rose would have downcountry. Gram had a few things stored in the attic, some of which she wanted Rose to have: a braided rug and dishes that had come down through the family and a cherrywood table. When they spoke of these things, Amos would leave the house, because it made him think of Joan. He wished that for him there was nothing but the fact of getting married instead of the desolation he felt.

It was a simple thing for Rose. She and Pete wanted to get married. They were suited to each other. They were going to get married so they could live together. It made a pattern of desire and need and fulfillment. It was not complicated, and when Amos thought of it he felt bewildered and hurt by his own situation.

At night before he slept he found that his tired mind would release him from the web of reality and show him the way it might be with Joan—Joan near him, Joan sleeping with him, living with him in Whichertown. Or the picture came to him of Joan with him in the woods, at the camp, with no necessities but to be together and fish and hunt and sleep, until he could almost smell the sweetness of her mingled with the woodsmoke and the balsam of the camp.

Rose's marriage affected him in another way. It upset the family relationship that had become established and he could feel the vacancy her going would leave in the farmhouse. It meant one less Jackman in Whichertown. How strange that in two weeks there should be such a break in the continuity of their lives—not only his and Rose's, but the family's. He could feel it now perhaps as his father had when Rose first said she was going away.

Pa couldn't quite resign himself to her leaving. On the evening before Decoration Day they were sitting in the kitchen.

Mort spoke of the work he had done in the cemetery.

"I scythed the graves where the grass was long," he said. "And I've picked the flowers to decorate them." He was silent a moment. "There's nobody to tend the Grimes and Lovejoy graves so I fixed them a little. I laid up the wall in two places where it had fallen down. Pa, you know how many Whichers and Jackmans are buried there?"

"Most of them," Pa said, in a bitter tone.

"No, how many?"

"Ten?"

"Eighteen."

Amos could see that Mort had become so familiar with the cemetery that it was part of his life and he spoke of it as he might talk about anything on the farm. But to Pa it signified the decline of the family and the decline of Whichertown. Amos thought he understood the weary sadness in Pa's face.

Pa stood up abruptly and shuffled to the stove where he turned his back to the warmth and looked at Rose.

"You and Pete can have the east corner of the lower field," he said, "if things don't work out downcountry. Cellar hole there from the old Whicher place and you could put up a little house cheap."

"Thanks, Pa. I guess we'll make out all right."

"You can come back, you know."

"Sure, thanks. I guess neither Pete nor me will want to be coming back."

"Likely not." Pa went to his chair. "I just wanted you to know."

Gram interrupted cheerfully, "Now, Rose, you get the veil and we'll try it on."

Amos went to the barn.

The next morning there was a misty rain falling and the wind blew chill across the valley. Pa wouldn't go to the cemetery and Gram said she'd wait until the weather improved. Rose had driven into town with Pete to get the minister. Amos thought that flowers looked better in the woods or on a lilac bush than they did in a mason jar beside a headstone, and he didn't care about decorating the graves, but someone had to go with Mort. Because Mort expected it to be an occasion, Amos made Whicher come with them.

They walked down the road to the cemetery. The fine rain seemed to be part of the clouds which had settled over the mountains. Although the road was muddy, it was not the deep mud of early spring, just top-slippery. The walled cemetery lay against the woods where the pasture ended and the road slanted down toward Whichertown. They passed the cellar hole about which Pa had spoken the night before. Here the field was really pasture; it had not been mowed for years and the young stock were turned into it during the summer. Birches and poplars and pines had seeded in from the woods. Amos looked beyond the barway at the granite foundation stones and at the trees growing from the cellar. Overlooking the valley and the mountains, it must have been a pleasant

[ 84 ]

spot for a house. He could imagine it on a clear day. It would be a good place for a house to live in with Joan.

They came to the cemetery. Mort, in his dark suit, a bunch of lilacs in his hands, left the road and opened the gate in the stone wall. His face was set in serious lines about the sad eyes. Whicher tagged along carrying a basket of wildflowers as though they were distasteful to him. He was cross not only because of the flowers but because he had wanted to work on the model railroad engine he was building of boards and an old box. His pointed face frowned under the close haircut Amos had given him the day before. Drops of rain clung in his hair. Amos carried a grain sack of empty preserving jars.

He could tell that Mort had done a lot of work in the cemetery. The bushes had been trimmed out along the wall and the fallen limb from the big pine in the corner had been cleared away. It was easy to tell, even if you didn't know, which grave was Ma's, for Mort kept flowers there and it was the newest grave, the headstone unweathered. They went toward it. Mort stood looking down, an incongruous figure in the dark suit with the purple lilacs in his arms and the rain wet on his face.

Amos found that it was easier to look at the woods beyond the stone wall. He heard Mort speak to him.

"You ought to take off your hat, Amos."

Amos reached up and bared his head. He wanted to say, "I guess it don't matter to Ma," but he didn't because there was no need to hurt Mort, although the sudden bitterness in him demanded that he make some defiance toward a God who could do such things.

Mort was saying, "I've got it all fixed up." He moved about the grave like a mother around the cradle of her child. He stooped to take a wilted moccasin flower from the glass by the headstone. He came to Amos and reached for the sack of jars and said, "There's a spring across the wall."

"I know. I'll go over."

Amos picked out two of the jars and walked across the cemetery between the graves. Whicher was looking at the headstones in the far corner. Amos climbed the wall and filled the jars at the pool in the woods. When he got back to the grave, Mort had selected two lilac sprays which he put in the jars and placed near the stone. He straightened up. "I'll say a prayer."

Amos called to Whicher, "Come here."

Reluctantly the boy moved toward them. He wouldn't look at the grave and faced the other way beside Amos.

Mort spoke in his deep voice. "Our Father which art in heaven,

Hallowed be thy name. Thy kingdom come. Thy will be done on earth as it is in heaven. Give us this day our daily bread. And forgive us our debts, as we forgive our debtors. And lead us not into temptation, but deliver us from evil, for thine is the kingdom, and the power and the glory, forever. Amen." Mort hesitated, looking down at the grave. Then he said, "The Lord giveth and the Lord taketh away. Blessed be the name of the Lord."

He stood quietly for a moment while he seemed to return to his brothers and the world around him. He said slowly, "I guess we've got jars enough for most of the family graves."

Amos put his hand on Whicher's shoulder. "You come with me. We'll fill the jars with water."

And that way they put out the lilacs and wildflowers on the graves of Jackmans and Whichers, and laid sprays of lilacs on the graves of the Grimes and Lovejoy families. It seemed to Amos, after a time, like an empty ritual—a ceremony with no meaning, for they had not finished when some of the wildflowers already appeared wilted. In a day or two they would be dead, although the ones in the jars might last a little longer. Withered flowers were only a comment on the deaths of the people buried here.

In an effort to throw off this feeling, he went with Whicher to the older section of the cemetery where the headstones of weathered slate showed worn carvings of willow trees and cherubs.

They knelt to look at one. He said to Whicher, "There's always been an Amos Jackman. I guess maybe this was the first." He read the inscription. " 'Amos Jackman.' A number I can't make out. 'New Hampshire Regiment, American Revolution. Died May 26, 1829.' That was a little over a hundred years ago."

Whicher's jaw relaxed. "Did he fight in the Revolution, honest? Did he?"

"That's what it says. Gram has a story about him. Something about over to Bennington. You ask her when we get home."

"Oh, I know that story," Whicher said. "It's about the cherrywood table she's giving Rose. He brought it all the way from Vermont on his back from a house that burned."

"Something like that." Amos stood up. "Let's start home. The rain appears to be setting in more."

Amos went to the gate with Whicher beside him. Mort was still standing by Ma's grave.

Amos called to him, "You coming, Mort?"

"No, I'm going to stay a little while."

Amos went through the gate and stepped into the road with a feeling almost of relief, as though he'd come back to life again. He turned to look behind him. Mort was kneeling beside the grave, bareheaded in the rain, a dark figure against the stone wall, while the woods beyond seemed to overshadow him.

"Come along, Whicher," Amos said needlessly, for Whicher was hurrying past him on the road.

Amos couldn't forget the picture of Mort kneeling beside Ma's grave. There was room in the cemetery for other Jackmans, there was plenty of room. When the cemetery was laid out, folks must have thought that Whichertown would be larger than it ever grew; they didn't think it would all be woods again sometime.

Mort kneeling in the rain. Amos felt the cold wind blowing off the mountains and the rain on his face. Ahead of him, Whicher had picked up a handful of stones and was throwing them at the fence posts. The dark spruce woods were behind them and the fields opened toward the house. He would welcome the warmth of the kitchen, but the house would be full of Rose's preparations for the wedding.

He went to the barn instead and took down the team's harness and found thread and beeswax and awl. He was glad of anything to keep his hands and mind busy. Whicher had gone inside. Amos worked until he saw Mort come back along the road and cut across the field as was his habit. And then he couldn't forget Rose's marriage, because she drove into the yard with Pete and the minister. Another car came behind, driven by Pete's brother, who was to be best man, and others of the Appledees. Pa appeared on the doorstep in his suit, his hair brushed carefully. Amos finished the stitches and hung up the harness. He put the box of awls and buckles on the shelf above the grain bin.

He had to change his clothes and get ready although he didn't feel much like it. He didn't care about going into the house and meeting all the Appledees and trying to talk to them. He didn't feel that it was a festive occasion.

The church was down near the interval on the way to the village, a small boxlike meetinghouse with a little steeple. Of course there was the big church at the village, but the Jackman and Whicher families had always gone to the little church, as had the Appledees before they moved away from Whichertown.

There were lilacs at the altar. Amos sat straight on the hard pew and stared at the back of the pew ahead while the organ music started and Pa and Rose came down the aisle. He looked up. In the white dress and veil, with the bouquet of flowers, she hardly resembled the sister he knew.

He listened to the ceremony, and wondered about living with a woman. The words of the minister in a way seemed unimportant. If you wanted to be married to a girl and live with her, the words and the ceremony and the marriage license were formalities you had to go through. But the important thing was the need and the desire and the want of two people for each other.

He thought of standing there with Joan. He thought of Joan standing like that in a big church with Ronnie. He realized that he might never see her again and he suddenly felt he had not made clear to her that they needed each other. Perhaps it had not been clear to him until he understood that what was lacking between them was this ceremony which would make allowable and right their being together always. He felt that he had to try to tell her.

He might write her, but a letter was only words on paper and he couldn't put them there very well. He'd have to go and see her.

He thought about it as Pete and Rose walked back up the aisle together. He planned it at the house where they had dinner and a cake. Pete and Rose went away and gradually the Appledees and people he didn't know drifted away. By late afternoon there was nobody left but the family, sitting down to supper after chores, everyone, Amos thought, feeling sad because Rose was gone.

But Gram began to brighten as she talked about the wedding and people she'd seen and what had happened when they lived in Whichertown years back. She told how long it had been since she had met each one—usually at a funeral, seemed as though, so it was nice to have a wedding. Of course it was sad in a way, but there it was, a wedding, and that was for making life, wasn't it, so why should it be sad? She had enjoyed it. At least it didn't end with the burying of another Jackman.

She talked on while Amos occupied himself with his own thoughts, and watched the clouds breaking up over Cobblestone. At last Pa got up and went to bed. Amos stepped outside. The May twilight had gone and the sky was almost dark. The rain had stopped. The cool air carried fresh smells of flowers and damp earth. He filled his pipe and lighted it, the match flaring in his cupped hands.

He was restless beyond anything he had ever before experienced. He tried to visualize what Joan might be doing, but Braemuir was so vague to him that he could only picture things she had talked about. He could not really connect it with what he knew. It seemed so distant in both space and in his experience that she might as well have gone to the moon.

But his mind told him that it was less than a day's drive away. He could go to her as he had decided he must while he was at the church. He understood that nothing he had ever known would guide him in how to act. He was afraid that in the strange place he might appear so awkward and stupid she would wonder why she had ever liked him. It seemed almost too much to risk. And yet if he didn't go, she'd be lost to him for good. All he could do was be himself and if that wasn't what she wanted, at least he'd have tried to get her back.

## Chapter 12

In the morning, after chores and breakfast, Amos went into the room he shared with Mort and changed to his suit and his good shoes. The suit was dark blue serge and the shoes black. He associated them with church and weddings and funerals. He didn't feel just right in them, but he knew he couldn't go to Braemuir in his dungarees and work shirt and leather boots. Still, he might take them along. He'd feel better if he had them with him. He rolled them into a bundle. He stood for a moment between the beds with their rumpled quilts and sheets. The room was still cool from the night air and shadowy for it was on the west side of the house. The early sun did not shine into it, but slanted on the backyard and clothesline, making west-going shadows of the clothes poles beyond the shadow of the house. West toward the ridge, the fields and woods were in sunlight.

Slowly he moved to the bureau and saw his face in the mirror over it. He saw the skin tanned dark under the straw-colored hair, the large features and jaw. He realized he hadn't shaved. He did not want to stop to do it because he was anxious to start before the strange emptiness inside him spread to his arms and legs. But he'd have to shave. Quickly he took his extra shirt from the bureau, a pair of socks and a tie and his razor. He found his wallet in the upper bureau drawer. He knew how much it contained—seven dollars. It didn't seem like much but it would have to do him. Picking up the bundle of work clothes, he left the room and moved along the little hall into the kitchen.

Pa and Gram were alone. Pa sat at the table with an empty coffee cup in front of him. He looked up.

"Well, now," he said, and took his pipe from his mouth. "Where you going?"

"Downcountry."

"You be?" He stared with open mouth at Amos, a shadow of fear in his eyes. "Now what you want to do that for?"

"See something different."

"You ain't going away?"

"I'll be back in a day or two."

"Well, that's reasonable. A young fellow ought to get around some." His voice lifted with relief and he held a match to his pipe.

Gram turned from the sink. "You know where she lives?"

"Well," he said. "Not exactly." He had to smile at Gram.

"You head for Boston and when you get pretty close, you ask. It's part of one of them towns outside the city, like Whichertown is part of Houghton. Mary Perkins' boy Ralph worked down there to a place they raise flowers and shrubs and such things. He told her about the house the Tarltons own. Big place on a little hill, he said."

"All right. Thanks, Gram."

Pa interrupted. "What you two talking about?"

"Joan Tarlton, who'd you think?" Gram said. "Now, Warren, you get Amos your satchel. He can't go traveling with his clothes in a bundle like a tramp. It's upstairs in the attic. And, Amos, you'll need soap and towel. You got to shave."

"I'm going to."

Pa stood up. "Well, I'll be damned," he said as he left the room.

Amos stood silent, not knowing just what more to say, but it was all right because Gram moved from the sink so he could shave, and sat down in the chair by the window.

She said, "Not that I can see any sense to it. There's girls here in town that would do you much better. What ever happened to you and Hazel Ellsworth?"

"Guess I wasn't fast enough for her."

"You've been fast enough about this one." Gram rocked with a determined motion. "Seems to run in the family and crop up every so often. No judgment where men and women are concerned. Puts me in mind of your Aunt Sally. She married into one of them Boston families. Good people and all that, but she had a poor time of it. She died when you was ten."

He wanted to say something about Ma marrying Gram's son, but it didn't seem fair, because she knew Pa wasn't any great shakes. He said, "I figure to bring her back here."

"That's it, is it? Make a farm wife out of her." Gram picked up her sewing and jabbed at it with the needle. "You're more of a fool than I thought. Can you feature Joan Tarlton here in Whichertown?"

"I can," he said, wishing Pa would return with the satchel. He wiped his face. "Likely she won't have me."

Gram glanced at him quickly and continued her sewing for a moment before she said in a gentler voice, "I guess you're in for a sad time of it, Amos."

"I don't know."

Pa returned with the little leather satchel. Amos put his shirt and things in it, leaving out the work clothes. Old folks were always looking on the sorry side of things. He didn't think he was in for a sad time. He didn't know what he was in for, but he intended to find out and he felt that there was a possibilty of wonderful things ahead. Gram's talk, instead of discouraging him, gave him a sensation of hope and defiance because he felt so much stronger than either her or Pa.

And now Pa was saying, "You ain't figuring to leave the place here, Amos?"

"No, I ain't, Pa."

"Got any money?"

"Enough."

"Take the Ford."

"All right, Pa. Much obliged."

He went out into the early morning sun. Tossing the satchel and the bundle of work clothes into the back of the Ford, he cranked it and backed from the wagon shed. Mort and Whicher came from the barn and stood beside Pa under the maple tree. Gram waved from the doorway. He raised his arm and started down the road.

The mountains were morning clear with the sun over the eastern ridge. He felt the sudden joy of going on a journey in the freshness of the day. The smell of gasoline seemed to suggest the power to travel distances over the earth. He had lost the empty sensation he had felt in the bedroom.

Everything along the familiar road appeared clear and sharp to his eyes, the flowers and young ferns, the ruts and the stones, as though the world had been touched to brightness by the dew. Although many hundred times he had been over the road since he was born, and it was the same road he had traveled with Joan, the road where Ma was killed, and he knew each turning, yet it was different.

[ 91 ]

The sensation stayed with him all through the meadows after he left the hills, and continued as he drove into the village. He waved to Lije Willis at the garage and turned south; he'd get gas where he didn't have to answer a lot of questions.

The road was known to him as far as Fallsburg. He drove down the June-green valley of the river. The mountains dropped behind. Fields stretched to wooded hills. The Ford ran smoothly in the cool morning air. He guessed he must be making close to thirty-five miles an hour. He could watch the countryside, for there was little traffic—a car now and then, a few buggies with milk cans or grain bags in back, a load of lumber pulled by two big bays. The road unrolled under the Ford.

He stopped at Fallsburg for gas. Across the street a mill gave out sounds of machinery through its open windows, and Amos could see men moving about. He wondered how they could work there, away from the open air and fields and woods. The filling-station man lifted the hose to drain out the last of the gas.

"Eight gallons, bud. That'll be a dollar sixty."

Amos passed over the money, thinking of the five-forty left.

"Oil and water?"

"It's all right."

He had a can of oil in back and there were brooks along the way. He wanted to be driving on, but he stopped at a store to get crackers and cheese. It was a grimy little store without the smell of groceries and vinegar and dry goods like the one in Houghton. He began to feel strange and out of place as he drove down the busy street, slowly, never quite sure when a car would pull out from the curb or a side street. He felt better when he was in the open country again and had passed the sign pointing to Concord.

The country flattened out and the sun became hotter. At times there was more space between him and the horizon over the long fields. He noticed the large herds of cows and the big barns. And then the road wound through woods of small birches and poplars; he saw hardly any good timber. The land seemed to change. There was a winding river and sandy flats with scrub pines on them and the cuts along the road showed a strange gravelly soil.

He didn't stop at Concord, although he had never been to the state capital before. He drove past the domed capitol building with its statues on the green, past the buildings along the wide street. Again he went slowly and cautiously, watching the cars, and the people who walked across the street as though a car couldn't run into them.

He took the road toward Manchester, as indicated by the signs. He knew that he should go there, and then to Nashua, but after that he had only a general idea of heading for Massachusetts and Boston. He couldn't find the right route out of Manchester but he was getting used to driving in cities and he turned around and asked a man on the sidewalk for directions.

Again in the country he drove until he came to a brook where he stopped for lunch. He ate the crackers and cheese, thinking of the time he and Joan had stopped on the way to Whichertown and had picked mayflowers. He began to feel lonesome and less adventurous, thinking of Joan, while the cars kept whizzing by along the road. He couldn't finish the crackers and cheese. The water didn't taste right. He went to the car and filled the radiator and poured in a quart of oil.

He had a bad moment before he started on. He felt almost like turning back from the strange things ahead, the unfamiliar country where he wouldn't know how to act, and the strange people. It was the emptiness inside again, the lonesomeness, such as he had never felt even when he was by himself in the woods of Whichertown. But he remembered Joan and pushed down on the low pedal and started off. He knew that if he didn't go on, he wouldn't feel right when he got home—it would always be unfinished whatever way it turned out when he found Joan.

Soon he was glad to be going on. A car passed him and the man waved and the woman and kids smiled. He felt better. After he got through Nashua he'd stop and ask the way at a filling station.

But he saw a sign which read BOSTON and he decided to keep driving. After a time there was a big river on his left and the country was very flat. He didn't know he was in Massachusetts until he began to notice that the license plates of passing cars were not the familiar combination of green and white. He stopped at the next filling station and climbed out of the car.

"How do I get to Braemuir?"

The man in brown coveralls looked at him and glanced at the Ford and the New Hampshire plates. "There's different ways. You been down here before?"

"No."

"I'll mark a map for you." He took one from a rack by the gas pumps, and spread it on the mud guard of the Ford while he penciled a line through town after town. "There, just follow that and you'll be all right."

"Much obliged." Amos took the map and got into the car.

The man's accent had seemed strange and he wasn't sure he could find his way by the map, but he nodded and drove back on the road. He lost his way after he got to Lexington and found himself driving twice past the green and the statue. He had to ask his way at a garage. When he started off again he suddenly felt tired of driving. It was the longest stretch he'd ever driven, and the Ford wasn't acting right. Probably the plugs had fouled. He didn't want to stop to clean them.

The country was small now, cut up by stone walls and orchards and small fields, alternating with long gardens in rich soil such as he'd never seen. Filling stations and vegetable stands and corner stores and hot dog stands seemed to be around every bend in the road.

At last with a great lift of his heart, he saw a sign that said BRAEMUIR. He drove by glassed-in buildings with flowers growing inside, and soon after began to pass houses. Rooftops stretched beyond as far as he could see. There were streets with new trees planted along the sidewalks and then he came to an older section of the town and a street with trolley tracks. He followed them, surprised when they grabbed at the tires of the Ford. After that he stayed to one side, passing a white church and stores. He saw a railroad station on his right. He could ask there, and perhaps wash. He felt hot and dirty. He pulled into the curb. The afternoon was almost gone.

Cars with women and children in them were parked around the square near the station. As he walked toward the gray-green building, a train whistled down the line and came to a stop beside the roofed platform.

He watched men begin to step down from the cars. They wore suits and white shirts and ties as though they were used to them, and hats in a way that seemed natural. Their shoes were polished. Some of the men were tall and others thin and others fat, smoking cigars or wearing glasses, some carrying flat leather cases by the handles. Rapidly they dispersed across the platform. Apparently they knew just where they were going, and Amos decided this must be a daily routine for them although at first he had wondered why so many men were getting off. He watched them go down the street or to the waiting cars.

In what seemed an incredibly short time to Amos, the train had pulled out and the platform was empty except for a woman who kept glancing at her wrist watch and a man who stood at the far end reading a newspaper. Amos saw another man in railroader's overalls walk into the station. He followed the stocky figure.

The man stopped at the ticket window and Amos came up to him. "How do I get to the Tarltons'?"

"Couldn't tell you, son." He was gone across the waiting room.

From behind the ticket grille a hand appeared pointing back the way Amos had come, and Amos saw the station agent.

"Follow the trolley tracks, third left, first right, take the lake road about a mile."

The window closed. Trying to remember the directions, Amos looked up at the clock on the wall and saw that it showed five-thirty. He went into the washroom where the smell of pine oil and the urinals made him hurry to wash his face and hands. He went out feeling still dirty, while the strangeness of his surroundings lay heavy upon him. He got into the Ford and drove back to the streetcar tracks.

He was never sure just how he found the house. For a time he kept in mind the turns he had taken and the direction he was going, as he might in the woods. At last he began to think he had come too far and when he saw a vegetable stand at the end of a row of houses, he stopped to ask. An Italian with a heavy accent sent him back the way he had come, with new directions that took him past a lake. He remembered those places, but mostly it seemed to be street after street of houses. He had never believed that there were enough people in the world to live in all those houses.

Joan had spoken of her home town as small, which probably it was compared to a city. But all these places seemed to overlap in such a built-up way that they were not like the towns around Houghton where there was a village street and the rest farmland and woods, so you couldn't mistake it when you were in town.

He stopped finally at a drugstore among a cluster of brick buildings. It was clean and airy, with a white tile fountain, and heavy linoleum on the floor. The clerk in a white jacket smiled when Amos asked if he was in Braemuir.

"Certainly are."

"Can you tell me where the Tarltons live?"

"Sure thing. Down this street and turn first left. Go two blocks and take the drive on the right with the brick gateposts. That's it." Then the man added, "But you won't find them there. Gone up north to their summer place."

With a sudden pain which he resisted, Amos said, "I see. Thanks." He turned blindly and went out of the store.

It must be that the clerk didn't know Joan had come back. Why should he? Or had she gone again? He should have stopped at the Tarlton lodge to find out before he drove down. Maybe she had returned to Whichertown. There was an ache across his eyes as he drove off.

He turned at the first left street and passed houses set wide apart in big lawns. He didn't know what a "block" meant, but he drove on until he came to the brick gateposts. He turned into the drive. It curved under oak trees and bore sharply upward under a ledge. The grounds had a cared-for look, although they were woods, for there was no underbrush and grass and shrubs grew along the drive. The Ford pulled up the hill in choking bursts. He came to the top where a brick house loomed among bigger trees. Through the leaves, the low sun slanted on the rosy walls.

Then it was all right for he saw Joan sitting on a terrace beside the house. She looked up as the Ford chugged into the circle by the front door. With a little cry, she came running toward him, her legs slim and her dress fluttering behind her.

## Chapter 13

Amos climbed from the Ford and walked toward her.

"Why, Amos!" she said. "What are you doing here?"

"I came to see you."

"That's nice." She stopped as though she might have intended to come close to him. She held out her hand. "How did you get here?"

"Drove the Ford."

"Why, of course." She laughed. "I mean, you found it all right."

"Yes."

He took her hand and thought of all the things he had intended to say, but looking at her he couldn't find the words. Yet he realized it wasn't necessary for there seemed to pass between them that automatic oneness and he felt that she must be aware of it too. If only nothing came in the way of it: he mustn't do anything which would make her feel embarrassed he was here. He couldn't think of anything to say and in his desperation he understood that he could only act like himself. There was no use trying to pretend he was different. And for a moment it was all right, for she gave another little laugh of pleasure and slipped her arm in his and led him toward the terrace.

"I'm so glad to see you. Come over and sit down. Have you eaten? I've just finished supper and I'm having coffee on the terrace. Maud will get something together for you. Would you like a drink? Where are you staying?"

He had trouble following her. "Yes," he said slowly. "I wouldn't mind a drink. Couldn't say where I'm staying."

"We'll put you up."

Beside the iron table he faced her. "Joan, I drove down to ask you to come back."

"Did you?" she asked. "Yes, I know you did." She kept her hands straight at her sides. "I thought we had settled it. I don't want to talk about it any more. I've just finished my first day at my job and I have to get things ready for a party tonight." She wasn't looking at him. "I've got an apartment in town and this is the last party we'll have here, and I'm packing."

Amos looked at his hands, big and awkward below the serge cuffs. "Things weren't so good for me, and I thought maybe they hadn't been for you and you might change your mind."

"I've been busy," she said. "Job hunting."

"I've been busy, too. Sort of rushed the season and put in the potatoes and the corn and millet. It didn't keep me from thinking."

"I've had so many things to do," she said.

"I suppose. Well, how's Ronnie?"

He knew after he asked that it was probably the wrong thing to say, but he had to find out.

She glanced up at him sharply. "What about him?"

"He's been around, hasn't he?"

"Naturally."

"Are you going to marry him?"

"I haven't decided. We get along better down here."

"I see." He watched her until she looked at him, but he couldn't decide what she was thinking. He said again, "I thought you might come back with me."

"Oh, Amos, how could I?" She was annoyed. "We settled everything that night. We made the break and I can't see the sense in starting it over again."

"You can't? Don't seem like a wise thing if it made you cry like it did."

"Amos, I'm trying so hard to do what's right."

"Don't seem right to me." He paused. "You want me to go away?"

She didn't answer for a moment, then said quietly, "No. Sit down. I'll get you a drink."

She went into the house.

It was strange, he thought, how things could appear simple when you alone were thinking of them, but became involved when another person entered into them. You had to change your ideas to suit another individual's requirements. He realized he had counted on Joan's going back with him. It had been a trip to get her, not just to see her. That had been in the back of his mind under all his fears and misgivings. And now he wasn't sure. The pictures in his mind were not what was going to happen.

He sat back in the wicker chair. He felt tired, not the body-weariness and quiet of mind that came from work on the farm, but a tension of nerves from the drive, from the searching and from the hope he had carried so deep in him. He stared across the terrace at the trees under which the lawn was now in shadows. In the distance he could hear the sound of traffic and a train whistle. There was a sense of people and their activities all around this island of trees. He noticed that although the season was still spring in Whichertown, summer seemed to have arrived here, with a mellow warmth in the air and flowers blossoming beside the terrace.

Joan came from the house carrying a tall highball glass. She handed it to him and asked, "How was your trip?"

"Good, until I tried to find your house. I rammed around 'most two hours looking for it." He smiled at her. "Ain't used to this country. It's a sight worse than being lost back of Cobblestone Mountain."

She laughed in the quick way he remembered. "How is old Cobblestone? I suppose the trees are leafed out a lot more and summer's come."

"Cold and rainy yesterday. My sister Rose got married."

"She did? Where's she going to live?"

"Somewhere near here." He drank the last of his highball. "Somerville, I think it is."

"Well, that's near if you think from New Hampshire."

"I do."

"Yes, I know." She stood up. "Come on in the house. I'll show you your room and then you can have supper. Dave will be along pretty soon."

"Sure you want me to stay?"

"Yes."

He followed her across the terrace to the glass doors. The house was larger and more luxurious than anything he had ever seen. He walked across the deep pile of the living room rug and saw the big chairs and the couch and the mahogany tables. They came to the hall where they met a colored maid.

"This is Mr. Jackman, Maud," Joan said. "He'll be staying in the room next to Mr. Dave's."

"Yes, Miss Joan. I'll have the supper on the dining room table like you wanted."

Amos nodded at Maud and followed Joan up the wide stairs. He was aware of a spacious hall with pictures. Joan turned in at a bedroom door.

There was a double bed and a fireplace and an easy chair and carpet stretching to the walls and a big bureau. He saw his satchel on a chair.

"Jeff brought up your bag," Joan said. "The bathroom's in there. Come down when you're ready."

"All right. Much obliged."

She went out and shut the door.

He looked around him. The room appeared to be a spare, for there was no evidence that anyone had used it lately. He prowled slowly about, looking in the empty closet and into the tiled bathroom. He shrugged and stepped to the tub and turned on the faucets, watching the water a moment, puzzled before he pulled the lever which shut the drain. He began to undress and then on second thought locked the door. In the bathroom mirror he saw that the beginning of a stubble showed on his chin although he had shaved that morning. He'd probably better scrape it off again.

While he shaved, he thought of Joan and realized that he hadn't understood by a good deal the way she lived. He hadn't intended to get into anything like this, but now he had, he'd go through with it the best he could. There was no use worrying about how to act. If he didn't know, why, he didn't know, and that was the end of it except to try to learn.

He wiped his face and got into the tub. It was a long tub and half full of hot water which felt fine. He soaked slowly and soaped himself with a sweet-smelling cake from a little niche in the tile wall. When he got out and dried himself on a big towel he couldn't help smiling at himself in the long mirror—the big-muscled body, the tanned forearms and face and neck. He thought, "I bet this is the first time a farmer ever took a bath in here." And he suddenly felt good.

He dressed, putting on the white shirt and blue tie. The knot of the tie wouldn't come just right but after the third attempt he left it alone as the best he could do. He wanted to be with Joan again.

He found her in a room off the downstairs hall, standing in front of the bookshelves which lined the walls. He noticed a deer head over the fireplace, models of two sailboats on the mantel, deep leather chairs, a center table with magazines and books, a desk in one corner.

She turned half toward him as she reached for a book. She wore a green dress with a white collar. She looked lovely to him.

"I'm swiping some of Dad's books for my apartment. He never reads them anyhow and there are several I'm going to miss." She flipped the pages of the book. "He has them sent out from the Old Corner Bookstore every month or so, but I don't believe he's read a third of them."

He looked at the book over her shoulder. "How do you say that name?"

"Babbitt. Haven't you read it?"

"No."

"Pretty good." She put it on a table. "Come and have some supper."

She led him into the dining room where a place had been set at the end of the long table. There was jellied soup and slices of ham and cold roast beef and tongue, rolls and butter and a salad.

Joan sat down and watched him. He could feel her studying him. "Looks good," he said, and helped himself to the meats.

He ate heartily, even the salad, and finished with the jellied consommé. It seemed like a strange dessert, but he said nothing. If Joan was trying to bewilder him, she might succeed, but he wasn't going to let on. He wondered if she wanted to see how he would act in her home, if that was the reason she had asked him to stay. Perhaps she thought that he would appear so out of place she'd know she had been right to leave Whichertown. Well, if he disappointed her, it couldn't be helped. He couldn't change himself now, even if he wanted to.

Dave came in as she was pouring coffee from a silver coffee pot.

"For gosh sakes!" Dave shouted. "If it isn't Amos, the man from the hills. How've you been?"

"All right." Amos stood up and they shook hands.

"Sit down and finish." Dave pulled out a chair and straddled it. "Hey, Sis, how about a shot of the giant killer? I'm all in from exploring the marts of trade."

Joan went to the sideboard where there was a decanter. "Looks to me as though you've had a couple already."

"Couple, huh! A vice president invited me to a bar, but I don't think I want to work for him." He took the glass she brought him. "I can give you a few tips on the market. Utilities are showing a little strength. Copper stirred microscopically. These are straws in the wind." He stood up and grimaced. "Christ, what a place to go to work. I'm going to get a job importing Scotch whiskey. Importing—by God, there's the place for me."

Dave left the room, stopping to fill his glass on the way, and called over his shoulder, "I'm going to take a shower."

"Poor Dave," Joan said, after he had gone. "He's job hunting. Had a chance at Higgins-Morse, to start right after he finished school, and he felt he ought to take it because good jobs are so scarce, but he hated the idea of stocks and bonds."

"Why don't he move around and try different things?" Amos asked.

"Yes," she said with her abrupt intensity. "That's just what I told him.

He can't tell what he wants to do until he's tried different things." She looked at his cup. "More coffee?"

"No, thanks."

"Then I'll get a tray and clear off. This is Maud and Jeff's night out."

He helped her put the dishes on the tray and carried it for her through the pantry into the kitchen. He thought at first that the pantry, with its sink and cupboards and wide shelf, was the kitchen and he wondered where the stove might be, until he followed her through the next swinging door. The kitchen seemed big enough to serve a hotel. There was an electric stove and a range, a long sink and white refrigerator.

"I'll wash the dishes," he said.

"No need to. Maud can do them in the morning."

"I shouldn't think she'd want to see a mess of dishes first thing."

"Well, I do usually leave the kitchen cleaned up."

"Then I better wash them, hadn't I?"

"All right, and I'll see about glasses and ice cubes. The Robertsons will be along soon, and Anita—you remember her—and Ronnie and some others, mostly people I grew up with. I hope you'll like them."

"I'll like them all right, but are you sure you want me around? I don't want to butt into your party."

"You aren't butting in. They'll like to meet someone from Houghton. They know we've been going there for years."

"Likely they'll be disappointed."

She looked at him critically. "I don't think so." She went toward the door. "I think I heard a car in the drive." The doorbell up on the wall rang, twice long and twice short. "That's Ronnie, the nut. I'll be back."

Alone in the kitchen, Amos found a towel and wiped the dishes. He didn't know just what to do when he'd finished. Joan hadn't returned and he could hear voices in the front of the house, and cars coming up the drive. He moved about the room examining the cabinet with the marble-topped bench and the cupboards of cooking things and the rack of bright pans behind the stove. He had a mind to look into the ice chest but didn't think he should. He studied the bottles and glasses which Joan had set out on the table. He picked up a bottle and read the label: *Genuine Scotch Whiskey*.

He was holding the bottle when Dave came in.

"Having a quick one for a foundation?" he asked. "I'll join you." He reached for a glass.

Amos didn't bother to tell him he'd only been reading the label. He unstoppered the bottle and poured for Dave, as he seemed to expect.

"Hold it. Long evening ahead." Dave drank the whiskey straight. "I'm going to get old Robertson tight if it's the last thing I do—if the liquor holds out. Now let's see. Three gin and ginger ale. Some gals have the damnedest taste in liquor."

He set about mixing the drinks.

Joan came into the kitchen and said to Amos, "I'm sorry I couldn't get back sooner. They all came at once. Dave, hurry up. The party's dying a slow death. Mary Robertson is being prim and Jim's tongue is hanging out."

"Why the hell did you ask them?"

"Had to give the party respectability. You know how people talk—those Tarlton kids going wild up there on the hill with their parents gone." She took ice cubes from the refrigerator. "The Robertsons will mix all right after a while. You can pursue Mary a little, Dave, and that will please her. Or Amos. Why not Amos? I bet she'd like a strong silent man from the hills."

Joan picked up a tray of drinks and smiled at him, a mischievous speculative look. "Come on, I'll pass out the drinks and show you around."

He held the door for her into the pantry and followed her across the dining room to the big living room. It seemed to be filled with people. Ronnie was talking to a fat man with thin hair, and a blond woman in a tight black dress. Joan introduced Amos.

"Amos is a friend of ours from Houghton."

He shook hands with the Robertsons and with Ronnie.

"Glad to see you again," Ronnie said, and Amos wondered why he said so when he wasn't. He had to admire Ronnie's ease, seemingly at home and comfortable, well dressed in a tan suit, clean and fresh looking, although Amos noticed his eyes weren't quite right and he didn't seem altogether steady on his feet.

Joan took him around the room and the names and faces became a blur in his mind. He worried about remembering them. Anita, he knew, but he wished she wouldn't run on so.

"Did you come all the way from Houghton in that Ford? Just to see Joan? Aren't you thrilled, Joan? I think it's terribly romantic. I wish some man would do that for me. I'd throw myself at him." She sipped her drink as Dave came up to them. "Dave, did you put any gin in this drink? Honestly, I can't taste it."

Joan steered Amos back to the Robertsons. "Mary, you talk to him about your glads. He grows things, too." And she left him.

"Really, Mr. Jackman?" Mary Robertson's voice was pitched high, as though she spoke from a distance, but Amos felt that she was more aware of herself in her dress than of her distance above the party. She went on, "What do you raise, Mr. Jackman?"

"Well," he said. "Potatoes. We put in pretty near an acre of potatoes and maybe two acres of corn."

"Oh," she said, "you're a farmer?"

"Yes."

"Well, why didn't Joan say so? You wouldn't be interested in my glads."

"I might be. What are they?"

She seemed incredulous that he didn't know. "Flowers, of course. Tall flowers with leaves like swords and blossoms on a spike. The little buds are above the open flowers as they mature." She glanced at him. "They're very lovely."

Over his glass, her husband said, "Damn nuisance."

"You've got the soul of a pig, Jim. They're very lovely, Mr. Jackman."

"I'm sure they must be. I think I know the flower you mean. There are some nice gardens in Houghton, but we don't go in for that on the farm. Don't hardly have time." He spoke slowly and tried to think how it was going to sound before he said it. He didn't want to disgrace Joan in any way. Mrs. Robertson seemed pleased.

"I'm sure you'd love my glads," she said.

Mr. Robertson asked, "How's old Greg?"

Amos had to think a moment before realizing he meant Mr. Tarlton. "Well, he's fine, I guess."

"Likes it up there, does he?"

"Far as I know."

"Hmm, can't see him living there all the time, myself. Not old Greg. I'd give him three months." Mr. Robertson looked into his empty glass. "Young man, you can't retire after the life Greg has had. I say he'll either be back in business by fall, or traveling—he might travel. He used to talk about it." Dave came up with a glass. "Thank you, Dave. What's this I hear about your father selling the house?"

"This house? You got me," Dave said. "It might be so. Dad doesn't talk much before he decides to do something. He might take it into his head to sell. Mother says it's more house than she wants now."

"Poor time to sell."

"I suppose so."

"Still, your father has some good contacts. There's money if you know the right people." Mr. Robertson took a deep swallow from his glass. "If I were in his place, I'd sell before that man in the White House ruins us all."

[ 103 ]

"You've got something there." Dave moved off toward the corner where someone had started the Victrola.

Amos watched Ronnie and Dave rolling back the rug. Anita came by and remarked in passing, "That's Guy Lombardo." She moved on, humming to herself. Amos found that he was alone with Mrs. Robertson. Her husband had wandered away toward the kitchen.

"Do you dance, Mr. Jackman?"

"No, can't say I do."

"It's not difficult. Come out in the hall and I'll give you a lesson." She put down her empty glass.

"I guess it's a little out of my line."

"Come along." She took his arm and led him into the hall. "Now listen to the music and step like this."

He tried to do as she told him, moving beside her, feeling foolish and clumsy. At last he began to master the simple step.

She said, "There, not difficult, is it? Put your arm around me and we'll try it together."

Her hand was warm in his and she felt surprisingly light. He decided she didn't have on much under the dress. He tried to hold her farther away but she said, "I won't break in pieces, you know." Which, he told himself, was pretty evident.

"I guess," he said, "I've got the idea of it." He stopped dancing.

"Of course you have, but you need more practice. They're changing the records," she said. "Let's go find a drink."

They went into the kitchen. Mrs. Robertson joined Dave at the table. Amos stayed in the pantry with Joan, where she was arranging little sandwiches on a plate.

She smiled at him. "Having fun?"

"Well, yes. Sure."

She lowered her voice. "Do you like Mary?"

"I hadn't thought. She's been teaching me to dance."

"Don't get any ideas."

He looked at her doubtfully. "I'm not sure I know what you mean." She laughed at him and then said, "Anyone else I'd call a liar."

He began to understand. "You didn't think I was going to—to bother Mrs. Robertson?"

"Why not?"

"Well, I ain't. Not feeling about you the way I do."

She put aside the plate of sandwiches and came up to him. "You, Amos," she said. "Damn you, Amos!" And she stood on tiptoe and kissed him quick and hard. Then she went into the living room with the sandwiches.

As he followed her he became aware that the party was progressing. He could feel it growing and expanding. He listened to the laughter and voices and music around him. He felt a little lightheaded from the whiskey. For a time he stood in a corner of the living room by the terrace door and watched the dancers. They all seemed to belong at the party except him. They talked of things they knew about and laughed at the right times and at the same things. Someone spilled a drink near the Victrola and a slim girl, whose dark hair was cropped close to her head, came with a mop from the kitchen. There was laughter. Outside on the terrace he saw a boy and girl in each other's arms. The music went on and on. Dave passed by and handed him another drink. Then Joan walked over to him.

"Oh, there you are. I want you to show me what Mary taught you." She took his hand and led him on the floor.

"Now, Joan."

He knew he must be awkward, but he tried to dance. It was strange how easy she rested in his arms, and how right it was to have her against him. All he could do was the little step back and forth and he knew it must appear funny, but nobody seemed to notice. He bumped into the dark-haired girl, and her partner grinned at him from a flushed face. He tried to keep away from the center of the floor.

Joan was smiling up at him. "You don't do so bad," she said. And she pressed his hand, adding, "I guess I'm awfully fond of you, Amos."

As he was trying to think what to reply, he felt a hand on his shoulder and Ronnie's voice said, "If you don't mind."

He didn't understand that Ronnie wanted to dance with Joan or that he had the right, and he kept her in his arms and moved on, thinking he was in Ronnie's way.

The next thing he knew, Joan cried, "Ronnie!" and he saw Ronnie swing wildly at him. Ronnie was in his shirt sleeves and his face was pale. Amos pushed Joan out of the way and backed up. He raised his arm to ward off a blow but Ronnie's fist caught him on the ear.

"Hold on," he said. "What you trying to do?"

Ronnie shouted, "Goddamn hick! Don't you know what a cut-in is? I'll show you."

He came at Amos again and because Amos had a fear of hurting Joan's Ronnie, he merely put up his hands instead of hitting back. He heard shouting and the shrill voices of women. Mr. Robertson moved forward like a slow elephant. Joan grabbed Ronnie's arm and was shaken off as Ronnie moved around Mr. Robertson and Dave ran up.

"Leave him be," Amos said and slipped quickly between Ronnie's flailing fists and grabbed him around the waist, picking him up on his hip like a baby. Someone laughed and he realized he'd made Ronnie look foolish so he dropped him in a chair.

"You can have your dance now, if you've cooled off," he said.

Joan burst out, "Not with me!"

Ronnie glared up at her. "I suppose you blame me for trying to teach him some manners."

"Manners! He's got more than you'll have if you live to be a hundred." She looked ready to cry. "I'm going to dance with Jim. Someone start a record."

The dancing began again as the music started and Joan moved off with Mr. Robertson. Amos took out his bandana for he could feel his ear bleeding.

"You two," Dave said. "Come out in the kitchen and have a drink. Of all the damn fool things."

Amos walked toward the kitchen while Dave got Ronnie to follow.

Ronnie slid into a chair at the kitchen table. "Sorry, Amos. Lost my head." He reached for a bottle. "Been under a strain lately."

"Sure." Amos took the glass Dave handed him, but he didn't drink.

He felt responsible for the brawl because if he hadn't been there, Joan's party would have gone smoothly. Everyone must think he was stupid not to know that custom about dancing. Everyone must wonder what the man from Houghton was doing here anyway. He placed his drink on the top of the ice chest. He felt completely sober and more removed from the party than ever. Dave was prying ice cubes from a tray at the sink. Ronnie had put his head on his arms and appeared to be asleep.

Dave nodded toward him. "Had quite a load when he got here. Nuts about Joan. No way to act though. Nuts about Sis." He shook his head and looked at Amos. "You too, eh?"

Amos nodded. "Me too." He dabbed at his ear with the bandana.

Dave was solicitous. "Bled some on your shirt. Stopped now though."

"I'll go up and change it, I guess."

"Sure. Stairs right over there."

Amos left the kitchen by the back stairway and found himself in the upper hall. The sounds of the party came to him as though from a great distance. The hall was dimly lighted. He made his way to his room and switched on the lamp he remembered by the bed. Feeling quite alone, he looked around the room and his presence there seemed utterly strange. At once he understood what he must do. He'd pack his bag and leave. Now Joan knew how different he was from her friends. She must be ashamed of him. He never should have come to Braemuir. She would think of her friends who had seen what happened and wonder why she ever allowed the farmer at her party where he could be the cause of such a row.

It wouldn't matter that Ronnie had started it. He was one of them and there'd be all kinds of reasons to explain what he had done. They'd say Joan should know better than to put up with Amos Jackman. She must be out of her mind to have him at her party. Amos Jackman was a fool to think she wanted him around. Just because she had known him in Houghton and been normally kind to him, he'd presumed all kinds of things and chased her way down here. You'd think he'd have the brains to stay where he belonged. That's what they'd say. Well, he would go back where he belonged.

He changed to the shirt he had worn that day and put the rest of his clothes in the satchel. He paused with the bag in his hand. It wouldn't be right to leave without saying goodby. He'd take his satchel out to the Ford and then find Joan and tell her. He'd go out the back way so as not to call attention to himself.

He turned off the light and went to the back stairs, stepping slowly down them and waiting until the kitchen was deserted. He walked across to the back door where a gravel path led around through patches of window light to the garage and drive.

He was putting the satchel in the Ford when Joan came up to him. "Amos, what are you doing?"

"Well, I thought I'd put my things in here before I said goodby."

"You can't leave, Amos."

"Think I better. I don't want to spoil your party any more, and get folks to talking."

"Oh, Amos, it wasn't your fault. Nobody thought so."

"If I hadn't been here, it wouldn't have happened."

"Ronnie had too much to drink."

"All the same, I guess I'll go. I want to thank you for everything." He paused while she watched him without saying anything. He wished he could see her face better. He said hesitantly, "Well, I knew I didn't belong here, and now I can see there's no good in staying. But—but I'd like to kiss you before I go."

"Yes, Amos."

He stepped forward and took her in his arms with the bitter feeling that this would indeed be the last time he held her warm aliveness and smelled the sweetness of her near and stirring. He wanted to remember how she was in his arms and the pressure of her lips, at once yielding and firm.

Then she was whispering to him. "Amos, you mustn't leave me. I don't want you to. I'll go with you. I will. Wait here, Amos."

He wasn't sure how long he waited there in the dark while the music and voices came toward him from the house. He was aware of everything in sharp focus, the big house and the curtained windows and the expensive cars in the drive. A light came on upstairs behind a green curtain and then after a time went off. Joan was walking toward him with a suitcase and a coat.

"Hurry," she said. "I told Dave and we woke Ronnie and explained to him. I guess he finally got it into his head that I was through with him." Her voice became less urgent. "Everything's all right, but let's hurry, darling. I want to get away. I don't want any more of this and I don't want to live alone in Boston and work and think what might have been."

He put her bag in back and they started off. He had to drive across the grass to get around the cars. He was glad now, with a wild exhilaration, but he drove carefully so as not to spoil it.

After they reached the street, she told him the turns to make as they sat close together. He noticed that the Ford ran good in the night air, like a horse headed for home. He thought, "It'll get us there. I could drive forever. I don't feel tired."

She sat beside him with her arm linked through his as they drove north in the night.

They stopped to eat hamburgs and drink coffee at a diner in Nashua, and then drove on. The highway was deserted. They passed dark farms and went through the empty streets of Manchester. Joan fell asleep beside him soon after that and he drove steadily north with her head on his shoulder. Above Concord he had trouble staying awake and he turned into a side road where he found a wagon track through the woods. She awoke as he stopped the car.

"What's the matter?"

"Nothing. I've got to sleep a little."

"Oh," she said drowsily. "You'll stay with me, Amos?"

"No, I'll rest me under that tree."

*Chapter 14*

He awoke at scant daylight with the birds singing. He was cold and lame from sleeping on the bare ground and his clothes were damp. Near him under the trees, the Ford had dew on the hood and fenders. He stood up and stretched and shivered. In the car, Joan raised her head and blinked. Her hair was tousled and her coat collar twisted, but she smiled at him.

"Where are we?"

"North of Concord somewhere." He walked to the car. "I drove until my eyes began to close on me and I was afraid of going off the road."

"I'm sorry I fell asleep. I was going to stay awake, but I just couldn't. Wonder what time it is."

"Probably about four. We'll get you home in time for breakfast."

"Ugh, no thanks. I can just see Mother and Dad if we descended on them at that hour and announced we were going to get married."

"I see what you mean." He yawned. "Well, we can eat at Fallsburg and stop to get the license at the town clerk's in Houghton. By that time your folks will be awake."

"Let's get married first and then tell them."

"That don't seem right. Besides, we have to wait five days after we get the license."

"Not really, do we, Amos?"

"Sure. Rose and Pete had to."

"I wish," she said, "it could be right off."

"I know."

"I don't want a big wedding and all that nonsense. It could be to-morrow. Let's not talk about it any more until after breakfast." She took a comb from her pocket and ran it through her hair.

He went toward the sound of a brook and found a little pool beyond the trees, where he splashed cold water on his face. When he got back she was standing by the car.

"You look awfully clean and washed," she said.

"Just brook water."

"Where is it?"

He pointed the way.

She returned from the brook as he was starting the Ford. They got in and he backed out to the dirt road and drove to the highway.

She said, "I guess I never made such an early start as this."

"Nice time of day."

There was no traffic and the sun was not up as they came into Fallsburg. He drove around until they found an all-night diner. Joan was sure there must be one because she remembered eating at it after a dance.

They found the diner at last on a side street, deserted except for the sleepy short-order cook who laid aside his paper and gave the counter a swipe with a cloth as they sat down.

"I'm hungry," Joan said, staring up at the menu above the gas range. "I'll have orange juice and oatmeal, bacon and two eggs, sunnyside up. Toast and marmalade and coffee."

"Same for me," Amos told the cook.

The diner was warm and smelled of coffee and food. Amos watched the fat cook move quickly about his work, with a smoothness and economy of motion that fascinated him. Sipping his orange juice, he held the glass in his left hand and touched Joan's with the other.

He asked her quietly, "Are you that good in a kitchen?"

"Well, I can make scrambled eggs and popovers."

"Think we can live on them?"

"Until I learn to cook something else."

There were other things he wanted to talk about, but he felt embarrassed by the cook and their lack of privacy in the diner. At any rate, Joan was willing to be married right off. Although five days seemed a long time, he was glad there wouldn't be weeks of waiting and preparation. Their marriage was a certainty now. Nothing would stop them, not her folks or anything anyone could say or do. The knowledge gave him a quiet feeling of security. Men about to be married were supposed to feel nervous. He just felt certain and glad.

After a second cup of coffee each, he paid the check and they went out to the car. The sun was coming up beyond the city. He could see it on the tops of the buildings. A milk truck went by and a man wheeled past on a bicycle with his dinner pail strapped on the back carrier.

Joan moved near him as they drove out of town. She was quiet, while he felt like talking. Approaching the familiar hills, he seemed to return to himself, as though he had left part of him in Whichertown.

"I haven't the money for us to go anywhere," he said. "I thought we might go out to the camp for a while. 'Course most folks take a trip."

"I don't care about that," she told him. "I just want to be alone with you."

"It's all right then?"

"Yes, darling."

"We'll make out afterwards, you know. Nothing fancy, but we won't starve."

She laughed. "Don't worry, Dad wouldn't let us do that."

He glanced at her. "I won't either."

She put her hand on his knee. "I know, darling. I just don't want you to worry. I didn't mean you couldn't look after me, but if we got in a jam—financially, I mean—Dad would help."

"Don't want no help."

"Oh, Amos, you're thinking of Dad's money and you mustn't. I know you don't want to marry me for the money."

"Well, we never spoke of it and I thought it was time to get it straight." He added clumsily, "Wanted you to know."

"Of course, darling." She sighed comfortably. "I love you."

He felt warm and happy as he drove along. He began to think of living with her. He said, "I figure on getting a house started this summer. There's a cellar hole down the road a piece from the house. Pa offered it to Rose and Pete but they didn't want it. Guess we can have it. You wouldn't care to live at the old house." He tried to think how to tell her about his place in his family. "I couldn't leave the farm. Mort's kind of peculiar since Ma died, and Pa needs me to help with the work. I don't figure on Whicher staying on at the farm. But we'd have our own place."

"That would be nice. Maybe Dad will give us a wedding present to start it."

"No, I'm owed a little at the mill from last year's logs, and with what I'll cut next winter, Jed'll let me have all the lumber I need."

"But the wood is your father's, isn't it?"

"Yes, long's it's standing. I sell what I can cut. Sort of wages, you might say. Besides Pa'll be tickled to have us settle on the farm. Scared his kids will all go away like the rest of the Jackmans—like Rose."

"Not you," she said. "You belong in Whichertown."

"Well, I do, at that, but I'm not sure how you'll like it. Bothers me some."

"I'll love it, but Amos, I don't know anything about living on a farm. I'll try to learn, but I don't know a thing about it."

"Never mind. Not much to it."

"I hope you're right."

They drove on in silence while the green river valley opened before them, northward toward Houghton and Whichertown. Amos felt quiet now, with a deep ease that made him aware of the life of his mind and body like a river in spring. It was as though he could grow and sustain himself from the earth and air. He held the wheel with steady hands. He felt no urge to drive fast, just sure and steady toward home. He could lift his eyes from the road to the mountains on the northern horizon.

After a time, he said, "That's Cobblestone."

"That rounded one?"

"Yes, you can't see the north ridge from here."

They drove through Houghton before Cy Tillman had opened his store. Dew lay on the common and on the cobwebs between the grass blades. Beyond the village they passed through a hollow, still misty with the river fog of the night. He turned into Brook Road, leaving the valley for the hills where the town clerk's farm spread up a rocky slope.

Sid Bartow was going from the barn to the house, and invited them in. He didn't act surprised, a big slow man sitting down at his desk in the living room. He didn't ask a lot of questions, just enough to fill out the form, and Amos was grateful. Mrs. Bartow gave them coffee in the kitchen when they were through.

As they drove toward Whichertown over back roads, Amos for the first time began to feel nervous.

"Maybe," he said, "we better set a date so's we can tell your folks."

"That's easy—as soon as the license allows."

"Let's see. Friday?"

"Yes. And Amos, they'll be all right about it."

"They won't think much of it."

"They're used to me doing things they don't approve of. Anyhow, they like you."

"As a son-in-law?"

"Well. . . ."

"You know they won't."

She touched his hand on the wheel. "They'd better, because I love you."

"I'll be glad when it's over."

He turned from the dirt road onto the highway through the hills and right again, toward Quartz Mountain at the Knapp farm. The road climbed steadily over ledges and past fields surrounded by woods. Before he felt at all ready to meet the Tarltons, they had reached the lodge on the ridge above Whichertown.

Gregory Tarlton came out on the porch and called to them as Amos stopped the Ford. "Well, what's all this?"

Joan ran up the steps and threw her arms around his neck and kissed him, then waved the marriage license at him.

He took it, muttering to himself, "What nonsense now?" And then he looked down at Joan and at Amos, slowly climbing the steps. Amos thought the dark eyes flared at him from the fleshy aquiline face.

Joan was chattering on. "He came down to see me and I found I missed him so much I couldn't bear to let him go home without me."

"Wonderful," her father said. "Just wonderful." His voice was hoarse. "Am I to understand that the wedding hasn't taken place?"

"This coming Friday."

"I see." He cleared his throat. "Well, my dear, I'm sure you'll be very happy. Come in and we'll tell your mother. Come in, Amos."

They found Joan's mother clearing the breakfast dishes from the kitchen table.

"Alice," said her husband, "you better sit down. We have news."

"Joan! For goodness' sake, what's wrong at Braemuir? What. . . ."

Gregory Tarlton kept on talking. "These two are going to get married Friday."

Amos stood aside, watching while Mrs. Tarlton gasped, "Greg, you're joking!" Amos felt that she realized it was so, but had to protest. And then she seemed to gather herself together.

"Isn't that nice," she said. "I'm very glad you didn't go away and get married, because I want to be at the wedding. But why Friday? You can't get ready so soon—the clothes, the church, the invitations." She looked at Joan and sighed. "All right, you don't want all that, but I had hoped —well. . . ." She stopped talking and kissed Joan and came to Amos and kissed him on the cheek. "Now," she said, "I'm going upstairs for a moment." She almost ran from the room.

"There," said Gregory Tarlton. "Your mother can go up and have a good cry but I'm going to have a stiff double hooker." He reached up to the cupboard. "More sensible and just as salutary." He poured out the whiskey and drank it. "You're a couple of goddamn fool kids, you know."

"Oh, we know, Dad. We know just what we're doing. We're going to live in Whichertown and—and have a good life."

"No doubt."

Joan smiled at him. "Now we're going to Amos' place and tell his folks." Her voice was quick and eager. "You and Mother will want to talk it over. I'll be back later, but understand, I won't listen to you, if you scold."

"I suppose not," her father said, trying to smile as he walked with them to the porch.

Amos drove away from the lodge and Joan said, "You see, it was easy, wasn't it, darling?"

"Better than I expected. But over home it will be all right."

And it was. Gram made a lot of Joan, saying how pleased she was to have a new granddaughter and Pa told her how good Amos was at running the farm, and sat by the kitchen window smiling while Amos knew his thoughts dwelt with satisfaction on having a son who would stay in Whichertown. Mort came in and when he learned the news, solemnly shook hands with Amos and said to Joan, "It's mighty fine, Miss Tarlton," before he retreated to the barn. Whicher looked in the door and grinned and vanished.

The next few days passed rapidly in trips to the village, phone calls to Braemuir and preparations that left Amos bewildered, none more than the drive to Fallsburg in the Tarlton beach wagon, Joan at the wheel, to buy a ring. As Friday approached, and he managed to finish the work on the farm which he felt he should do before he went with Joan to the woods, he came to understand that the wedding was accepted by everyone in the two families, that he was almost the same as married. Just one more day.

But he hadn't reckoned on the night before that day. After he had kissed Joan good night at the lodge Thursday evening and had gone home, he couldn't sleep. He never remembered a time when he couldn't sleep, unless it was when his mother was killed. The night thoughts, he understood, were never good ones. He felt a vague fear and restlessness, not a yearning for Joan, but a strange feeling of unreality when he thought of her. He wasn't sure he wanted to get married. He wasn't sure of anything. He felt about her almost as he had near the bog that first day when he realized she had complicated things for him. It was difficult to make himself think of her as he had before he went down to Braemuir, or as he had on the trip back. Lying there in the room where he had slept for years, in the house where he was born, with Mort breathing heavily in the bed across the room, he felt that there was something wrong. He should be glad and happy and contented and sure of himself and the future, all rolled into one. But instead he lay there like a prisoner whose day of execution approached.

At last he got up and went outside where he sat under the maple and looked at the stars and the night horizon in the east. The air was cold, yet fresh with the odors of spring flowers and trees. He could hear the little brook below the field. An owl hooted in the woods. After a time he felt better and went back in the house and slept.

## Chapter 15

Behind the Tarlton lodge, against a screen of lilacs and evergreens, Amos stood before the minister and listened to the words of the marriage ceremony. He was aware of the soft grass under his feet and the scent of lilacs and balsam. He could look off toward the wooded ridge beyond the lodge where the granite ledges of Quartz Mountain gleamed in the sun. He felt that he was neither of the woods nor of the lodge, almost as though he were a stranger in a place where he didn't belong and he was glad that Joan stood beside him. Aware of the silent people behind him—the Tarltons and his folks—he understood that they were two small groups attending the same ceremony, but apart.

"Do you, Joan. . . ."

The words went on while Amos waited for Joan's reply. Almost holding his breath, he waited as though his part of the ceremony did not matter. Time seemed to stop and there was nothing but his desire to hear that voice and the two words. He waited and his whole being seemed concentrated and dependent on those words. They came, in a low tone, but clear and sure.

"I do."

For Amos it was the release of the suspended moment, the beginning of life again, and he felt the breath in his body and the blood moving and sight and sense restored.

The minister's voice continued. He looked small and old, standing in his robe, with the little book held in his thin hands before him. "Do you, Amos. . . ."

Waiting to reply when he should, Amos had a quick revelation of the lifetime meaning of the words. It was not just a ceremony that would make possible their living together. "In sickness and in health . . . till death do you part."

There was a cool breeze blowing from the west and the shadows of leaves moved on the green grass.

"I do."

He had spoken louder than he intended and his voice seemed to ring out on the afternoon air.

The rest of the ceremony was sharp and clear to him: his big hands placing the ring on her delicate finger, hers in return slipping the ring on his. Her hands were firm and cool and did not tremble or make a false move. He could feel the sureness in her motions. And then she was in his arms. It was right to be kissing her in front of their families and the minister.

He did his best to act at ease after the ceremony when Mr. and Mrs. Tarlton and Dave came forward and kissed Joan and took his hand. Gram and Pa stood a little to one side, with Mort and Whicher looking at him as though he were a strange animal in a cage. At last Gram came up to them, and Pa, and Rose and Pete. It seemed strange for Gram to be wishing them happiness and saying the things people said after a wedding, as though she were accustomed all her life to her grandson's marrying a wealthy city girl. He was proud of her and knew the next hour or two would be all right, with her to represent the Jackmans. He thought Pa might speak up a little more; usually there was nothing lacking in his ability to talk, but not today. He acted as though he were afraid he might say something wrong. But it was funny to see Joan kiss Mort and Whicher. They both turned pink and scarlet under the tan and Whicher retreated hastily behind Gram.

Walking to the house for the reception, he had a moment of loneliness, although Joan was holding his arm, for he looked down from the terrace into Whichertown and through the leaves of the trees caught a glimpse of the farm. The buildings appeared small and gray and shabby, the fields as always surrounded by the forest. It was home but somehow it had no reality seen from the big lodge after the wedding, and he felt a softness of fear inside him, inexplicable and beyond reason.

Among the people at the reception were friends of the Tarltons who had come from Braemuir, as well as people whom the Jackman family had known for years. Amos met them all, until he thought the smile on his face would crack; he wondered how Joan could continue to converse sensibly and brightly with everyone. He thought that the reception would never end. He and Joan were prisoners and the others their jailers, surrounding them, moving about the big room. It seemed to Amos that he and Joan stood forever in front of the fireplace in the living room. After two glasses of the punch, Amos realized it was strong and didn't have any more. Mr. Tarlton and Dave kept the glasses and the bowl filled. People milled about and the noise of their talk was a roar and a babble in Amos' ears. He felt that he and Joan would never escape.

He leaned down and whispered to her, "How much longer?"

"I think we can leave any time now. Come upstairs."

He became possessed of the need to escape, and it seemed foolish, for these people should know that he and Joan wanted only to go away alone. It must be some unnatural twist in folks' minds that made a custom of hindering the going away of a bride and groom. Amos found that it angered him with a deep sense of wrong. Why couldn't he and Joan be let alone, without the reception and all the elaborate planning of escape?

It was better when they reached the top of the stairs and Joan had tossed down her bouquet. She pulled him quickly into her room and locked the door.

"There," she breathed and went to him. "My darling, how are you bearing up? You did so well, I'm proud of you—all those people from Braemuir to see what sort of a guy I married. I love you. We showed them."

"It was all right?" He looked about him at the feminine room and felt clumsy.

She said, "You were wonderful!"

"It helped, having you there."

"We make a good team," she said. "Let's hurry. I'm all packed. Did you get everything hidden away in the woods?"

"It's all ready."

In one quick motion she took off her veil. "Help me with these damn hooks." His hands were awkward, and then she was in her slip, laughing at him. "You can look, you know," she said, as he tried to keep his eyes from her. "Going away in slacks and checked shirt and you in dungarees and work shirt—good thing we let everyone think we were going north to camp out."

Dressed and ready at the door at last, he took the little knapsack from her and asked, "How do we get out of here."

"Down the front way and make the best of it."

"I feel like a man escaping from jail and it's all foolishness."

"Don't get mad, darling. It's almost over. You remember what we were going to do?"

"Yes."

Hand in hand they went down the broad stairs and Amos thought it was like stepping into an ocean of faces. Rice and confetti were thrown. He was pushing his way past Dave. They ran down the steps of the porch among other people, toward the roadster they had arranged with Dave to borrow. It had been hidden across the lawn behind a thicket of spruces.

Dave had been made a conspirator and had promised not to tamper with it. "Joan, you know I'd never think of such a thing."

And now she pointed to the decorations and a flat tire. "Just as I thought," she said.

They ran toward the gate in the stone wall. Amos stepped to the big rock which formed one side of the gate. Putting his shoulder to it, he released all his pent-up anger and strength. He knew he could move it, and it tilted. He heaved again and Joan struggled with it beside him. It toppled into the driveway. They ran to the Model T parked near the road. For once, it started on the first twist of the crank. Amos heard shouts of frustration from Dave and Anita, from the Youngman boys wrestling with the stone, as he and Joan drove off down the road. He steered the jouncing Ford over the rough road, straining at the wheel. Maybe they could move the rock back there, maybe they were coming now. Another two or three minutes and the turn would be at hand where nobody would think to follow. Everyone would expect them to turn right but they would turn left toward the Grimes place and the end of the road and the beckoning woods. The road was almost impassable, bushes close on either side.

Joan, hugging his arm, said, "We made it, Amos. We're all alone."

"Pretty near," he answered, as the bridge over Carr Brook rumbled under the wheels.

"Will anyone find the car?"

"Sure. I told Gram."

He stopped in front of the deserted Grimes farmhouse. A window was broken and above it a swift darted into the crumbling chimney. The barn roof had fallen in and young trees grew in the small fields.

He took the knapsack from the back seat of the Ford. Joan was waiting for him. He looked at her. "All set?"

She smiled and nodded. "I guess I've been ready ever since I met you, darling."

"You mean what I suppose you mean?"

"Yes, darling."

"Don't seem like it ought to be talked about."

"Do I embarrass you, Amos?"

"I guess so."

She laughed and kissed him. "Where do we go?"

He led the way toward the woods and the rough logging trail at the edge of the field. "I hid the pack and the fishing rods here this morning.

Hope there's grub you like. I just went into the store and bought stuff. Don't know what you like."

"I'm not fussy. Isn't it strange not to know what we each like to eat?"

"Yes."

He moved behind a clump of balsams and brought out the big canvas packsack containing the food and blankets and cooking utensils and tarpaulin for a tent. He had made the pack when he built the cabin and needed something to carry heavy loads.

"It looks like enough for a month," Joan said, slipping into the straps of her little knapsack.

"I didn't figure on going hungry."

"I guess not," she agreed. "I haven't done this since I was a Girl Scout. Well, yes, I did, one summer at camp. We climbed Mount Washington."

"I've never been there."

"Honest? We'll have to go sometime."

He was anxious to move on into the woods and he shouldered the pack, but he didn't walk fast up the trail. He didn't want to walk too fast for her. He glanced back and saw that she followed easily. His pack was heavy but it made him feel free and secure because it contained shelter and food and everything they'd need in the woods. It was like carrying a home on your back.

The woods closed around as he walked through the last of the bushes and thickets above the Grimes place. The briars and wild apple trees were behind them. The trail followed up the brook beyond the gorge where he had first met Joan and into the familiar ledges and big hardwoods of the mountain. Here he had shot a partridge last fall, right under that beech tree. Here he had dragged out a deer two falls ago.

He stopped to breathe when he felt that there was enough distance between them and the world beyond the forest.

"Are we going up to your cabin?" she asked.

"No, I think that's too far for this afternoon. I've got in mind a place to camp."

She stopped to pick a moccasin flower. "That will be nice. I like to be outdoors. What if it rains?"

"I've got a canvas. If we get a real rainy spell we can go up to the cabin."

She put the moccasin flower in a buttonhole of her shirt. "I suppose I shouldn't pick it."

"There's plenty of them." He pointed to another group of the pink flowers. "Are you tired?"

"No, darling."

They climbed up the ridge. The trail ended near the height of land. He turned left toward the brook and crossed it where a tributary came off the mountain. The walking became rougher as he led the way through the woods beside the stream which tumbled down rocky ravines.

"It's not much farther," he said.

"I'm doing fine. I like this." She looked about her. "All the evergreens and the soft moss and needles underfoot—and the birds, they're everywhere. And flowers. I love it, Amos."

"Wait till you see where we're going to camp." He wanted to tell her how pleased he was to be with her in his woods and have her so happy. "Glad you like it. You won't be sorry we didn't go traveling?"

"No, never."

"There'll be more black flies, when we stop walking."

"I know, you warned me."

"Did I?"

"Last night you told me how awful this would be. You don't need to worry. I just want to be with you alone."

He wished he could say things like that so easily, but he was choked with words of love that wouldn't form. He could only walk on.

They came to a level area on the side of the mountain where the spruces grew close together, and the brook flowed more gently. There was the sound of falling water. He pushed aside a spruce branch and waited for Joan to come up beside him.

"Amos," she said, "it's lovely. Is this the place?"

"Do you like it?"

"It's beautiful."

He walked into the little opening among the trees where the brook formed a long pool beneath a waterfall. The water slid in a thin cascade from a high ledge and splashed into the pool.

He eased his pack to the ground.

She asked, "How did you ever find this?"

"I was fishing and took this branch. Trout in there all right."

She came to him and put her arms around his neck and kissed him. "I knew you'd pick a lovely spot like this. I just knew it." She smiled at him. "I think you're a poet at heart, Amos."

" 'Tain't likely." But he was pleased and held her close and kissed her, realizing that they were alone at last, that this was not like kissing her before they were married, although he had felt that they belonged together. Now they also belonged to each other and this was only a beginning.

"I guess I better make camp," he said, releasing her.

"I'll help."

"I can tend to it."

"I'd like to help. I want to, darling. I can't sit by while you work."

"Well, all right."

He unbuckled the straps on the pack and rolled out the canvas and picked up the small axe. He didn't expect her to do much, but after he'd cut saplings and stretched the canvas and brought a great pile of balsam boughs to shingle into a bed, he found that she had gathered a stack of firewood. He had wanted to do everything to make the camp comfortable for her, but it was better this way, doing the work together. And the wood was dry—dead tree limbs—and all of it good for a fire.

"You see," she said proudly. "I'm not helpless."

"That's right," he said and smiled at her.

He moved stones together at the edge of the brook to make a fireplace. Then he started a little fire. He spread the blankets on the boughs under the canvas.

"It's like home already," she said, arranging the coffee pot and frying pan by the fire. "This is the kitchen and that's the bedroom and this flat rock is the dining room."

"And what are the black flies?"

"Damn intruders."

"Want some fly dope?"

"No, this cigarette keeps them at a distance. You wouldn't love me all smeared up with pine tar and citronella."

"I guess I would."

She stood up and looked about her and he noticed how the late afternoon sun came through the trees and outlined her body and made little lights in her dark hair. "I love it here, Amos."

"It's all right, I guess, ain't it?"

"Yes."

She was taking off her shoes. She touched the water with one toe. "It's cold, but I'm going to have a shower under the waterfall."

Almost before he realized what she was doing, she had dropped her shirt and slacks and slipped off her underclothes and was wading across the shallow end of the pool toward the falls. Her slim but full body was white and he felt an abrupt tightening of his throat. She gave a little cry as she stepped under the waterfall. It poured over her in silver rivulets. She laughed and held her arms across her breasts, her short hair wet and her face dripping. She lifted her arms to the water, moved aside and called to him.

"Do come try it, Amos. You mustn't sit and stare at me. You'll see me without clothes a lot now, you know. It isn't cold, not very, after the first splash."

He became aware that without a thought he was taking off his shirt and dungarees, that something had released him, the picture of her under the waterfall, the innocence of her. He slid off the rock quickly into the deep water of the pool and swam toward the far end. The water was icy cold and washed him over like a primeval cleansing of inhibitions and all previous ideas of women and marriage, which he had vaguely understood didn't apply to himself and Joan, but had yet been a part of him. And he stood up in the shallow water of the pool beside her, taking the hand she reached down to help him, smiling. They stood together under the cold water, splashing and laughing like children. They held hands and faced each other in the tingling spray.

"Oh, Joan," he said. "I love you."

"Darling, you never told me that before."

"Well, of course I do. I couldn't say it, that's all. I love you."

"And I love you. But I'm getting cold. Aren't you?"

"Some."

They waded across the pool and went to the shelter. Joan took a towel from her knapsack and they dried each other. Her lips were cold when he kissed her and held her to him, reaching for a blanket to warm her.

"Amos, I do belong in your arms, don't I? I knew all along but now I'm sure, darling."

"Joan."

"Yes, Amos. Yes."

## Chapter 16

In the evening coolness after supper, they watched the fire while the woods became dark. The twilight lingered under the trees and then still lingered at the tops of the pointed spruces where the sky was clear. For a time no stars showed. The birds continued to sing near the treetops, although the lower branches and the canvas shelter were in shadows. Lying on a blanket spread over the balsam boughs, they listened to a small bird perched on the uppermost spike of a spruce, whistling in a lonesome descending scale.

"It makes me feel so much with you," Joan said. "I wouldn't want to hear that alone."

"It's a good song for the mountains," he told her. "I've listened to them often."

"Weren't you ever lonesome?"

"Not until I met you, I guess. I always felt at home in the woods." He realized that there would be a difference now, but it made him glad, for he would have her near him. "This is better," he said.

"I hope you always think so."

She was lying on one elbow, her head on his shoulder, so that he couldn't see her face in the firelight. She reached back and stroked his cheek and moved against him.

"I wish," she said, "we could go on like this. Sometimes I get scared."

"What do you mean?"

"We're so different, and know different things, but this is perfect and we're just right." She sat up quickly and went on in a brighter tone. "I'm going to wake up at daylight and while you're still asleep, I'm going to catch four trout and make the fire and get your breakfast. Bacon and trout and pancakes and coffee."

"If I'm awake, do I have to get up?"

"Not unless I make a mess of the pancakes, and not if you won't laugh at me trying to cook over a campfire."

"I won't. You thought of the rest of the day?"

"Why, yes. We could go back to bed until the sun was on the pool and then we could swim and have dinner and—well—have a nap." She laughed and lay down again beside him. "Am I shameless?"

"Just a mite." He moved his hand lightly against the soft swell of breast under her shirt and he could feel her breathing quickly.

"You're so gentle, Amos."

"I thought I should be careful of you." He searched for the words he wanted. "Like, like you should treat any small fine thing—careful."

"Not too careful, darling." She raised her arms and pulled his face suddenly to her and he felt her warm lips on his cheeks and eyes and against his mouth, the teeth hard and parted. She sat up. "There, that's enough." She stood up and tossed a stick on the fire. As he waited and she didn't return to him, he got slowly to his feet and went toward her.

"Joan."

She had moved beyond the fire and he reached for her hand. She let him take it and he drew her toward him and for a minute she pressed against him and passed her hands over his back and thighs. Then she had wrenched away and was walking away from the fire.

[ 123 ]

He stumbled after her, but she ran. She must be able to see in the dark. Blinking, he tripped and caught himself. She was only a flash of white shirt ahead of him. His head seemed to clear and he hesitated, confused and hurt in his desire for her. And then she laughed. He understood that she was just plaguing him and he followed after her and caught her by the waist as she tried to slip around a spruce tree. He pulled her down, his knee gouging against a rock. He hardly noticed. He was aware of ferns brushing his face and their scent mingled with the sweet smell of her hair and neck, and her lips against his.

"Ah, Amos, you must think I'm a bitch."

"No."

"I love you so many ways."

Later when the sky had darkened, bringing out the stars, the air became cold. Amos could feel it blowing down the brook from the falls as he lay beside Joan under the blankets. She was curled toward him, breathing regularly, her hand on his shoulder. He felt quiet and contentedly sleepy with a warm pleasure in not being alone. Thinking of all the times he had slept out in the woods, in the cold of fall, in rain and sometimes snow, he understood that there had been a singleness to his life, and it was strange now to find that he wasn't alone.

Joan moved and turned closer to him. She mumbled sleepily, "You awake?"

"Sort of."

She kissed him. "Isn't it nice to wake up together?"

"Yes."

She raised her head. "Not so dark. And there are some coals in the fire still. I can see the trees against the sky."

"The woods ain't really dark except on a cloudy night. Not like a house, that is."

"I'd never noticed. I like it. And the cold air and so warm in here."

She sighed and pulled the blanket around them. In a minute he knew she was asleep. He closed his eyes and listened to the falling water and slept.

## Chapter 17

He awoke before daylight. The birds were beginning to sing in the woods. One called from across the brook and another, as though just awakened, answered with half a song. Amos looked out through the front of the shelter. There was a growing light among the trees. He could see the white cascade of the brook and the gray ledges and the dark pool. The near trees stood out distinctly but he couldn't see into the woods, although even as he watched, they seemed to open up. The sky was growing lighter above the pointed spruce tops. And the birds sang everywhere. He turned to look at Joan and tried to remain quiet for fear of waking her.

She slept on her side facing him, as peaceful as a child. He noticed for the first time how long and dark her eyelashes were, brushing her face above the high cheekbones. A balsam twig had become tangled in her hair, dark green needles against the chestnut of her hair. She looked as though she were just napping, for there was a touch of color on her skin and her hand rested lightly against the soft flesh of her neck and shoulder. Her lips were formed in the beginning of a smile.

He lay back and stared at the canvas roof, listening to the wood's sounds. He felt that he should get up. The habit was strong, but he knew the day stretched before them without demands. He could get up and start the fire, but even that wasn't necessary, for she had said she wanted to do the morning chores. And he realized that he didn't care about anything except to have her wake up and smile at him and be with him through the day.

He thought of the days ahead of them, so many days to be together. Somehow this was different from awakening alone like an animal that belongs in the woods without time or history. He found that he was thinking about the wedding, he was thinking about last night, he was thinking of their return to the farm.

He lay there restless and wishing that he could get up without waking her.

And then she turned and he closed his eyes, pretending to be asleep, while his heart beat in his chest. He felt her feet against his legs before she moved away from him. She must be sitting up. He opened his eyes.

She was yawning and stretching. Her skin looked soft along the curve of her neck and breasts, down to the slim waist.

"Oh," she smiled. "You're awake." She leaned over and kissed him while her hair touched his face and he could feel her warm against him. She lay down again and pulled up the blankets. "I was going to sneak out and start breakfast. Isn't it fun to wake up beside each other? My nose is cold." She pushed her face against his shoulder. "Cold morning, but lovely first morning of married life."

"You cold last night?"

"No, darling, I wasn't cold last night." She laughed and sat up again, throwing back the blanket as she reached for her clothes. "Isn't it funny, we don't know how we behave in the morning. Are you ever grouchy?"

He lifted himself on one elbow and felt the air cool on his bare chest. "Not very often. You always so lively?"

"I'm apt to be." She put on her shirt. "Darling, where did you get such muscles?"

"I don't know."

"I think it's nice you look well without clothes. I suppose if you were thin and frail, I'd love you, but I love you this way more." She kicked her feet loose from the blanket and pulled on her slacks. "I'm going to get breakfast, you know. You stay in bed."

"I'd sooner get up. I ain't much on lying a-bed in the morning."

"Well, all right, but you mustn't interfere. I want to learn how to do everything. You'll have to tell me, but don't scold. I'll cry if you scold before breakfast. After breakfast I'd hit you with the frying pan. That's what coffee does for me. Goodness, I'm hungry."

He watched her step out of the shelter in her bare feet. She glanced back.

"The ground's wet and cold," she said.

"It's the dew. Want your boots?"

"I guess I better. Why, it's all over the ferns and bushes."

"It'll dry off in an hour or so when the sun gets up." He handed her the boots and socks. Then he got dressed.

As he stepped from the shelter, she was trying to start the fire with spruce twigs as she had seen him do. He knelt to help her and before long the smoke was rising into the still air. She looked at him. "I'll do it all right alone the next time."

"You told me you were a Girl Scout."

"Yes, but I used to cheat and use paper and half a box of matches. It was a lark and we used to giggle about it. I never thought I'd be building fires on my honeymoon or I might have paid more attention."

"Things work out peculiar."

"Isn't it nice, though?" As she picked up the coffee pot, she kissed him. "I'm so happy, Amos."

"That's good," he said. "Sometimes I wondered if you—if you'd like being married to a farmer."

"Darling, I'd love you no matter what you were. I think we're just right. I feel so good to be with you."

"I do, too," he said.

She filled the coffee pot with water from the brook and measured out the coffee. He helped her hang it over the fire on a stick, before he rigged a rod and line. The trout rose at once when he cast out and the worm hardly hit the water before he had a fish. He let her take the rod then and cleaned the fish as she caught them.

"I'll do that next time," she said.

"I guess I can take care of it."

While the trout were frying, he watched her mix the batter, and although she had said she didn't want him to interfere, he found little ways of helping her and she didn't object.

The sun was coming up as they sat down on a log near the fire and ate from tin plates set out on the flat rock. The newly caught fish were curled crisp on the plates.

Joan said, ruefully, "I didn't do much of it myself."

"There'll be plenty of other times."

He felt the warm sun on his face and he could see trout in the clear water of the pool. Birds sang and a chipmunk scampered under a spruce tree. He emptied his coffee cup.

"I'll get you some more," Joan said, and brought the coffee pot.

They lazed in the warming sun and drank coffee and kept the fire going slowly just to watch the smoke blow past them across the pool where the breeze caught it and carried it down the valley.

"My," Joan said. "We might be the only people in the world. I wonder if anyone knows where we are?"

"No, except I told Gram we were going toward the camp. The smoke won't show above the trees. I guess no one will bother us. Folks don't come up here much. I've been here only once. Never went above the falls."

"You don't know what's farther up the mountain?"

"Well," he explained, "not exactly. I've hunted over on the east shoulder."

"We can go exploring this afternoon."

"All right."

With the sun higher now, the black flies began to hover in the air. Amos got his bottle of fly dope from the pack. "It smells kind of strong, at first."

"I'll wait a little while," Joan said as she sniffed at the bottle.

"Then I will." He lit his pipe.

They washed the dishes and Amos chopped wood. When the sun was full on the pool they went swimming.

After the first cold shock of the water, Amos felt refreshed and alive, slicing through the clear pool to the gravel bar at the shallow end. With Joan beside him, they reached for white pebbles on the bottom. He brought up one after another and Joan, standing knee-deep in the water near the ledge, took them from him and arranged them to form initials on the rock. *A. and J.J.*

"Joan Jackman," she said. "I like that name." She cupped her hands in the water and tossed crystal drops into the air. They splashed on her laughing face and white shoulders. "Joan Jackman," she said. "In some ways she's a new person. She loves you because you're her husband, but she likes to play in the water without a care in the world. I'm not sure whether she's a woman or a girl or someone I never knew. Darling, do you feel like a different person today?"

"Maybe a little—sometimes."

"Very strange. And do you love me? You haven't told me today."

"I love you."

"Do you find it easier to say?"

"Well, yes."

"Say it again."

"I love you."

"Do you want to go to bed now or would you rather I started dinner?"

In the afternoon they took a fishing rod and climbed around the falls. Amos led the way up the rocky bed of the brook. The water rushed over and between boulders on the steep side of the mountain. It was bordered by spruce trees which clung to the ledges, the bare roots here and there exposed under the covering of forest earth. He felt eager to climb on where he'd never been before and he hardly paused to fish.

"We can catch enough coming back," he said.

[ 128 ]

He was surprised when Joan answered him from some distance back. He turned and saw that she lagged behind. He hadn't realized how fast he had been climbing. He waited for her and they went on together, while the brook grew smaller and tributary streams joined it from springs on either side of the valley. At last he stopped again to let Joan rest.

"I shouldn't wonder," he said, "if we'd come almost to a cliff I saw one time from the east shoulder."

She was out of breath. "Why don't you go ahead, if you want to? I'll fish back to camp."

He hesitated, although he suddenly realized he wanted to go on alone. He felt an opportunity for freedom, as though a door had opened in front of him, and yet he'd been unaware that he wasn't free. He looked down at her. She sat on a rock below him and she seemed almost like a person he might have met on the brook.

"Go ahead," she told him. "I'll be all right."

"Well, maybe I will." He handed her the rod and the bait can. "Always wanted to find out what was up in this valley."

"I'll be at camp." Her expression was reserved and her eyes sought his, demanding. She asked, "When will you be back?"

"Don't know. Shouldn't take me too long."

He started up the brook. When he stopped at the next boulder, to wave, she was busy fishing and didn't look toward him.

He climbed on, feeling a twinge of uneasiness at having left her, but it passed and he began to find pleasure in leaping up the rocks, pushing ahead rapidly at his own pace into the new country.

The brook became a trickle, overhung by bushes and small trees. He located easier traveling through the spruce woods parallel to it. He was entering a section of jumbled ledges and great blocks of stone surrounded with thickets of mountain maple and hobblebush and small evergreens. Some of the rock slabs were as big as wagon sheds and they lay one over the other on the steep slope, forming caves and damp crevices that opened into the earth.

He could no longer hear the brook and concluded that he must have passed its source in some hillside spring he hadn't noticed. Pushing through the brush toward a light ahead, he reached the foot of a high cliff, among rocks that had apparently fallen from the mountainside centuries before. Almost at his feet a crevice showed between two huge slabs. He moved into it and found that it angled upward. It was a shadowy slit in the granite, with porcupine dung underfoot and dampness against his hands as he climbed up into a cave. There was light above him between the rocks. He looked around the cave.

Something about the place appealed to his sense of wildness and he realized what a good shelter it would be if he was caught out late on a hunt. A roaring fire would heat the cave like a room and the crevice above him would carry off the smoke.

He climbed on and stepped over an opening in the rock from which blew a stream of cold air, almost like a spring breeze from woods where the snow still lingered.

At last he pulled himself out into sunlight on a shale slope directly below the cliff and made his way across to a weathered slide which led to the top of the sheer ledge. He was out of breath when he reached the topmost rock but he could look across all the forest he had hunted on the east side of Quartz Mountain and Cobblestone. It gave him a wild lift of excitement. He knew the contours beneath the trees and now he could study it from above, as a bird might see it. The first landmark he noticed was the pond near his camp, and farther east another pond where he had shot a deer two years ago, or three. Closer, he could make out the bog where he had rescued Joan.

Joan—he thought of her with a start, and realized he had no idea how long he had been away. The sun was getting low in the west. He would have to start back, but he found that he was annoyed at the thought of anyone waiting for him or needing him or expecting that he be at a certain place at a certain time. It was, he knew, a strange way to feel about Joan and although he tried to put it from him, it clung in the recesses of his mind and he started back reluctantly.

He knew he should hurry, but at first he went slowly, circling above the cliff and rocks before he swung down the mountain to reach the brook. When he came to easier walking, he moved through the woods fast, for he had turned not only his feet but his thoughts toward Joan, and he wanted to be with her. He was anxious to rejoin her and he was no longer a man alone in the woods.

He came to the brook a little distance above the falls and climbed rapidly down to the ledge above the pool where he could see the camp. Joan was sitting beside the fireplace. He pushed through the trees around the ledge and came into the little clearing. She looked up as he approached.

She ran toward him. "Amos!"

He took her in his arms without understanding what bothered her. Clinging to him, she burst out, "I was worried sick, you'd been gone so long."

Somehow the joy of returning to her faded because of the demands upon him which it involved. He didn't like to think of anyone worrying about him. It seemed to lessen his individuality, and although he understood he ought to be glad that he was necessary to her, that she should worry about him, still he felt it changed their relationship and took something from him. He patted her shoulder and went to the fireplace and began to arrange twigs for kindling.

"Probably," he said, "I did take longer than I thought."

"Don't ever leave me again, Amos. Say you won't."

"But Joan, I'll have to, sometimes."

"I don't want you to."

He saw that she was crying. Tears ran down her cheeks and her face was twisted by her misery and anger.

"Oh," she sobbed. "I wish I didn't love you!"

It seemed to him such an unnecessarily desperate outburst that he wanted to tell her to shut up and not be a little fool. At her suggestion, he'd been gone two or three hours and now she was carrying on in a way which made him wonder why he ever wanted to marry her. He went to the pool and sat down on a rock, while harsh thoughts and words raced through his mind.

Before long, watching the swift-flowing water below the pool, he felt calmer, and then lonely, there on the rock. She came and sat beside him. He was aloof, but felt a bittersweet pleasure in her nearness.

"I'm all right now," she said. "I was just so awfully worried."

"It was my fault. I never should have left you."

He held her close and kissed her, bewildered at the recollection that he had wanted to be away from her—up there on the brook—and that a few minutes ago it had been as though he'd never loved her. Impossible as it seemed, he now wanted to share with her what he had found. He began to tell her about it.

"I'll take you up there tomorrow," he said. "It's real interesting. Caves like you never saw, and a cliff where you can look out over all the woods."

"I'd like to see it," she told him.

And then they began to get supper and afterwards passed the evening by the campfire.

*Chapter 18*

The sun was bright the next morning, with a lingering red as it came over the spruce tops. By the time they had eaten breakfast and packed a lunch, there were streaks of cloud above the clearing. Amos looked up at them as he tucked the sandwiches into his fish bag.

"Shouldn't wonder if we got a little rain before night."

Joan went to the shelter. "I'll fold the blankets and put them away inside."

"Likely we'll be back before it rains."

When she was ready, he started off around the falls, climbing slowly so that Joan could keep up with him. At the top of the ledge, he turned to her. "We'll have better walking in the woods. You want to go first?"

"I'd like to, Amos. I never walked through woods like these without someone showing me the way." She spoke eagerly. "I should learn, shouldn't I? To make you a better wife? Goodness, there isn't any way through them."

"Just walk along and keep the brook in hearing."

He watched her move ahead with hesitating steps where, to him, the way seemed clear past that little spruce, around a birch, toward the next opening among the trees. He followed slowly, saying nothing. Before long, he saw that she was making better progress, not waiting so long to decide which way to go when faced with a new group of trees. She'd catch on, but it was strange to think that anyone didn't walk through the woods naturally.

She looked back, questioning. He smiled and nodded. He was pleased to see her learn, and this was better than yesterday. This was for them both, not just for himself.

"Walk along easy," he said, "and decide which way to take while you walk."

Trying to analyze what he did when he went through the woods, he discovered that there were many little tricks to make it easier. He'd never thought about it before. You didn't watch your feet, but looked beyond and remembered the branches and rocks in the way. You timed your pace until you knew almost without glancing down what was in front of you while your eyes moved on ahead. You kept in mind the sun, when it showed through the clouds, and the sound of the brook. You used your hands to fend aside the branches and you balanced easy on your feet to suit the roughness of the ground and twisted your shoulders to slip around the trees. He told her these things bit by bit as he came to understand them.

They were moving steadily up the valley and he noticed by the diminishing noise of the brook that they had almost reached the upper end. He showed her that it was easier to walk around a blow-down than to climb through it. When they had reached the far side, and could no longer hear the brook, he laughed at her bewildered expression.

"It's gone," she said. "It's been growing fainter, but now it's gone. Have I been turning away from it?"

"No, it ends somewhere along here." He pointed below them. "Probably a hollow down there and two or three springs."

"Where do I go now?"

"Bear off to the east a little."

"That way?"

"No, that's north. About like that."

"How do you tell?"

"I don't know—remembering where we came from, where the sun was before it clouded over."

"Oh, I see." She made a face. "There's so many things to think of."

"Don't have to, when you get used to it. They take care of themselves."

"I don't think they ever will for me."

She walked on and soon they came to the first of the big rocks. Amos led the way then, helping her over the steepest places, until they stood in front of the cleft ledge leading to the cave. She stood beside him looking up at the rocks and cliff.

"Golly," she said. "What a place! I feel as though I'm a million miles from anywhere. I wonder if I could ever find my way back if you should fall and hurt yourself and I had to go for help."

"Sure you could. Just back the way we came."

"I suppose so." She moved beside him and said after a minute in a happier tone, "Where do we go now?"

"Into the cave." He was peeling a strip of bark from a birch tree. "I'll show you. Come on."

He led the way slowly into the split rock. He could sense Joan close behind him as they climbed up the crevice to the cave. He stopped and she took his hand.

She said, "Scary, isn't it?"

"I hadn't thought. Wait until I light the torch." He felt for a dry rock at his feet and struck a match, holding it to the birch bark which caught fire with an oily crackle. It threw a flickering light against the rock walls. In an angle of the ledge and floor, something moved. Joan started to cry out and clapped her hand to her mouth.

"Just a hedgehog," Amos said, picking up a stone and tossing it at the humped form. The quills rose and the tail slashed the air as the porcupine pressed its head into the joint of rock and waited with tail alert.

"Wish I had a club," Amos said. "There's twenty cents bounty."

"Oh, no, Amos, not for twenty cents."

"Well, all right."

Carrying the torch, he went on through the cave, to the chimney leading upward. "There's a crack in the rock here. Feel the cold air?"

"Yes."

"Hold the light for me, will you?"

"Where are you going, Amos?" Her voice was almost trembling, though she seemed to be trying to steady it.

"Just down here a little. Don't fret, it's all right."

He began lowering himself into the slot between the rocks. In the shadows, he had to feel for footholds and then he was on solid rock again, standing with his head below Joan's feet.

"Cold down here," he said. "Move the torch over that way."

She was kneeling beside the crevice, her face worried in the flickering shadows cast by the flames.

He knelt down and saw a patch of rotten ice. Kicking at it with his heel, he broke loose a piece and handed it up to her. "Look at that! Snow falls down the chimney in the winter and stays here right into summer."

"Yes," she said, taking the ice. "I see. Come up now, Amos. It's so cold and dark down there."

He lifted himself up the rock and stood level with her. "You want to go out?"

"Yes."

"It's just a step up this way." He crushed the torch under his foot. Almost at once they climbed out into the air and daylight again, the sun bright, shining through a break in the clouds before it was hidden again.

Joan still clutched the crystals of gray ice.

"It's like holding a piece of the winter," she said. "Isn't it strange?"

She watched a trickle of water drip through her fingers, and she shivered a little.

He said, "We'll climb up the cliff and rest."

He was looking forward to the moment when she would stand beside him on the cliff and see all his woods and hills spread out before her. He helped her up the steep rock, then over the last edge. She stood beside him with the wide eastward view spread out below them.

Abruptly she stepped back from it, against him, breathing hard. At first he thought the height had startled her, but she said in a tense voice, almost whispering, "What an awful wilderness! It's so far from anything and nothing but woods. Amos, it scares me!"

"No need to be scared of it," he told her gently. "I been all over it."

"I didn't know there were so many trees in the whole world."

"Shucks, it's only five, six miles across. One winter I trapped along the ridge beyond that second pond. See, there's the bog you fell in."

"Goodness, if I'd known what a forest I was getting into I'd never have dared start out alone that day." She added thoughtfully, "It's so different when you're down there. It's doesn't come over you so. I feel helpless when I look at it."

"Yes, I suppose so, if you ain't used to it." He pointed to the nearest pond. "You can almost see the roof of my cabin."

She sat down and placed the ice she'd been carrying on the rock beside her. It began to melt into a little pool. She didn't look at the forest any more and when he turned to sit beside her and open the lunch, he saw that she was still nervous and unhappy.

"You want to start back to camp?" he asked.

"No, you like it here." She tried to smile. "I'll be all right. I'll think of you here with me and it'll be all right."

He held out a bacon sandwich. "Eat something and you'll feel better." He was disappointed, but he tried not to show it. He munched on a sandwich and let his eyes wander over the woods below them. Black flies gathered in the air and bit his neck and hands. He hardly noticed. He heard Joan slapping at them.

At last she said, "Amos, I think it's going to rain."

He had been aware of the clouds piling in from the east and the wind blowing the leaves of the trees so their lighter green undersides showed, but he had not given these things much thought. You got wet when rain fell and that was all there was to it. Joan, of course, was different. She would want to stay dry.

"Well, if it does," he said, "we can go down to the cave and get out of the wet. Be a good place to sit out a storm."

She shook her head. "No, Amos, I want to go back to camp."

"Well, all right."

Soon after they started, the rain began to fall. It came with a rush of wind off the mountain. The sky darkened like night and the rain came down in torrents. Amos took shelter under a thick spruce. Joan huddled next to him, saying nothing. They were silent until the rain began to reach them through the sheltering boughs.

"We might as well go on," he said. "Going to get soaked anyhow."

She only nodded, and followed him through the stormy woods. A branch cracked and dropped to the ground behind them after they passed under it. Wind roared in the treetops. They were wet twice over, once by the rain and once by the dripping bushes. Amos stopped to let Joan rest and saw that her shirt and dungarees were plastered to her body. Her wet hair clung to her face. She looked cold and scared and miserable.

"Amos," she asked, "are you sure where the camp is?"

"'Course I'm sure." He let his hand rest on her shoulder. "Don't worry about that." He started off again, adding, "We'll be warm and dry before long."

He was sure of it, but after a time he began to wonder. They should have reached the brook by now. He had been careful to head for the brook after they left the cliff so he'd strike it above camp and be able to follow it down if the storm got worse. He'd been careful not to take the route by which he had returned yesterday, for fear of passing by the camp. He walked on and on through unfamiliar woods, not panicky but worried about Joan. He didn't care about himself. He felt that in time he'd come to a place he knew, but he didn't want her to walk any more in the rain and cold wind.

He realized she must sense that something was wrong, because when he stopped next, she asked, "We're not lost, are we, Amos?"

He smiled at her. "No, but the camp is, for a little while. I must have missed the head of the brook when we came down off the cliff." He looked about him. "Want me to build a fire to warm you while I look around? Seems as though I been through here once."

"No, Amos, no. I don't want you to leave me. If we don't find the camp soon I'll wash away to nothing."

She was shivering and he felt that she reproached him for this, although she tried to joke. She had counted on him in a strange place and now she wasn't sure she could rely on his help.

He felt afraid about her, a dull emptiness in his stomach that reminded him of the first time he'd been lost when he was a kid. It was taking his mind from his task, and he almost walked across a faintly marked game rail where there had once been a logging road. He remembered it and he pointed it out to her.

"Camp's right over that way," he said.

"Are you sure?" Her eyes brightened.

He nodded and turned back up the slope, while their route oriented itself in his mind. He had gone past the source of the brook and too far down the mountainside. But he knew where he was now. Soon he heard the brook above the rush of the wind and rain in the trees. He pushed through the trees to the stream, a little below the camp.

With a sudden shock, he saw that it wasn't the camp they had left. Helping Joan to cross the brook, he saw the falls and the pool and the rock fireplace. But the canvas shelter had vanished under the dripping boughs of the big spruce which had stood behind it. He realized how much he had counted on the protection of that canvas. Now their blankets would be wet, the canvas torn by the spruce limbs, and their food smashed under the tree. He stopped by the fireplace and looked at the wreckage, while the rain pelted down. Taking Joan's hand, he drew her to him and held her against his wet shirt. She wept and shivered.

"Amos, we might have been in the shelter. We might be dead or crippled, away up here on the mountain. It's such a cruel forest, Amos. I'm frightened."

He hushed her and quieted her and tried not to think that if he was alone, he'd strike for the cabin on the pond and spend a dry night. She could never walk that far, and neither could she go back to Whichertown. He wouldn't go back there even if they could. He'd make her comfortable. He'd show her that he could take care of her and that the woods were all right.

Crawling under the spruce, he found his old jacket and a blanket. He dragged them out and put the jacket on her and wrapped her in the wet blanket. Then with the axe, he cut into a dead stub for dry wood and built a fire while the wind and rain continued. As he worked, and although he was working for her, he felt separated from her because she sat there by the fire and watched him with dull eyes.

He cleared away the spruce and set up the canvas on a frame of poles. It was torn so that he had to cut it and overlap three sections to shed the rain. Then he picked Joan up and carried her under the shelter. He brought her a pot of steaming coffee he had made from wet grounds salvaged out of the torn package.

He built another fire close to the shelter and chopped the spruce trunk into firelogs which he laid up behind the fire to reflect the heat toward Joan. He lost himself in work, moving methodically, asking occasionally about her comfort. The wind was going down, but the rain still fell in a steady drizzle and the air was cold, as night came on. He chopped more and more wood, until the growing shadows forced him to put down the axe.

Squatting by the fire, he raked out coals and added twigs and split wood which gradually caught flame and burned across the entire front of the shelter. He looked over the food in the flattened packsack. The bread was a soggy mush, the corn meal wet. The jar of butter had been smashed. Flour and spruce needles and coffee grounds had mixed with rain water to make a soupy mass of the crackers and cheese. The bag of sugar was torn. He slowly wiped off the slab of home-cured bacon, and searched out the potatoes and onions. He stared bleakly at the ruin of their food. Bacon and potatoes weren't much of a supper for Joan. He wished that he could provide something better.

He knew that Joan was watching him. She must be hungry, far hungrier than he, for he was accustomed to going without regular meals when he hunted or fished. Looking at the shelter and at the fire, and the rain falling in the twilight, he realized what a hardship it all must be for her—primitive and fearsome and painful. And he couldn't even offer her a good supper. He picked up the bacon to begin slicing it. He was about to ask her if she felt any warmer, if the blanket was drying all right. . . .

A rabbit hopped from the darkening woods into the light of the fire. It was a big hare, long legged and long eared. Amos could see its wet fur. Nose wrinkling, it sniffed the ground and hopped closer. Amos thought of hot rabbit stew for Joan and reached slowly for a stick of wood. The law was on rabbits, but she was hungry and deserved something better than potatoes and bacon. He waited while the rabbit hopped forward again. He didn't move, except to raise his arm a little. His fingers sought a firm throwing grip on the stick of wood.

He turned his eyes toward Joan. She was watching the fire in front of her. He looked back at the rabbit. It might not come any closer. He flung the stick of wood and struck the rabbit in mid-leap. The rabbit squealed sharp and piercing as it made off brokenly into the shadows. Amos jumped after it and caught it by the legs and swung its head against a rock, silencing the squeal in a crunching thud.

He came back to the shelter and held up the rabbit. "Now we'll eat."

She cried, "Amos, how could you!" There was a look of horror in her eyes. "How could you!"

She hid her face in the blanket while he stood in the rain with the rabbit limp at his side and stared at her sobbing form. Her reaction was beyond his understanding. He stood in front of the fire with the feeling of aloneness coming over him. He did not know what to do. He felt dead in the part of his mind that loved her and wanted to look after her. At last he made himself drop the rabbit and kneel beside her under the canvas.

He put his hand on her shoulder. "I was just trying to get you something nice to eat."

"Don't touch me! Go away, go away!"

He heard the rain on the canvas and her muffled sobs. He stood up and moved to the fire.

The rabbit lay on the ground where he had dropped it. He picked it up and slowly went to a stone on the far side of the fire where he began to skin the animal. When he had finished dressing it, he fried bacon in the large kettle and browned the quarters and saddle of the rabbit. He added water and sat by the fire for a long time tending the stew and drying the other blanket, while the rain changed to a mist and finally stopped. He peeled potatoes and sliced onions. He salted the stew and tasted it, occupying himself with his task so that he wouldn't think.

When it was cooked, he spooned some of it into a tin plate and turned to the shelter. Joan was sitting with her back against an upright, the blanket wrapped around her.

"Want some?" he asked.

"No."

He began to eat. She watched him. He ate greedily, careless of what she thought about his manners. Squatted by the fire, he chewed on a rabbit leg and tried to imagine what she was thinking, wondered if she could ever live his way of life.

She said at last, "You look like a caveman sitting there filling his belly. You're not a pretty sight."

"Got to fill it somehow," he replied.

He remembered some things she had said the first day on the brook, talking about hunters and Western scouts and woodsmen.

He asked, "Those men you told me about the day we met—Leatherstocking, wasn't it, and Dan'l Boone and them. How you figure they filled their bellies? Off the pantry shelf?"

"I hadn't thought what it looked like."

He said with more gentleness, "Likely not." He spooned more stew into his plate and blew on it.

[ 139 ]

She looked at the plate and then at the fire. "It's not the same any more. Us, I mean."

"I'm no different."

"I see you different, maybe." She straightened up and leaned forward. "I love you, though. Isn't that funny?" She paused. "Is the stew good?"

"I've had better, but I don't know as I had any that tasted better."

He filled another tin plate and handed it to her. She lifted the spoon to her mouth, watching him, and swallowed. "It is good." She smiled at him.


*Chapter 19*


When he awoke in the morning long after daylight, he could feel the east wind blowing down the valley and he saw that the sky was dark and overcast, or he would not have slept so late. The wind smelled of rain, not from the storm of the day before—clear air blowing through wet woods—but of rain on the way. It stirred the great heap of coals left from the fire and brought their warmth into the shelter.

Joan slept between him and the fire. She lay curled against him in the same position where she had fallen asleep the night before, after eating the plate of rabbit stew and undressing to roll into the blankets which he had dried before the fire. She might hardly have moved all night. He could see her clothes hanging in the front of the shelter and they gave him an abrupt awareness of her presence, evidence that this was her camp, too.

She moved against him, her smooth shoulders warm against his chest. He knew the soft pleasant sensation of her sleeping with him, the exciting comfort of her near him. Its strange newness fascinated him and created a wonder that he could not understand. With her sleeping beside him he was alone and not alone. Their trouble of the previous night seemed like a bad dream.

Shifting her head, she opened her eyes and blinked. She stretched and rolled over to face him.

"I'm lame," she said, "but I feel fine. Would you believe it? After all that. I was sure I'd have pneumonia this morning."

"You must be tough, but getting wet don't hurt as much as you might think."

"We were wet, all right."

"Going to rain today, too."

"No, is it, Amos?"

"Expect so. We ought to decide what to do." He thought a minute. "Since you feel like you do about the woods here, maybe we better go home—take a little trip somewhere."

She shook her head. "No, that would spoil everything. I'm all right today. I don't know what was the matter with me last night. Let's move to your camp."

Doubtfully, he said, "It's not much of a place. One room and bunks and stove, that's about all." He added, "Roof leaks in one corner."

"I don't mind. I want to stay there, Amos."

"It's a lot farther on into the woods."

"I know. I want to go there."

"Then we better start or we'll be walking in another rain storm."

She nestled closer to him. "I hate to get out of bed. It's so comfortable here."

He had been prepared to roll out of the blankets and start the fire and make coffee and heat the rest of the stew. He had thought of packing and the walk to the cabin. The rain wouldn't hold off forever.

She stroked his cheek. "I'm sorry about last night, Amos."

"That's all right."

He was thinking of the wet woods. Rain or not they'd be wet through before they'd gone a hundred feet from the camp. Perhaps there was no need to start at once, yet he felt he should get up and begin the day. Of course here in bed it was warm and dry and Joan was kissing him. He didn't want to leave Joan and still he did. All his habits urged him to get up. He'd overslept—the day was well into the morning. A man should be about the day's business.

Joan moved against him. He yielded to her caresses, at first almost with reluctance and then in complete forgetfulness, with only a slight sensation of defeat as an individual.

As he had expected, later, the rain began to fall in a steady drizzle. The only good thing was that it had held off until they had eaten breakfast and taken down the shelter, saved what they could of the food, and put out the fire.

He shouldered the pack and glanced around the campsite where only the black ashes of the fire and the poles of the shelter and the bough bed were left.

Joan said, "Doesn't it look deserted? Almost as though we'd never been here."

"We have," said Amos.

"Haven't we, darling?" She laughed and kissed him. "I suppose that's why I feel a little sad about leaving."

"The cabin will be better if we're in for a spell of rain."

"Doesn't it ever stop raining in New Hampshire in June?"

"Sure does," he said. "This is just to make the grass grow."

"June ought to be perfect weather."

"Well, this is early June, sort of the tag end of spring up here." He shifted the pack on his shoulders. "You all ready?"

"Yes." She picked up her little knapsack.

They got wet as soon as they left the camp and walked into the dripping bushes, but it didn't seem to matter so much today because they knew there were walls and roof and stove at the end of their journey. When they reached the main brook, they climbed up to the bog where Joan had fallen in, then over the next ridge to the stretch of brook running under the dark spruces.

Familiar as the country was to him, he saw it new for Joan's benefit and tried to make her understand it not as the wilderness she remembered below her yesterday on the cliff, but as woods with interesting plants and animals and trees. He talked of the different times he had been along this way. He showed her a partridge clucking in the bushes, and deer tracks in the mud of the brook. He wanted her to see it as he did, but he realized this was impossible; there remained the difference of birth and background between them. She was a visitor while this was his own country.

So he felt a certain diffidence as he led the way around the pond to the cabin. He hoped that the mice and squirrels had not made too much of a mess out of the place. He hoped she wouldn't be afraid of them. And as he climbed the little path from the pond inlet, he saw the cabin with her eyes. It was not the shelter and haven which he had built in the woods. Instead it appeared to him as a rough log cabin with a flap of tar paper loose on one corner of the roof and the windows dark and uninviting, the rain dripping from the eaves. It seemed a poor place to bring a girl whose idea of a log cabin must be based on her father's big lodge.

He stood quiet while she came up to him and brushed back her damp hair. He thought of the last time he was here, wet as now and needing shelter, after pulling her out of the bog that rainy day last month. The cabin had been lonely after his return to it. He had thought of her here but it had never seemed possible.

He waited while she looked at the cabin.

[ 142 ]

"Amos!" she said. "It's wonderful. Did you cut those logs and build it alone?"

"Yes."

She glanced behind her across the inlet and pond. "It must be a pretty spot on a nice day. Now I want to see the inside."

He opened the door for her.

"Don't you lock it?" she asked.

"No, there's nothing in here anyone would want. Besides, it's too far away for anyone to bother." He followed her inside and lowered the pack to the floor. "I'll start a fire."

"It's going to be cozy, Amos. It's just right." She was moving around to look at the canned food on the shelf, and the bunks.

"It ain't much," he said, "but it's dry except over there in the corner and I'll fix that. Stove draws good." He replaced the stove lid and listened to the dry spruce sticks crackle in the firebox. He took the broom from the corner by the woodpile and began to sweep the floor.

"My," she said, "even a broom. Who'd think there'd be a broom way off here in the woods?"

"I lugged it in one day after I got sick of trying to sweep the floor with a spruce bough." He brushed at the twigs and needles in the cracks between the boards. "Mice and squirrels strew stuff around when the place is empty. Do you mind them? Little wood mice and red squirrels."

"I don't think I will. I never exactly lived with them before."

"The wood mice are sort of pretty, not like house mice, but white and soft brown."

"I think I'll like them." She took the broom from him. "How'd you ever get the stove here?"

"Well, I unbolted it and carried the pieces in and put them together again."

"I should think it would have been easier to build a fireplace."

"A fireplace don't heat much," he said. "It uses a lot of wood. And I'd have had to lug in the cement."

"Yes, that's true."

He looked about the cabin. "Well, I might go catch us some trout while I'm still wet. Don't know's they'll bite after the rain, but I can try." He picked up his rod. "You want to come?"

She shook her head. "I'd rather stay here. It's my first house, you see. I like that roof over my head and I want to dry out."

"Sure." He started for the door and then remembering, turned and kissed her. "I won't be gone long," he said.

[ 143 ]

"That's all right. I won't mind, like the other time."

"Good."

He went out the door into the rain, stopping to make sure he had enough worms in the bait can before he walked through the woods to the brook.

He knew it would be a poor day for brook trouting. The water was high and dark, running swiftly near the top of the banks. In places it had flooded among the trees, and flowers and green leaves floated, root moored, against the current. He had no enthusiasm for the fishing. He was aware of Joan left behind at the cabin. He could almost see her moving around the strange room, perhaps trying to make it more home-like or more in keeping with her ideas of a log cabin. Or perhaps she was just sitting on a bunk and staring at the rough floor and log walls or looking out the door at the wet woods, and wishing she had never married him.

He felt a desultory tug on his line and for a few moments occupied himself with hooking the trout. It didn't bite with the sudden rush of a hungry fish, but slowly, as it mouthed the bait down there under the roily water. He caught it at last and put it in his fish bag. When he had three or four more he could go back to the cabin, but if they didn't bite faster than this, he'd have to go back anyway.

It was strange to have an anchored sensation, a feeling that he was tethered to the cabin on a rope which was slack and allowed him to move away, but would eventually bring him up short. He didn't like it and he couldn't fish properly. He missed several trout and continued to push on from one pool to the next, saying to himself, "Just one more pool and I'll go back." He caught two more fish and then started back reluctantly. He felt that it was foolish to stop fishing with only three trout in his fish bag, but he could no longer move away from the cabin.

He found that he was hurrying as he went back down the brook. As he approached the pond, and the woods opened up toward the gray sky and falling rain, he could hear the sound of chopping. He came into the clearing. Joan stood at the chopping block with the axe in her hands. She swung it clumsily and it glanced from the stick of wood—he caught his breath—and drove into the earth near her foot.

He came up to her just as she lifted the axe and stood glaring at the jagged edge of the blade which a moment before had been razor sharp. She looked at him and dropped the axe like a guilty child and stooped to pick up the kindling that lay around the chopping block.

She asked, "Did you catch any?"

"Three." He laid his rod across spikes on the side of the cabin. He was torn between relief that she hadn't cut her foot and anger at the damage to his axe. "You shouldn't be splitting wood," he said. "There's plenty in the cabin."

She stood up with the kindling in her arms. The rain formed in drops on her dark hair. "I wanted to get the oven hot and it wouldn't seem to heat with the big wood."

"There's kindling aplenty under the bunk."

"I found it, but I thought it was something special. I'm making biscuits," she said.

"All right," he told her. "But you better leave the wood splitting to me." He said nothing about the axe. "You'll get hurt chopping."

He followed her into the cabin. The table was spread with dishes and pans and covered with flour. A can which she had apparently used for a rolling pin lay at one side of the flattened dough. He could see that the dough was stuck to the table in several places. It all looked to him as though six little girls had gone on a cooking spree.

Joan went to the stove and filled it with kindling. There was a smell of scorched food in the air. Amos lifted the lid from a kettle on the stove and watched the smoke pour out.

"Oh!" Joan cried out. "The potatoes!"

She snatched at the kettle and dropped it in mid-air when the handle burned her fingers. The steaming, smoking mass of potatoes spilled over the floor and the kettle rolled under the stove.

Filled with abrupt anger, Amos controlled himself and said nothing. He moved the frying pan of bacon to a cooler spot on the stove before he turned to Joan.

She wasn't crying. She stood there amid the ruin of her dinner and looked at him as though she was afraid he'd hit her. Although he was hungry and irritated about the nicked axe and the spoiled cooking, frustrated with his fishing and the new ties that held him to the cabin, yet he realized above everything else that she was afraid of him. It struck him as an awful thing, and the words that were forming in his mind about her clumsiness and thoughtlessness and inability to cook a simple meal wouldn't come to his lips. He looked about the cabin.

She had spread the blankets on the rafters to dry the dampness from them. She had cleaned the shelves and washed the windows and hung up the pots and pans behind the stove. Everything about the cabin spoke of her eagerness to please him and make things pleasant within the first four walls they were to share.

The fact that she was afraid of him would have been enough to soften his heart, for he could not bear to be feared. His size and strength had always worried him because they made hurting people or animals so easy. He had always tried to be kind and gentle because he hated the thought that anyone would be afraid of him.

He went to her and took her in his arms. "Don't fret about it," he said. "It's just a kettle of potatoes."

"I know, but I can't seem to do anything right, and I wanted everything to be nice for you." She didn't weep, but her voice was tight and her body stiff. "I don't want to keep on making a mess of whatever I try to do."

"You aren't afraid of me?"

"Not now. For a moment I thought—something about the way you looked at me. . . ."

"I didn't mean to. I wouldn't hurt you for anything. Don't you see?"

She nodded her head against his chest and he felt her relax in his arms.

"I'll learn," she said. "Honest, I will, Amos. I promise. If you'll be patient with me, I'll learn to do everything right for the way we're going to live."

"Sure, of course you will."

She began to clean up the potatoes. He helped her. Then she scraped the dough from the table into the kettle. He went outside with it to throw way her first attempt at a stove-cooked meal for them. And when he returned, it was almost funny. She was trying to open a can of soup. The old can opener didn't work easily, but she struggled with it until she could pour the soup into a pan. He pretended not to notice, busying himself with the fish.

There was soup for dinner and bacon and trout. Although Amos felt hungry when his bowl and plate were empty, he said nothing, but lit the damp tobacco in his pipe and set the open can on the back of the stove to dry a little. He found a file on a shelf and brought in the axe. While he filed a new edge on the axe, Joan washed the dishes in a pan. He realized that they weren't talking much, but it seemed unnecessary, for he felt closer to her.

The rain came down outside in a steady gray drizzle. Through the window, Amos could see the dark pond and beyond it the low clouds. The cabin was shadowy and the rain made a sleepy whispering sound on the roof. Joan finished the dishes and sat down on a bunk. She watched him sharpen the axe with a pocket stone.

He asked, "You all right?"

She nodded and smiled.

He said, "I been thinking. There'll be a lot of days like this for you. The winters are long, and spring ain't very pleasant. When we have our house, it won't be one room like this, but there's days and days when you'll be shut in."

"I won't mind."

"It'll be a hard way for you to live."

"It's what I want," she said. "I knew what I was doing, Amos."

"Sometimes I worry about it. And my family. I kind of have to look after them. Mort ain't right since Ma was killed, and Pa's just sort of all wore out. Whicher won't be around much longer, not after he can make his own way, but there's Gram. She'll need looking after."

"I know. We talked about that before." She stood up and went to the window. "You don't understand how I feel about it. I want to live a—a fundamental life. Ever since I was old enough to think about it, I've felt artificial and useless at home. I don't care about money and society and all those things you think mean so much to me." She faced about and frowned a little as though she were trying to say exactly what she felt. "I've had enough of them to last me all my life because they never made me happy. Something's all wrong with the values—wealth and big houses and big cars and people who don't know what it is to be cold and tired and hungry, talking about their stocks and bonds, new clothes, golf games and all that. It's no good and I want to get away from it . . . besides loving you." She came and kissed him. "See? So what's the sense of talking about it?"

He smiled at her. "All right. I just hope it ain't all in your head."

"What do you mean?"

"Well, that it might be something you dreamed up and thought you liked and would find a lot different when it really came to happen."

"I certainly never dreamed up you."

"No, but maybe I came along at the right time to fit in."

"Oh, Amos, stop talking about it. Talking can spoil anything. And it's all in the future. I want to enjoy this, now. I love you and the cabin and the rain and being here alone with you and I'm sick of talking."

"Never thought much of talk, myself," he said as he stood up slowly and put a stick of wood in the stove.

# Chapter 20

The rain continued. Amos heard it in the night and it was still falling when he awoke. It seemed to shut them into the small world of the cabin and circle of woods and the pond. He felt that it divided the past and the future until there was nothing but the cabin, windows showing the dark spruces, and the warm blankets.

Joan had awakened before him. She lay on her back smoking one of her cigarettes, which had miraculously stayed dry in the bottom of the packsack. She was close to him in the narrow bunk on the quilts and balsam boughs, with the blankets over them. A mosquito hummed above the bunk.

He watched a mouse run along the logs to the corner where it darted to a shelf and crept along, white and brown, long tailed, sniffing at the cans of beans and the flour and cornmeal and bacon. It skittered on, with the peculiar footless motion of mice, down the window frame to the table. It paused to nibble a crumb. Joan moved and it whisked into the stack of wood.

Joan said, "I've been watching him for a long time." She leaned over and dropped her cigarette into a tin can on the shelf beside the bunk. "I could sleep some more," she added, moving down beside him.

"Good day for sleeping," he said, and realized it was a new thought, sleeping in the daytime. He had always been eager to get up and start the day but now he wanted only to hold Joan in his arms and listen to the rain on the roof.

After a time, he awoke and got up. He put on his pants and shirt and went outside into the cold rain. The woods were a heavy green and the earth cold and wet underfoot.

He returned to the cabin and met Joan coming toward him from the edge of the woods. She had put on his jacket and her bare legs and feet below it made him laugh.

"So I look funny," she said. She took off the jacket and tossed it at him. "I always wanted to feel the rain on my bare skin. I wish it weren't so cold." She looked up at the sky and let the rain fall on her face. She shivered and ran ahead of him into the cabin where she slid under the blankets of the bunk. She laughed at him, with the blankets pulled up to her chin. "Don't look so startled. Make the coffee and we'll drink it in bed and then I might get your breakfast."

"Biscuits and boiled potatoes?"

"No, probably canned beans."

"I'll show you how to make johnnycake."

He started the fire in the stove. As he took the coffee can from the shelf by the window, he noticed that the day was no brighter than when he first woke up. He put the pot on to boil, and yawned, wondering at his quiet contentment. There was nothing at all but Joan and the cabin and the rain falling outside. He didn't feel imprisoned or restless. Sitting down on the bunk beside Joan, he realized that there were timeless worlds other than those of the hunter and fisherman.

The coffee boiled and he brought it to the bunk with two cups and spoons and the jar of sugar. They drank it sitting in the bunk with a blanket around their shoulders. And then they lay down together and he told her about the winter trapping and the deep snow.

The rain fell, and they slept and then made dinner while the fire crackled warmly in the stove. Amos knew that the day was passing, but there was no sign of it except at last the gathering darkness. They had spent the entire time as though there were no such things as noon or sunset, merely their being together, the comfort of each other and the quiet of the cabin, slow talk between them. Joan told him odd bits of her childhood, remembered and related, and his own voice replied in short sentences between silences—accounts of his life—until he felt that they had exchanged their lives and each had taken over a small portion of the other's, not experienced but still a new part of mind and memory.

He lit two candles. They cast flickering shadows on the walls, leaving darkness between the rafters. The shadow of Joan at the stove moved slowly across the logs. She was getting supper. She had been working on it for the past hour or more. She had made spaghetti with tomato sauce and added things she thought should go into it, such as onions and bacon. They ate with the candles between them on the rough board table.

It was late when the dishes were done and Amos realized the rain had stopped.

"Probably clear tomorrow," he said. "I'll take you out on the raft on the pond."

"That would be nice." She came and sat on his lap. "I love our evenings together, Amos. Thinking of sleeping with you all night, and looking forward to the next day."

"I like them too." He held her against him. "You getting sleepy?"

"Well, we could go to bed."

In the morning, the sun came through the window to the east, the birds were singing and the woods looked fresh and clean. Amos thought of the previous day as almost a dream. Joan, stirring beside him, looked at the sunlight on the wall and said, "Why, Amos, it's just as though the world were starting up again."

After breakfast, he took her down to the pond. The raft, which last fall he had hauled up on a slanting rock near the inlet, was made of spruce logs spiked to cross pieces, and it floated well when he pushed it into the water.

He went to a balsam tree near the rock. "I laid up an old bamboo pole somewhere here, with a line and spoon hook, and a paddle I made out of a board." He found them and returned to the raft. "Better take off your shoes," he told her.

While he unlaced his own shoes, he watched her move carefully across the floating logs and sit down on a cross brace. Taking up the peeled spruce sapling which lay across the raft, he pushed off into the still water. There was no breeze. He poled the raft slowly along the shore where the pointed spruces were reflected in the blue water. It carried them across the reflections as though they moved in the sky. At a cove where lily pads covered the surface of the pond, he drove the pole between the logs into the bottom to moor the raft. He tested the line wound on the end of the bamboo cane and fluffed out the feathers of the treble hook below the spinner.

"Here," he said. "Take it and skip the spoon over the top of the water."

"You try it."

"No, go ahead. There's nothing to it."

At first she caught lily pads, but then she found the open water between the pads and a pickerel came at the spoon with a splashing lunge. She swung the pole back and Amos caught the fish as it lifted clear of the water.

"Amos, what a big one! What is it?"

"Pickerel. Bigger ones in there, too."

She began casting again and caught another. He moved the raft, now she had the knack of it, and poled slowly among the lily pads toward a point where logs, fallen from the woods, rested in the water.

"My," she said at last, "that's fun. Don't you want to try it?"

"Just a little. Can you pole the raft?"

"I guess so."

It went in a wide circle, and he had to help her with the paddle, but finally she managed to keep it near shore, and he caught three pickerel.

"We've got more than we'll want to pick the bones out of," he said.

"All right."

"How about a swim?" He looked at the sun. "Nice and warm now. The shore's mostly mud, but we can swim off the raft."

He pushed out into deeper water until the pole would scarcely touch and there moored the raft, leaning on the pole to ram it into the bottom. Joan was taking off her clothes.

"It's cold," she said.

"You don't have to go in."

"I want to."

She made a little leaping dive and her body cut the water in a short arc of grace that caught at Amos' heart and made him wonder in how many ways she would continue to appear beautiful to him. Her head slid up and she turned toward him, laughing. With three quick strokes, she reached the raft and pulled herself up and sat with her legs dangling in the water.

"Go on in, sissy," she said. She splashed water toward him. "I'd say from the way you're looking at me a little cold water would do you good."

"I like to look at you."

"I like to have you." She smiled. "Go on, dive in."

He dropped his clothes on a cross piece out of reach of the lapping water. He gripped the edge log with his toes and pushed himself up and out. The cold water surged over him and above him. Surfacing, he swam back to Joan. He rested one elbow on the raft.

She said, "Your face is so tanned and your shoulders so white in the sun." She touched his neck. "A line right around here. Someday I should like to get tanned all over."

"If you tried it here, the black flies would carry you off."

"Yes, they've found me already." She slapped at one on her arm. "I'm going to dive once more."

She poised a second and sprang out into the water, her arms slicing the surface beside him, legs sliding through the circle left by her hips. She swam slowly away from the raft and back to meet him.

"I've had enough," she said.

He reached the raft first and pulled himself up on it and helped her beside him.

"I wish," she said, "the flies would wait a while. I'd like to dry off."

"You can have my shirt for a towel."

"No, I'll dress wet." She put on her shirt, and then suddenly bent to examine her leg below the knee. "Amos, there's something on my leg! Ugh, what is it, Amos?"

He shifted his position and saw a blobby worm on the calf of her leg.

"Bloodsucker."

"Get him off, Amos, quick!" Her voice was high and frightened.

He reached for his pants and took out his knife, opening the sharp blade.

"What are you going to do?"

"Shave him off."

She was trembling and he saw how pale her face was. He slipped the blade under the bloodsucker and peeled the creature from her skin. A trickle of blood appeared and spread thinly with the water on her leg. He dropped the bloodsucker on a log and carefully cut it in two and flipped the pieces into the pond. The separate pieces stretched and contracted in the water, disappearing under the raft.

"Won't hurt you," he said as she sank on the log beside him.

"Aren't they poisonous?"

"No. Old folks call them leeches."

"Was that a leech? I've heard about doctors years ago applying leeches." She shuddered. "Horrid, nasty things. Brr." She dabbed with her shirt tail at the bleeding spot on her leg. "Won't it ever stop bleeding?"

"Takes a little while. Always does. I mind one time I had six on me after skipping for pickerel with bare feet and legs." He talked on slowly to calm her. "They don't usually bother in deep water. It must have been on the underside of the raft."

Color was coming back into her face. "I didn't scream or anything, did I?"

He put his arm around her. "No, you did fine."

"Why is it that something awful has to happen just when everything is perfect? Now I won't want to swim here again."

"Well," he said, "they don't really hurt you any."

"I hate them. I hate the slimy, squiggling damn things." She stood up and drew on her slacks. "But I suppose I can get used to them."

"Sure you can. Want to go back and eat these pickerel now?"

"Yes."

He put on his shirt and pants.

As he started poling the raft toward the inlet, he heard a partridge whir up through the bushes near the lower end of the pond. He stopped and looked back.

Joan asked, "What is it?"

"I don't know. Nothing probably." And then he saw Whicher's tow head appear through the bushes toward shore. Whicher waved and shouted, "Amos!"

Amos raised his hand and faced about to pole back. The raft grounded in the shallows a few yards from Whicher.

The boy spoke as though reciting a piece he had memorized. "Gram says she's sorry, but Pa's sick and Mort ain't acting right and she thinks you better come on home."

# PART II

## Chapter 21

In the late afternoon sun, as Amos drove the Ford up the hill from Whichertown, he did not feel that he was coming home. It was strange, but with Joan beside him, this return was unlike any he had known. Always he had come back with a sense of belonging at the farm but now he approached it more as a visitor. He looked carefully, slowing down, at the cellar hole and field where he planned to build his house.

It seemed necessary to have his own place. He thought of the work that would have to be done to the foundation: he must clear out the brush and level the granite slabs for the sills. Beneath his concern about Pa and Mort, he was anxious to start work on the house. With annoyance, driving on, he saw that the corn he had planted in the upper field had sprouted, along with the weeds, and needed cultivating. Somehow it didn't seem like his corn any more and he didn't want to put in his time working it when he should be building his house.

Joan sat silent beside him, Whicher in the back seat, silent, too.

The farm had not changed, although the season seemed further advanced, the grass tall and the leaves of the trees more luxuriant. Gram came to the door as he drove into the yard. She looked smaller and older than he remembered.

He climbed out of the car and went around to Joan and they walked toward the house.

Gram said, "It ain't right, but I had to have help."

"Sure, Gram."

She reached out and patted Joan's hand and led the way into the house. "I've fixed up Rose's room for you two," she said.

Amos saw his father on the couch by the kitchen window. He was dressed in work clothes and he stood up when they came in. He hadn't shaved and he looked old and gray.

"Guess you'll have to handle things, Amos, till I get my strength back." He sat down. "Can't seem to keep going. Hello, Joan."

Amos asked, "Did you have Doc Parsons?"

Pa motioned at the medicine bottle and the pills on the window sill.

"Says I'll come out of it all right. I reckon I'm just run down like an old clock that ain't been wound."

"You can rest up now. What's the matter with Mort?"

"Took off by himself and built a crazy shack in the woodlot."

"You want me to go see him?"

"You better, when you get a chance." Pa sighed. "Whicher's been doing the work, but things are creeping ahead of him, and he can't handle Mort."

"I'll bring in our things, first."

Outside by the Ford, he tried to smile at Joan. "Nice homecoming," he said.

"Never mind, darling."

He took the packs and went with Joan toward the house. He noticed the worn granite doorstep and the weathered door opening into the kitchen and the unpainted screen door. Tight and neat and clean, not in need of repair, but worn. Perhaps he noticed it because Joan was with him. Perhaps he saw with different eyes when she was beside him at his old home. The gray walls of the kitchen and the scrubbed floor were plain and harsh. He led the way upstairs.

Gram had rearranged Rose's room. The bureau stood against the north wall and there was a double bed which Amos remembered seeing in the attic. A hooked rug and an extra chair were new.

Joan said, "I'll have to go home for my clothes."

"Can you drive the Ford?"

"I don't know."

"If you can wait a bit, I'll drive you over."

"That would be better," Joan said. "We both ought to see Mother and Dad."

Amos didn't know where to begin. There was the work to do in the fields, and Mort to talk with. He didn't want to leave Joan alone in the house, almost a stranger, first thing, but he couldn't see any other way.

"You be all right for a little while?" he asked, looking down at her.

"Yes, why not? I'll help Gram with supper." She glanced toward the door, then pulled his head down and kissed him quickly. "Isn't it funny to wonder if anyone's looking?"

"It don't matter."

"I know, but it's not the same." She smiled. "But didn't we have a nice honeymoon? Now you go along. I'm all right."

"Probably I'd better get it over with."

They went downstairs, and in the kitchen he said to Gram, "I'm going to see Mort. Joan'll help with supper." He turned toward the couch. "Where is he, Pa?"

"Over beyond the sugar house somewhere. Ask Whicher." Pa looked at him with lusterless eyes. "I'd go along with you, Amos, if I could."

"Sure, Pa."

Gram said, "You talk him into coming back, Amos. He's got no business out there in the woods. Everlasting fool ideas he gets. Joan and I'll get along."

Amos nodded at Joan and went out.

He found Whicher in the barn, milking. The late afternoon sun came in the cobwebby west window, shining on Whicher's forehead against the black and white flank of a cow. Whicher said nothing, while his hands worked fast and strong at the cow's bag.

Amos asked, "Where's Mort?"

Whicher pointed with his chin. "You know where we saw the owl last winter? Over beyond the sugar orchard?"

Amos nodded.

"He's built him a lean-to in them birches."

"I'll find him."

" 'Twon't do you any good. He's crazy as a tick. I watched him. Sets there with the Bible on his knee just a-staring at nothing."

"He ain't crazy, Whicher. You don't want to say that."

"Well, this place is enough to make him." Whicher turned his head down. "Can't wait till I'm old enough to get a job on the railroad."

"There's worse places than Whichertown," Amos told him, and went out through the open door and across the barnyard.

He took the road beyond the house. In the early days it had led over the ridge and into the next town. There were stone piers of vanished bridges across the streams which ran down the rising slope of forest. But the houses to which it had led were gone, like so many in Whichertown, and now the road was no more than a trail beyond the sugar house.

He came to the big maples with their high green tops and passed the gray-boarded sugar house, its cupola shuttered and windows dark. He turned into the woodlot, walking between the sprouted stumps of the clearings where he and Pa had cut cordwood in past years. He reached the birches and moved on among the straight white trunks. Smelling smoke, he headed into the breeze until he reached a little clearing.

Mort sat with his back to a birch tree beside the smudge fire. Beyond him was a low shelter of birch bark and boughs. There was a tin can by the fire, but Amos could see no other utensils. Mort's face looked thinner and his eyes were shadowed above the stubble beard on his jaws, but he nodded quite normally at Amos, as he closed the Bible on his lap.

Mort said, "See you got back."

"A while ago." Amos squatted by the fire so the smoke would drive off the flies. "Staying here right along now?"

Mort looked about him as though the birch woods and the shelter were surroundings of which he'd just become aware, but found familiar and right when he looked at them.

He said in his deep slow voice, "I plan to, for a time, Amos."

"Seems to me you'd be more comfortable to home. Besides we need you around the place."

For a long time, Mort didn't reply.

Amos chewed a twig and stared at the woods—white trunks on a slope, graceful, like Joan. He knew there was no use to hurry Mort. He wondered if Mort went to Ma's grave each day. He slapped a black fly on his wrist.

Mort said, "You recall the day I got cowslips for Gram?"

"Yes."

"Well, I felt something like that coming over me again, only worse, and I was afraid of myself." He touched the Bible beside him. "The Book tells about fasting and meditation. I think it's helped me. I think I'm going to be all right."

"Good."

Amos waited and listened to a bird singing, off in the birch woods, a clear note that seemed to come from far away.

"Seems like I've taken the right turning at last," Mort said. "I'm not real sure what done it, because I've prayed for help a long time. Maybe He was just waiting to see if I was strong enough to bear it, if I was going to help myself, because quick as I felt that spell coming on, and made up my mind I'd go away, and fast and meditate and read the Book, I begun to feel better almost right off. You see, He was helping me."

"I see."

"There's nothing you need worry about, Amos. The Lord is helping me in His infinite compassion."

"Nothing you need?"

Mort shook his head. "I've enough for the time I'll be here. I don't eat but a little bread twice a day." He looked quietly at his brother. "I will help you on the farm in a few days, Amos."

"All right."

Amos stood up and nodded at Mort. He reached into his pocket and took out the bottle of fly dope he was still carrying. "You better take this."

"No, thank you, Amos. The smudge will do me."

Amos thought he understood and didn't urge Mort because Mort figured the flies were part of his starving and thinking.

He wondered, as he turned back through the woods, if Mort was as near right as he seemed. Gram and Pa wouldn't think so. He thought about telling Joan. It wasn't very good to have to tell your wife that your brother had gone into the woods to fast and meditate. Of course she knew about Mort and would be kind about it but perhaps she'd worry about the family into which she had married.

The sun had set as he came up the slope toward the house. Drum bayed at him and Whicher came to the door of the cow tie-up and turned back inside. The light from the west softened the square lines of the house and barn. There was a robin in the top of the maple tree, the sunlight still touching his red breast. Amos looked for a moment at the shadows in the valley of Whichertown, and at the sunset colors on the upper slopes of Quartz Mountain, turning the ledges pink, and on Cobblestone, showing the dark green of the spruces reaching down into the paler leaves of the hardwoods.

He felt suddenly at home and he understood that his wife was waiting for him in this house and on this land of his ancestors, and Mort wasn't so important, nor Pa, nor any of them, as important as Joan and him, for they were the new Jackmans and this was their place, just as it would be their children's place—not the house particularly, but the land and the mountains and the sky above and the forests and fields.

He went into the kitchen. Joan was sitting at the table opposite Gram and she smiled at him as though she wanted him to know how well she was getting along in his home. Gram and Pa looked quickly at him.

"Mort's all right," he said. "Claims he didn't feel good and wanted to be alone for a while. Wanted to read his Bible and think."

Gram snorted. "He didn't take enough food to keep a bird alive."

"That was part of it, like in the Bible."

Joan helped him. "Like the old prophets."

"That's it. Claims he's feeling better than he has for a long time."

"Well, I'm glad of that," Gram said, and added to Joan, "Mort ain't been right since his mother's accident."

Joan nodded. "Amos told me."

[ 159 ]

While Amos washed at the sink, Whicher came in and joined him. Amos said, "You all done at the barn?"

"Yes."

"I'll help you in the morning."

When Gram and Joan had laid out the supper, Amos saw Pa make an effort to act well. He sat at the table to eat the baked ham and boiled potatoes, but he took his wedge of rhubarb pie back to the couch and his hands were shaking as he fed himself. The veins of his hands were transparent like an old man's. Amos thought it was not possible so many things had happened to people while he was gone only a few days. When he had remembered the farm, up there at the brook camp or at the pond, he had thought of everything being just the same as when he left, but it wasn't, and he wasn't, and there never would be the farm as he had left it for he was with Joan now and his family had changed.

After supper, as he and Joan drove through Whichertown, he spoke about his father.

"You suppose Doc Parsons knows what ails Pa?"

"Your grandmother says the doctor called it a mild heart attack. She told me when we went down cellar to get the potatoes."

"He'll be hard to get along with if he can't work."

"That's what your grandmother says."

Amos turned into the Ridge Road leading up the hill to Joan's house. "The farm must seem like a sorry place to come to."

"It's all right, darling, as long as I'm with you."

"We'll see about starting a house tomorrow."

"I'd like to." She braced herself with a hand on the seat as Amos pushed down on the low pedal and the Ford lurched over a water bar. "We'll be all right for a while," she said, "but we ought to have a house of our own."

"We will. You can look at the place tomorrow and soon's I get caught up on the work, I'll start it. Evenings before that."

"We could move in when the roof's up and finish it while we live there. I can paint. I painted a sailboat once."

He looked sideway at her. "You won't settle for a tar paper shack?"

"Well," she said, "if we had to. . . . You're teasing me."

"Just a mite, but paint's kind of scarce around Whichertown."

"We'll go to Fallsburg."

"Wait till your folks hear you're going to live in a tar paper shack."

"They wouldn't put it beyond me." She laughed. "You know, it's

[ 160 ]

funny, I do look forward to seeing them, now that I'm a separate person."

He glanced at her curiously. "You feel you don't belong here any more?" He pointed at the lodge beyond the gate and swung the steering wheel. "Seemed to me everything was changed at first when I saw our place this afternoon."

"There's something funny about it," she agreed. "I belong, all right, but not to stay and live here."

Amos stopped at the porch. Mrs. Tarlton opened the door of the lodge and came down the steps to greet them as they left the Ford.

"Joan—Amos—isn't this wonderful!" She kissed Joan. "Greg," she called, "they're back."

Joan said, "I had to come and get some clothes and see my dear old parents. Hi, Dad." She went to him as he came out the door.

He took her in his arms. "How's my girl? Great to see you again!" He shook Amos' hand. "Come in, come in! We'll have a drink."

Mrs. Tarlton spoke up, "We didn't expect to see you for another week."

Joan looked at Amos and he understood she hesitated what to say about his family.

As they walked into the big living room, he spoke for her. "Pa and Mort took sick at the same time and Whicher couldn't do all the work."

Joan added, "We were just up in the woods camping out, you know."

"Yes, Amos' grandmother told me," Mrs. Tarlton said. "Is it serious about your father and brother?"

"I guess they'll be all right," Amos told her.

Joan interrupted the silence that followed. "We're going to start building our house."

Gregory Tarlton smiled as he poured whiskey into glasses. "I've got a little surprise for you there." He squirted soda water and handed around the glasses. "I deposited five thousand to your account, Joan, in the Fallsburg bank. Thought you and Amos might be doing a little building."

"Oh, Dad!"

Tarlton waved his hand while his hawk's face softened. "Great pleasure for me, to be able," he said. "No strings, you understand, no strings."

Amos had not quite believed what he heard but as it slowly came into meaning in his mind, he wanted to reject it. Before he spoke, he realized there was no way to tell Joan she couldn't have the money; he had to accept it to that extent. And then he saw how it would make him look, working to pay a lumber bill which his wife's bank account would reduce to insignificance. It belittled him and his efforts. It wasn't right. He had known all along she was rich, or her folks, yet it hadn't made any impression on him before.

She was saying, "I'll change it to a joint account as soon as we can get to the bank."

"As you wish, my dear," Tarlton said to her. He walked about the room and growled into his drink. "As you wish. Wanted to see that my daughter had a dowry—best tradition. Kids need money."

"Isn't it wonderful, Amos! Now we can start right in and build. You won't have to do the work between taking care of the farm. We can hire carpenters!"

Amos said slowly, "Yes, we can, but I don't guess we will." He looked at the Tarltons and back to Joan. "You save your money for a rainy day. I'll build the house."

"Oh, Amos, it's not my money, it's our money."

"All right. Let's save it till we need it. Don't need it to build a house."

"You don't, eh?" Tarlton was standing with his glass poised, the whiskey bottle in his other hand. Behind him, through the glass doors, the hills had darkened. Mrs. Tarlton moved to a floor lamp and switched it on. Tarlton poured his whiskey and asked, "How would you build a house?"

"Lumber from the mill," Amos said quietly. "With what they owe me, and the pine and hemlock I'll get out next winter, there'll be more'n enough to build a house."

"I see." Tarlton smiled. "Jackman pine and hemlock?"

"Well, mine. I chop my wages."

"Oh, that's it." He laughed and downed his drink. "Joan, he didn't marry you for your money."

"Dad! I knew that!"

Tarlton laughed again. "So did I, so did I." He took out a cigar case, while Mrs. Tarlton rebuked him.

"Greg, you stop teasing these kids. Come on, Joan, we'll go upstairs and pack you a bag."

When they had gone, Tarlton didn't speak and Amos was silent, thinking about his wealthy wife. He hadn't married her for money and he didn't care about money. But there it was and it made him wonder what Joan was thinking about his plans for a little house, maybe three rooms. It wouldn't seem like much to her. There it was between them. He wanted to tell Gregory Tarlton to keep his money.

Tarlton interrupted his thoughts. "Amos, you're all right. Goddamned if you aren't. Have a cigar?"

"No, thanks. I'll light my pipe." He waited silently while Tarlton poured them each another drink.

And then they talked of brook trouting and the rain and hunting in the fall. That kind of talk was easy. Amos didn't mind it. When Joan and her mother came down he listened to their conversation about friends who had been to visit, about her brother Dave, about putting the wedding presents away until they should have their house. Amos sat quietly and did not think about Joan's money any more than he could help.

And yet it was there. Joan sensed it, for after they had said goodby and drove down the steep road to Whichertown, with the lights making a tunnel under the overhanging trees, she didn't speak until they reached the meadows by the brook.

She said at last, "I'll make Dad take it back, if you want."

"It's your money."

"It's ours."

"You can call it that."

He turned up the hill toward the farm, aware that she was no longer sitting close to him. He saw in the headlights the wall of the cemetery on his right and beyond it to the left, the barway leading into the field around the old cellar hole. He could not think of the house location as he had, with hope and anticipation.

Gram was in the kitchen, knitting in the Boston rocker. Pa and Whicher had gone to bed. Gram took her lamp and said good night, and they were alone again.

Joan looked at him. "I don't see why it should bother you so."

"It makes me feel kind of small." He glanced around the kitchen and out the dark window. "I suppose you know you could buy this whole place for less than that?"

"I hadn't thought. Anyhow, what does it matter? Oh, Amos."

She came toward him and put her head against his shirt, her hands on his shoulders. "I'll make Dad take it back tomorrow."

"No, sometime you'd want something I couldn't give you and you'd think of it. You keep it. Someday you may be glad you have it."

"Whatever you say."

"And there's no need to talk about it any more."

"No, not now, not now. Darling, I've had enough talking for tonight."

[ 163 ]

## Chapter 22

There was an urgency in the land which Amos could feel as he held the cultivator between the rows of young corn. The field slanted up toward the pasture, and the cultivator tended to inch downhill. Whicher had driven to town with the other horse, so there was nobody to lead Dick. Amos kept him between the corn by the reins over his shoulder. He pressed down on the cultivator handles so the tines stirred the earth deep and uprooted the weeds and turned the stones, damp side up, to the hot sun. Below him the rows of cultivated corn were neat and straight with the loosened earth between them a darker color from the exposed dampness, marked by the lines of the cultivator teeth and the windrows of young weeds drying in the sun.

The cultivator struck a rock and leaped aside in his hands, uprooting a few stalks of corn. Dick stopped while Amos dragged it back. Dick was an easy horse on a cultivator: he never bulled ahead and he reined good. Amos clucked to him and kept on, to the end of the row. He could feel the warmth of the earth, as though it had never been frozen hard as rock. It was made to grow things, like the grass at the end of the row, which reached to his knees, every blade with the green strength of life in it. He turned Dick and stopped to wipe the sweat from his face. The sun beat down, not a dry destroying heat, but a heat for growth.

He saw Joan leave the back door of the house and come up the hill toward him. It was strange to see his wife step out of the house where he had lived all his years and for a moment she seemed like a visitor, someone who had stopped to call on Gram, a transient from the world beyond the hills. He watched her move up the wagon track through the field while the breeze rippled the grass on either side of her in the same billowy motion with which it pressed her skirt against her legs. She had caught her hair under a green ribbon and the curls in back danced as she walked. Her arms were brown against the white blouse. And then she smiled at him and she was no longer a figure moving up the field, but his wife come to see him because she missed him even after the short hours he had been away from the house.

"We've done the dishes," she told him, "and cleaned the house and started dinner. My, don't you get a lovely view from here?"

"Well, I guess so, now you mention it."

"Where did we camp out—over there?"

"No," he said, "more to the left, at that notch between Quartz and Cobblestone. The brook comes through the low place there and the pond is out beyond."

She nodded and turned to him. "I like it here, Amos. I was a little afraid how I'd get along, but it's going to be all right."

"You hit it off with Gram?"

"I think so." She laughed. "As long as I do things her way. And, Amos, I'm learning to cook. I like it here. You don't know."

"Well, that's fine." He paused and looked at her, smiling at her enthusiasm. He was pleased and yet he couldn't help but think that she was so different, and the way she had lived was so different, he had to say, "I hope you keep on feeling like that."

"Of course I will!" She frowned and her voice was quieter as she went on. "I've tried to explain how I feel about it and I wish I could make you forget what I was and how I lived. Probably when we're old and gray and our grandchildren are running this place, you'll still think I wasn't cut out to be a farm wife."

Abruptly she knelt in the grass. "Oh, Amos, look! Wild strawberries! We can have them for dessert with cream and sugar. Aren't they wonderful? Here, try these."

She stood up and held out her hand with the small ruby berries in the palm. He took them one at a time in his big fingers and ate them, dropping the hulls. They were juicy and sweet, sun warm and ripe.

"Aren't they good?" She started down the hill. "I'm going to get a bowl and pick some."

She was gone before he could reply. He smiled to himself, watching her run down the slope toward the house. It was comical to see anyone excited about a patch of wild strawberries. She wouldn't be so happy about them by the time she'd hulled them. But he looked at the berries by his feet with a feeling that he took them too much for granted.

There had always been wild strawberries in the fields, as long as he could remember. He liked them, one or two picked as he walked through the grass, stopping to bend down and pick them and go on again with his mind on the farm work. He could remember back when he was a kid, but that was not the same. Then he would search out the biggest patch and stay there for a long time, eating the berries as fast as he could pick them, while the sun beat down on his back and the grass reached higher than his head and he lived in the circumscribed world of the grass blades, with the ants and small grasshoppers and spiders close to the earth where the fine blades grew beneath the taller stalks and the straw-berries clustered beside their dark green leaves. And standing up was like emerging into a new life of wide blue sky and sun and hill horizons.

That was the way it had been.

He clucked to Dick and went on with his cultivating. Joan came back and began to pick the strawberries into a dish. He could see her bent shoulders and her dark hair from the far end of the corn piece. When he cultivated back and turned Dick, she hardly looked up. Each row took him farther away from her, until at last he reached the end row up by the stone wall, and turned the cultivator on its side and drove Dick back down the hill. He stopped near her.

She got to her feet. "Look, Amos, I've almost filled the bowl."

"Who's going to hull them?"

"Why," she said, "I did that as I picked. They're all ready to eat."

He smiled as he looked at the berries. "So you did."

"Well, I don't know why not. It seemed like the sensible way."

She walked beside him down to the house and he felt a warm pride in her and a sensation of contentment in walking down to dinner with his wife. At the table he was pleased by the way she helped Gram serve the meal, jumping up to get things from the stove or pantry and setting out the dishes for the berries, and the sugar and cream.

"My," she said, "just look at that cream. It all came from one setting pan. Isn't it wonderful?"

Pa smiled at her as he helped himself to the thick cream. "Amos, she's a good girl, even if she did burn one batch of the molasses cookies."

"I declare, Warren," Gram told him, "if you'd get a stove that was worth a hurrah, 'twouldn't have happened. A woman has to be a wizard to make that thing heat right."

"It's a good stove."

"I never did have any use for it."

"Likely it's the only stove there'll be."

"Doubtless." Gram sniffed to herself and Joan poured her another cup of tea, winking at Amos, while Whicher laughed.

There seemed to be a new feeling among them, almost gaiety. Amos was aware of it and he hoped it would continue. He wanted Joan to have an easy time until they could move into their own house. The thought came to him that he hadn't spoken to Pa about building.

"Pa," he said, "I figured on starting to clear out the old cellar hole later today."

"Don't know why not. Rose and Pete ain't interested in it. You go ahead, or you can stay here, just as you're a mind."

"I guess we'll build."

Gram nodded. "Young folks do better in a place of their own."

Amos said nothing about how he would build the house. He knew Pa understood about the lumber. And he didn't intend to say anything about Joan's money. That was between them and nothing to do with the family. He'd go ahead with the house his own way. When Mort came back, there'd be an extra hand on the farm. He thought of Mort alone in the woods and he supposed that both Pa and Gram were thinking of him although they didn't speak of him.

That evening after he and Whicher had milked the cows and they had all eaten supper, Amos took his axe and went with Joan down the road to the cellar hole.

It was a warm summer evening and the sun had barely set. The air was still. Amos could hear the brook below the field on the edge of the woods. A growth of trees along the wall hid the farm as he let down a pole at the barway so they could step into the field. He led the way to the cellar, past blackberry bushes and an old lilac. They stood looking down at the stone foundations and at the young trees growing up around the big slab of granite which had supported the fireplace.

There were two poplars and a pine in the cellar, their tops higher than Amos' head as he stood on the doorstep. A rotted beam projected from the cellar. It crumbled as he put his hand to it and lifted. He climbed down into the hole and reached back for the axe. Joan hadn't said a word. He began to trim out the bushes to get at the trees. When he could swing the axe, he started to chop, cutting deep into the soft poplar wood with each stroke. He could smell the sweet musky odor of the slashed bark. The tree toppled slowly and came to rest on the foundation. He lopped off the branches and tossed them up to Joan. She dragged them into a pile in the field. He cut the tree into lengths and slid them up to the top of the foundation.

They worked until he couldn't see to chop and then he climbed out of the cellar and they stood side by side looking at it. The granite-walled hole in the ground now seemed as though it might become the cellar of a house. He had taken it back from the woods. The fresh chips, the torn earth where he had uprooted bushes, gave an appearance of human activity.

Joan said, "I can begin to see it now. Honest, darling, at first I couldn't believe we'd ever be living above it on a wood floor with a roof over our heads."

"It's a start."

They sat down on the doorstep. A whippoorwill was calling from a

[ 167 ]

ledge below them. Amos could make out the dark form of the bird on the rock, and the repetitious call came over and over again, clear in the quiet dusk.

"This is lovely," Joan said, looking past him at the twilight hills and the shadowy valley.

Amos was thinking of the work ahead of him. Now that he had started, he felt better about it. With Joan here beside him, the house began to take on a reality which it hadn't possessed and it no longer seemed like a small thing compared to her bank account, not when they were both working at it together.

"There used to be a barn down below," he said. "We can fence off this end of the field easy. The old walls are standing."

"How long since anyone lived here?"

"I don't know exactly. Back in the nineties, I guess. This branch of the Whichers kind of died off and scattered. I think I've got some cousins out in Iowa." He took out his pipe. "Don't seem reasonable anybody'd want to leave here."

"No, it doesn't," she said. "I can't imagine it. I feel as though I'd come home. Isn't that funny? I just feel all relaxed and happy as though nothing could ever hurt me here." She added thoughtfully, "And we've been city folks for generations. I don't understand it, but I like it."

He put his arm around her and they sat there on the granite doorstep and listened to the whippoorwill and watched the darkness settle over the hills.

## Chapter 23

Two days later Mort came home. Amos was hoeing potatoes, his eyes turned down toward the first green tops, yet he saw the motion in the valley. Mort was walking steadily up the old road from the sugar orchard. Amos leaned on the hoe and watched him come toward the house. Mort walked with a purpose, as though he were returning from a journey and was anxious to get home. In his overalls and blue work shirt, carrying his denim jacket over his arm, he didn't show any weakness from his fasting in the woods. The growth of beard on his face was dark. He disappeared beyond the woodshed and Amos went back to his hoeing.

Before long, Mort came toward him with a hoe in one hand. Saying nothing, he went to work. Amos could see that he had lost weight. His cheekbones were prominent above the beard and his body had shrunk inside his clothes. Amos moved more slowly along the row but Mort kept up and passed him in the adjoining row and Amos had to return to his normal pace.

At last Amos stopped and walked to the stone wall where he had set a jug of water in the shade of an ash tree. Mort finished his row and joined him. Amos held out the crockery jug. Mort took a drink and nodded toward the potatoes.

"Coming along," he said. "Don't seem like I'd been gone long enough for them to break through the ground."

"Good growing weather, since the rain."

"That's so. I guess the Lord is kind to us." Mort set the jug by the wall and looked at the field of potatoes and away at the hills. "Seems like everything shows His goodness. I'm glad to be back home, Amos."

"That's fine."

Amos looked at Mort and saw that his eyes were clear and peaceful. Amos could think of no explanation for the change; it didn't seem possible, but if Mort had found some assurance of God's goodness, it must be what he needed since Ma's death and it had changed him back like he used to be. Amos remembered their talk in the birch woods and waited for Mort to say something further, but Mort was silent, just standing there quietly with the shadows of the ash leaves moving across his face as the breeze stirred the branches.

Amos went back to the potatoes and took up his hoe. Mort joined him and they worked on through the morning.

Amos was reminded of other summers when they had hoed potatoes or corn together. Of course, away back, it had been Mort who set the pace and kept Amos at the job. Mort was older, and serious and steady. When Amos felt like dropping the hoe and taking off into the woods, he was always aware of Mort's purposeful eyes on him. But there had been the day when Amos threw the hoe over the stone wall and leaped after it, running like a deer across the pasture, on and on through the woods with wild strength until he came to the big pool on Carr Brook below Whichertown where he stripped his clothes and dove in and splashed and swam and chased minnows all the rest of the afternoon. Mort never told Pa, but worked harder to make up for him and only looked at him in a disappointed way when they were together again.

Funny to think of that now, and to remember Mort on the day of the fence mending, this spring. There was something similar about their actions on those two occasions. He wasn't sure just what, unless it might be that he had been a kid breaking loose from work and Mort had tried to break out of his life. One you could do and one you couldn't.

Today Mort seemed to enjoy the work. This was steady work together. But Amos knew that in some way he had grown up more than his older brother and he took the lead and set the pace, a little ahead of Mort, chopping the weeds, covering the potato plants with loose dirt, hoe tunking against the stones, steady and not straining, along the rows.

He found that he was thinking of the farm and the family as complete, now that Mort was back. They all took their places in a proper pattern to which the summer day gave serenity and warmth that seemed impervious to change. Everything was all right. When he and Joan had returned from the woods, he had thought that the family was broken forever, but now the feeling was gone. Even Pa had seemed better the last day or two; he walked about the dooryard and into the barn where he found fault with the stable and set Whicher to cleaning it. The boy had done a good job, too, with Amos keeping an eye on him. It all gave Amos a feeling of family security that was new to him. He had never felt so much a part of the farm. He wondered if it was because he had married and Joan was with him here—Joan about the house, Joan in bed with him at night, Joan going with him to the cellar of their house where already he had started to level the foundation stones for the sills.

He looked down the slope toward the line of trees which hid the cellar. Now he could spare a few days to work there all the time, before haying. He hoed on faster, toward the end of the last row, and when he finished he stopped while Mort caught up with him. He looked at the hills and the woods around the farm. They didn't seem to be pressing in any more. The Jackman farm wasn't going back to trees.

Next spring, or even maybe in the fall, he could start clearing the land north of the cellar toward Whichertown. If he cut the young pines and hardhack out of it—the poplars—it would make good pasture. There was a spring in the sidehill which would keep the grass green all summer. And then he could plow up and seed to hay the pasture around the cellar. There wouldn't be much rock to clear because it had all been field once.

His mind was filled with plans for the future. He wanted to improve the farm and make it a better place for Joan to live with him. He felt that he didn't want her to be ashamed of it and he wanted to work. He felt strong and confident.

He said to Mort, "It's a good farm. It's a good place to live, ain't it?"

Mort nodded and smiled a slow smile as though he understood.

That afternoon, Amos drove to town with Joan to see about lumber for the house. They hadn't been away from Whichertown since they were married and he felt a little shy about taking his wife with him, a little worried about how to act, but he liked the road along the brook and he thought of the first time they had gone down it together, driving Dick through the spring mud. Now the road was dry, although the ruts still showed, crumbled over and packed down into parallel hollows. The Ford steered easily under the trees. On the left the brook which poured over the rocks was clear and sparkling in the sun and shaded and dark in the pools under the pines.

Joan asked, "Do you remember our first trip?"

"Sure."

"I hadn't any idea of being your wife, yet here we are married, about a month later—well, going on two."

"Seems sort of quick, at that, don't it?"

"Yes, nice." She sat closer to him.

The sawmill was over on Brook Road, beside its rotting dam. Jed Peabody used steam for power now and the mill pond drained away through a hole in the plank and timber dam, while grass grew on a sand bar extending into the channel. The water wheel wasn't turning. Instead, smoke poured from the sheet iron stack above the tin roof. There was a smell of pine logs and sawdust and smoke as they got out of the Ford. With a whine like a giant cicada, the saw cut through a log and filled the hot yard with sound which echoed from the piles of lumber in the field next to the mill.

Jed Peabody ran the table back and nodded to Amos. He was a big man with a mop of sawdust-filled white hair. His eyebrows were peppered with sawdust. As he yelled at the helper and threw a lever and came toward them, mopping the sweat from his face, he brought the smell of pine resin with him.

"Mighty hot in there," he said.

" 'Tis warm."

"Not much air stirring." Jed glanced at Joan, who had stayed near the Ford.

Amos found it hard to start talking business, as though he couldn't begin in front of Joan, but at last he said, "I been thinking of getting some lumber."

"What kind of lumber?"

"House lumber."

"Heard you'd got married." Jed moved toward the lumber piles. "Nothing here you want, probably. Now over this way. . . ."

Amos wasn't sure how long they talked, dickering while Jed figured footage, but it was quite a spell. He'd forgotten Joan until he found her waiting for him in the car. She looked hot and annoyed.

"Are you through?" she asked and, without waiting for an answer, "Why didn't you introduce me?"

"Why didn't I what?" He climbed over the side of the Ford into the driver's seat.

"Introduce me."

"Oh. Well, never thought about it. You must know Jed Peabody. Anyhow, there's no need to be formal, I guess."

"I don't know him," Joan said. "And besides, I want him to know I'm your wife."

"Likely he knows that already."

"That's got nothing to do with it. And I wanted to see the lumber. I think it's exciting to pick out the boards for our house."

"Didn't suppose you'd be interested. Just men's talk and a lot of lumber stacked around. You want to go look at it now?"

"No."

He drove off slowly, back toward the village. Finally he said, "We don't always seem to hit it off good in town."

"No, we don't."

"Probably I didn't act just right, but you take it easy and I'll learn." He hesitated. "Maybe you will, too."

"What do you mean by that?"

"Well, just that I won't never be like you expect a man to be, and I hope you can make the best of it."

She didn't reply and he glanced sideway at her. There was a flush on her cheeks and he thought she was going to say something sharp, but she fooled him, slipping her arm through his, at last, and saying quietly, "I know, Amos, I'll try. I like you just as you are and I love you."

He stopped the car in front of Cy's store on the main street of the village and before he got out, touched her hand.

They went into the shadowy store past the shelves of canned goods and the rack of axes. Joan was beside him as Amos walked up to the counter. Cy looked up from his newspaper and grinned at them. His round face beamed and his brows lifted toward his bald head.

"Well, well," he remarked.

"This is Mrs. Jackman, Cy," Amos announced.

"Why, I'm pleased to meet you." He smiled, winking at Amos. "Now that she ain't a Tarlton, I've a good mind to call her Joan. How's everything out to Whichertown?"

"About the same. Potatoes coming along pretty good."

Joan had taken the grocery list from her pocket. "You can call me Joan and I don't see why you haven't before."

"I didn't know you very well, but you're married to Amos now and that makes you an old resident." Cy took out his account pad. "Make the slip out to the Jackman's account?"

Joan glanced at Amos. He nodded.

"One thing, Joan," Cy went on. "You married into a bill-paying family."

"Usually," Amos said.

"Don't have many, do you, Amos?"

"Can't say we do. The farm takes care of us."

While Joan went through the list with Cy—flour and sugar and yeast and baking powder and so on—Amos stood in the doorway and watched the long street with the maples over it. The sun was hot and he could smell the gasoline from the pumps in front of the store. Beyond the brick town hall, red in the sun, three boys played baseball inside the board and granite post fence around the common. It was the same fence on which Amos had sat the night of the dance. That seemed years ago. He could remember how he felt when Joan said she was going away. And now he listened to her voice behind him, speaking to Cy about flour and sugar. It was the voice of his wife.

He watched the boys throw the baseball back and forth. He'd never learned to play ball. They didn't play ball in Whichertown when he was a kid, but went fishing instead, or roamed the woods, or worked— always work on the farm. There hadn't been anyone but Mort and his cousin Jake and Pete Appledee of an age to play ball and it had never entered their heads. No place to play anyhow in the sidehill fields of Whichertown. But he could throw a rock. Once he had struck a red squirrel with one, knocked him clean off a stone wall where he skittered around in the leaves before he came to his senses and ran up a nearby tree, too scared even to chatter. Joan wouldn't have thought much of that.

She was talking now about her folks' mail. "I don't think we'll take it. Probably they'll be in, or they can wait till it's delivered tomorrow."

Amos said, "We can swing around that way."

"No need to, dear. They may be driving in now."

The "dear" struck on his ears with a strange sound and he waited for Cy to notice it and make a joke, but Cy was at the candy case, scooping chocolate creams from the dish with a little tin scoop and sliding them into a brown paper bag.

Joan watched him put the bag with the groceries. "Did I order them, Cy?"

"Nope, they're my present for the newlyweds. Amos will remember." And Cy winked at him.

Joan looked puzzled before her eyes lit up. "Oh, those delicious chocolate creams. I remember, too. Thank you, Cy."

Amos saw Mrs. Hardy coming along the porch of the store. He could see her through the windows and could hear the determined tread of her shoes on the boards. She appeared in the door, wearing her apron over a cotton dress, and moved toward the counter like a purposeful bell cow. Amos thought of her as a friend of Gram's but somehow not of them in Whichertown. It was the difference between living in the town and in the hills, and not being really neighbors, although Gram shared a lot of memories with her because Mrs. Hardy used to live on the road out of Whichertown, years back. They could talk for hours about the old days.

She came toward him and nodded, pressing down her double chins. He felt awkward but made up his mind to carry off the introductions right. He was a married man now and it brought obligations toward people. Things were easier at Whichertown, but he felt Joan eyeing him and he'd try to do it right.

"How do, Mrs. Hardy," he said. "Like you to meet my wife."

"Well, if it ain't Joan Tarlton grown up and changed into a Jackman." She took Joan's hand. "Child, I haven't seen you to talk to since I was librarian and you came in to get books. At first it was adventure books like any boy and then love stories. Girls do change, don't they, Joan?"

"Yes, they do, Mrs. Hardy. Now I'll be coming in for books on farming."

"Well, you'll have to see young Mrs. Smart. She's librarian now. I had to give it up. My sciatica kept me to home so often I didn't feel I should try to do it. 'Twasn't fair to people not to have the library open some days when it was supposed to be and then Amy, that's Mrs. Smart, helped me out and finally we decided she better take it over altogether. Well, I am glad to have seen you young people. Amos, do come in and bring your grandmother."

"Yes, I will."

He moved to the hardware and began looking over a box of files.

When Cy had waited on Mrs. Hardy, Amos said to him, "Guess I can use two of these."

"You must be going to sharpen a saw."

"Well, I figure to build us a little place."

"You'll need some nails."

"That's so. Probably I'd better take about ten pounds of them eight penny and five pounds of six-inch spikes."

Amos watched Cy weigh them out. It seemed to bring the house nearer reality.

He helped Joan carry out the groceries and nodded to Cy.

It was good to be driving back toward the hills. Always he felt a lift as he headed back to Whichertown. The village was all right, but he felt closed in and there were too many people around. This was better, to be driving the Ford back toward Quartz Mountain, distant and white-crowned with granite, on the eastern horizon. It was a sensation of homing, deeper, now that Joan sat beside him.

She said, "You did very well." She leaned over and kissed him quickly on the cheek. "Now don't pull away. Nobody'll see except the birds and they don't care."

"Cushman place coming around the bend."

"Well, I'm proud of you. You're awfully good to me, Amos."

"I try to act like you think I should. You see, I'm real fond of you." He smiled.

He drove on comfortably. They were nearing the mountains, although still only among the first hills east of the river where farms lay along the oxbows of Carr Brook and pastures spread up the slopes beyond the meadows. Elms grew in the fields along the brook. Here the road seemed to rest after the steep climb from the river valley. Beyond the farms were the last miles of uphill grade through the woods, deeper and deeper into the mountains. They drove past the waterbox where they had picked mayflowers, up Footstep Hill, to the clearings of Whichertown where the eastern mountains rose like a wall ahead and forced the road to turn right across the brook and along the ridge to the Jackman farm.

Amos stopped the Ford. He saw that the cows were waiting by the barnyard gate and the afternoon was well along.

"I'll help with the chores and there'll be time to work on the foundation before dark."

"When will the lumber come?"

"Tomorrow. I'll be ready for it then." He lifted packages from the back seat. "Took some talking to get Jed to bring it so prompt, but I guess he will."

"I like to think of it," Joan said. "By the time it's built, I'll be a good cook and can take care of you." She smiled. "I'm glad I have Gram. Think of the meals you'd eat without her."

"You do all right."

They were walking toward the house. Pa came around the corner of the woodshed. The knees of his overalls were dirty and he slapped at them.

He said, "Been weeding the garden. Easy work, but I've had enough."

Joan told him, "You couldn't do that a few days ago, Pa."

"That's right, girl, but time was I laughed at being tired." He brushed the knuckles of his right hand across his moustache. "We all come to it, I suppose."

He followed them into the house and sat down in the rocker by the window. Gram was setting the table.

"Joan, I forgot the cream of tartar. Don't know what possessed me, I didn't put it on the list."

"I remembered, Gram."

"Well, that's a blessing. I used baking powder for the dumplings but they won't be so good. They're all mixed dry and when the men finish with the chores I'll show you about adding the milk and putting them on the stew."

Amos could smell the chicken stew. "I'll go out and help Mort and Whicher."

He found Mort in the barn, pitching hay down from the mow. This year there was hay to spare, but he could remember some years when they were scraping the bottom of the deep mows beside the barn floor, when the platforms overhead and above the tie-up were long since empty. There'd be another good crop this year, enough for a few more head of young stock. He might raise some of the heifers to milk and another pair of steers.

The bull in the far corner moaned deep in his chest as Whicher came in the door. Amos could look past him at the fields and the blue sky and woods. Whicher made a little gesture at the bull as he passed.

Amos asked, "You been plaguing that bull, Whicher?"

"Nope. Me and cattle don't get along, that's all."

"Well, you leave him alone. He's clever and I don't want him spoiled."

"I wouldn't bother to plague the old fool." Whicher's face brightened as he went toward the grain bin. "Amos, I'm building me a toy railroad. I've got the engine all made except I need some wheels."

"Saw slices off a stick of wood."

"Golly, I never thought of that. Will you help me, Amos?"

"If I get time. I've a lot of work to do, Whicher."

"Yes, I reckon." He was scooping dairy ration into the mangers through the dropped-down doors between the tie-up and the barn floor. "Well, I figured I could build an engine and a few freight cars and make a grade out by the garden where it ain't planted, by the bank. I wouldn't have any tracks, 'course, but maybe a tunnel and a station. Gee, you'd ought to see some of the sets in the Sears catalogue." He added, "I've grained them horses, Amos."

Amos lifted a fork full of hay, catching it under the near edge and lifting to dig the fork into the middle.

"They cost money," he said, and went into Dick's stall. "Gee over there."

Dick whinnied and reached back for a mouthful of hay before Amos put it in front of him. Pal kept nickering and pawing the floor of the next stall until Amos brought his hay.

He went through the tie-up and out into the barnyard to let down the pasture bars. The cows filed past him and up the ramp into the barn. He watched them pass. They were grade Holsteins and a Jersey, not the scrubby cows of most hill farms. Pa always said if you were going to keep a cow you might's well keep a good one; they didn't eat any more than a poor one.

While he was milking, Joan came into the tie-up and stopped beside him.

"How long before you'll be through?"

"I don't know. Pretty soon."

"Gram wants to know when to start the dumplings."

"Well, I've got two more. Mort and Whicher each have one. Guess that's all."

"And that should tell us when to start the dumplings?"

"Godfrey," he said. "It should give you an idea."

"How long to milk a cow?"

"That depends on the cow." He smiled up at her. "Never noticed by the clock, you might say, but some take longer than others, varying with how much they milk and how they milk."

"Well, now I see."

"It's simple if you look at it that way."

She reached over and pushed his hair over his eyes and let her fingers rest on his neck. "I'll tell Gram there are four cows to go and she can judge it."

"All right. Don't forget the washing up."

"Oh, yes."

After she had gone, Mort said, "Dumplings have got to be timed just so."

"Appears that way," Amos agreed.

"I don't recall Gram ever fussing about them much."

Whicher called over his shoulder from down the row of cows, "Shucks, Joan just wanted to come out and see Amos. He's been away 'most half an hour. Women!"

Amos listened to the milk in the pail and smiled to himself. The cow twitched her tail extra hard at a fly and pulled it from the grip he had on it in the bend of his knee.

He said, "You didn't spray these cows any more'n you had to, Whicher."

He tucked the hair of the cow's tail under his knee again and went on with his milking, finger and thumb closing, grip, squeeze, open and close, while the cow reached into the manger for stray particles of her grain. He stripped out the last of the milk and carried the milking stool and pail to the next cow.

The routine of the work left his mind free. He thought with pleasant ease and well-being of the afternoon in the village. There wasn't anything so terrible about being a married man among people, after all. They sort of expected it of you and took it as a matter of course. Somehow he felt better now that he knew.

But Whichertown was the place to be. He'd acted somewhere near the way Joan wanted him to, and made out all right with people, but the village wasn't the same as Whichertown. Here he could think of Joan and himself together, whereas something separated them when people were around—not the family, for he was used to them now and could think of Pa and Gram and Mort and Whicher as part of the pattern in which he and Joan lived. It was a strange thing.

He wondered how it was with her. Not the same probably, because she hadn't lived all her life in Whichertown. Perhaps she liked the village better, liked people better. But he felt that she was glad to get back home here.

His thoughts wandered to her money. It must be comical to go into a store and buy plain things like flour, when you had enough money in the bank to buy out the shelves and then some. And yet she had asked the price of flour, questioning Cy about one brand and another. Perhaps she was the saving kind. He had no way of knowing. It was peculiar to think how many things he didn't know about her. Made their sleeping together seem not quite proper, if you twisted things around and looked at them for a joke. He'd have to tell her that.

And when he went in with Mort and Whicher to supper, he saw her new, still thinking of what he didn't know about her, almost like a stranger working there around the kitchen, taking off the cover of the stew while the fragrant steam rose up.

She turned to look at him and became his wife and, as the songs said, his true love. He smiled at her and went to the sink.

At the table, Pa began to talk about haying. "If you boys don't start, you'll miss the weather."

"Next week's time enough," Amos said. "The hay's still growing."

"I can remember when we got two crops, some years like this, mowing early and again at the end of the summer."

Mort said slowly, "I mind one good rowen crop we had a few years ago."

"Crimus," Whicher put in. "Seems like haying once a year's bad enough."

"You may be out there helping twice this summer," Pa told him. He blew on his spoonful of chicken stew. "Any rate, I don't want none of this late haying when all the good's dried out of it."

"We'll get to it, Pa," Amos said, "but first I'm going to make a start on my house."

"At least this summer you're around the farm instead of helling off in the woods. I should say marriage done you a world of good."

"Warren," Gram said, "just because you're feeling better, you got to talk. I don't see why the boys can't help Amos a few days. That way the house will get a good start and he won't have to fret about not working on it during the haying."

Amos didn't say anything for a time. He had thought of the house as something he would build for Joan and he had to accustom himself to the idea of help. It would go up faster with Mort and Whicher working on it, but at first he didn't like the thought; he'd intended it to be his personal job, but there was no reason for thinking like that. The main thing was to build the house.

"The lumber's coming tomorrow," he said. "A load or two. Get the north side of the foundation level tonight and we'll be ready for it."

"I'll take my shotgun," Whicher said. "There's an old he woodchuck down in front of the cellar." He grinned at Amos. You wouldn't want a woodchuck right in your dooryard."

"No, I don't suppose we would, Whicher."

"I'd just as soon help," Mort said.

[ 179 ]

Joan seemed to feel, like Amos, that it had lost some of its privacy between them, for she asked, "Can I come, too, Amos?"

" 'Course you can. Got to have someone to boss the job."

She smiled. "Oh, good. I think it's wonderful to have help."

After supper as they were going down the road, Amos recalled that he hadn't walked this way with Mort and Whicher since Decoration Day. Looking at Mort as he strode along with his firm steps, steady and sure, Amos thought that he didn't appear to be the same man.

Whicher hurried on ahead with his single-barreled shotgun, hoping to catch the woodchuck away from his burrow before the others came and scared him. Joan walked beside Amos. The sun was low over the hills to the west and the heat of the day had gone. It was the time and season when the grass became cool in a hill field and a man could lie on his back and rest and watch the sky change from blue to purple, and think about fishing or hunting. Now he had no inclination to rest or loaf; he wanted to work and he felt that the days weren't long enough to make the farm right and to build their house.

They turned into the field, through the bars, which Amos put back into the double posts in case the steers or the young stock should wander up the hill.

Whicher had sneaked past the cellar and was crouched behind the pile of brush. Amos saw Whicher raise the shotgun and pause; then his shoulder jerked back and the gun roared. Whicher raced out of sight down the hill. When they reached the cellar he was coming back, disappointment all over his thin face.

"Goddamn it, I never touched him."

"Mind your tongue, Whicher," Amos told him. "Where was he?"

Whicher pointed down the slope toward a clump of birches where a pile of dirt marked the burrow.

Amos smiled. "Shucks, that's two rods farther than the gun'll carry. You ought to have sneaked up on him. It ain't a cannon."

"I know," Whicher protested, "but I was afraid he'd duck into his hole. Do you think he'll come back out?"

"Shouldn't wonder. At that distance you didn't even scare him. Likely he just wanted to go back in and take a nap."

"Aw, go on."

Mort was looking at the lines which Amos had strung for squaring up the old foundations. He picked up a crowbar and began to pry at one of the big granite slabs on the north side.

Amos said to Whicher, "You can go find us some rocks for shims."

"I can do that, too," Joan said. "Ones like the other night?"

"Sure, over around that ledge."

Amos moved around the cellar to help Mort.

With the two crowbars, they worked at one of the foundation blocks which had been tipped on its side by years of frost and erosion. Mort would pry, and then Amos, while Whicher, coming up with smaller rocks, would trig it in place until they were able to maneuver a greater lift with the bars.

Amos could see the little half holes made by the stone drill where the slab had been split from a ledge, years before. He remembered a ledge with similar marks, in the woods above the road. Probably these slabs had been drilled and split from it and hauled down by oxen.

At last the slab was upright and almost level with the line strung from the corner of the foundation. Amos went to the end and sighted down it, then took a flat stone from the ones Joan had dropped near the foundation.

"Just a whisker, Mort," he said.

Mort put his weight on the crowbar and Amos slid the stone under the slab.

"That ought to do it." He pushed against the granite. He couldn't budge it. "Sets firm," he said and went along the foundation to the next.

They finished with the last one before dark. The foundation was ready for the sills. Joan stood beside him as they looked it over. Mort was a few steps away leaning on the crowbar. Whicher had gone down the slope to try for the woodchuck. Amos felt that they had completed one part of the job, like when you finish planting a field and stop to think about it, kind of letting the sense of accomplishment sink in. It wasn't the end of the job, by a long sight, but on the way. Tomorrow morning he'd touch up his saws and get his tools together before the lumber came. By tomorrow night they'd have the sills laid, with Mort helping, and some of the joists in place.

"My goodness," Joan said, "I can't wait to see the walls and roof up. I get all excited and want you to hurry, Amos."

"It'll take a little time. I ain't much of a carpenter."

"We could hire one," Joan said.

"No, Mort and I'll make out. I ain't paying wages for work we can do."

He wished she wouldn't talk about it in front of Mort. Probably she'd have said more, if Whicher hadn't fired at the woodchuck then. Almost at once, he came racing up the slope carrying the chuck by a hind leg. He stopped before them, out of breath. He held up the woodchuck. A drop of blood trickled from its nose and Joan turned away.

"Ain't he an old socker?" Whicher panted. "He come out just as I was sneaking down the hill and I pulled up quick and let go at him." He stopped for breath. "I'm going to skin him. I'll get another and make a pair of mittens out of the hides."

"The fur ain't much good," Amos told him.

"Well, I'm going to skin him anyway." Whicher set off for the house. Mort smiled slowly. "You'd think he just killed a buck deer."

"Between hunting and railroading," Amos predicted, "he'll need some prodding to do any work."

Joan said, "I wish he'd stick to the railroading."

Amos tried to explain. "A kid's got to shoot a woodchuck once in a while. I'll help him with the hide so it won't go to waste, if he's set on a pair of mittens."

"I didn't mind as much as I thought I would."

"In a way," Mort said, "you could almost think the Lord made wood-chucks for kids to shoot. They ain't good for much else."

"In a hay field or pasture," Amos added, "they ain't good for anything."

He led the way back to the road in the gathering dusk. He liked to be walking down the road with Joan while Mort followed quietly. Some-how he felt more than ever that he was strong enough to run the farm and make a home and living for the whole family and look after them all. He wondered if Pa had ever felt that way when he was young on the farm. There must have been someone like that in every generation of the Jackmans or the farm wouldn't be here in the family now.

Whicher was working on the woodchuck by lantern light on the barn floor. Amos helped him skin out the hide and then they went into the kitchen to wash up. Whicher was still talking about hunting. Amos wondered if he had forgotten about the railroad, but soon he was sitting at the table with the catalogue spread out near the lamp, open to the toy railroad pages. Amos thought how easy it must appear to Joan to buy one. Perhaps she'd say something. She didn't, and they sat on in the kitchen for a time, Mort reading the Bible, Gram knitting, and Pa dozing on the couch. Amos smoked and whittled shavings from a stick into the woodbox. Joan sat at the table reading through a stack of *New England Homesteads* which he had brought down from the attic for her when she said she wanted to study up on farming.

She read with her chin in her hand, elbow on the table. The lamp light made a little shadow behind her ear where her thumb rested against the brown hair. A cooling breeze blew in the open window and moved the curtains. He could still feel some of the warmth from the stove, which Gram had let out after cooking supper. He moved his eyes from Joan to the stick he was whittling, and back to Joan. It would be good to have their own home. Although he liked to sit here for a while with the folks around him, the evenings were too long. Sometimes Gram didn't go to bed until late, sometimes eleven o'clock, and Mort would stay up reading the Bible. It was hard to get Whicher away from the catalogue. Pa would go early. Amos was ready now, but he didn't like to seem too eager about going to bed with Joan, for of course that's the way they'd take it and he felt a little embarrassed about it. When he and Joan had their own place they could do as they pleased and if they felt like going to bed with the chickens, they could, and nobody the wiser.

Tonight, as usual, Pa left the room early, likely tired out from working in the garden, and soon Mort carefully closed the Bible and put it on the shelf behind the stove and said good night. Whicher didn't want to go, and hung on at the table, standing on one leg and yawning while he stared at the pictures of electric trains, until Amos told him to get a move on.

After a decent interval, Joan looked at him and said, "I'm sleepy."

Amos got up and went out to look at the sky and stood there beyond the maple tree while he watched the stars overhead and thought how outlandish it seemed that a man's mind could wander off toward the unknown while his body was hitched here to the earth. He went back in the house.

Gram looked up and said, "You young folks go along to bed. I want to finish the toe of this sock."

Amos took a lamp from the shelf and lit it. They said good night to Gram and went into the hall. It was empty except for one chair. The front door was closed. They passed the door into the bedroom which Mort and Amos had shared. Joan went up the stairs while Amos followed with the lamp. The gray paint looked as old as the faded yellow wallpaper. The darkness closed in behind him, like the door of the bedroom he himself closed behind them at the top of the stairs.

The small room with the double bed was no longer Rose's and had lost the personality he had associated with it for so long. And yet it wasn't a man's room. Although a clean pair of his dungarees hung over a chair and his heavy boots stood by the closet, it was more of a woman's room, with the white curtains Joan had fixed and her mirror and brush and comb on the bureau.

He sat down on the bed to take off his shoes. He slid out of his clothes and tossed them to the chair and rolled into bed with the sheet over him. The room was warm. A June bug zoomed against the screen and outside he could hear a whippoorwill. Joan slipped her nightgown over her head and stood in front of the mirror brushing her hair.

[ 183 ]

She said, "Amos, I think I'm going to have a baby."

He raised up on one elbow and stared at her, his first thought being that she ought to look different, but her belly was still flat under her nightgown. She laughed at him.

"You don't need to act so startled."

"I'm not," he said. "I'm just thinking about it."

He watched her turn down the lamp and blow it out. She slipped into bed beside him. She seemed to be waiting and he said, "It's fine. Want you to know I'm glad." He touched her gently, the roughness of his hands catching on the silk of her nightgown. He couldn't think of any way to tell her how he felt about it and wasn't clear himself, only that it seemed to tie him in with the past and the future and make him more than he had been, making them more than they had been with the new sensation that they were not alone. Joan held his hand against her breast and whispered, "I think it's wonderful. I hope it's twins and they both look like you. I love you so."

He moved his hand over the soft curve of her side where her hip rounded under the nightgown.

Joan said, "I'll take it off. I like your hands on me."

She sat up and pulled the nightgown over her head and dropped it off the side of the bed. He watched her profile against the window and felt a pang of compassion, thinking that he must always care for her, and be kind and comforting to her and their love and their unborn child.

## Chapter 24

Amos couldn't hurry the work on the house. He wanted it built right, because he and Joan might raise their family in it and live there all their lives. A house ought to be square and put together so it would last. He knew he wasn't a fancy carpenter, but working in the hot July sun, measuring, laying out, fitting, while Mort cut the sills, he was sure he could build it sound and rugged. A small house ought to be just as well built as a bigger one, and although he and Joan were anxious to have their own place soon, he wouldn't rush and make a tinker's job of it.

The second day, while Joan and Whicher cleaned old bricks in the cellar, and he and Mort put in the floor joists, Amos heard a car in the valley. Holding the square and pencil with which he was marking the two-by-sixes, he straightened up from the saw horses and watched the Tarlton beach wagon come over the brow of the hill from Whichertown. He said to Joan, "Here's your folks."

She climbed up the short ladder from the cellar and ran across the pasture to the bars where Gregory Tarlton had stopped the beach wagon. In the dirt road by the stone wall, the car's shining varnish and polished black paint looked out of place. Amos walked toward it. The Tarltons were getting out and Joan and her mother were laughing and her father kissed her. Amos supposed she had told them about the baby. He wondered how they felt about their grandchild being born a Jackman.

Gregory Tarlton held out his hand, saying, "I understand I'm going to be a grandfather. I think it's wonderful." He nodded toward the house frame. "I see you're building already."

"Well, made a start before haying."

They were walking toward the cellar. Amos couldn't think of any special reason for the Tarltons coming to visit. They'd hardly come just to be sociable. At any rate Joan would be pleased, and maybe that was why they had driven over.

It seemed to be, for they had nothing particular to say, but admired the view and the progress on the house. Joan and her mother sat down on a pile of boards.

Tarlton said to Amos, "See here, don't let us hold up the work. I'll pitch in and help. You know, I resurrected the family fortunes by contracting." He laughed. "Carries me back. Certainly does."

Before long he was helping to place the joists and then suggested they start the floor. "Whicher and I'll lay the boards while you and Mort put in those last joists."

The morning was well along when Amos said, "You folks better stay for dinner."

"Yes," Joan said quickly. "Come along, Mother, we'll go up to the house and help Gram."

"Well, I don't know—such short notice for Mrs. Jackman." She glanced at her husband.

"Please, Dad," Joan said.

"It would be a pleasure, of course," Tarlton told her. "Certainly we'll stay, if it's no bother."

Amos understood that they wanted to see how he and Joan lived, and what sort of people Joan had married. The wedding and reception had been formal, and in the Tarlton home. Joan's folks didn't really know much about the Jackmans, come right down to it, although they had been summer neighbors for years. Summer neighbors: that meant not really neighbors at all, each leading different lives, in different worlds. Amos had no misgivings about the visit. He knew his people were not like the Tarltons but that didn't mean one or the other was better.

And it worked out fine. They drove to the house in the beach wagon, Gregory Tarlton, Amos, Mort and Whicher, and washed up and sat to dinner at the big kitchen table. Everybody talked, except Mort, but he appeared pleased about the visitors in his serious way. They ate boiled potatoes and fried ham and canned corn and biscuits, finishing with pancakes and maple syrup and mince pie. Amos realized that Gram and Joan had done a lot in the short time allowed them, probably with Mrs. Tarlton helping, for he was aware that the baked beans in the oven were to have been the dinner.

He saw that Joan was happy. She must have thought a good deal about her folks over across the valley and wondered when they'd come to see her, or whether they would, since it meant visiting the Jackmans, but here it was and everything had turned out fine. She smiled at him across the table.

After dinner, Pa went back to the house with them and sat and watched the work or talked with Tarlton about Whichertown. When the afternoon had passed, they'd finished the flooring. The women came down the road. It was the first time Gram had seen the house.

She said, "I remember the old one well enough. It was in disrepair when Jabez Whicher moved away. The oldest boy, he was ten or twelve years older than me, came back from the Civil War and stayed on a few years before he talked his father into going West." Gram looked thoughtfully into the valley as though seeing back over the years. "Suited Jabez well enough. He always had a mind to look for greener pastures over the hill. Peddled hardware in York State and sailed out of Boston and I don't know what all. He was my uncle, married my mother's sister."

Joan asked, "When did they go West?"

"I'd say about eighteen-seventy or seventy-one. We rented the place some, but nobody kept it up. It was a small, low house."

"That's what this'll be," Amos told her.

"I should think," Mrs. Tarlton remarked, "you'd be pleased to see it built again."

"Yes, I am. I'd like to see Whichertown the way it used to be, but I don't expect to."

"Why," said Tarlton, "it may become a thriving village again, if half the people who talk about moving to the country come here. Say, maybe I should buy a likely tract and subdivide it."

"Oh, Greg," Mrs. Tarlton admonished.

"Who knows? I'd like to see it. There's not much doing here now." He took out a cigar and lit it. "Well, Alice, we'd better be running along."

"We really must," she said to Gram. "We've had a lovely day, Mrs. Jackman."

"Come again when you can."

"And you must come to see us."

Amos walked with them to the beach wagon and stood next to Joan as they drove off. On the way back to the new house, she said, "You know, I think they had a nice time. I think they were lonesome."

"Shouldn't wonder, over there all by themselves."

"I'm awfully glad they came, Amos."

"Sure, so am I."

They spoke of it again that night in bed, Joan saying, "I am so pleased about Mother and Dad and your folks getting along well. I knew they would, but I wasn't sure, if you see what I mean."

"I guess so." He drew her close. "The Jackmans didn't show up so bad, you mean?"

"That isn't it at all—just I'm pleased everyone really knows each other better now."

"Well, anyhow, your father's pretty good with a hammer. Now the floor's done, I guess we better get at the haying."

"Oh, Amos, can't you work on it any more?"

"Not now. This weather won't hold and we need it for haying."

Joan sighed. "I suppose so. I can wait, but the house has gone along so fast, I'd begun to think of it all done."

"I'll get at it again in a week or two. We'll move in by the end of the summer."

"That will be nice," she said sleepily.

Amos yawned, thinking of the frame to be raised, planning the location of the doors and windows. He'd have it figured out by the time haying was done. He fell asleep.

The weather held dry and hot. In the mornings, Amos mowed with Dick and Pal while Mort scythed around the walls. Amos liked to ride the mowing machine and watch the grass fold over the cutter bar. He knew the fields so well that he could anticipate the rocks and woodchuck holes. He remembered the projecting ledge which looked low enough for the machine to clear but was just the right height to break a Pitman rod.

Except for the heaviest stands, the hay cured in a few hours and they put in the barn by nightfall the grass Amos had mowed in the morning. Whicher drove the horse rake in the afternoons while Amos and Mort tumbled the windrows of hay into piles for loading. And Whicher dragged the bull rake after the loaded hay rack to gather the scatterings. Amos wouldn't let him pitch on because the work was too heavy. Joan helped tread the load, riding on the rack with Amos and sometimes driving the horses from one haycock to another. Mort pitched on as Amos built the load carefully around the edge of the rack, filling in the center, layer after layer, at last rounding over the top securely to bind the load during the drive to the barn.

The sun beat down and the west breeze was hot. The barn was hot and airless. Sweat soaked Amos' shirt and trickled into his eyes and down his sides while he pitched off the hay into the dusty mows. It was good to drive out again into the bright sun, blinking against the brilliance, for the breeze felt cool after the heat of the barn.

Amos couldn't remember when the haying had gone so well. Some years the weather seemed to be against them all the way, showers alternating with rainy days, when even the sunny mornings were deceptive because they ended in rain after the hay was on the ground. But this year, all week, the hay made well. It dried fast, like green tea, with all the life still in it. Each day more of the fields had the new shaved look. After the first week, there were showers one night and the next day, but the disturbance passed and the sun came out in the blue sky, brassy hot by midmorning.

The house was hot, particularly the upstairs at night, and stifling because no air stirred although outside the darkness was cool. One night after lying naked and sweating on the bed, they went outdoors and slept with a blanket under the maple tree, dozing until the mosquitoes drove them back into the house.

Another day of rain came the second week. After breakfast, Amos was content to sit in the kitchen and smoke and look out at the falling rain and the clouds hiding the mountains. Mort had gone to his room to read, Whicher was in the shed working on his train, and Pa had moved his outdoor chair to the barn floor. Amos heard Joan and Gram talking in the pantry. Their tones caught his ear.

"Land sakes," Gram was saying. "I should think you'd remember to put in the shortening before you add the milk."

"Well, I was thinking of something else, I guess." Joan's voice had a defiant quality. "I can't help making a mistake once in a while."

"I've told you often enough." Gram paused and Amos heard the sound of a spoon on a bowl. "Feed it to the chickens and start over. Shameful waste."

"Goodness, it's just a few cups of flour!"

"Flour's dear and I can't abide wasting it." Gram added sharply, "Least it's dear to a Jackman."

"Never mind," Joan said. "I'll buy you a barrel of it."

She came from the pantry, saying to herself, "Fussing so over four cups of flour." She saw Amos and made a face as though he would understand and then she turned to the dishes in the sink.

Amos couldn't believe his ears. He'd never before heard anything like sharp words between Gram and Joan. He was inclined to think that Joan had taken offense when she should have been sorry. After all, Gram was right. Four cups of flour were four cups of flour. He didn't like to hear her speak as though she could buy a carload of the stuff, which she could, but no need to boast about it. He realized that being in a family way probably made her touchy, yet just the same, Gram was right. He'd talk to her about it when they were alone, and for now, he'd best get out to the barn.

He decided later that he perhaps should have stayed in the house and talked to Joan alone, because at dinner Gram and Joan were hardly speaking. She announced that she was going to visit her folks that afternoon and might even stay to supper.

"I'll take you over," Amos said.

They reached Whichertown, driving along through the rain which had turned the road to mud, before Joan said, "I wish you'd hire carpenters to build our house. I can't wait to move into it."

"Can't wait another month or so?"

"I don't believe I can. Gram and I are getting on each other's nerves something terrible. I don't think it's all me, Amos."

"Well, you came back at her this morning more than you'd ought, seems to me."

"You think so? You should have heard her yesterday about my using too much soap in the washing. Damn it all, it's nothing but old yellow soap she makes at home!"

Amos suddenly wanted to laugh. "That's why she thinks so much of it," he pointed out.

Joan sighed resignedly. "Probably. But she's hard to get along with if you're independent at all." After a little she brightened. "I feel better already to be away alone with you. I'll try to be meek and mild for a while longer. You won't hire any help on the house?"

"Nope."

"I think you're a stinker about it."

"All right, I am."

They drove in silence up the hill and turned in at the lodge. They found Joan's folks surrounded by travel folders strewn about their chairs in the living room. Gregory Tarlton waved his hand at them and tossed aside a colorful pamphlet on Switzerland.

"We're going to Europe," he announced. "Maybe around the world!"

Joan's mother explained, "Greg's getting restless."

"Yes, I am. Finding my children grown up and doing well, the daughter married to a fine young man and the boy settled with a good firm of importers—the simple life here having palled—I intend to see the world." Looking at Joan, he added, "If you don't mind, my dear."

"Heavens, no, I don't mind."

Her mother said, "He means the approaching event."

"Oh, that. It's a long way off and anyhow we can attend to it." She laughed. "Give me a drink, Dad, will you? No, never mind, I'll make it myself. You wouldn't put enough in. Amos?"

"Yes."

They sat in the living room while the rain fell outside, cool and misty, hiding the valley of Whichertown in a soft gray curtain. He looked at the folders on the floor: England, Spain, Germany, India, places all around the world, including some he'd never heard of.

Joan turned to her father after she had put down her glass. "Are you serious?"

"Never more so. We're driving to Boston tomorrow to see a travel agency."

"Well, I think it's fine. Don't you, Amos?"

"Yes, seems though."

He had trouble grasping the idea that anyone could take off across the ocean just for fun, but he made himself think about it and poke at the notion until it didn't seem so strange after all. If you had the money and no work to do, there was nothing to prevent. Joan could go herself, any time. She had money that would take them both. He didn't feel any inclination to go, but there it was. They could go if they wanted to, except for the farm.

He found in the next few days that leaving for Europe didn't mean planning a long time. The Tarltons packed and were ready to leave for New York before a week had passed.

Amos and Joan drove with them to the station. The grimy building beside the tracks had a new significance for Amos. You could leave from it for any place in the world.

They sat in the beach wagon and waited for the train. Talk came as slowly as the time passed.

"Joan," her father said. "I want you to use the car here, if you'd like to."

She glanced at Amos. "Thanks, Dad, but I don't think we'll need it."

Amos said, "I'll block it up for you in your garage."

Tarlton laughed. "I guess that won't be necessary. You make it sound as though we'd be gone a year. At that, I expect it will be several months, if we find many places we'd like to visit a while."

"Greg wouldn't hear of a regular tour," Mrs. Tarlton said.

"You'll have a wonderful time," Joan told them. "And don't worry about us."

"I'll write regularly," her mother promised. "I'll send you forwarding addresses."

Amos felt that he was a little out of place, and left the car to wander along the platform and talk with the agent in the station. When he heard the train whistle to the north, he returned to the beach wagon and took the bags to the platform.

He was surprised at how composed the Tarlton family appeared. Joan acted as though her folks were leaving for Braemuir.

The train came in with a rush of the engine. Amos helped carry the bags in the car. Joan kissed her folks. Her mother kissed him and whispered, "Take good care of her." He shook hands with Joan's father. Then he and Joan were on the platform waving as the train pulled out.

Joan turned quietly away. She drove back to Whichertown, where they left the beach wagon in the garage at the lodge and returned to the farm in the Model T. Joan got out quickly and walked around the corner of the house, while Amos stopped to speak to Pa about the last of the haying.

He followed Joan and found her on her knees in the garden, weeding a row of carrots while tears streamed down her face.

"Joan, what's the trouble?"

"Nothing," she sobbed, pressing her hands to her face.

He knelt beside her and put his hand on her shoulder, not knowing what to do or say. She wiped her eyes with her arm as a child might.

"All of a sudden I was lonesome," she said, trying to smile. "Isn't it silly?"

"No," he said. "They're your folks."

"For a moment everything felt strange, like when you're a kid and get left at school the first day. I'm all right now."

She bent to her weeding and he stood up. There was a load or two of hay yet to bring up from the lower field and he felt anxious to finish the job. By way of comfort, he said to Joan as he left, "I'll be starting on the house again tomorrow." She nodded but didn't look up and he couldn't be sure whether she was crying again or not.

## Chapter 25

It was early for August thundershowers, but to Amos, working on the roof of the new house with Mort and Whicher, the oppressive air made him think of the afternoons which would come later in the month. There was the same breathless saturation of heat and moisture that kept you sweating while you waited for a cooling breeze which didn't come. There were the same thunderheads rolling up in the southwest, but instead of darkening the sky, they faded away behind Cobblestone and the sun pressed down through the still air like a hot weight.

Pausing for Whicher to pass him another strip of asphalt shingles, Amos could see that the hills and fields had gone beyond their lush green to the darker shades of midsummer, as though growth had stopped and the leaves and grass were in suspension, resisting the heat instead of flourishing under it, waiting for the end of the season.

From the roof of the house he could look over the fields and across to the hills from a position he had never been in before. He felt proud that he had built the house here and could be near to the ridge on the plank scaffolding, almost ready to close in the roof against the weather. He could see over the line of trees along the stone wall to the farmhouse where Joan was hanging the wash in the dooryard. She looked toward him and waved. He lifted his hand with the hammer in it.

Whicher passed him the shingles and he and Mort lined up the new strip and nailed it in place. Two more, three more, finish the row, one more row to nail. Mort climbed down the roof for another bundle of shingles. Amos saw that Whicher, waiting below him on the roof, was nearly ready to quit. They had been working hard. The frame and the boarding and the rafters and the roofers had gone up day after day as the three of them worked steadily from sunup till dark. And Whicher'd had enough. It showed in his quietness and in his eyes wandering off down the valley. Amos remembered when he himself had been young and work was different. He thought of telling Whicher they were near done, he could quit.

But when he turned around from nailing the last strip, and only the capping of the ridge was left, Whicher had climbed down and was walking toward the barway with a stiff tenseness about his stride that told Amos he expected to be called back.

"Hey, Whicher, where you going?"

Whicher didn't turn. "Swimming."

"Go ahead," Amos called, and smiled at Mort who was slipping the last bundle of shingles off his shoulder. "He's had enough and I can't say I blame him. Why don't you go with him, Mort? I'll put on the ridge cap."

"No, I'll stay and help you."

"I can finish it easy. Go along. He's all hot and sweaty—he oughtn't to be swimming alone."

"Well, that's true, Amos." Mort looked toward the road. "He's running now."

Glancing in the direction Mort pointed, Amos saw Whicher running fast across the upper pasture, toward the woods that lay between them and the pool on Carr Brook, over the ridge. He laughed. "Puts me in mind of the time I skipped out."

"I remember," Mort said. "Well, probably I better go with him."

"Sure, go ahead."

Mort made his way down from plank to plank set on hangers at right angles to the roof, and backed down the ladder, head and shoulders passing from Amos' view. He reappeared again, walking toward the field, tall and steady in his overalls.

Amos worked on alone. He cut the strip shingles into sections with tin shears and nailed the squares over the ridge. Now, he thought, anytime we can move in, if Joan and Gram don't get along better than they have been. There was furniture, some things in the loft over the woodshed, a table or two and a bedstead with holes in it for ropes; he'd have to buy springs and a mattress, and he'd had a mind to cut down the post, but Joan wouldn't let him. She wanted to buy a lot of furniture. Of course they'd need a stove. Probably down to Fallsburg they could find a secondhand one.

There'd be perhaps a year's work finishing up the inside, and they'd need a woodshed and a backhouse. Joan kept talking about a bathroom but that would have to wait until he got the water piped in and the finish work done. It wasn't as though you had to have a bathroom.

He worked steadily in the sultry heat. He had finished the capping when he looked up and saw Mort coming down across the pasture with Whicher in his arms. Amos noticed at once the dangling naked legs and arms and the  head rolling on Mort's shoulder. Mort was trying to steady it with his free hand.

Amos caught his breath and hooked the claws of the hammer in the ridge and climbed down the roof, down the ladder. On the ground, he could still feel the gasping emptiness inside him. His legs were weak but he began to run toward the road. He met Mort at the pasture wall. Mort's blank face framed desperate eyes which sought Amos, traveling over him in an appealing search.

"Amos, I think he's dead."

Amos could see the gash on Whicher's temple where the crude bandage had slipped, and the blood on his face and neck.

Mort continued to hold him, pressing the loose shirt and overalls around him with a gentle hand, as he stood on the far side of the wall. Amos climbed over the piled stones, tearing his dungarees on the barbed wire at the top.

"Put him down, Mort." Amos helped him lower Whicher to the grass. "What happened?"

Mort brushed a big hand across his tortured face. "He dove from that high rock at the end of the pool. Struck his head on the bottom." Mort looked down at Whicher. "Time I got him out, he'd bled a lot and was full of water. I done all I could, Amos."

Amos was kneeling over Whicher. The beardless face looked so young and girlish, the arms so unformed in a man's muscles, that Amos could not realize it was Whicher. He tried to wipe the blood from the cheek but it had already started to dry.

He said to Mort, "We'd better get his clothes on him."

Mort looked at Amos. "He's dead, ain't he?"

"Yes."

"I done all I could, Amos."

"I guess he was gone by the time you got him out of the water."

And he was thinking that if Whicher hadn't been helping him with his house, he wouldn't have been so hot he had to go swimming, he wouldn't have been in such a desperate way he needed to dive from the high rock. Of course it could be done. He had done it himself, but you had to judge nicely between the rock on shore and the ledge that stuck up in the middle of the pool under the water.

Amos took the overalls which Mort had tried to wrap around Whicher. He pulled them over the limp legs.

"Help me, Mort."

Mort moved slowly and without apparent understanding. Amos kept telling him what to do. And then Mort seemed to come back and he looked at Amos across the body of Whicher.

"I don't think the Lord had any right to do it. Whicher was a good boy. There wa'n't no need of it."

"No." After a moment, he said, "Why did he have to dive off the rock?" He asked it not of Mort or anyone, but only to express his wish to turn time back and stop Whicher.

Mort was kneeling beside Whicher. He didn't pray. He didn't look at Amos, but kept his eyes on the still figure.

"The Lord made him do it. That's the way the Lord is."

"It ain't that at all, Mort. It was an accident. He's dove from there before. He must have slipped."

"Who made him slip?"

"I don't know." Amos got to his feet. "Come on, we got to take him up to the house."

Mort didn't move and Amos reached down and shook him, feeling a strange unreasoning anger, suddenly almost on the verge of tears. "Help me, damn it, don't just kneel there."

Mort stood up slowly, not helping much, and they lifted Whicher over the stone wall.

Whicher was an awkward load and Amos said, "Wait here."

He went to the house and took off a door and carried it back to the road. They lifted Whicher on the door. Mort looked at him for a moment and then put his bandana over Whicher's face. They carried him along the road slowly, Amos trying to walk steady with his hands behind him under the edge of the door.

They came to the house.

He saw Pa sitting under the maple. Pa stood up and came toward them without a word, helping to lower their load, his breathing harsh behind Amos.

"What happened to him?"

Instead of answering, Amos told him, "He's gone, Pa."

"I know. What happened to him?"

"Dove off the high rock into the swimming hole."

Pa knelt down and took Whicher's hand and lifted aside the bandana. He stood up. "I'll go tell your grandmother. Bring him into the house." He went up the slope.

Carrying Whicher in their arms, Amos and Mort passed through the door into the kitchen. Amos could see that neither Joan nor Gram really believed Whicher was dead. They came after him and Mort, to stand in the living room as they eased Whicher down on the couch.

Gram came forward then, saying, "Are you sure, Amos?" She went quickly to the mantel and took from it a little hand mirror which she wiped on her apron. She knelt beside Whicher and held it over his mouth. After she looked at the mirror, she shook her head and carefully took Whicher's hand and laid his arms across the overalls on his bare chest. "I'll get a blanket," she said.

The words sounded strange to Amos as he stood in the humid room with Joan beside him. Her hand to her face, she whispered to him, "Are you sure?"

He only nodded and turned to lead her out of the room.

"Call Doc Parsons, Joan," he said and steered her toward the telephone on the kitchen wall.

Back in the living room it didn't seem strange to see Gram and Pa spreading the blanket over Whicher. He looked cold.

## Chapter 26

After the funeral, Amos could not go back to work on the house. He didn't return the door on which they had carried Whicher to the farm. Driving down to the church for the funeral, he had seen the empty door casing and it looked in keeping with the unfinished appearance of the house.

The August days continued and thundershowers came with lightning that spread in flashes across the kitchen where they all sat silently. The blue flame played across the pipes at the sink as it always did. It used to fascinate Whicher but he wasn't with them to see it.

Rose had come for the funeral and three days later went back to Massachusetts.

Sometimes the storms came at night with crash upon crash of thunder directly over the roof, and lightning which flared in the room until Joan, lying beside him tense and far away, would turn to him and huddle against him while he couldn't bring himself to put his arms around her. He didn't understand why they were not as they had been before Whicher's death. He knew that he should be comforting and kind, because she didn't always feel well, especially in the mornings, but it was all he could do not to speak harshly. He went around silent for fear of what he might say if he let go of the bitterness that filled him.

He talked no more than Mort, who shambled about the business of the farm like a man doing work automatically. Amos noticed that Mort never read his Bible any more and his eyes had the dark look which Amos remembered from the days before his fasting. With his black beard, he resembled some tortured prophet from the Old Testament, driven by his lack of faith.

On a morning when the weather had turned cool, and the life of the farm seemed to have been suspended for days, Joan awoke and said to him, shivering as she pulled up the quilt, "We've got to move into our house, Amos. I can't stand it here any more."

"The windows ain't in yet and there's no furniture."

"I don't care. We'll hire a carpenter to put in the windows and we'll buy the furniture."

"No." He looked past the curtains at a single branch of the maple tree turned orange. "I can't see my way to leaving the family now."

"Goodness, it would just be moving down the road. And you aren't helping them. You act as though you'd been sick. You—you haven't even cleaned out the barn decently since the funeral. Pa says you've got to dust the potatoes. What's the matter? What is it, Amos?"

"I don't know. Expect I'll be all right."

"If you'd only move to the house with me, we'd be better off. You'd feel better." She was staring at the ceiling. "Just to get away from here a little would be good for both of us and you'd feel more like yourself, be able to do something here on the farm."

"I can't stand to think of our house. If I hadn't made Whicher work so hard on it, he'd be alive today."

"Amos, how can you say such a thing? He might have gone swimming during the haying and done the same thing. You talk as though we were to blame."

"I should have left you alone, three months ago."

"That's not so!" She sat up in bed and gripped his shoulder. "You

[ 197 ]

should have hired help on the house, that's what, if you want to look at it that way."

"No."

He could never remember being so confused and torn by thoughts he was unable to control. He got out of bed and dressed without saying anything more.

The sun had not come up as he went into the kitchen and started the fire. Gram came downstairs and he went out to the barn.

Usually Mort was there before him, but this morning Amos could not find him. The air was cool and clear when he let the cows into the barn for their morning feed and milking. He heard the cawing of crows beyond the corn piece and he stopped in the doorway to look up towards the woods.

He saw Mort appear beyond the corn on the edge of the field. He was carrying a shotgun. The crows hadn't seen him yet, for he stood in the shelter of the woods. One flew over and lit in a tree above him. Now Mort would raise the gun slowly and poke it through the bushes and shoot the crow. Amos waited, but nothing happened and then the crow flew away, cawing. Mort sat down on a stone with the gun cradled between his knees.

To Amos there was something wrong about the scene and he felt a sensation of dread as he left the barn and began running up the hill.

"Mort," he called. "Hold on there!"

Mort looked up and saw him coming and put aside the gun.

Panting, Amos stopped in front of Mort, who didn't move from his seat on the rock. "What you doing?"

"Thought I might shoot a crow."

"Why didn't you? You had a chance."

"Well, Amos, I decided they wa'n't what needed killing." After a pause, he looked up and said, "Amos, did you ever get so's you didn't want to live?"

"No, I ain't."

"It's a gnawed-inside sort of feeling."

"You'll get over it." Amos picked up the gun.

"Abandoned by the Lord," Mort said, almost to himself. "Deceived or made a fool, I don't know which."

"That's no way to talk." Amos took the shells out of the gun. "Let me have the rest of them. Come along," he said. "You ain't put flowers on Ma's grave lately. There's some pretty blue ones down by the corner of the field."

"I don't do that any more, Amos."

[ 198 ]

"Time you started again. Come along."

He led the way to the clump of asters by the barnyard.

"Here," he said, pulling at the flowers so abruptly he tore a few out by the roots. "Take them. Put some on Whicher's grave, too. Go along now and then come back and help with the chores."

He watched Mort walk slowly down the road beyond the house. He felt that Mort needed to be ordered and guided harshly, that the hurt workings of his mind could rest by following directions from outside. And yet there was a listlessness about Mort's figure and walk which bothered Amos. He couldn't forget the dread which had come over him as he saw Mort sitting by the wall with the shotgun cradled between his knees.

Instead of continuing with the chores in the barn, he returned to the house and went to the closet off the kitchen where the shotguns and rifles were kept. He put away the gun Mort had carried. He took down the boxes of shells and cartridges.

Gram asked, "Where you going with them?"

"I'll keep them out in the barn. Don't want Mort hunting. The way he's mooning around, he's apt to hurt himself."

She looked at him sharply. "Is that what you mean, Amos?"

"That's all I mean now. He ain't fit to carry a gun, not now."

Joan watched him from the stove with a worried, frightened look. Pa asked, "What's the matter?"

Amos told him about the crows. "He was thinking of shooting himself."

"I don't believe it."

"It's so."

Amos went to the barn and put the shells and cartridges in a corner of the haymow under a beam. He was milking when Mort came back from the cemetery. Wordless, Mort sat down and began to milk.

Amos felt that there must be some way to change things back to the simple days of early summer. He could not quite believe that he was caught up in relationships and problems which had not existed before Whicher's death. Yet he was aware he should do something to bring Mort back to normal, to release his own frozen strength and will, to change the tension between him and Joan. If he could correct these things, living might again resemble the earlier summer weeks.

But he couldn't think of anything to do. He felt that he should begin with himself. Joan had been right that morning when she said he was no use around the farm now. But he didn't know which way to turn.

[ 199 ]

He was reminded of being lost in the woods. He remembered a late afternoon on a cloudy day, back among the ridges, when he was a youngster. Since noon he had been walking, with every step bringing him almost to familiar country, but never actually to a known place, and darkness coming on. Finally he had not the will to walk any farther because he was so afraid he wouldn't come to landmarks he recognized and he was afraid before long he'd give in to the urge to run and run in search of a trail or logging road or a contour of land with which he was familiar. That's the way it was now, in his mind, and the strange woods were people's needs and tangled relationships. The lethargy and deadness and underlying panic in him were the same.

He thought about it during breakfast. He found he couldn't look at his family around him, eating in silence, and when his eyes met Joan's there was no message passing between them. He left his coffee unfinished.

He went out to the woodshed and sat down on the chopping block where he could look through the arched door. He had no plans for the day. There was work to be done, but he couldn't start. Under the maple in the yard he could see the door to his new house. He hadn't touched it since they carried Whicher home on it. He looked across the lower field to the wooded ridge of Cobblestone. Although the rising sun was warm and the grass green and the leaves of the hardwoods thick, he felt a chill in the air from the cold night and he noticed a tinge of color on a few branches of the swamp maples in the valley.

He got to his feet. With an effort of will, he walked across the yard and stood looking down at the door.

Pa came out of the house and sat in the chair under the maple and then he got up and moved the chair into the sun. Amos turned to him.

"Can you watch Mort, Pa?"

"Watch him? What for?"

"I told you this morning."

Pa shook his head. "Somehow I can't believe he would. It don't seem like a son of mine could do such a thing."

"Just the same, you watch him."

"Where you going?"

"Down to the house."

"I'd rather you stayed, Amos. It's a bad time to leave me."

Amos looked away. "I know." He felt the impossibility of acting for himself alone, and yet he knew he must act for himself now or succumb to the morbid apathy that was overcoming him. "I got to go for a while, Pa. Make a start at doing something."

He walked to the door and picked it up. Rain had washed its panels. He carried it down the road. It was heavy and he set it down several times before he reached the new house.

Goldenrod was growing beside the old lilac bush. The yellow blooms waved in the breeze. He found that he could look at the house easier, now he had picked up the door and brought it back. He made up his mind to work on the house and he felt better.

The ladder still leaned on the low roof. The planks from which they had shingled the roof were still in place with trimmings of shingles lying on them. He saw his hammer hooked over the ridge. Nothing had changed, except perhaps the bare walls which the sun and rain had weathered a little from their fresh-milled cleanliness.

He had not built the steps and he slid the door up through the casing and climbed after it and hung it on its hinges. He'd build the steps next. There ought to be a porch, but he didn't have time to build one. Steps would be enough for now, so he and Joan could go in and out. Two would serve, for the house lay close to the ground on its low foundations.

As he worked, marking and notching the two-by-sixes, he found that the action seemed to help him. He didn't feel so tangled in his thoughts and he had a sensation of release. He cut boards and boxed in the steps and when he was through he knew that he was going to be all right again.

He walked up the steps and opened the door into his house. The window frames were stacked in a corner of the kitchen near the brick chimney he had built using the old bricks from the cellar. He wanted to start setting the frames into the walls, but he thought of Mort and Pa. He had been gone a good part of the morning. He had been absorbed in thinking of his house and of Joan and himself living there. Now he remembered that he had other responsibilities. Reluctantly he put away his tools. Although the incident of the early morning had faded temporarily from his thoughts, it had been with him and now he felt that he must go back.

As he walked down the road, he began to stride faster while a feeling of impending trouble grew in him. He should not have gone. He should not have stayed so long. He was hurrying when he reached the house. He went into the kitchen. Gram sat reading to Mort from the Bible. They were across from each at the table. Mort looked up absently as though he were not paying attention to Gram. She kept on reading.

Amos turned about while the reaction of relief almost made him laugh. He went out. Pa was in the garden hoeing onions. Beyond the bean rows,

Joan picked tomatoes into her apron. She walked with him back toward the house.

Amos said, as they reached the woodshed, "I started work on the house again. Figure we can move in before long, if you don't mind sort of camping out."

She turned to him quickly. "Of course I don't mind. I think it would be wonderful!" She held her apron with one hand and slipped the other around his neck and kissed him. "That's the nicest thing you ever told me."

She was smiling as she used to do. He picked up a tomato which had rolled from her apron. He held it out for her to bite into. They ate it together, standing there just looking at each other.

## Chapter 27

The tops of the potato plants had grown across the rows and the field was a blanket of green, the lower half tinted white-green by the dust which Amos sprayed from the whirring duster slung over his shoulder. He walked along the rows, the plants brushing his legs, and cranked the duster, making a thin cloud blow out the nozzle. The sun had not come up and the cold dew still lay heavy on the plants. His dungarees were wet and stained by the dust. When the sun rose the dust would dry on the plants. It was to prevent a late blight and would be the last time he'd have to tend the potatoes before digging. He felt that the summer was over and he thought of preparing for winter. He thought of his house.

In the past week he had finished putting in the windows and had tacked felt building paper over the outside and shingled the walls. It could be lived in now. Indeed, he'd promised Joan they would rent a truck and go to Fallsburg for the stove this afternoon, the stove and the bed springs and mattress, as well as the things Joan wanted, a bureau and chairs and tables and dishes.

He felt that he had given in too easily about spending money for furniture. She wanted nice things and last night as they talked about it in bed, he had not been able to resist her any longer.

"It's your silly pride, Amos," she told him. "I know you'd make everything nice in time, but why should we wait? We've got the money."

"You've got the money."

"Oh, Amos, don't be that way. It's our money." She took his hand and placed it on her breast. "I love you. Let's have a few nice things in our house."

He had finally agreed, but somehow he seemed to have lost a little of himself. He was not happy about it now and felt a vague discomfort.

Perhaps it was partly because he still worried about moving to the new house, and leaving Pa and Gram with Mort. Yet during the past few days Mort had seemed better than he had since Whicher's death. The episode of the crows might almost have been a bad dream. Mort had taken up the routine of the farm as though he were again at peace with the Lord. He did the chores in his old steady manner, he spoke quietly and his eyes above the black beard were calm. Right now Amos could look down the hill and see Mort in the barnyard putting up the bars behind the cows which were grazing back into the pasture. There was an everyday peacefulness about the scene that reassured Amos and he told himself no harm could come from moving with Joan to the new house.

That afternoon, he and Joan drove to the village in the Ford. They left the milk at the creamery and drove back to the garage to rent the truck. Amos had never driven with four shifts forward; he'd not often driven with a shift lever. He had to remember that the pedals at his feet were not like those on the Ford. Lije Willis, in dirty coveralls and black cap, leaned in at the window of the cab and pointed with a greasy hand as he explained how to shift. Amos felt ill at ease and annoyed, especially with Joan on the seat beside him.

"I guess I can handle it," he said at last, anxious to get away.

He stalled once as he started, and then, co-ordinating better, drove slowly out on the road. The cab seemed high above the road and the truck jounced emptily behind him.

Joan laughed. "Don't frown, Amos. This is fun."

He felt better after he had driven a few miles, and when, on a clear stretch of road, he stopped and started for practice, and backed, he made up his mind he could drive through the streets of Fallsburg without any trouble. He caught some of Joan's gaiety. The day was clear with the high clouds and sharp blue sky of late August. Joan sat close beside him and talked and looked about her like a child on an excursion.

"Isn't it a beautiful day, Amos? I'm so glad to be going somewhere—to a city, a big city like Fallsburg." She smiled. "Remember when you told me you'd been to Fallsburg?" She leaned over and kissed his cheek. "And now you're going there again with your wife to buy furniture."

"Seems though I am."

"Isn't it nice to get away from Whichertown for a change? I think we ought to take a trip every week."

"Whichertown's all right."

"Of course it is. I love it. But this is all right, too." She looked out the cab window. "I love to see the country roll by. Amos, I'm going to spend a lot of money. I can feel it in my bones."

"I'll bet you can."

"Did you get the measurements of that nice old bed?"

"Yes."

"I want a box spring and a good mattress, not too hard and not too soft, probably a hair mattress. And a bureau and a kitchen set. I might even buy one of those kitchen cabinets so you won't have to build cupboards. And a sink. Why don't we buy a bathroom and all the fittings and you could put it in this winter?"

"Now hold on, hold on."

"Well, then we won't. But rugs, we'll need some rugs." She tapped his leg. "You don't know me when I'm on a buying spree."

"I can see that."

She turned serious. "Amos, is Mort going to be all right?"

"I guess so. He's got hold of himself, I think. And then I don't know. He usually tells me how he's getting on with the Lord, but he hasn't said anything lately."

"Maybe a doctor—maybe we could take him to Boston."

"He ain't crazy, Joan."

"I know, but maybe someone could help him, someone who knows about such things."

"It would make him worse. He'd get the idea we thought he was crazy." Amos turned out to pass a wagon and team. "He'll be all right. I'll watch him."

"I was scared that morning."

"So was I." He added slowly, "I still don't know if I did right to leave today and get ready for us to move into the house. I don't want Mort to feel more alone. I guess you can feel alone enough when you figure you been abandoned by the Lord, like he says."

"It sounds so strange and old-fashioned."

"Not when you think of Mort," he said.

"No, I guess not." She went on in a forced way. "Cheer up, Amos. He'll be all right and your father is better. He's going to help with the chores tonight. Don't be sad. This is our day."

"Well, your day. I reckon you got something coming."

"I'm all right. I love you."

He saw the small houses and shacks and old car dumps on the outskirts of Fallsburg, and the roadside signs.

"We're almost there."

He drove slowly through the streets, cautious with the big truck among the cars and people.

Joan said, "We'll stop first at the bank and change my account to a joint one."

"Now, Joan, I'd rather you didn't. I don't want your money."

"Please, Amos. Let's not argue about it any more. Please, for me."

He thought she might be going to cry and he said hastily, "All right, if you really want it that way."

"I do. I've kept telling you it's ours."

"All right."

He parked the truck and went with her into the brick bank. He waited at the high writing desks along the wall and looked at the inkstands and forms and blotters. She came back from the teller's window and showed him how to write a check.

"There," she said. "That's all there is to it. Now we'll go to the furniture store."

They walked down the street to the store in whose big windows were sets of furniture for any room in a house.

Amos made himself lead the way inside among the rows of chairs and couches and lamps set out over the floor. He went to the nearest clerk, and dreading what he had to say because it was about beds, he told the carefully dressed man with the graying hair that they wanted to see some bed springs.

"And mattresses," he added.

With this start, Amos felt that he could let Joan decide what she wanted. He hadn't hung back or put Joan to shame by not speaking up. Now he tried to keep his face from giving away his feelings about the prices. He tried not to say anything to Joan about the way she bought. She was different from the time she bought flour and sugar in Cy Tillman's store. She walked around without saying much, bending to look at a label or to sit on a mattress—while Amos looked away—pressing it thoughtfully before she said, "We'll take this one." And she moved on, serene, not excited or voluble as he might have expected, nor careful about prices as she had been at Cy's.

Stepping daintily along in her navy blue suit, she rejected various kitchen sets and then at last said, "We'll take this one." She seemed to know just what she wanted, and after a while Amos saw that there was pleasure to be had in watching the face of the clerk. The man, looking at him, had probably thought to sell a few cheap items. And then as the list grew, the clerk must be wondering about the money, for he'd look at Amos doubtfully, saying to Joan, "Yes, Madam."

Gradually there came to Amos a realization of what you could do with money if you had enough of it, when you wanted something. It was a power that he had never experienced before and could only try to understand with a sensation of wonder. He suspected that you had to be born to the use of money, like Joan, for at the back of his mind each thing she bought was reducing her—their—bank account at a startling rate, yet it didn't seem to bother her in the least.

When it had all been added up, at the desk, they were handed the bill and the clerk excused himself. "I'll get the manager. He'll arrange with you about payment and delivery."

Joan looked at the clerk and then smiled to Amos, lowering her voice so the girl behind the desk couldn't hear. "Now, darling, you just take out the check book and pay them."

He did as she directed, writing in his large hand, "Six hundred and twenty-four dollars and 52/100." His fingers trembled a little as the sum of money flowed off the end of the pen, but he signed his name with a strange sense of power. The feeling lasted until the manager, concealing surprise at the check, asked about the delivery, while the girl made a discreet phone call and nodded slightly to her boss.

Then Whichertown came back to Amos in a flood of images and memories and he said slowly, "We'll take it along. I've got a truck."

And he remembered it wasn't his money and he had been pretending it was, like a boy in a daydream. But it had been so real he felt an abrupt fear that he would never think of money again as he used to, and there seemed to have been a slight erosion of his soul.

By the time the truck was loaded at the back of the store and the canvas lashed down, Amos could tell from the sun over the buildings that chore time had arrived at Whichertown and he felt restless about being away. This was not like fishing or hunting when he never gave a thought to chore time because Pa and Mort and Whicher had been home to look after the stock. Now he wondered if Pa was strong enough to help Mort and if Mort was all right. He ought to be there.

But Joan wanted to go to the hotel and have a drink and supper.

"No sense to that," he said, as he started the truck. "We can eat when we get home. I should be helping with the chores. Besides, I ought to unload this furniture and take the truck back to Lije."

"You can put it in the barn for tonight and take it back in the morning.

And Pa and Mort will have the work done before we could get back, now. Please, Amos, I do so want a good time."

"I don't think I ought to."

"Please, Amos. We'll have fun. It would be almost dark anyhow if we started home now."

"Well, I suppose that's so."

Joan showed him how to get to the hotel. They parked the truck and went into the lobby and Joan led the way across the carpeted floor past the people in armchairs, past the desk clerk and elevator boy to a door at the back where they entered a bar whose curtained windows barely let in the late afternoon sun. They sat in chairs at a table. Men and women were seated about the room at other tables. Behind the bar a man in a white jacket and apron worked before shelves of bottles. A waiter came up to them.

"I'll have a martini, please," Joan said.

Amos nodded and the waiter went back to the bar. Amos looked at Joan and she smiled.

"You can relax," she said. "Nothing's going to bite you. Sit back and relax and don't look at that girl's legs."

"I wasn't."

"You noticed them."

"Difficult not to."

"Well, you may, if you want, in a discreet manner." She lit a cigarette. "Isn't this fun? I do love bars."

The waiter set down two little glasses of pale liquid. Joan lifted hers and looked at him over the rim. "Try it, Amos."

He picked up his glass gingerly, almost afraid it would break in his big hand. "There's something in the bottom of mine."

"That's an olive, silly."

He tasted the strange drink and, finding it not unpleasant, drank it down and chewed the olive's salty meat.

"You aren't supposed to gulp it," Joan said. "It's not like a shot of whiskey."

"I'll learn."

He could feel the drink's warmth spreading through him. He sat back. The farm and Whichertown seemed far way. He listened to the low music coming from the radio near the bar. There was a quiet, soothing effect to the sound as it blended with the murmur of voices. The shadowed room and the people in intimate couples or small groups around the tables talking, talking, the clink of glasses, all seemed to shut out the world.

"Shall we have another?" Joan asked.

"I don't mind."

He drank the next one slowly, thinking of the ways into which he had fallen, while he let himself forget the cares of the farm and his family and Whichertown. They were part of another man in a different life, distant and not touching him in this quiet retreat. Pa and Mort would be all right; they had nothing much to do with him. Only Joan across the table from him was real.

The faraway effect stayed with him through supper, which they ate in the dining room at a white tablecloth. He found that he was not even worried about behaving and eating right, and he knew this was peculiar because he had never eaten in a hotel dining room before. He watched Joan and followed her manners and discovered that there was nothing difficult about it, feeling the way he did. The soup was good, though thin, and the roast beef tender. He had a strange sort of frozen raspberry juice for dessert with little cookies. Although he knew there must be a cook in a kitchen beyond the dining room, his wonder was that the food should appear on the table through no apparent work of anyone except the waiter who brought it. Money, he saw, could do many things besides buy furniture.

Afterward, he felt sure that he behaved all right, for Joan took his arm as they were going out through the lobby and said, "You're fun to be with, Amos, and I'm proud of you, even in that old blue suit. We'll have to get you a new suit some day. We'll come down and do this again and buy you a suit."

"All right."

They drove back to Whichertown in the darkness, and Amos felt an impossible sensation: regret because the afternoon was over. He did not at first realize that he wasn't anxious to get back to Whichertown, that he didn't look forward to the increasing familiarity of the road, until he noticed how much of his mind was taken up with the past hours. He had a somewhat guilty reaction because home and the farm and the hills had always meant so much to him. But after he stopped in the village to tell Lije he'd return the truck in the morning, and they were driving toward the mountains, he seemed to return to himself, and the stars and quarter moon over the ridge of Cobblestone were bright as ever.

There was a car in the yard. It looked like his cousin's—Jake Whicher's. And then in the lights of the truck he recognized another car. Doc Parsons'.

## Chapter 28

Jake Whicher met them at the door, a short stocky figure against the lamp light.

"Hello, Amos."

"What's wrong, Jake?" He formed the words slowly, trying to control his sudden feeling of guilty dread.

"Your Pa's sick and Mort's gone off somewhere."

They went into the kitchen. Gram stood by the sink. Doc Parsons, in his shirt sleeves, was saying, "I believe he'll come out of it." His shirt was wrinkled and his jowled face looked tired.

Gram's eyes passed over Joan before she spoke to Amos. "If you'd been here, Amos—I wish you'd been here." She sighed and went on in a quiet voice, "Your pa went looking for Mort before I could stop him. He got back as far as the doorstep. I give him his medicine and covered him up and called Rob, here." She nodded at Doc Parsons, and sat down in the rocker by the stove.

Amos went to the closet and looked at the guns. They were all there. He took his overalls from a hook and, removing his suit coat, put on the overalls. He changed to his work boots and put on his denim jacket.

He asked Jake, "Where've you looked for Mort?"

"Marvin and I been scouring around. Went through the sugar orchard to the place he stayed last month and down to the cemetery. Marvin's up on the hill now, hollering."

"We better go over to the pool where Whicher was killed."

Amos went into the front room. His father lay on the couch covered by a blanket. The lined face was shadowed by the turned-down lamp, the moustache and closed eyes singularly lifeless, although he breathed heavily. Amos stood in the doorway looking at him. He could not think of Joan or the trip to Fallsburg or of the furniture in the truck outside. It was too late now to correct what he had done. He could not move the hours back to this morning. He returned to the kitchen.

"We may be gone quite a while," he said.

Jake followed him to the door with a lantern. Marvin Hostetter was coming toward the house, a lantern swinging at his side in rhythm with his gangling walk. His smooth old face was serious.

"Hello, Amos."

"Will you come with us over to the swimming hole?"

"Sure."

They started around the house. Amos heard Joan call him, and paused. She ran from the lighted kitchen door and gave him the little flashlight she kept in their bedroom. As he took it from her he noticed that her fingers were cold.

"It wasn't my fault," she said.

"No," he said. "No, it wa'n't."

"But I'm sorry, darling."

He touched her shoulder. "Maybe he's just mooning around somewhere trying to figure out God."

He left her and followed Jake and Marvin. The light from the lanterns cast moving shadows around their legs. Amos couldn't help thinking that Mort had killed himself. He tried to put the thought from him, but it remained in his mind and brought to him again the pang of conscience which had gripped him when he and Joan first got back to the farm. It was his job to look after Mort and instead he had been away with Joan. But under his remorse he felt angry that he should have the responsibility. He and Joan ought to be by themselves. They didn't need anyone else and people were spoiling what they had. He gave up thinking and concentrated on his feet in the shifting light.

Jake asked, "This way, Amos?"

"Yes, up to the old trail."

They reached the woods at the end of the wagon track through the back field. Crickets chirped loudly in the grass. Amos led the way to the corner of the wall. The trees were a dark cave beyond the lantern light. He climbed the wall and took Jake's lantern from him, holding it high on the far side while Jake and Marvin climbed over. He searched along the edge of the woods for the faint path which in daytime was so plain. Now bushes and rocks looked different and there seemed to be no trail in places, only the ranks of tree trunks receding into the darkness.

Amos thought of the times he had gone looking for Mort. There had been the day last spring when Mort let out the cattle. And the time he and Joan got back from the woods, Mort down in the birches beyond the sugar orchard. That had been a poor sort of return from a honeymoon. He let his mind dwell on the days when he and Joan had been alone. He thought of them with an aching nostalgia, realizing he and Joan alone were not troubled or complicated or torn one way and another.

The trail led over the ridge. Amos thought he saw deer tracks in some damp moss and lowered the lantern to make sure while he felt surprised he could be interested. Deer kept open the trail now, more than boys from Whichertown. He wondered how old the trail was. Of course, from the valley you could reach the swimming hole easier by the road, with a short walk through the woods where the brook left the road and formed the pool. This trail was mostly a Jackman and Whicher trail.

Jake and Marvin were silent behind him, but he could hear their feet in the leaves and twigs. He bent under a branch and circled a fallen tree. They reached the top of the ridge. He heard the brook below them. Now that they were approaching the pool, moving downhill fast through the open pine woods, he couldn't help thinking what they might find at the brook. Of course he wasn't actually sure Mort would be there. It was only a likely hunch. Yet as he saw the moonlit water through the trees, he suddenly hated the brook and feared it with an unreasoning panic which belonged to the darkness. It had killed his mother and Whicher and maybe Mort. But it was the same brook on which, back in the hills, he and Joan had camped. It seemed to flow through his life.

He stopped at the rocks and found that he was trembling. He didn't want to climb down among the pine roots to the ledge where the blown spray from the falls made the footing slippery. With an effort he forced himself to hand the lantern to Jake. Taking out the flashlight, he played the beam on the rocks, moving the circle back and forth and out toward the pool where the current from the falls rushed white into the opaque water. He raised the light to the high rock from which he knew Whicher had dived. He felt Jake grip his shoulder.

Mort was standing on the narrow ledge. A pine grew up from a cleft in the rock and his hand rested on it while he stared at the dark pool.

Amos called above the sound of the water, "Mort, it's me—Amos."

Mort took no notice.

Jake whispered, "The crazy bastard's going to jump."

"Shut up, Jake," Amos said and then called, "Stay there, Mort! Don't move, stay there!"

Amos started across the slippery rocks, not heeding Marvin, who cried, "You can't go up there after him."

"I'm going to talk to him."

[ 211 ]

Mort was near the edge now. Fearful that the flashlight would surprise or frighten him, Amos kept it trained on the rocks in front of his own feet, but he could see Mort in the faint light from the moon and the sky. His beard and hair obscured all but the white triangle of face from forehead to cheek. His overalls were pressed against him by the breeze which always blew from the cascade.

Amos began to talk. "Time we was going home now, Mort. I'm bringing a light so's you can get off the ledge." He hoped his voice would reassure Mort and he kept speaking words that meant nothing, as he might talk to a nervous animal.

He reached the steep ledge up which a boy might climb to dive into the pool. The flashlight showed the familiar crevice and hand holds. He looked up. Mort was standing on the point of rock, seemingly absorbed by the depths of his own mind. And then he stepped out with arms wide, as though to embrace the empty air, which must not have been empty to him, for his face was expectant and glad.

As Mort plunged from the ledge, Amos scrambled across the rocks to the water. Perhaps Mort wouldn't hurt himself, for diving was the dangerous way, toward the jagged rock angling up from the bottom of the pool. Amos waded out into the cold water, slipped and struggled to his feet. His head went under and he was swimming, as Mort came to the surface. He grabbed Mort around the neck from behind, found the bottom with his feet and pulled Mort to the pebbly beach at the foot of the pool.

Mort staggered up, looking back at the deep water. Amos held him firmly by the arm. Mort turned in the shallow water and stared at him.

"You, Amos?"

"That's right."

"Let me go, Amos." He moved toward the pool. "It's lovely in the water at night, Amos, when it closes over you. . . . Let me go."

"Stop it, Mort. You come along home with me and Jake and Marvin." Mort said, "They here? Gosh, Amos, they'll think I'm crazy."

"No, they won't. I'll tell them how you were bothered about Whicher. I'll fix it up."

"I don't want to see them."

"Well, then they can go along." He called to them, "You boys can start back. We'll make out all right." And to Mort, "Come on now, it's cold and we're both wet." The flashlight was gone from his hand and he called over to Jake, who had come around the pool, "Leave us a lantern."

Jake put down his lantern and the two men went back into the woods.

Amos could see their light moving slowly away and then only a gleam of it as they waited at the top of the ridge.

"Come on, Mort."

His brother waded ashore and Amos moved beside him slowly among the rocks to the lantern. He waited patiently while Mort climbed up the bank over the pine roots, to the trail. He followed him up through the dark woods. Cold and tired, his wet clothes clinging to his body, he could think of nothing to say and yet he felt that there should be some words which might help Mort. He was overwhelmed by a feeling of distance separating them. Although he had known Mort all his life, there was nothing he could say to him. He did not know what to say to a man for whom death was a bright and beckoning vista where he would leave behind all his anguish and self-doubt and perhaps—and to Amos this seemed the most poignant appeal—perhaps find again the Lord by whom he had been deserted in this life. Perhaps that was it: Mort had to be sure. Mort didn't know, and he had to find out. But there must be that dreadful question in his mind; perhaps even in death he would not find his God.

Amos looked at Mort's bent, slow-walking figure ahead of him and he wanted to cry.

They came to the top of the ridge. Jake and Marvin had gone on. Mort stopped and looked back past Amos.

He said finally, "I love Him so, Amos."

"Whicher?"

"Yes, but I mean the Lord." He put his hand to his heart. "Sometimes it hurts me here. I love Him and want to be with Him." His eyes shifted to the ground. "And then I don't know. He's all I care about. He is my whole life and I don't know."

"I guess you can be sure. I guess you can rest easy about that, Mort."

"Sometimes I am sure, but I can't help wondering." Mort turned and started off slowly. "Someday I'll have to find out."

He kept on through the woods. Amos followed him. They didn't speak again. They went across the field to the house.

The kitchen was brightly lighted with extra lamps. Mort hung back at the door and Amos opened the screen for him and touched his arm, and led him inside. Joan sat at the window looking out into the darkness. Doc Parsons slept on the couch, his old hound's face dewlapped and patient. Jake and Marvin sat at the table over their coffee cups. Joan looked quickly toward Amos. Jake and Marvin nodded. Doc Parsons opened his eyes wide awake and sat up. Amos felt Mort shivering, his arm trembling. He guided Mort toward the hall and the bedroom. Gram stood aside as they went into the hall. Amos coud hear Pa's breathing from the parlor.

"Cold swimming, tonight," Amos said. "Mort's going to bed now."

"I'll bring a lamp," Gram said.

In the little room which they had shared before Amos was married, he helped Mort undress. Doc Parsons came in and sat down on the chair with his bag on the floor beside him, waiting while Mort shivered into dry underdrawers and lay down beneath the quilts.

Doc asked, "How you feeling, Mort?"

"Tired. Cold a little."

"Amos, get a cup of that soup Gram is fixing."

His feet slipping wetly in his boots, Amos went into the warm kitchen. He nodded at Joan when she looked at him, and she tried to smile. Gram poured the soup into a cup. He took it to the bedroom. Doc Parsons slipped off his stethoscope and folded it into the bag. Mort raised himself to one elbow and took the pill Doc Parsons gave him and washed it down with the soup. He lay back and closed his eyes.

Doc Parsons said, "You better go change your clothes, Amos. I'll stay on a while."

Amos went upstairs, carrying a lamp from the kitchen. The bedroom was warm from the day's sun and smelled faintly of Joan's face cream. He took off his wet overalls and pants. They were his best pants, wet and wrinkled now. He folded them and hung them on the back of a chair. Ironing would fix them, but it didn't matter. He and Joan wouldn't be going to Fallsburg again. They shouldn't have gone at all. And yet he enjoyed the memory of the afternoon. It wasn't right, but he liked to think of buying the furniture and of going to the bar and dining room with Joan. He could think about it like a dream from which he'd come back to the farm. But he knew they should not have gone. He thought of the furniture out in the truck and of the house down the road. They couldn't move in now. He'd have to stay with Mort. They'd better not even sleep together up here. He'd have to sleep downstairs in Mort's room.

He put on dungarees and shirt and dry socks and his spare boots. At the door he paused and looked at the bed and Joan's things in the room, at her nightgown hanging inside the open closet door. He turned and went downstairs with his wet clothes over his arm, the lamp in his other hand.

Jake was saying, "He'd have drowned himself sure, if we hadn't got there. Amos hauled him out of the pool." Jake stood up and went to the stove where he knocked out his pipe.

[ 214 ]

Marvin pushed back his chair and crossed his legs.

"Coffee, Marvin?" Gram asked.

"Had enough, thanks."

Doc Parsons came into the kitchen. "He's asleep."

Amos turned from the rack behind the stove, having finished hanging up his wet clothes. He asked, "What had we better do about him, Doc?"

"Take care of him. Watch him. Keep him working. That's all I know. He may be all right." Sitting down at the table, Doc Parsons began shaking pills from the little bottles in his bag. He shook them into envelopes and wrote on the envelopes with a fountain pen. He stood up and closed the bag. "Warren should have one of these when he begins to stir around, maybe in two hours." He explained about the other pills. "That's about all for now. I'll stop out in the morning." He looked at Gram. "Don't worry or I'll be prescribing for you."

"I'm all right, Rob."

"You're a great girl." He put on his coat and went to the door.

Jake said, "Probably you folks don't need me and Marvin no more."

"Want to thank you," Amos told him.

"That's all right."

Amos followed them through the door and watched the lights of the two cars disappear down the road. Joan stood beside him. A cool breeze blew across the valley and the moon was low. The stars had the brilliance of fall and winter.

Joan said, "You must be tired, Amos."

"Guess not. Just need a little time to think about things."

"Amos, you won't let it hurt us, will you?"

"No, it won't hurt us, but you can't just push it to one side."

"I know. I'm awfully sorry about Pa and Mort and I wish we'd never gone away. Why should it always be when we're away?"

"Just happens, let's say." He hesitated. "You know we can't move into the house right off?"

"Yes."

"It won't be easy, with Gram."

"She thinks it's my fault. It isn't, is it, Amos?"

"No," he said. "I can't see that it is."

"Well, I'll get along all right with her."

"Sure you will. Another thing, I'll have to spend the night downstairs."

"I'll sit up with you."

"No, you better get some rest." He put his arm around her shoulders.

"I shall miss you," she said.

He kissed her and she pressed close to him.

"Love me always, Amos."

"Yes." He could feel her rounding belly against him. "How's the young one?"

"Just fine."

"We're all right."

"We are, aren't we?" She sighed. "When we're together, everything is all right."

## Chapter 29

In the passage of time, Amos found a numbing comfort. As the days moved into September and Pa made again his slow recovery and Mort worked beside him cutting corn and digging potatoes, Amos returned deeper into the ways of the farm and Whichertown, ways which had been his for years and went back through the generations of Jackmans on the farm. Sleeping downstairs in the room with Mort, seeing Joan only at meals and evenings around the kitchen table, he felt that his marriage was almost a thing of the past. He and Mort worked hard. He wanted Mort to be tired at night because he thought, with Mort sleeping exhausted, he and Joan could have some time together. But he found that he was afraid to leave Mort, who slept lightly and sometimes lay awake in his bed staring at the ceiling. And so he continued to work because it was a man's job and made him forget. After a time he did not long for Joan or try to kiss her when for a moment they were alone.

He didn't think nights any more of the house down the road with the furniture moved in and the rugs down and the stove connected to the chimney and the bed waiting for them. He had carried in the furniture the day after Mort tried to drown himself. Although then he had known they could not use it until an indefinite time, it had yet been in the future, when Mort and Pa were better. But after a while he could not quite imagine himself with Joan in the little house, for the lives of the family surrounded them and separated them until she hardly seemed like his wife and he her husband.

The work went on and on. He and Mort dug the potatoes with

long-tined forks, working each in his row while the brown tubers dried in the sun. They bagged the potatoes in the late afternoon when the air had begun to chill. Amos sorted out the best for seed. It was a good crop, enough for the coming winter and plenty more to swap at the grain store.

The corn stood in shocks in the upper field and they began to feed it out to the cattle as the pasture grass dried. Mort liked to braid the seed corn and hang it under the eaves of the barn. Bags of the golden ears were ground up at the grainstore for winter feed.

They brought in the squash and pumpkins to the woodshed and dug the turnips.

In the mornings the crickets were silent in the cold grass. There was a smell of fall in the air, of ferns dying in the woods. The leaves of the butternut trees behind the barn had fallen and the squirrels, red and busy, worked on the nuts, scampering along the stone wall to store them in hidden caches or, sitting on the limb of a tree, gnawed with small scratching sounds which could be heard a surprising distance. Sparrows flocked among the bushes by the walls and robins passed over the treetops in purposeful flight. Jays, silent all summer, called from the woods and raided the corn shocks. They flew in the skulking manner of jays as though they might be caught in their stealing. The leaves of the swamp maples down by the brook turned bright red.

And when the regular work was done, Amos began to plow. He turned over the entire lower field and with Mort, cleared the rocks, breaking in the young steers on the stone boat. He harrowed and fitted the land. He took a great deal of satisfaction in it because he couldn't remember when they had reseeded a field. He felt that he and Mort were building up the farm. It gave him a feeling of belonging. He cut the brush along the walls and on a rainy day they burned it on the brown earth, leaving patches of gray ashes beside the wall. Pa told him he was a fool to seed down a field in the fall, but he went ahead. Harry Foster at the grain store said the winter rye would grow and hold the land and in the spring he could harrow it under before he seeded the field to hay. He knew Pa was better by the way he objected to the new methods. If Pa hadn't felt well he wouldn't say a thing. Amos liked to be trying something new on the farm. It satisfied his urge to preserve the farm and turn back the woods that marched on Whichertown. The work made him feel that better days were coming.

And Mort got well. He talked to Amos easily, never mentioning God or Whicher or Ma. The day they broke the colter on the plow,

Mort helped put in the spare. He used the wrench with his old sureness and he looked at Amos and smiled.

"I ain't done that for a spell," he said.

Amos nodded. "Didn't know's I'd ever see you use one again."

The next day in the afternoon when they had finished the chores and supper, Mort shaved off the black beard. Standing at the sink in the late sunlight, he trimmed the beard with Gram's shears and then shaved with his straight razor. The long line of his jaw appeared and he stroked carefully up his throat; he washed and slowly rolled up the newspaper of hair and suds.

Pa smiled. "Glad to see you again, Mort."

Amos looked at his brother. He appeared younger now with the untanned skin of his face as smooth as a boy's. Amos felt that they had all passed through a strange time. He let his eyes move on to Joan, who was polishing the stove.

She must have been unhappy. She had not been able to understand why a husband could work and work and find satisfaction in his life, but she hadn't complained. She had waited for him to return to her, not able to share his feelings about the land and the family, but patient, sleeping alone upstairs and working with Gram, silent for the most part, a wife separated from her husband. The only thing he noticed which gave her feelings away were her visits to the new house. She puttered around her home that had never been a home, hanging curtains and dusting and cleaning where there was yet no reason for it.

Now Amos felt a startling release, as though he had finished a tedious piece of work or had completed a tiresome journey. He looked about him in the kitchen. Pa was reading a paper which Amos had brought from the village when he took the milk to the creamery the day before. He looked well and rested, the lines around his mouth fainter and his hair brushed and moustache trimmed. In his clean overalls and shirt, he seemed to possess the wiry toughness that he used to have. Gram hummed to herself as she clicked her knitting needles, sitting by the window where the light struck her wrinkled cheek and moving hands. Mort sat at the table with a magazine open before him. Joan was by the stove working with brush and polish can.

Amos felt a sudden warmth as he watched her move about the stove, her arms in the short-sleeved dress firm and brown, curls at the back of her head, the print dress covering the fluid motions of her body as she scrubbed, leaned over, or crouched on her heels, polishing.

He said, "It's about time Joan and I were moving to the new house."

Nobody commented for a while, but Joan looked at him quickly and turned back to her work and scrubbed over places she had already done. He could tell she was holding her breath and listening and he felt a sharp pain in his throat as he watched her.

At last Pa said, "Appears to me you'd better, if you're going to get set for the winter."

"Yes, I want to sheathe up the inside before cold weather."

Gram said, "You'll need some groceries. Joan and I can take care of that. There's enough to home here without going to the village."

Joan put away the stove polish and brush and cloth. She washed her hands at the sink. "I'll go up and pack, first."

Amos got to his feet. "I'll still be helping with the chores," he said.

He felt that if he didn't do something, he would break apart. He went out to the barn and walked through the tie-up and around through the barnyard, past the pigpen and the hen house and the wagon shed. He looked at the bare fields and scuffed the fallen leaves under his feet. The poplars and birches were turning yellow on the mountains. He felt the last rays of the sun hot on his face and the breeze cool from the valley as he moved beyond the wagon shed.

Amos was sure it was right for him to go with Joan to their house. Mort was himself again. He might never have another spell. He was better than Amos could remember since Ma died. Everything he did indicated his health of mind. He would repair machinery on the farm now. He didn't need looking after, if he'd do that.

Pa and Gram wouldn't worry, Amos told himself, or they'd never have agreed so quickly to his moving. Anyhow, he'd be only a step down the road, still part of the farm, part of his family but living with Joan as they should. He thought about it, and the baby coming. He had never felt such joy and supreme contentment. It came through all his senses and flooded his body with awareness of the familiar buildings and the hills and fields. This was his place. He could live his life now as he wanted.

He went to the house. Joan had packed her bag and put it by the door. Amos saw the box of groceries on the table. There didn't seem to be anything to say, and he picked up the groceries. Joan took the suitcase.

Pa said, "Drive the Ford, if you want."

"We can walk, thanks."

Mort came to the door with Gram and Pa and the three of them stood there while Amos and Joan went across the yard and down the road. Amos turned and raised his hand. Joan waved. He faced about toward their new house. The road stretched ahead of them. He shifted the box of groceries under his arm.

Joan laughed. "Isn't it funny that going down the road this little way should be so important?"

"Seems kind of foolish, but it ain't."

"I didn't even stop to change my dress, I was so afraid something would happen. I've still got my apron on."

"You're all set to start housekeeping, then."

"It's going to be wonderful having my own things. Wait till you see the curtains. You haven't been in the house since I put them up."

"No," he said, "I haven't been there since I moved in the furniture. That was last month."

She took his arm and skipped a few steps. "I'm awfully happy, darling."

Amos could see their house beyond the row of trees that lined the wall. It seemed to hug the ground. The new shingles on the walls were a clean sand color and the green shingles of the roof made a pleasant contrast against the blue sky. Over the ridge was the granite summit of Quartz Mountain.

They walked toward the house through the barway and along the path made by their feet that summer and by the lumber truck crushing down the sweet fern and hardhack bushes. The path had a new look, and there were board ends around the house, and the brush pile in front from the trees and bushes he'd cut in the cellar hole. The leaves were faded brown and drooping on the twigs. It all looked raw and new to Amos, but he'd clean it up and in time the house would appear as much a part of the landscape as the old granite foundations under it.

He opened the door for Joan. He would not let himself think about that door. He went in and set the groceries on the natural-finish pine table Joan had bought. She looked about her with a little sigh and took the suitcase to the far corner of the room where the bed had been set up. She came back, making a little dance step as she smiled at him and threw her arms around his neck.

"Our house, Amos," she whispered. "Our house." And she kissed him.

He saw that there were tears in her eyes.

She hid her face on his chest. "I'm an awful sap. I'm so happy I have to cry." She wiped her eyes with her knuckles and burst out laughing while the tears still came to her eyes.

"Darling," she said, "build me a fire. See, I've brought in wood." She pointed to a box of board ends beside the stove. "You didn't want them, did you?"

"No, they'll make a good fire to take the chill off. I'll haul out some real wood in a day or two, from the woodlot. Cut last winter—dry birch and maple."

He built a fire of shavings and shingle trimmings and added the board ends.

"It draws good," he said, adjusting the drafts and listening to the crackle of the fire. He could smell the heating newness of the stove, a faintly acrid odor of hot new iron.

"Now," Joan said, "you sit down and I'll make you a cup of coffee."

He pulled out the bench which went with the kitchen table and looked past the pink and white curtains at the valley and the long ridge of Cobblestone. In the fading light there was a purple cast to the sky and a single star shone brightly above the mountain.

He turned to Joan and watched her rummage in the box of groceries, setting out flour and sugar and a slice of ham and coffee and eggs.

"What will you use for water?" he asked.

She looked at him in surprise. "I hadn't thought."

"You still have faucets and city plumbing in your mind."

"Well, not really. I bought two pails. So there. I carried water from the brook when I mopped the floor."

He got up and went to the corner beside the kitchen cabinet where two pails were lined carefully along the wall under the pots and pans which Joan had hung by nails to the bare studding.

"Not that one," she said. "I mopped with that one."

He took the other pail and went to the door. "There's a spring nearer than the brook. I'll show you. Bring a cup."

They went out into the cool twilight. She held his hand as he led the way down the slope in front of the house. He said, "It's over by that clump of birches."

The pool of water lay in a hollow below a ledge. He knelt, and using the cup, dipped a pail full without disturbing the silt on the bottom of the spring. He held the cup to her. "Try it. It's cold."

He felt that they were very alone in the old pasture below the house. He stood near her while she drank the water. He could hear the little brook in the valley. There were more stars in the sky now, and as they went back to the house, the ground was dark, and the sky in the west fading into night.

The house was warm and shadowed.

"I have a lamp here," Joan said. She didn't move away from him.

"Never mind. I don't know's I care about any light now, or coffee."

"I don't either."

# Chapter 30

There was a touch of frost on the grass as Amos started toward the farm the next morning. He turned to look at Joan in the doorway, still in her nightgown, arms folded across her breasts against the cold. She waved and closed the door. He saw the curtain at the window move and he smiled at the image of her face. With an exulting pressure in his heart, he took a deep breath and stepped out toward the farm to help Mort with the chores.

The sharp air caught in his lungs and the freshness of the morning was all around him. He strode along the dirt road, looking at the fields and hills. He felt so glad to be alive that he wanted to laugh and run. Strength seemed to flow through him like a flooding river. His mind was full of the warmth of sleeping with Joan, while his thoughts raced with plans for finishing the inside of the house, adding a porch, and laying a pipe to the spring. With a hand pump at the sink, Joan could have water. He'd better do that soon, before the ground froze. The inside work could wait until winter.

He was ahead of Mort at the barn and he set about the chores alone. He fed the cattle and the horses and cleaned out, thinking it strange that Mort was sleeping so late. Usually Mort was awake before daylight. He started to milk, while a growing fear came to him. Finally he finished stripping the last cow and went to the barn floor, carrying the pail, and then abruptly walked toward the house.

Gram was starting the fire in the stove. Pa washed at the sink.

"Where's Mort?"

"Ain't he out to the barn?" Gram stood there with the stove lifter in her hand and looked at Amos.

"No."

Pa stared at him over the towel with which he was wiping his face. "Likely he's still asleep."

Amos set down the milk pail and went into the hall. The door of the little bedroom was closed. Not knowing what he'd find, hoping it would be Mort asleep in bed, but afraid he wouldn't be—not asleep —if he were in bed, Amos opened the door. The bed had not been slept in. Mort's work clothes were on the chair. Amos lifted aside the curtain to the little closet. Mort's black suit and shoes were gone.

Amos returned to the kitchen while his world fell away from him and he had the sickening feeling that everything had been too good, too right. He knew again the guilt of having left Mort alone. And then his mind began to work on the practical side, considering what Mort would do, where he'd go, in his best suit.

"He's gone," Amos said. "Put on his church suit."

"I don't understand it," Gram murmured, almost to herself. "I can't understand it." She looked at Pa. "He was all right last night after Amos left, wa'n't he, Warren?"

"Yes, like he used to be." Pa stood in an attitude of distress and ineffectuality, passing his forefinger over his moustache while his eyes became tired and bewildered. "We played a game of checkers like we used to do."

Amos asked thoughtfully, "You suppose he had some notion of visiting Rose or something—putting on his suit and all?"

"Probably headed for the village, anyhow," Pa said. "Likely that's it."

Amos went to the telephone on the wall. He rang up the Hostetters. Marvin hadn't seen Mort go by. Amos thanked him and rang Central. He made several calls, to the station, to Cy Tillman, to Mrs. Hardy, to Jake Whicher. Nobody had seen Mort. He turned from the phone at last, shaking his head.

"He ain't in the village. One of them would have seen him."

Pa said, "Maybe ain't got there yet."

"If he'd headed that way, the Hostetters would have seen him." Thinking of the places around the farm where Mort might have gone, he walked to the door. "I'll go have a look in the cemetery and then over at the pool."

He saw that Pa and Gram knew what he meant, Pa sitting in the rocker staring at the floor and Gram watching him closely. He tried to reassure them. "Expect I'll find him easy enough. Expect he's all right." He went outside.

Walking down the road, the thought came to him that Mort must have been planning something the day before, because he'd shaved and cleaned up. He'd likely been thinking of it then. The suit was part of it—the suit didn't mean traveling to Mort. It meant church and weddings and funerals. They were wrong to think that it meant travel to Mort. He had never been anywhere.

Amos stopped at the new house to tell Joan. She was dressed and getting his breakfast. He took the coffee she poured for him.

"I can't stay to eat," he said.

[ 223 ]

"You ought to have something."

"Couldn't."

She said, "You mustn't blame yourself, darling."

"I don't know's I do, come right down to it. I can't watch him all my life—all ours. But I don't feel good." He put down the coffee cup. "You'll go stay with Pa and Gram?"

"I'll start over now."

"That would help."

"I could go with you to the cemetery first."

"No," he said. "There's no telling what I'll find."

They went to the road together and parted. Amos turned to the right and walked toward the little cemetery beyond the new house. Looking back, he saw Joan hurrying along the road in the direction of the farm.

He climbed up the short bank and opened the gate in the wall. He could feel the sun warm on his neck. It shone on the headstones and the sparse grass and moss and blueberry bushes and on the faded leaves and dead petals of the wild pinks. It shone on the black suit Mort wore. Amos saw the black-clad legs and the open black coat and the bloodstained shirt of the figure lying in the grass. He ran forward, heavy footed and stumbling, and then he saw there was no need to run. Mort had cut his throat. The open straight razor lay near him.

Amos understood that he had intended to do it all along. He had said, "Someday I'll have to find out." Now perhaps he was happy in his final knowledge of his God.

But Amos could only think of Mort getting up from the bed in the little room at home—the bed in which he had not slept, perhaps only sitting there with his head in his hands—and putting on his best clothes, not to travel the earth but to meet the Lord. Shaving that afternoon for the same reason, the razor at his throat giving him the thought of the means to use. Not saying anything out of the way. Playing checkers with Pa. Wanting them to think of him as he had once been.

And Amos could see him walking down the road in the dark to the cemetery, past the new house where he and Joan lay in each other's arms, walking past to the cemetery where Ma and Whicher were buried, and the other Jackmans. If Amos had only known, if he could have done something, if Mort had only come to the house. It was terrible to think of Mort passing so near him in the night. Had Mort wanted him? Hoping to talk to him but finding the house dark, had he walked on to the graveyard? Amos told himself that Mort was bent on his own plan, probably didn't think of his younger brother except

[ 224 ]

to hope that he wasn't awake. For hadn't Mort been planning his death since afternoon? Amos knew this but he could not put away the feeling that he had failed to be ready when Mort needed him.

He passed his hand over his face and felt the tight muscles of his jaw. He looked across the stone wall at the mountains where the trees were turning yellow and orange and red. Words formed on his lips. "Maybe he's better off. And yet it don't seem right a man should be driven so."

He took off his denim jacket and spread it over Mort's face and chest. Turning to the gate, he walked back to the road and on toward the farm. It looked small and lonely to him now, the fields barren and the mountains and forest overpowering around the old buildings. He didn't know what to say to Pa and Gram. He walked slowly toward the door. They came out with Joan.

Pa asked, "Did you find him?"

Amos nodded. There was no gentle way to tell them. He said harshly, "He killed himself. In the cemetery."

"How could he?" Pa cried. "How could he? He was all right."

For a moment Gram said nothing, but stood on the doorstep with her apron raised in her hands as though she might lift it to her face, and then she let it drop. "Poor boy. Poor soul."

Amos led his father into the house and made him lie down on the couch. Gram handed him the medicine and his father took it meekly, dazed, and kept asking, "Why, Amos, why?"

Amos said, "He wanted to find the Lord." Realizing that sounded impossible, he added, "Mort told me the night we found him at the pool." He hesitated, at a loss for words, while he thought of Mort saying, 'I love Him and want to be with Him. And then I don't know.'

"Go on, Amos," Gram said.

"Well, he loved God, but he wa'n't sure because of things like Ma and Whicher getting killed, and he had to find out, one way or another. It bothered him, and he'd think he had it figured out and be all right, then he wa'n't sure. So he had to find out."

Gram was crying silently, her face toward the window. "If we had got the minister to explain to him again. . . ."

Amos interrupted her. "It don't appear to me anyone could tell him what he had to know."

He felt that there was no sense talking about it, but Pa kept on.

"Why did he do it? That ain't reason enough, Amos."

"Reason enough for Mort," Amos said. He watched Joan go to Gram and put her arm around the trembling shoulder and move Gram to a chair by the couch. Joan sat down on the edge of the couch.

Amos went to the phone. "I'll call Doc Parsons and then go back to the cemetery."

## Chapter 31

There was a branch of orange leaves near the church window. Amos watched it and it seemed to reassure him about the world outside the church. He could hear the minister's voice and he could feel the presence of his family, sitting like himself in the hard pew—Joan beside him, Rose beyond Pa and Gram, and Pete beyond her, and the friends and neighbors who had come to Mort's funeral. Mort lay in the coffin before the simple altar, his big features in repose.

"It is not for us to judge him," the minister was saying, "without compassion in our hearts. His were compulsions which we find hard to understand, but let us realize that he was in his way devoted to God beyond the capacity of most men."

Amos could feel the people behind him in the little unadorned church. He looked past the minister in his gown and past the coffin and the flowers in formal array, again to the window and the colored leaves that moved in the sunlight as a breeze touched them. The minister's voice went on and Amos scarcely heard. He was thinking of his older brother through all the years when they were growing up, through all the days they had shared, and he felt there was nothing to be said in comfort or justification for either the living or the dead. He wished the ceremony were over. He stared at the floor in front of him.

And then they were carrying out the closed coffin, he and Jake and Pete and Marvin, while the undertaker and his helper directed them. He thought of the other times he had performed this same office, with Mort then and Whicher in the coffin—Ma in the coffin.

They drove slowly behind the hearse to Whichertown. It was a clear and sunny day under the blue sky as they slid the coffin from the hearse and carried it through the gate to the waiting grave. The minister stood bareheaded beside the earth and spoke the service. Pa's eyes did not move from the grave and coffin. Pa could not yet quite believe it, Amos thought. It should be a familiar pain to him, for Pa had seen his father buried there and his wife and two sons. Amos wondered if Pa felt, as he did, that the family was draining away into the earth of Whichertown. He looked beyond the wall at the woods.

He waited in the cemetery for a time, although there was no reason to, after the service. Rose and Pete were taking care of Pa and driving him with Gram to the farm; cars were moving up the road to turn at the house, the long black hearse coming back, and he could not bring himself to leave at once. And then he couldn't stay any longer and walked down the road past the new house to the farm and under the red-tinted leaves of the maple to the kitchen door.

Rose, very citified in her black dress and trim hat, pretty in a different way, was saying, "Why don't you come, Pa? We've got an extra room, and it would be a change."

"I don't know. I might." Pa's face was grief worn and he looked small in his wrinkled dark suit.

Gram had taken off her hat, but she still wore the gray dress with the narrow strip of lace at her neck. In the farm kitchen it looked out of place to Amos. Pete stood by the window, tall and unobtrusive, awkward.

"Yes," Pete said. "Do you good, Pa."

Amos almost expected to see Mort there by the window, but it was Pete, asking Pa to come visit them. Amos thought perhaps they were right, it would do Pa good, keep him from brooding. If Pa was well and could work, that would be better, but now he'd only sit and think or do light chores around that didn't amount to much, and think.

"Maybe I'll go," Pa said.

Gram seemed to be waiting for him to set his mind on going. Then she spoke up in her abrupt way, "All right, I'll go visit Nance Hardy. We haven't had a good visit in a long time. No need of my staying here."

She looked at Amos. He nodded. "Joan and I can look after the place."

It was easy to say, but a little time passed before he realized that he and Joan would be alone on the farm. The strangeness, the suddenness of the new pattern made him feel alone for a moment. He had been used to thinking of the farm and Pa and Gram and Whicher and Mort—yes, still thought of it with Ma. Just himself and Joan on the farm, alone in Whichertown. He had not grown accustomed to Mort gone, and now this was more than he could accept all at once, but he'd do it. He would have the work now anyway. He could do it.

He looked toward Joan. She sat at the table, somehow apart from the family, silent and waiting. She didn't say anything, but glanced from one to another of them. Amos wondered what she thought about this change. With her folks gone, perhaps she would feel deserted. The cards and letters from her folks in far places must give her little comfort. He wanted to tell her that he and she would be all right. Together they always got along. But she must understand that herself. He sat down beside her.

Rose said, "You don't have to decide now, Pa. I'll stay on till Sunday and Pete will come get us then. He has to drive back tonight."

For Amos there was an unreality in the way life continued on, and people went their ways and about their business, planning for the future as though there was nothing final to them about the grave in which they had buried Mort. It seemed to him that there should be an interim of suspension from ordinary living, but then he realized that he himself was thinking ahead. Nothing stopped because a man died—or killed himself after walking past his brother's house in the dark to the cemetery. Soon chore time would come around, just as it had every other day.

He stood up. "I'll be going back to the house. Got to put on my old clothes for the chores."

He and Joan went out together. They started down the road toward their house.

"There wasn't any need for me to stay, was there, Amos?"

"No."

"I thought they'd rather be together without me—the family, I mean."

"You're family, now."

"Yes, but not the same."

"Well, new."

She said quietly, "Your father's taking it so hard, Amos."

"His son killed himself."

"Yes, but he doesn't seem to understand."

Amos tried to express what Pa must feel. "I think he figures he made a mistake somewhere along the way, raising Mort. I guess he thinks he failed or didn't do just right by Mort."

"He shouldn't."

"Well, he seems to." They walked on in silence until he said, "Will you mind being alone here?"

"I don't think so. I love you, Amos." She hesitated, looking about her at the empty fields and the mountains. "It's lots of space and no people, isn't it, Amos?"

"I suppose so. I'm used to it more, but I never been here without someone at the farm."

He didn't look past the new house toward the cemetery, for it would be deserted now and the mound of fresh earth lonely against the surrounding woods.

The little house was warmed by the sun through the windows. He stood in the single big room after he had closed the door and for a while he shut out all the grief and pain he had felt, shut out his family and his dead brother and the farm, in the warm, late-sunlit room with its new stove shining and the enameled sink and the cabinet, the pink and white curtains framing the mountains under the blue sky. He turned to the far end of the room where his clothes hung on nails against the new boards.

Joan had taken off her shoes and was pulling her dress over her head. He hung his coat on a nail and unbuttoned his shirt. He untied his low black shoes. Knowing that he had come here to change into work clothes for doing the chores at the barn, he still couldn't bring the past minutes and hours back to him with any meaning. They remained beyond the door of the little house. And yet they were a part of him, for he had a pressing sense of time, time that would not release him, and living that was not forever.

"Joan," he said, and went to her and took her in his arms.

Questioning him with her eyes at first, she then turned her lips to him, the soft-firm, yielding, seeking lips for which he longed now with a passion that obscured his thoughts.

"Amos, Amos," she whispered and he didn't know what he answered in his urgent need for her.

Later, he slept for a moment beside her, then awoke almost at once, back to himself and the world he had left.

They got up and dressed. Joan, at the mirror, asked, "Shall I go back to the farm with you?"

"I think so. I think Pa and Gram would like it."

"All right." Joan put a green jacket over her blouse and skirt.

On the road to the farm, they met Pete driving away. He stopped the car.

"I'll be back Sunday, Amos, to get Rose and your pa."

"Appreciate your taking him, Pete. It'll do him good."

"Well, I hope so. He's welcome to stay as long as he wants."

"It may be quite a spell, if he don't want to come back right off."

"That's all right." Pete nodded and drove off.

Amos was left with a vague sense of the outside world which he had visited when he went to see Joan in Braemuir, a suggestion that Whichertown wasn't the universe. But it passed as they continued along the road. He felt close to Joan and not alone. He thought of the baby she was carrying and it seemed to mean they had a future beyond their own lives. It seemed to place them in the stream of life. He thought about the baby, wondering if it would be a boy or girl. He would like a boy, but that didn't seem as important as the fact the baby was living and growing, because of them, in Joan's womb.

# PART III

*Chapter* 32

From the barn door, Amos looked across the valley to the slopes of Quartz Mountain and Cobblestone where now, in the second week of October, the hardwood trees had all turned color. The ridges were flame red and yellow and orange-gold under the early morning sun. He felt restless with the crisp air of the hills in his nose. He smelled the tangy woods as the breeze lifted from the valley.

The hound Drum had been baying at the end of his chain that morning as Amos came along the road from the new house to the barn. He was accustomed to the walk alone now in the mornings, but at first after Pa and Gram had gone, it had been strange to see the blank windows of the house. All his life there had been lamp light in the windows when he was up early, or smoke rising from the chimney. The barn had seemed empty without Pa or Mort or Whicher, and the cattle somehow left behind as though they stayed on at the farm but did not quite belong there. He cared for them and did the milking and fed the horses and chickens and pigs, but they were not connected with the little house down the road where he lived with Joan. He couldn't understand the way he felt about them, yet he realized he'd had enough of them. He was tired of the farm and farming. Perhaps, he told himself, he needed a change.

Abruptly he left the barn door and walked to the kennel by the barn-yard wall. Drum stood up and wagged his tail and raised his muzzle, great ears drooping as he bayed excitedly. Amos unsnapped the chain, and the black and tan hound was gone across the road and into the field, nose on the ground, working back and forth through the stubble.

Amos moved quickly to the house and opened the unlocked door. Already there was a deserted look about the kitchen and a closed stuffi-ness in the air. He went to the closet and got his double-barreled shot-gun. Reaching for the box of shells on the shelf, he remembered Mort and the day he had seen Mort on the edge of the corn field with the shotgun. He went back to the barn and climbed into the mow and took a handful of shells from the box under the hay.

As he went outside again into the clear air and sunlight, he thought of Joan and he realized he had almost set out after Drum without telling her. He started down the road, while Drum's baying suddenly echoed across the hills. It stirred Amos' blood and made his heart beat faster. It came again from the valley. Drum had found a fox track. Amos hurried on at a trot toward the new house.

Joan met him at the door. "I saw you coming down the road. What's the gun for?"

"Drum has a fox track down there. I'm going after him."

"But you haven't had your breakfast."

"Well, that's so." He looked at her, thinking of leaving her alone. "Would you want to come?"

"Yes, but I haven't had my coffee. I've been waiting for you."

He laughed then. "I guess there ain't any great rush." He leaned the shotgun against the house. "Drum's working out the cold trail. Take him a while. We can eat before he starts the fox."

He didn't feel very hungry and he kept listening for the sound of Drum's baying beyond the open door. He ate the bacon and eggs, and the toast Joan made in a wire toaster on the stove. He drank his coffee and went to the door.

"Drum's working along the valley. He'll jump the fox soon. We better get over on the ridge. Come on."

"I haven't done the dishes." She glanced at the table and sink, undecided and amused. "Well, it doesn't matter."

She took off her apron and got her green jacket. She was wearing dungarees and moccasins and a white blouse. He waited impatiently until she joined him outside the house. Then he started down the hill into the valley.

They passed the hole where Whicher had shot the woodchuck. Amos climbed over the wall into the woods, and turned, remembering Joan, to help her over. He could hear Drum baying in the cut-over slash to the north. In his mind there were two stands he might take on the hardwood ridge. One was by a beech tree at the head of a little valley through which trickled one of the tributaries to the stream they were now crossing. The other stand was by an overhanging ledge farther up the ridge. He wouldn't be sure which to take until Drum started the fox. And the wind. In the morning the wind would be uphill.

Joan couldn't quite step across the brook and one moccasined foot went into the moist earth and leaves.

"Never mind," she said, and followed him.

He led the way on through the hardwoods whose leaves made a red and gold ceiling over them, penetrated by the sunlight above. The bushes around them were yellow, and fallen leaves rustled underfoot. He felt the blood-pumping excitement of the hunt and tried not to walk too fast for Joan. Drum's voice was a distant, intermittent baying to the north. They were climbing steadily up a short ridge, part of the broad slope of Cobblestone. He paused at the top, and Joan came up beside him. She was breathing rapidly.

"All right?" he asked.

She nodded.

He noticed a change in Drum's baying. "There, listen! Hear him?" The hound's voice shifted in pitch and frequency, echo-waking and excited, a steady belling cry. "He's jumped the fox. They're headed back this way."

Amos strode down into the ravine, dodging bushes and rocks until he came to the big beech whose smooth trunk lifted up into the yellow leaves. There was a clear place under the great tree, covered by crisp leaves fallen the year before, and twigs cut off by feeding coons, and beech nuts in bristly husks on the leaves. Beyond it the stream trickled down the slope into a stand of smaller beeches and yellow birches. Amos could see clearly the full range of the shotgun. He moved in front of the gray trunk.

Pointing to the hollow of moss between the roots, he told Joan, "You better sit down."

She rested her back against the tree and pushed up her hair.

"Don't move," he said.

He took a step away from the tree. Waiting, he thought of the fox track which Drum had followed. The fox had been hunting through the night and in the early morning hours must have passed through the field below the barn where Drum picked up the trail. Then the fox had wandered through the spruces along the brook and over into the slash, trotting back and forth and weaving an intricate pattern of tracks as he hunted field mice and moles in the grass of the logging roads or stalked rabbits in the brush piles. Going on toward the cellar holes of Whichertown in the second growth woods and berry bushes, perhaps there the fox first became aware of the hound and turned to trot away toward the upper slopes of Cobblestone, loping for a distance until the slow and noisy hound had been left behind, baying on the hot scent. Now the fox would be moving like a red shadow through the golden woods toward the valley where Amos waited.

Drum's baying came closer and closer until it seemed to fill the woods with its clamor. Amos raised the shotgun to his shoulder and thumbed forward the safety catch, ready.

He first saw the fox as a flicker of red below him in the ravine. He waited and the fox appeared again, coming straight up the slope toward him, bushy tail flowing behind. He sighted along the gun barrels and followed the fox with a steady motion which would be imperceptible. He made no sudden move but stood quiet as the fox came straight on. He could feel his heart pounding. Joan must keep still. Any abrupt move would send the fox away like a red flash among the bushes. He could see the pointed ears and floating gait of the fox, as though it didn't touch the ground, but he could hear the paws in the leaves. He sighted carefully on the black nose of the fox and pulled the trigger.

The gun roared against his shoulder. The fox rolled in the leaves. With legs clawing it gained its feet and, belly low, tried to crawl away. Amos fired again. The fox kicked and lay still. He ran forward and stood over the bundle of red fur. It was quite dead and the mouth was open showing the sharp little teeth. Amos picked up the carcass by a hind leg and turned grinning to Joan.

"I guess you bring me luck," he said. "You'll have to come with me every time."

She was standing halfway between him and the beech. She held her clenched hands at her sides and looked at the fox. Then she raised her eyes.

"He was so beautiful, Amos," she said. "How could you kill him?"

Amos looked at her in amazement. At last he replied, "It's the easiest way I know to make a few dollars."

Drum came along the trail, baying wildly until he stopped and nosed the fox. He lost interest almost at once. Tongue out, he turned brown eyes to Amos a moment before he trotted off through the woods. His great voice silent, he disappeared with his nose on the ground and ears brushing the leaves.

Joan turned away and Amos could see that she didn't want to look at the fox or touch it.

"We might as well go home," he said.

The excitement of the hunt was gone and the exhilaration had subsided. He realized how much he had counted on her enjoying the hunt and admiring the fox. He had been pleased to be successful so easily. She might have followed him all day from stand to stand, waiting in the woods while the fox slipped past them or holed up in the ledges at the top of the ridge. Instead, this had been a hunt to remember, yet she had only looked at the fox and said, "He was so beautiful, how could you kill him?" She made him feel he had done something wrong.

"We might as well go back to the house," he said again.

They returned in silence, Amos leading the way back as they had come, down the ridge and across the brook and into the open pasture below their house.

At the door, he said, "Maybe you'll feel different after I've skinned him out. Maybe you'd want a little coat. I can get quite a few this fall and winter, better pelts when they're real prime."

"I wouldn't wear the poor thing's fur."

"All right, but I've hunted foxes since I was old enough. They're extra cash. They're part of my living."

"I don't care," she said. "We don't need the money."

He looked at her coldly, knowing that her feelings about killing animals would never change. "I still figure to make a dollar when I can. Besides, I like to hunt."

"Go ahead then."

"I will."

He turned away and put the carcass of the fox in the shed behind the house. He could hear Drum baying again far up on Cobblestone. Without a glance behind him he strode off down the hill.

Walking rapidly, he was soon among the trees and climbing fast. His anger died in him with action, leaving an empty urge to press on and on toward the upper slopes of the mountain. At last he stopped to listen. He could not hear the hound. The chase must have gone over the ridge. In other years he would have followed, and sometime late in the afternoon would have shot the fox in the spruce forest beyond the mountain, where, if the day were too far gone to return to the farm, he could spend the night in his camp on the pond.

But now there was Joan—the chores and Joan. Thinking about other hunts when he had been free of responsibility, he tried to recapture some of the feeling of patient ease which had always come over him when he was in the woods. He tried to forget Joan.

The desire to follow the hound and the powerful call of the hunt gradually returned to him. He hurried on up the slope until the yellow birches and maples changed to spruces high on the ridge and he could hear Drum again.

He stood on a ledge among the spruces and looked out to the east over the forest which stretched to the edge of the sky. He could see one end of the pond in front of his camp. He remembered standing with Joan on a similar ledge over on Quartz Mountain, when she had been overwhelmed by the extent of the woods. He thought of her and listened to the baying of the hound faraway, toward the spruce swamp. He wanted to go after the fox, but in his mind he saw Joan alone in their house, alone in Whichertown.

He stayed for a long time on the ledge, thinking and listening to Drum's baying. He knew that he should start home, but the more he waited, the clearer became his vision of the chase below him. If he judged the sound of Drum's voice right, the fox was trotting along ahead of the hound on the edge of the spruce swamp, circling back again and again on the same hardwood ridge. He knew the country and he could see the spot he'd pick to wait, where the ridge fell away into the swamp. The fox wouldn't go into the water but would leap across the dry hummocks among the spruces.

He glanced at the sun overhead. There would be time. Joan could wait for him a little longer.

Yet he felt guilty as he plunged down over the rough ledges and gained the woods below where he trotted downhill fast, dodging spruce tangles and rocks. He came at last to level ground and a scattering of hardwoods, yellow among the spruces. He stopped to catch his breath and rest his legs. Listening for Drum, he was aware of the blood pounding in his ears. The baying came to him faintly in the maze of ridges.

He strode on until he saw water ahead of him through the spruces, narrow pools under the green boughs. He turned north around the edge of the swamp and, when he saw a rise of ground ahead of him, stopped in front of a rock and waited.

Nervous and anxious, wishing he felt the quiet patience with which he used to keep a stand, he waited while Drum's baying came nearer, muffled a little behind the ridge. Not until the sound had passed on his left would he admit that the fox had gone around him. And the fox did not return. Time slipped by while he tried to control his counting of the minutes. Drum had followed the fox out of hearing.

Now he began to feel he had to shoot the fox to justify staying away from home so long. Not that Joan wanted it, but for himself.

He followed the hunt north around the swamp. Twice more he waited and the fox passed out of range, as he could tell by Drum's voice. The day was well into the afternoon and he was hungry and worried about Joan but he wouldn't give up. Perhaps he was moving too often. The next time, he'd say put. He'd pick one more stand on the fox's circle, and wait and wait. The mere act of waiting might deceive the fox, for the scent of a man seemed to die down as he stood motionless for a long period.

Amos chose an opening in the woods where he could lean against a slanting birch.

But he hadn't the patience. He kept thinking of Joan and of the farm until the conflict within him grew too strong and with an abrupt snapping of tension, he stepped away from the tree. He would go home. He had to. The sun was down and he couldn't stay any longer. His motion seemed to break the charm of the woods around him and changed him from a silent spectator of the trees and little birds and squirrels to an intruder walking through the woods.

And then he saw the fox leap off between the trees like a floating red shadow.

If he had waited a minute or two more, if there hadn't been the need to return to Joan and the chores, he would have shot the fox and brought the hunt to its proper conclusion. He knew his failure was not her fault, but he couldn't help resenting her and resenting the circumstances which put him in charge of the farm.

With a sick and weary disappointment, he began to climb the ridge of Cobblestone. He did not try to pick up Drum. The hound would stay with the fox until it holed up or laid a trail too difficult to follow. Drum would stay with the fox, just as he used to do. Drum didn't have a wife back in Whichertown, nor a farm and stock to look after. There was only the trail scent in his nose and the fox ahead, for Drum.

The sun was almost down as Amos climbed the pasture toward the little house. It did not appear as it had in the morning—almost like another day—for the sun was in his eyes now instead of behind his back and it threw the house shadow toward him and made the chimney smoke misty and the sumacs near the road blood red. His legs were tired and the shotgun weighed down his arm. He saw the Ford in the barway. He took the shells from his gun as he came to the door and went inside.

Joan looked up from the big chair in the part of the house which was to be the living room. She had on a yellow dress and silk stockings on legs curled under her. She held a book.

"Hello, darling," she said, and the "darling" was a term that didn't mean much.

"Where've you been?" he asked.

"Oh, here and there. Down to the village where I bought a lot of things we don't need."

He glanced at the pile of canned foods on the table, cookies and candy and magazines.

"I've had a lovely time," she continued. "After the shopping, I went to the lodge and played records all by myself and drank Dad's whiskey and got out all my old books." She laughed and held up one book after another and read the titles, *Deerslayer, The Covered Wagon, Riders of the Purple Sage, Tales of the Rocky Mountain Trappers.*

"I suppose none of them ever shot foxes?"

"Oh, yes, and buffalo, and ate the livers with gunpowder. Very bloody. I've had a delightful time. I'm a little tight." She pointed at the kitchen cabinet. "Have a drink. Dad won't mind—he's got half a case in the cellar of the lodge. Dad's chasing all over the world seeing strange and wonderful places. He won't mind. It'll do you good."

"Won't hurt me none," Amos said, and feeling like a stranger in his own house, he went to the cabinet and poured himself a drink.

Joan asked, "Did you get the second beautiful fox?"

"No."

"I'd hoped you'd bring me another."

He drank the whiskey. "I'm going down to the barn."

He went out and got the fox carcass from the shed. Walking down the road with the fox over his shoulder, he realized that he felt cheated because Joan had not acted as he thought she would while he was gone. Instead of remaining alone there in the house while he hunted the fox, she had gone driving around town and enjoying herself at the lodge. He need not have worried his head about her. He felt that she did not need him, that she could have a life of her own without him. It was a new sensation.

He could feel the whiskey warm inside and yet it did not relax him. At the barn, he hung up the fox and skinned out the pelt and stretched it while there was daylight. Then he went about the chores methodically, aware of the tension within him. He understood that the pattern of his life seemed to be shifting into forms that he could not understand.

The cows had been waiting in the barnyard and he let them into the barn where they took their places in the tie-up as he went along the row fastening their chains. He grained them and the horses, and set about his milking. He was drying up two of the cows; soon he'd have two less to milk. He thought ahead toward the fall and winter. He might as well forget about fox hunting. He could not go through the feelings of today again, nor could he leave Joan if he had to worry about where she was and what she was doing. With a sense of loss and disappointment, he forced himself to put aside all thoughts of the days on the hills with Drum.

There was cord wood to haul and after that he could start to get out some pine logs. He did not look forward to the winter. The farm and Joan seemed to own him now and he could feel his independence slip-

ping away from him. But he would go deer hunting. They needed the
meat. Next month he would go. That was necessary. But abruptly he
realized that with Joan's money they could buy a side of beef if they
wanted to. It wasn't important to shoot a deer, as it had been other years.
He thought of butchering the hogs later on. How would Joan feel about
that? Perhaps he might as well sell them. And the steer he had been
raising. He and Joan could never eat the meat of two pigs and a steer,
even if Joan would consider the idea. He had the feeling she wouldn't
want to eat the animals they had raised. He could sell the steer.

When he had finished milking, he strained the milk and put it in the
cooler. There would be ice to cut alone this winter on Pout Pond. Then
he got down the hay for the cows, working by the light of a lantern hung
in the barn door. He mixed the slop for the pigs, filled a pail of mash for
the hens, and went to the pigpen in the barnyard where the two white
pigs grunted and rooted at their trough. He moved on to the hen house.
The hens had gone to roost, but he dumped mash in the hopper anyway
and threw a few handfuls of grain on the floor. He collected the eggs in
the empty pail.

As he went out, he passed Drum's kennel and saw the hound lying
beside it licking his paw. Amos knelt and held the paw gently but
found no cut or thorn. It must be merely sore from the first run—and
last run—of the fall. He felt a cut on the edge of one of the long ears
where it had snagged in the brush. It had stopped bleeding and would
heal. Both soft ears were scarred on the ends. Amos went to the barn and
mixed a pan of mash and filled another with water at the trough. Taking
them to the kennel, he snapped Drum's chain to his collar.

The chores done, he took a two-quart can of milk from the milk room,
and eggs in a split-ash basket. He shut the barn door. He never used to
shut the door until cold weather. One of the barn cats came up to him and
rubbed against his legs. He opened the door and poured milk into a
pan on the floor. Another black and white cat came from the shadows
and joined the first one at the pan. He went out and closed the door
behind him.

The moon was rising over the ridge of Cobblestone, big and yellow.
He walked along the road in the cool air, without really looking forward
to his return to the little house.

When he went inside, he found that Joan had changed her dress for
dungarees and blouse. She was getting supper. He set the eggs and
the can of milk in the icebox. He blew out the lantern. Joan came toward
him.

"I'm sorry about today, Amos." She stood looking at him, her face soft in the lamp light. "I don't know what was the matter with me. I want you to go hunting and shoot lots of foxes."

"Well," he said, "it's not something I have to do."

He knew he wouldn't go, but he was pleased that she was trying to be good, and he kissed her.

"See," she said. "I've made you a nice supper. I haven't started the steak —I was waiting for you—but there's mashed potatoes and shell beans and tomato salad. And a cake. I baked a cake. Would you like a drink?"

"Yes."

"I bought some oranges and lemons. I'll make you an old-fashioned."

"I never had one."

"They're good. Lots of whiskey."

He sat down and watched her at the kitchen cabinet. He was happy to be with her, but he was aware that somehow she appeared different. He was aware for the first time in a long while that his wife did not understand things or react to them as he did or as a girl from Whicher-town, like Rose, would. She had fitted herself so easily into the life of the farm that he had almost forgotten what she was. Except for her tiffs with Gram there had been almost nothing to remind him that she was a Tarlton, brought up different and thinking different. Now as she came to him with the glass of ice and fruit sections and amber whiskey, he saw her new after the past months.

She brought her glass and sat down on his lap. "There," she said. "Isn't this cozy? Drink up and we'll have another before I cook the steak. Isn't it good? You can suck the orange and lemon slices, if you want, and eat the cherry."

He sat in the big comfortable chair with Joan on his lap, her firm legs against his and her warm fragrance around him, and drank the whiskey and felt he was very lucky, for he might be alone on the farm, or he might be looking after Gram and Pa, sitting with them in the kitchen of the farmhouse and thinking about Mort and Whicher.

## Chapter 33

Amos did not go fox hunting again. Instead he hauled out wood which he had cut the winter before, from the woodlot, using a drag and the front wheels of the dump cart. He found that he was unaccountably lazy and slow about the work. Often he wouldn't finish the chores until mid-morning. There was no real reason for getting up at daybreak. It was pleasant to lie in bed with Joan in the morning. The work of the farm had been done, he told himself, and this was an interval between seasons.

The frosts came regularly at night and the leaves were falling. He hauled out eight cords of wood and sawed some of it with the circular saw rig he and Mort had made from an old car engine. Joan helped him for a while, tossing aside the chunks as he pushed the four-foot lengths against the singing saw. She wanted to help, but the work was too heavy for her and he made her stop. He'd ask Jake to help him, or Marvin. But he didn't get around to it, and October passed into November while the late rains set in and whipped the leaves from the trees. The saw rig remained in the yard beside the split wood, a canvas over the engine. There was wood enough for the present and he'd saw the rest of it up sometime. He began to sheathe the inside of the house with wallboard. Rain fell outside, cold and bleak in driving sheets across the valley, obscuring the slopes of Cobblestone.

At last one morning the weather cleared and the sun came out on bare mountains. Through the window near the bed, he could see the twigs of the trees like lacework on the hills and against the sky. The trunks of the birches were white and the distant slopes smoke-blue under a gray sky in which clouds appeared cold and winterlike. The house was cold and they lay in bed, warm under the wool blankets Joan had bought.

"Let's go somewhere today," Joan said. "Let's go to Fallsburg and buy you a suit and me a winter coat. I'll buy a heavy one shaped like a tent." She placed his hand on her belly. "I won't want to be seen much longer. Feel him kick, darling. I think he's going to be awful lively."

"He'll have to be, so's he can help around the farm."

"Do you suppose he'll like it here? He won't have anyone to play with."

"Got all the animals and the woods around."

"Yes, but if he wants to play baseball?"

"I never did."

"No, I suppose not." She looked out the window, turning her head away from him. "That's funny, isn't it? I thought all boys played baseball."

"Some don't," he said, and threw back the blanket to put his feet on the cold floor. He stood up and covered Joan.

She tried to smile at him but there was a little twist to her lips. "You'll have to get some winter pajamas, darling. You look awful funny in that nightshirt."

"It suits me."

[ 241 ]

He went to the stove and scraped around in the cardboard carton they used for a woodbox—he'd have to build a proper one this winter—and found a handful of bark and chips with which to build the fire.

"When shall we start?" she asked.

"I ought to saw up the rest of that wood. Get Marvin to help."

"Oh, Amos, I want to go on a trip. We'll take the beach wagon from the lodge. Dad said we could use it. We'll fill up the tank with gas and do our errands in Fallsburg and then drive to Braemuir and see the house. We'll turn around in the drive and see what it looks like with someone else living there. Then we'll visit Dave."

"Joan, there wouldn't be time. I have to get back for the chores."

"You could hire Marvin to do them."

"Don't think I will. Besides, it'll be noon before we can leave."

"Sometimes I wish you didn't have those damn cows."

" 'Twouldn't be much of a farm without stock." He began to dress. He wasn't sure he wanted to go even as far as Fallsburg. He remembered the last trip and somehow he felt that it had been responsible for Mort trying to drown himself. The idea of leaving the farm still bothered him, although Mort was dead. Nothing could happen to anyone on the farm now in his absence. There wouldn't be anyone, and the cattle could look after themselves. Just the same there was a feeling of guilty neglect conflicting with his obligation to please Joan. He'd go, but it would not be quite right.

And yet he knew he would enjoy the change, just as he had before. It would be pleasant to go to the now familiar hotel with Joan. He'd know how to act in the bar and dining room. He could relax and enjoy himself and forget the farm. And it would be fine to drive the beach wagon, although something in him reacted against taking it because it wasn't his. He couldn't afford to run it, either, and if he smashed it up he'd need years to pay for the damage. But there was Joan's money. She had said, "Fill up the tank with gas." The phrase stuck in his mind. He had never filled up a gas tank in his life. He always bought a few gallons at a time, enough to get from the farm to the village and back.

But they took the beach wagon because Joan insisted, and he didn't protest very much.

They drove north to the end of the Ridge Road instead of through Whichertown, for the beach wagon wouldn't clear the washed-out water bars between the lodge and the corners. They passed the Knapp farm as they turned onto the main road and Amos knew Fred Knapp would see him and think that he was taking over Tarlton property, but he felt the power under the hood of the beach wagon and he didn't care.

At the store in the village, when Cy came out to the gas pumps, Amos managed to say without a lift in his voice, "I guess you better fill her up."

He took out money which was Joan's and paid for the gas. She wanted to go to Fallsburg. It was all right to use her money for the gas.

"Going on a little trip?" Cy asked.

"No, just to Fallsburg."

Cy looked up at the sky closing in behind gathering clouds. "Shouldn't wonder if it snowed before you got back."

"Looks as though."

"Air feels like it." Cy counted out change from the handful he carried in his pocket. "Well, it's due."

Amos nodded and got into the beach wagon. They drove down the street past the Hardys' white cottage.

He thought of Gram. He had stopped to see her the day before when he came to town with the milk. She had looked smaller, not quite the same person who had ruled the kitchen at the farm since his mother's death. She was wearing a second-best dress under an apron and she and Mrs. Hardy were taking a cup of tea at the dining-room table before going to the church to help other Alliance women with preparations for a supper.

"I'm glad you stopped, Amos," she said. "I had a letter from your pa this morning. He wants to sell that flusher. Said you'd know which cow he meant. He wants some money. He's going to pay Rose board and stay on longer."

"All right," Amos agreed. "I had a mind to sell the pigs and steer, too. It's more meat than Joan and me'd eat in a month of Sundays."

"I'll tell him when I answer his letter."

She hadn't said anything about the length of time she'd be staying at the Hardys', but thinking of it now, as he drove past, he felt that she wouldn't be coming back to the farm. He wondered if Pa would come back. Although Pa had lived on the farm all his life, perhaps he was glad to get away, now that he'd gone.

Amos drove on fast down the valley. The slate-colored sky seemed to press down over the purple hills and withered fields. They passed a shanty where coonskins were stretched on the shed wall. He did not point them out to Joan and he wasn't sure she saw them. Snow began to drift down before they reached Fallsburg. It melted on the asphalt of the road but collected on the frozen gravel shoulders. In the streets of the city it shrouded the bricks and pavement and softened the harsh lines of the buildings.

Joan became happily excited. "Isn't it lovely, Amos? I do like a snowstorm in the city. It makes everything so mysterious and new and romantic." She put her hand out the window to feel the snow on her palm. "Will we be able to get back to the farm? Just think, maybe we'll be snowed in on the road and have to take shelter at the nearest farmhouse."

"I'd have to hoof it back to the farm and milk the cows." He eased the beach wagon along the curb and stopped. "No, I guess we'll get back before it amounts to much."

"We'll buy your suit first, before we do anything," Joan said, as they started down the street.

From the window of the men's clothing store, he could see the snow falling. He tried on suits before the triple mirror. The only mirror he ever used was the one over the kitchen sink where he shaved. Now he tried not to study his big features in the mirrors, but he couldn't help it because he kept wondering if that was the way he really looked to people. It wasn't the way he thought of himself. Perhaps the suits made the difference.

Joan sat in a chair by the suit rack. "No," she said, about the blue pin stripe which the clerk had him put on in the little closet. "No, you aren't the type, darling. Try that tweed."

They finally settled on a brown tweed with a nap like a dog's coat. It felt odd and bulky to Amos and didn't have the hard lines and tightness of the blue serge to which he was accustomed. And it cost more money than he'd pay for a cow. He shrugged. Joan liked it.

She wanted him to buy a hat and coat and pajamas, but something in him rebelled. "I don't need them."

"Well, you'll have to get some shoes." She looked at the clerk. "A pair of cordovan brogues," she said. "Don't let him buy anything else." And she wandered off among the counters, while the gray-haired clerk smiled and nodded.

When Amos finished buying the shoes, he found that Joan had assembled coats and hats she liked, with the help of another clerk.

"If you won't buy them," she said, "I'll pick out what you need."

"I don't need them."

"You haven't a felt hat that's decent and your coat must have belonged to Gramp Jackman."

He wished she wouldn't talk like that in front of the clerks and for fear what else she might say, he tried on the coats and hats until she chose one of each. And then she herself bought socks and shirts, pajamas, and ties.

"There," she said as they were leaving the store, "now you're all fixed to take me to the hospital when the baby comes."

[ 244 ]

"Hospital?" His voice sounded startled even to himself. The baby wasn't due until sometime in March.

"Naturally." Joan smiled at him. "I've been thinking of going to Braemuir when the time comes."

"Oh, you mean then—but Doc Parsons would come to the farm. And we'd get Gram to look after the house."

"No. You don't think I'm going to have a country doctor delivering our baby?"

"Why not? He's a good doctor. After all, he tended to me. Nothing to it. Shucks, I bet I could do it. Helped enough animals around the farm."

She burst out laughing. "Darling, I'm not a cow. At any rate, it won't be until March. Come along and help me buy a winter coat."

She took his arm and they walked through the snow to a dress shop down the street. He paused before the windows displaying girdles and underwear as well as dresses and coats. He looked inside at the women by the counters.

"Guess I'll go down to the hardware store," he said.

"Now, come on in," Joan urged him. "Those females won't bite you."

He shook his head. "There's some things I need for the house."

"All right. Meet me at the hotel bar. I may be a little while."

After she had gone into the store, he moved slowly along the street. Suddenly he felt quite alone, although people were hurrying by on the sidewalk and cars passed in the street. He wanted to be home at the farm. The snow would be coming down over the hills, covering the dead leaves and sifting down through the bare branches. Tomorrow would be the day to go deer hunting. Every track would be fresh and easy to follow. He remembered the deer he had seen when he was hauling wood, before the season was open. Often in the past two weeks he'd thought of going deer hunting but he hadn't been able to bring himself to tell Joan, to leave her, to risk what she might say if he shot one and brought it back. For her the deer were beautiful and mysterious woods dwellers which she had seen one summer evening in the lower field.

But now she had gone into the dress store and he was alone thinking of her as though she didn't affect him. He knew it was strange he should feel thus cut loose from her. He stopped in front of a hardware store window, looking at the saws and planes and chisels and tool boxes, things he understood. He went inside and asked to see some hinges. He looked over several pairs which the clerk laid out. He handled them and tried the way they opened before deciding on the pair he wanted for the woodshed. And then he realized they were for the new house, for Joan's house.

[ 245 ]

Again in the street, he stood near the curb and looked at the snow which was already turning dirty gray and wet, tracked by the feet of people and by the tires of cars. He wanted to go back alone to Whichertown. He wasn't sure that he longed for the other days of other Novembers, when Ma and Pa and Whicher and Mort and Rose were all on the farm. He didn't think that was exactly it. He felt more that he wanted to be away from Joan, in Whichertown, on the farm with the mountains behind the falling snow. And no Joan. Only himself as he was now, himself, as he had lived and as he had been brought up, just himself. The urge to start back was so great that he found himself walking toward the car. Yet when he saw the beach wagon, instead of the old Ford he'd had in his mind, he stopped and knew he wasn't going back alone.

Maybe Joan by now had gone to the bar at the hotel to meet him. He couldn't be sure how long he'd been standing or walking along the street, couldn't be sure how long he'd been at the hardware store. The hotel was across the street.

Almost blindly he stepped from the curb. He didn't understand that the approaching truck was so near. With a sudden reflex, he jumped as the driver slammed on his brakes and skidded to a stop against the curb of a concrete island in the middle of the street.

The driver yelled, "Son of a bitch, whyn't hell you look where you're going!"

Amos knew he had been in the wrong and yet he felt a rising fury at the truck driver and his strident voice. He leaned over and picked up a handful of snow, carefully stepped forward and reaching through the cab window pushed it against the driver's fat unbelieving face. He stood back.

"Why, you bastard!" The driver opened the cab door part way, glaring at Amos. "I'll. . . ." His eyes passed up and down Amos. He shut the door and drove off.

Amos jammed his fists into his coat pockets and watched him go. Probably going after a cop.

He waited but nothing happened. Apparently nobody had seen or cared about the incident. Cars and trucks continued to pass and people moved around him on the sidewalk.

He went into the hotel and entered the remote atmosphere of the bar. He could not see Joan at any of the tables. He took off his coat and hat and sat down. His hands on the table were trembling. He ordered whiskey.

Drinking it quickly, he ordered another, but he realized he didn't want it. The whiskey did not warm or relax him. Alone, he didn't care for it and he stared without interest at the ice floating in the glass of amber liquid.

He was still looking at his glass when Joan came in and stood in front of him.

"Hello, darling," she said. There was snow on her coat and hair. "I found it—just the right cut for my new figure, and soft and woolly but durable for a farm." She sat down. "It'll be ready the same day as your suit and coat. I had to have it shortened. But if the snow keeps up I don't think we'll get out from the farm till spring."

"Coming down, is it?"

"Regular blizzard. I want a martini."

After the waiter had brought her drink, Amos said, "We'd better start back pretty quick."

"Must we, Amos? I'm having such a good time. And I'll have to eat something. I'm starved."

"We'll buy some crackers and cheese. If we don't start we'll never get up Footstep Hill."

"Where's that? Please order me another martini." She set down her glass.

"It's the last steep pitch up into Whichertown."

He waited while she drank her second martini and then he stood up, leaving his highball untouched. He put on his coat. He felt like a spectator at an event which didn't concern him. The bar and the people at the tables and Joan shrugging into her coat were players on a screen. He could not enter into it. He paid the check and they went out into the storm. The falling snow dimmed the afternoon light into a grayness which enclosed the buildings and hurrying people. Traffic on the street moved slowly.

Amos stopped at a grocery store. "We'd better get something to eat."

"Poor substitute for a steak dinner," Joan remarked, turning her collar against the snow. "You go in and buy something. Buy me some sardines, too. I have an awful yen for some. I'm going to the liquor store. Meet you at the car."

He went into the lighted store and bought cheese and crackers and sardines, a dozen cans of them. She wanted sardines; she could have them. The impersonal clerk passed him the paper bag and took his money.

Outside, the snow came over his shoes and his feet were wet before he reached the car. He ought to be in boots and sensible clothes. Joan was waiting for him. She had taken off her shoes and sat in the front seat with her feet tucked under her coat.

"I laid in a supply," she said, motioning to the packages beside her. "If we're going to be snowbound we don't want to run out of liquor." She huddled into her coat. "This is too much of a good thing."

He started the beach wagon and pulled away from the curb with the wheels spinning. Then gradually he became accustomed to the feel of the accelerator and the action of the tires of the strange car on the snow. He drove slowly through the streets into the country.

The snow came toward the car in an opening white cone. There were tracks in the road of a few cars. They met a logging truck going south toward Fallsburg, but little other traffic. A wagon loomed up out of the snow as a farmer crossed the highway from house to barn. Amos saw it in time and slowed almost to a stop. Further on he passed a Model A coupe. The beach wagon handled easily on the road but it felt light in back and he wondered if they could make Footstep Hill. Joan ate crackers and cheese. He wasn't hungry.

He stopped in the village to get the mail. Cy made a comment about seeing him next spring, and laughed. Amos put the paper and a letter on the seat beside Joan. He turned on the lights as he started toward Whichertown.

Only one pair of tracks marked the road leading away from the river valley. Although he started fast, Amos could feel the engine labor as it pulled up the hills heading to the flat along Carr Brook. The wheels started spinning but the car slowly crawled over the top.

Joan let out her breath in a sigh when they moved faster and the snowy fields slid past again.

"Any chains?" he asked.

"No."

Soon they were in the woods and Amos turned off on the dirt road to Whichertown. Beyond the Hostetters' place there were no tracks ahead of them, only the unbroken snow in the lights of the car and the flakes coming against the windshield. He shifted into second gear and drove hard at the steady grade. The trunks of the trees on either side of the road passed by in the snow and the weighted boughs of the pines and spruces hung over the car so low they at times brushed the windows. The beach wagon climbed steadily, jouncing and skidding over the stones and ruts, but continuing up.

Amos knew they were approaching Footstep Hill and he stepped down on the accelerator as the road slanted upward. The wheel was alive in his grasp and he tried to steer straight while the back of the car began to sway. They were halfway up the hill.

The steep incline and the snow seemed to be holding the car back. It moved slower and slower and then the tires wouldn't grab any more and the rear of the car swung off to one side, the wheels singing high-pitched in the snow as they slid off the road.

He pressed in the clutch pedal and let the motor idle. In the stillness he could hear the radiator boiling, a deep forward gurgle.

"Wish I had the old Ford," he said and, setting the brake, got out to look at the road.

In the reflection from the headlights he could not see clearly at the rear of the car. The snow was over his ankles. His feet were wet and cold. He could feel the snow falling down his neck. Throwing open the back of the beach wagon, he felt around in the body hoping to find chains which Joan didn't know about.

He heard her say, "I need a drink," and the sound of tearing paper and the clink of a bottle. He found nothing in back but an old canvas wrapped around the jack.

He got into the car.

"Here," she said, holding out the bottle.

"No thanks."

Carefully he backed up and maneuvered the car onto the road and eased it to the bottom of the hill. While he waited for the engine to cool, he loaded rocks behind the rear seat, making several trips to the stone wall beside the road.

In the car again, Joan said to him, "I don't like this."

"Who does?" he asked, and added, "I think we'll make it this time." He lighted his pipe and sat silently beside her.

"Can't we try it now? I'm cold."

"Wait a little."

At last he saw by the temperature gauge that the engine had cooled and he started fast along the level stretch before the hill. He could tell that the car was climbing better with the rocks in back and the road broken out. If he managed to keep it in the tracks, it wouldn't have to push against the snow. They were past the ditch where they had slipped off the road. Amos felt his muscles tense as the car began to lose speed. They must be almost up. A little more gas. In the driving snow he couldn't tell how much farther to the top. He heard Joan drink out of the bottle. Hardly creeping, they passed a big pine on the left. It wasn't more than a rod or two from the top. In a last desperate effort, as the wheels began to spin, he set the hand throttle and stepped out to put his shoulder against the door frame. "Get out and push, Joan!"

"I haven't any shoes on."

"Then steer."

He dug his heels into the snow and forced the car over the last few yards. Panting, he jumped behind the wheel and kept on toward the corners.

[ 249 ]

"My God!" Joan burst out. "What a road! What a way to go home."

"Should think your folks would have chains," he said.

"We never expected to use the beach wagon getting into this God-forsaken place in a snowstorm."

"Chains are handy." He turned over the bridge across Carr Brook. "Now if we can make the hill up to the farm, we'll be home. Anyhow, we could walk from there."

"I'm not walking anywhere tonight. I'll camp in the car. Or you can carry me."

"I guess you'd walk."

He saw that the snow was deeper here in Whichertown. He turned past the abandoned Lovejoy place and steered up the hill toward the farm. The beach wagon took the gradual slope without skidding. Then it bounced over a water bar and lurched toward the woods while Joan braced herself on the dashboard. Amos swung the wheel and they were heading straight again. The road leveled out and they drove past the cemetery wall. He turned in at the barway. The car lights flashed on the house. He shut off the motor.

"Guess we're here."

"Thank goodness. You wouldn't get me on that road again in a blizzard."

"This ain't a blizzard. Just a November snow."

"I call it a blizzard." Joan opened the door and looked out. "I suppose you won't carry me into the house?"

"Well, all right." He switched off the lights.

He went around the car and lifted her into his arms. She clutched the package of bottles. Wading through the snow to the steps, he set her down so he could open the door.

She cried out, "My feet!" and darted into the house. "Would you get my shoes, Amos? They're on the floor of the car. And the sardines."

He said nothing but made his way through the blowing snow to the car for the things she wanted. Back in the house, he found that she hadn't lighted a lamp in the shadowy room but was lifting the lids of the stove and peering into the firebox.

"Out," she said. "And I'm cold as hell."

"Of course it's out. Light a lamp and start it. I got to change my clothes and go tend the cows."

"Damn the cows, you start me a fire, Amos!"

"Start it yourself. There's kindling in the woodbox."

He struck a match to a lamp and took it to the far end of the room where he quickly changed to his work clothes and boots. The dry socks were warm. He put on his overalls and denim jacket.

Joan had made no move to start the fire. Instead she had lighted a lamp, poured herself a drink, and opened her mother's letter. Shivering, she held it close to the lamp on the table.

"They're in Bali," she said, almost to herself. She hugged her arms across her breasts and stared down at the letter.

Amos put kindling into the stove and poured kerosene over it and dropped in a flaring match.

Joan said to him, "I wish I were in Bali."

She walked to the window, drawing her coat around her, and looked at the snow falling beyond the glass. She came back to the stove and and held out her hands.

The fire crackled in the stove. Amos added split wood. Joan watched him but he felt that she didn't see him. Then she burst out, "I hate it! Oh, how I hate it!"

He thought she was going to cry, but she didn't. She continued speaking in a strained voice.

"It's so far from anything, and now the snow coming down so hard it would smother you after a while and you couldn't get out if you wanted to, not even if you had to. It's a prison!" She looked up at him. "I won't be able to stand it all winter. I know I won't."

He was aware of an abrupt emptying of his mind, as though all his plans for the future and his thoughts of them living together on the farm had shattered and dropped from him. He felt barren and destitute and he said harshly, "I guess you'll have to stand it."

She turned away and then faced him. "What makes you think so? I'm perfectly able to leave here when the storm's over and walk or drive down off this damned hill and go where people live like human beings!"

"You'd go alone."

"I could do that, too."

He realized that she could and he didn't know what to say, for he saw himself alone on the farm, as he had wanted to be that afternoon standing on the street of Fallsburg. But now the picture brought him only a desperate loneliness. Without Joan there would be nothing for him here, though he continued to farm the land and hunt and fish. He would be a poor excuse for a man, without Joan. Living to himself, he would be no part of anything. Thinking of Joan leaving him, he suddenly wished he had some experience beyond the farm and mountains. If he had that, he might know what to do. His mind rebelled at the thought of leaving Whichertown; it filled with a millrace of confused images and and wandering ideas. Out of this came the realization that Mort must must have been confused in some such way, faced with a thing he couldn't understand and a love that twisted his heart. "I love her so," he thought, "but I don't know what to do."

At last he said, "I'm sorry you feel like that. I want you to be happy."

She held her coat around her although the room was getting warm. "I know you do, Amos. It's me and—and this place." Her arms stiffened at her sides and she looked about her at the stove and the bare studded walls and at the window beyond which the snow drifted down in the lamp light.

"Well," he said, "it ain't much."

"I don't mean just the house, but the outside." She motioned toward the mountains. "Probably you can't understand."

"Never thought about it."

She said no more, and he turned away, taking a lantern from a nail on the wall. He lighted it and adjusted the wick carefully.

"Well," he said, "I'd better go do the chores. You all right?"

She nodded and because there didn't seem to be more he could say, he went out into the snowstorm.

He walked toward the farm, scuffing through the snow, and for the first time in his life he felt that there must be something about the land here and about the weather and mountains which was opposed to people. He had always liked the snow. It meant deer hunting and logging in the woods, and the mountains white in the sun when the storm cleared. The cold didn't bother him, nor the mud in spring nor the heat of summer. He had never thought of the farm as remote and shut in at any time of year. He had never worried about the poor living the farm gave them. They ate three meals a day and were clothed and housed and had a little money. It was the life he knew and wanted.

But now as he walked along the narrow road in the snow with the lantern casting shadows ahead of him, he could feel the mountains pressing in beyond the darkness and feel the frozen inhospitable earth beneath the snow. He thought of the months ahead—December, January, February, March, April—before the green leaves came again and the doors and windows of the house could be opened. Yes, and May, too; May was often cold and rainy. And then there would be the long days of work to scratch a living from the farm.

He felt tired and discouraged. He understood why people left Whichertown.

As he came to the barn, Drum's baying did not arouse him. He did not think with pleasure of fox hunts during the winter. He didn't think of deer hunting the next day. He went into the warm tie-up where the cows turned their heads toward him with their eyes dark in the lantern light. He set about the feeding and milking listlessly, through long habit, but his thoughts were not on his work.

He had finished milking when Joan came into the barn. She had changed to dungarees and overshoes and a jacket and had tied a scarf around her head. He set down the milk pail and went toward her, quick alarm and fear catching at him.

"What's the matter, Joan?"

"Nothing. I just wanted to come and help you. I thought I ought to after the way I acted." She stood before him with the snow on her shoulders and a flashlight grasped in her mittened hand.

"You shouldn't have come," he said, "in the snow and all."

"I'm fine. I want to help. If I could help I think I'd feel better."

He stepped forward and took her in his arms and kissed her. But he didn't quite dare to give way to the feeling of relief and love which passed through him. He wanted to, but he wasn't sure of her or of himself or their life any more. She could help, but he was afraid it wouldn't change the way they were.

And then he didn't know what job to have her do. There was hay to pitch from the loft. She couldn't do that, not when she was four months along. The tie-up was cleaned and swept, but he wouldn't have asked her to do that anyway.

"You could feed Drum," he said. "And the pigs."

"All right."

He helped her mix the pail of slop for the pigs and the dish of mash for Drum, holding open the grain bin while she scooped out the feed and mixed it with water from the waterbox in the tie-up. He took a pail of mash for the hens and went with her to Drum's kennel and the pigpen. He was reminded of visitors at the farm who wanted to help but had to be shown how.

After he'd put out the hay for the cows, they walked back to the house through the snow. He knew that he should feel close to her and glad of her presence, but somehow they were not the same as they had been before she said she hated Whichertown. He tried to tell himself everything was going to work out and she would get used to the winter and they would be happy and have a good life. But at the back of his mind there was a ghost of insecurity to haunt him, for he knew sometime he would have to decide between Whichertown and Joan.

## Chapter 34

The snow continued the next day. It came down light and steady all morning. After the chores, Amos stayed in the house with Joan. He did not work on the sheathing although his tools were in the corner and two sawhorses supported the wallboard he had been cutting up. He felt tired and lethargic. There seemed to be no point in working on the house. He sat in a chair by the stove while Joan did the breakfast dishes. He watched the red gleam of coals in the ash pit of the stove. Joan finished her morning work and took a book to the big chair in the living room part of the house.

After a time she said, "Don't you want to read, Amos? I don't see how you can just sit there."

"I never was much of a hand to read." He looked around him and the house seemed cramped and small. "What would you think of moving into the old house? Maybe you'd be more comfortable there."

"I wouldn't like it, Amos. This is our house. It's all right." She closed her book on a finger. "Anyhow, your father will be coming back sometime, and Gram."

"I doubt it."

"You don't think so?"

"He's had enough of the farm, with Whicher and Mort dying, and all. He won't be back."

As Joan took up her reading again, he found that he was thinking of the past months. The events seemed to press in upon him as though they might crush him, too, into the earth of Whichertown. He sat thinking about Mort and Whicher. Nothing could bring them back and the farm would never be the same again.

He watched the snow let up and stop. He could see Cobblestone under the gray sky. He sat silent for a long time.

At last Joan stood up. "This is a dreary day. I'll make us a drink."

After his second whiskey and water he felt better and sat back while Joan talked of Braemuir and college and dances and places where she had worked. They ate sandwiches and drank whiskey and talked happily together. The day passed into the afternoon and they went to bed and slept and, waking, drank again together while they lay in bed listening to the wind outside. It blew the snow from the trees and piled drifts across the road and whined at the eaves. Amos didn't want to get up and feed and milk the stock, for he and Joan were having a gay happy time, and Joan was fun to be with in bed.

He was a little drunk when he finally dressed and waded along the road through the deep snow late in the afternoon. The wind had fallen and the sky was clearing. It was dark when he finished the chores and came back by lantern light to the house.

The next day Amos awoke and looked out the window near the bed. He saw that the sun was bright in the blue sky above the white hills. Joan stirred beside him and opened her eyes.

He said, "I ought to go out and shoot us a deer for Thanksgiving."

Joan laughed. "It is a lovely day. Why don't you go out and kill something, Amos?" She sat up in bed. "I'm high as a kite. How are you?"

"I'm fine," he said.

She held the blankets around her and looked out at the snow. "How would we get out, if we had to?"

"I'd hitch up the team and we'd drive out. The town plow will be around in a day or two and then we'd take the Ford. Nothing to worry about."

"I don't like it." She slid back under the blankets and crawled beside him. "Would you take me away from here if I asked you? Would you, darling?"

He lay suddenly tense beside her. "I'm not sure."

"I'd feel better if I knew you would. I'd feel almost free. Not that I'd ask, but just to know you would."

"I couldn't." He wanted to pull away from her but the soft warmth of her body against him held him beside her and although he willed that he resist her and throw off the blankets and get out of bed, he was unable to. "And leave the farm and Whichertown? Don't seem as though you ought to ask me."

"I'm not asking you. I'm just asking if you would."

"No," he said and went on desperately, "I've got no trade. I couldn't make a living."

"We have money."

"It won't last forever."

"I can get more."

"That's no way to talk. That's no way to live." He felt weak and helpless. "I don't think I could ever leave Whichertown."

"Not even if I asked you?"

"I don't know."

"Don't you, Amos?" Her lips were at his ear and he could feel her teeth as she whispered to him, "And no more of this, darling, and this? Don't you know?"

"I thought we were going to be all right here."

"Maybe, but I have to know you'd take me away. Tell me you'd go anywhere with me—and this, darling."

"Well, I might. Joan, no, leave me be."

"Say you'd do anything for me. Promise."

"All right, I promise."

"That's what I want. Amos, my darling, my love."

At last he got up and dressed and started the fire in the stove, while Joan watched him sleepily from the bed. She smiled at him and closed her eyes. He made coffee and fried bacon which he put between slices of bread and washed down with scalding coffee. He felt an inner shame and he wanted to get out of the house. He was not a whole person any more. He felt divided and weak in his heart, as though he could not trust himself because he had given in to Joan, as though his personality had been sheared off, leaving him naked.

He went out into the blinding sunlight on the snow. Already the white drifts had become soft and heavy from the sun and the warming air. They would not last. On the way to the barn he stopped where a deer track crossed the road. He could see that the deer had paused to sniff at the marks his boots made the day before. Then the deer had leaped the stone wall and left a trail across the lower field. Probably it had gone to the corner where the old apple trees grew.

At the barn, he hurried through the chores and went to the house for his rifle and to the hay mow for cartridges. Sometime he'd have to put the boxes back in the closet, now that Mort was gone, or take them to the new house. He looked up at the chimney to see which way the wind was blowing the smoke, but of course there was none. He felt the breeze on the side of his face and making up his mind which way to go, he circled toward the sugar orchard and cut through it to the brook. He kept to the woods which bordered the lower field.

As he moved slowly along he began to feel better. He watched the snowy woods ahead of him and stepped silently in the covering of snow. He came to the wall near the apple trees and there saw the deer tracks leading off into the woods. He brought up the rifle and looked at the slope of hardwoods. Perhaps the deer had recently stopped feeding on the apples and was still on the ridge there, maybe behind that clump of spruces. He watched for a motion, an ear flicking or the turning of an antlered head beyond the spruces. He scanned the openings between the birch and maple trunks. A flock of little birds flitted through the woods, feeding among the twigs of a birch and then taking wing with little notes falling behind them as their skipping flight carried them away.

Perhaps the deer had gone along up the ridge. If Amos had gotten here at daylight he might have seen the deer under the apple trees. The morning was half gone now and the deer had likely moved up the ridge. He should have gotten up early. Yes, early. And of a sudden he could feel Joan pressing against him again and whispering in his ear and he felt ashamed and undecided what to do. There was not the clear urge to follow the tracks in the snow, not the sweet pure hunt before him in the snowy woods with the deer at the other end of the tracks, elusively drawing him on.

He walked a little way along the track and when he saw that it no longer wandered about among the trees, but headed directly up the hill, going away steadily, he became oppressed by the thought of the time he'd have to spend following the deer to its bed on an upper ridge and he became aware of the days which had passed without work.

He'd go back to the barn and get the axe and one-man saw, take his rifle with him into the stand of pines where he had planned to get out his winter logs for the mill. He'd begin that today and maybe see a deer, too. He started back to the barn and after the tracks were well behind him he became glad that he had not followed the deer.

With the axe and saw over one shoulder, the rifle in his right hand, he strode through the sugar orchard to the logging road which led to the pines. He wanted to work. That would be the only thing for him. Work. Get out his logs. Make his living as he always had. He tried not to think of Joan.

He came to the end of the logging road, sweating and out of breath from walking hard in the wet snow and sun. He passed the stumps where he had cut last winter. Ahead of him the tall pines grew along the ridge, dark green against the snow, with straight trunks and openings between them that were white and clear. He made his way around a pile of last winter's slash. There were young pines here whose tops barely came to the surface of the snow. They'd be about right for his great-grandsons to cut. The Jackmans had never gone in for full-scale logging. The farm included stands of spruce and pine, like this one, which would provide pulp and timber logs all his life and the lives of his sons and grandsons. If a man cut what he could alone, or with a little help, and sold the logs, he had cash coming in. Not much, but a little, to go with the money from the maple syrup and the milk. It all added up to a living. That was the way the Jackmans had always farmed it. They didn't have much, but they got by and they didn't owe anyone. That was the way he should live.

He stamped down the snow by a sapling and leaned his rifle in a crotch. Then he trimmed out the bushes around the pine so he could swing his axe. He chopped a notch in the pine and went to sawing on the opposite side. He and Mort used to be able to make the sawdust fly when they cut together. They were good together with a crosscut saw. But he was alone now and he'd better not think of that. He'd make out alone with the one-man saw. He worked steadily and stopped to breathe and look around the woods. Sometimes a deer would come right up to a man cutting in the woods, if the wind was right. The sound of an axe or saw didn't always scare them.

He took up his work again. After a time the tree began to pinch the saw. He chopped a wedge and drove it in behind the saw, until he could again draw the blade back and forth. The tree began to sway. He got up from his knees and looked at the top. He sawed some more. The tree leaned gradually toward the notch he had chopped and then it toppled, slowly at first and then faster, falling with a rending crash, its upper boughs coming to rest where he wanted them near the pile of slash.

Resting for a time, before he trimmed out the branches, he thought about the money from the logs and about the time he had spent cutting the tree. He thought about it still as he began to chop off the green boughs. It was small pay for the work he put into the logs when you considered money like Joan had. There was a lot of sweat and labor for a few dollars.

He tried not to think about it and for a time he worked along, but the pleasure was gone and he had to drive himself to saw the trunk into lengths. At last one of the sections pinched on the saw. Alone, he couldn't raise the log enough to free it. He needed a cant hook, or the team to swing the log.

Noontime had passed. He was hungry and tired. Picking up his rifle and axe, he turned to go. But something in him hated to leave the saw there in the log. He put down the rifle and chopped out the saw, which he shouldered again beside the axe. He took his rifle and started back the way he had come.

He stopped at the barn to leave the axe and saw. It was not time for the chores and he went on down the road to the house.

Joan got up from the easy chair. "Hello, darling. I kept your dinner hot." She went to the stove and ladled a dish of stew from a kettle. "I made your favorite beef stew. It's canned but I fixed it up the way you like, with more onions and potatoes."

He washed at the sink and thought that perhaps she was so changeable because of the baby. He couldn't understand why she was so unpredictable, trying to be a good wife and do everything right, trying to like the farm, when a short time later she'd want something different, want to get out of Whichertown, want to drink or make him give in to her. He couldn't understand her, but again, like the evening at the barn after their return from Fallsburg, he was ready to accept her in her new mood on the hope that it would last.

And this time it seemed to. The next day he hitched up the team and they drove down to town through the melting snow, to take the milk to the creamery, to see Gram and to show Joan—Amos thought—that Whichertown wasn't snowbound.

The following afternoon, the town plow came chugging up the hill with Lije Willis in the cab of the tractor. He waved and thundered on toward the farm where he turned around by the barn. The wide wings of the plow thrust back the snow and left the road open for a car. The tractor always sounded strange and outlandish to Amos with its hammering treads and roar echoing from the hills. Lije came in and they gave him a drink and a bite to eat and when he went on, back down to the main road to plow out other hill farms, Joan seemed to relax now there was a clear road from Whichertown. Amos understood that the ride out behind the team had not convinced her the farm wasn't snowed in, for after Lije had gone she stood at the window and looked at the snow banked on either side of the road and she turned back to smile at him.

"I feel better," she said.

"I'll go and shovel out the beach wagon."

A week passed and they had their own Thanksgiving dinner of turkey which Joan insisted they buy, although Amos couldn't see how they'd ever eat it up alone. In the afternoon they drove to the Hardys' to visit Gram. She had a letter from Pa.

"He says for you to do what you think best about selling the hogs and the steer and that cow. He says you're running the farm now."

Running the farm, Amos thought, as they drove back to Whichertown. He wasn't running it. He hadn't gone back to the pines. He was just feeding the stock and puttering around or sitting in the house with Joan. He had no will to work; the days of work which formerly he used to put in from daylight till dark, the chores done before daylight and after dark, because the days were so short, had become things of the past. Now he didn't work that way. Nor did he go hunting. In the years before, he always hunted and trapped much of the fall and winter, letting Pa and Mort and Whicher look after the farm. He didn't want to go into the woods any more. It was not important to get a deer for meat, nor foxes for the money their pelts would bring. And he had lost the hunting urge which would have taken him into the woods in the old days whether they needed the meat and money or not.

A cattle dealer from down the river came and bought the steer and the cow and the two pigs. And at the last moment Amos agreed to sell the matched steers he had been breaking to work. He couldn't see that he'd need them now. He yoked them and showed the dealer how they handled. He was proud of them and disgusted at the offer the dealer made. They dickered back and forth.

At last Amos said, "I'll let you have the lot."

It wasn't much of a price—beef and pork didn't bring much—but he sent it all to Pa in a letter with a money order.

He spent a lot of time one evening over the letter because he knew Pa would want to hear about the farm and the hunting and how everything was going on the old place. In the back of Amos' mind was the knowledge that it wasn't going well and he couldn't bring himself to write a long letter. In the end he just spoke about the sale, asked how Pa was feeling and said they were fine. It wasn't a good letter and he knew it, telling himself he wasn't any hand to write. But that wasn't the trouble. The fact was he didn't care about the farm any more.

He had to admit it to himself as he sat there with the sheet of paper before him, looking at his heavy handwriting. He raised his eyes to the lamp, staring at the flame, while the realization came over him. He almost couldn't believe it, but there it was, come to the surface at last after the past month or two. He felt alone with the knowledge, lonely. It must be that he had been more dependent on the family than he ever understood. It wasn't all Joan. It was an accumulation of the summer's events. He had never thought much about the family and had gone his own way a lot, hunting and fishing and spending days at the camp. But there had always been the farm and the family to which he returned when he wanted. And that was gone now, Mort dead, Rose married and moved away, Pa gone, Whicher dead before he grew up, and Gram moved to the village. And Joan was not really happy here. He thought momentarily that he should never have married her, but he could never have done otherwise, feeling the way he had, feeling the way he did.

Thinking was no good. He folded the letter and sealed it and then remembered he had to put in the money order. He got another envelope from the bureau drawer and wrote out the address in Massachusetts.

That week, the snow came again. There was still snow in the woods from the first storm, but it had gone from the fields and the cold had frozen the ground deep and made the snow in the woods crusty, as he discovered one day when he had wandered along the brook below the house. This was more of a winter snowstorm with cold small flakes. There wasn't much of it in the morning, but the gray days continued and more snow fell, and it all stayed. It would be good sledding snow. He ought to be working in the woods. There were the pine logs to get out and cord wood to chop for the next year. He ought to get at it before the snow became too deep for working easily in the woods. But he didn't. He was far behind on his work. Christmas had almost come.

He tried to think what to get Joan for a present. She seemed to set a lot of store by Christmas and he wanted her to have a good time. She talked of Christmas parties and dances when she was home from school during vacations at Braemuir. He cut her a tree and they set it up in the house by the living room chairs near the front window. They bought decorations. There were a few at the old house but mostly his family had made their own ornaments, popcorn strings and paper balls. Joan wanted tinsel and glass balls and lights. Of course they couldn't have lights without electricity.

She stood back after they had finished decorating the tree. "I suppose it doesn't matter. There'd be nobody to see it. Half the fun of Christmas is the lights in the windows for people to see." She moved restlessly away and came back to look at the tree. "We used to drive around Christmas Eve and see all the lights that people had put up. Everyone hung lights on the evergreens outside the houses. It was awfully pretty. And Christmas carols. I'd like to hear some."

He bought her a silver bracelet at Fallsburg the day before Christmas and they had dinner at the hotel. He wore his new suit. They had drinks in the bar and he should have enjoyed it but he didn't. They drove back home in the cold of the late afternoon. The stars were coming out when they reached Whichertown—bright winter stars over Cobblestone, looking remote and cold as he walked with Joan from the beach wagon to the house.

He was carrying a heavy box which she had him set on the kitchen table. "It's your present," she said. "I want you to have it tonight. When you get back from the chores, you knock on the door and wait till I open it."

He changed his clothes and went down the road, boots squeaking on the cold snow, and did the feeding and milking, and then came back, knocking as she had directed.

After a moment, he heard music in the house. She opened the door and cried out, "Merry Christmas!" and kissed him.

On the kitchen table a Victrola was playing, "Silent Night."

"It's your present," she told him. "There's lots of records. You know," she admitted, "I wanted it, too. I hope you like it."

"Why, it's just right. I'm real pleased."

He brought her the bracelet and watched while she opened it. She held it up.

"Oh, darling, aren't you sweet!"

They had a good time together that night, drinking and listening to music and he was glad she took so much pleasure in the Victrola. He was surprised when she announced the next day that she wanted to go to Braemuir for New Year's.

## Chapter 35

They were standing by the beach wagon. The morning was bitter cold. Amos had backed the car into the road for Joan and left the motor running. He had put her suitcase on the rear seat. She stood by the door, the collar of her coat turned up and a little felt hat on her brown hair. She didn't look like the wife of a hill farmer. She didn't look like his wife at all and he couldn't realize she was and that he should kiss her goodby. He was conscious of his overalls and denim jacket smelling of the barn, and his crumpled red hunter's cap. He knew he needed a shave.

She stood on the toes of her little fur-trimmed overshoes and kissed him on the lips. "I'll come back Friday. Be good."

He could see that she was already gone; her mind had traveled south to Braemuir and she had really left him earlier that morning as she packed her suitcase after breakfast. She opened the door of the beach wagon and slid into the seat.

"Goodby," he said and shut the door.

She raised a gloved hand from the wheel and formed her lips in a kiss before she shifted and started off. She was remote behind the glass of the window. He stood there watching the beach wagon disappear down the road. He didn't wave. The beach wagon was gone between the white banks of snow where the road dipped toward Whichertown.

For a time he did not move. He looked about him at the house and the snowy mountains beyond. Smoke drifted up from the chimney. The low December sun gave no heat. He knew that the short days at the end of the year would pass and the sun would climb higher each week into the long days of spring and summer, but he did not feel the lift which usually came to him with the thought. The interminable winter and the lonely hills seemed to press around him. He was alone in Whichertown.

He could have gone with her. He could have arranged with Marvin Hostetter to do the chores. She had wanted him to go, she said. But he felt that she needed to go by herself and had looked forward to the trip as her own. Besides, he could not bring himself to stay with her friends, as she planned to do. There would be an endless series of situations in which he would not know how to act. And the thought of leaving the farm chilled him and made him afraid. He clung to the idea of the farm while he felt at the same time that it could not help him. He sought refuge in his past and in his established ideas and memories of the farm, yet he was aware that it had all changed.

That was why he felt so lonely now. He had thought of going hunting with Drum. The snow was not too deep for the hound to run well. He had thought with eagerness of the days by himself. Perhaps somehow he would be able to gather himself together until he felt whole again. Now there was only the fact of his solitary isolation in Whichertown.

He walked back to the house. It was warm inside but the fire had burned down. He put another stick of wood in the stove, thinking that he ought to set up a chunk stove in the other part of the house. Joan had done the breakfast dishes. He looked about the unfinished room. The north and west walls were sheathed with wallboard, and he had put up a partition where the bedroom was, but the rest of the walls were bare studs and boards with the nails of the outside shingles sticking through. He could work here for the next few days and perhaps finish it, and Joan would return to a complete house. It would be a nice surprise for her. But he could not make himself believe it was important enough to undertake. He did not really think she would ever be contented in the little house.

He had planned to make this time his own and here he was thinking about her. He was aware of her presence all through the house. Abruptly he closed the drafts on the stove and went outside into the cold.

He walked to the barn where he had not yet done the morning chores. The next few days passed in a steady routine to which he held himself while actually he was only waiting for Joan's return. There were meals to get and the chores to do, morning and night. During the day he worked in the pine woods, taking sandwiches, and a bottle of coffee which he warmed in a can of water over his fire at noon. He cut trees and limbed them out and sawed the trunks into board-length logs. The work kept him busy and made the days go by quicker. He did not chop with his old energy and he seemed to tire easily. Often he would sit down and stare at the log he had been sawing.

In the mornings he forced himself to start again by sheer effort of will. The work did not seem to have any connection with the farm and his life. His mind and body appeared to reject it. He knew he was not sick. He ate and slept normally although he felt lonesome in the house alone. There was something in him which had given up, and every stroke of the axe was an effort. With steady longing he looked forward to the end of the week.

Friday, the day she was to return, he cleaned the house. He mopped the floor and washed the dishes which had been accumulating in the sink. He wanted the house to look nice and he wanted to be there when she arrived. If she started in good season that morning, she ought to reach Whichertown by early afternoon. But as that time came and passed, he realized she had probably put off her departure, visiting her friends to say goodby. He sat at the window and watched the freezing drizzle which had begun to fall. The thought came to him that she might not be coming back. She had written once, telling him about the good time she was having and about the show she went to in Boston with Anita and Dave. He could not help thinking that she must have seen Ronnie. He wondered if she would put off her return another week, and then another, finally writing to say she couldn't bring herself to come back at all.

By late afternoon, he became too restless to stay any longer in the house. He wrote a note and left it on the table before he walked to the farm. After the chores, he started back in the driving sleet. The road was slippery under his boots. Perhaps the weather had been worse farther south. Perhaps she had not been able to leave Braemuir, and had called the Hostetters or Mrs. Hardy to leave a message. He turned back to the farmhouse. The kitchen was cold with a deserted chill as he rang up the Hostetters on the phone. Marvin answered.

"Well, yes, I see her go by 'most an hour ago."

"Maybe she's down at the new house." He tried to keep his voice steady. "I been doing the chores. Thanks, Marvin."

Outside, his boots slipped on the hard-packed icy snow and he almost fell down. Thinking about the road, he felt sure Joan could not drive the beach wagon up Footstep Hill. He went toward the wagon shed, kicking his heels into the crunching snow. In the fading light, he took chains from a beam of the shed and jacked up the rear wheels of the Ford, one at a time, and stretched the chains around the narrow tires.

Darkness had almost come as he drove down to the new house. The beach wagon was not in the barway. Perhaps she had been forced to walk. Leaving the motor running, he went quickly to the steps and opened the door. The room was dark.

"Joan?"

There was no answer.

He hurried back to the Ford and switched on the lights. Sleet had frozen on the windshield and he leaned out to drive, squinting his eyes against the sharp particles of ice.

Near the bottom of the hill leading into Whichertown, the lights of the car picked out a figure hunched in the snow of the ditch. Amos saw Joan lift her hand and struggle to her feet. He braked hard and stopped. He jumped out and ran to her, catching her in his arms.

"Darling," she said. "I'm so glad you came."

"Are you all right?"

"I guess so—just awfully tired. I've been resting." She leaned on his arm. "What a hell of a place to live. The beach wagon is in the ditch on Footstep Hill."

Her gloves were wet and her coat streaked with dirt. She bent to look at her knees.

"There's not much left of my best stockings." She rubbed one knee and her hand was bloody. "I think I crawled most of the way."

He picked her up, slipped, and had to put her down. He helped her to the car.

"I'll have to drive down and turn around at the corners."

He could feel her shivering beside him. While he was driving slowly past the Lovejoy place and turning beyond the bridge, he kept wondering if the Ford would make the hill back to the house. The road was a sheet of ice in the lights, but the chains continued to bite through it as he pulled down on the throttle. Near the top of the hill, the front wheels slid off the road and a chain broke as he kept the throttle down. The chain banged with a deafening clatter on the fender but the Ford charged sideway up the last pitch. He righted the front wheels and drove on to the barway.

The footing was safer in the soft snow leading to the house. He was able to carry Joan. He kicked open the door and put her down on a chair by the stove. Lighting a lamp, he filled the stove with wood and opened the drafts.

"I'd like a drink," Joan said, trying to smile at him.

The teakettle was still hot and he filled the half glass of whiskey with steaming water. She gulped it down, shuddering after each swallow.

He helped her undress and get into her nightgown. He brought a basin of warm water and bathed her bloody knees. Then he put her in bed with hot bricks wrapped in towels at her feet. Her face was pale around her shadowy eyes.

"I guess," she said, "I should have waited till tomorrow, but I wanted to come home to you." She shivered and lay still. "I won't be much good for you now, darling."

"Don't talk. Would you like another drink?"

She nodded and he went to the kitchen. When he got back she was lying on one elbow, her hand to her mouth.

"I think I'm going to be sick. You'd better bring the basin. Hurry."

He brought it and held her head while she retched and spasms shook her whole body. At last she lay back. He wiped the sweat from her forehead with a towel.

"I'm all right now," she said. "I drank that too fast."

"Have you any pains?"

"Not really. Just a low feeling there. Don't worry, it isn't that."

"Did you fall down hard?"

"Well, once or twice."

He nodded, looking down at her. He patted her hand and smiled while he tried not to think what might be happening to her. He said, "Would you like a cup of coffee?"

"Tea, darling," she said slowly. "In the cupboard. With sugar and a little whiskey."

He made the cup of tea. Wishing that there was a phone in the house, he wondered if he could leave her to go and call Doc Parsons. He thought of the farm and Whichertown with a bitter hatred because they were responsible for Joan being here in the half-partitioned bedroom, her dark hair spread on the pillow and her face almost as white as the sheet. But she had not been required to go to Braemuir. If she had been content to stay here, it would not have happened.

He took the tea in to her. She frowned a little and made a face before she took the cup.

"Something's going on down there," she said. She reached for the cup and her hands were trembling.

He watched her sip at the tea. "Will you be all right while I go to the house and call Doc?"

She nodded. "But don't be gone long, darling. I'm scared."

"I'll be right back."

He went out and drove to the farm in the Ford, with the broken chain clanking against the fender at each turn of the wheel. He did not bother to light a lamp in the old kitchen, but from long habit stepped directly to the phone on the wall.

The connection was poor and Mrs. Parsons' voice came to him faintly above the whirring roar. He thought absently that icy branches would soon break the wires.

"This is Amos Jackman. Out in Whichertown."

"Who? Oh, Amos, yes."

"My wife's sick. I think she's going to lose the baby."

"The doctor's out on a call."

Amos could feel the receiver cold against his ear. "When will he be back?"

"I don't know. He should be here now, but the traveling is so bad. I'll call you in a few minutes."

"Never mind. I can't wait. I'm calling from the old house where the phone is. My wife's alone in the new house."

"How's that? New house? Oh, yes, the doctor said you'd built. I'll tell him you need him right away. I'll. . . ."

Amos interrupted her. "Have him stop at the Hostetters'. Marvin can drive him here with his team. He'd never make it in his car. And ask him to bring Gram."

"All right, but your grandmother's laid up with the flu. No, not bad, but she couldn't come out."

"I see. Thank you."

Amos rang off. He stood for a moment in the darkness, the old familiar kitchen around him but no longer a part of him. He rang the Hostetters and asked Marvin to drive up with Doc.

"Glad to, Amos. Anything else?"

"No."

"Don't worry."

Marvin's voice faded and the line went dead. Amos hung up and walked across the kitchen, feeling cut off from the world for the first time he could remember. He closed the door behind him. He drove home.

Joan looked better when he went inside. She had more color and she opened her eyes as though she had slept a little, but she didn't smile at him. "Is he coming?"

He nodded. He didn't tell her when.

He brought in wood and warmed a can of soup. Joan tried to eat a cup of it but put it aside half finished. He sat by the bed and they talked a little but Joan's words were often interrupted and he knew it was the pain. There was nothing to do except wait. The clock ticked on the shelf in the kitchen and the sleet rattled against the windows. Amos wondered if Doc could make it to the Hostetters. There were the hills outside the village. They would be glare ice. And perhaps he had not been able to get back from his call. Perhaps he couldn't reach Whichertown for hours. Amos took Joan's hand. She pressed it hard and then relaxed.

"Tell me," she said, "what you did while I was gone."

"Worked in the pine woods, mostly. And got my meals and did the chores. Took the milk to the creamery. I'm milking only three cows." He shifted in his chair. "Gram's got the flu, Mrs. Parsons said."

"Is she very sick?"

"I guess not."

They were silent and he saw Joan's eyes turn toward the window as though she expected to see the lights of Doc's car swing toward the house.

"He'll be a little while," Amos said. "Marvin's going to drive him up with his team."

"I hope they can get by the beach wagon."

"If they can't, they'll move it."

Joan said, "I think you better get me some towels, darling. Something's happening."

As he went to the kitchen, he saw by the clock that an hour had passed. He brought towels from the chest. Joan's eyes were closed and her hands gripped the blankets. He could see the tightened cords in her neck and the flush on her damp face. He pulled back the covers and lifted her by the knees to tuck the towels under her.

"My nightgown, Amos, it's my new one." She was crying and for a moment he thought she didn't know what she was saying, then realized she was concerned about spoiling the nightgown. He drew it back and covered her up.

"I'm cold, darling. Please get me another blanket."

He brought a spare blanket from the chest and spread it over her.

"The pain's gone for now," she said. "I thought I was coming apart. They always say this is worse than having a baby. I hope it is." She turned her head away. "I'm so sorry, darling. Nothing seems to go right for us."

"I know, but it's not your fault."

"I shouldn't have tried to walk up here."

"Don't fret yourself. It's this country, it's not you." He brushed the tears from her cheeks.

Suddenly she clenched her fingers. "There again, oh, Amos."

She snatched at his hand and he watched her body heave as she went away from him in her pain. He was overwhelmed with a feeling of helplessness because there was nothing he could do for her and her suffering seemed so cruel and unnecessary. He felt that someone, something, should be called to account for it. She did not deserve it; she had no debt to a cruel world or a harsh God, and it was an evil thing for which there was no excuse.

He was not aware how long it continued. He had given up hope of the doctor arriving. He did what he could, changed the bloody towels and folded them over the dead baby and put wadded sheets under Joan and raised her hips on pillows and tried to stop the bleeding which came in gushes while she moaned and sank her teeth into the covers. As she grew paler and weaker, he realized that he might not be able to do enough for her, and her life might drain away while he remained helpless to stop it. To himself, he cursed Whichertown and the remoteness of the farm and the storm's icy wind. He blamed himself for her being here in the little house among the mountains. But that was all beyond changing and there remained the fact of her suffering and fading away.

The room was cold and he went into the kitchen and put wood on the fire. The clock showed eleven-thirty. And then outside he heard the thud of horses' hoofs and sled runners creaking. From the window he saw a lantern beside a figure approaching the house. He went to the door.

Doc Parsons came in, with Marvin behind him. Doc said nothing but set his bag on the kitchen table and took off his frozen coat and cap. He glanced around and went at once to the bedroom. Amos followed him. With one hand on Joan's pulse, Doc lifted the blankets. After a moment he faced about and looked at the towels on the floor.

"Did she pass it?"

Amos nodded.

Doc went into the kitchen and took off his suit coat and the sweater he wore under it. He rolled up his shirt sleeves. From the sink, as he washed, he said, "Get me a basin of hot water, Amos."

There was the smell of antiseptic as Doc poured liquid from a bottle into the basin.

"Bring that rubber sheet, Amos. You, Marvin, stoke up the fire."

Amos went with him into the bedroom. Doc pulled on his rubber gloves. He looked tired but his hands were steady.

"Now, my girl," he said quietly, "you're going to be all right."

While Doc worked, Amos held Joan's hand and tried not to look at the rubber sheet. Joan cried out and pressed his fingers to her mouth. He smoothed back her hair and wiped her face with the corner of a towel.

At last Doc said, "That's all. Now we'll fix you up for a good rest, my girl. Amos here will get you some hot bricks and we'll warm you and everything's going to be hunky-dory."

Joan lay exhausted under the covers as Amos tucked her in with the warm bricks wrapped in cloths. She didn't seem to go to sleep but drifted off into a weak unconsciousness. Doc sat by the bed with his hand on her wrist. Amos returned to the kitchen where he made coffee. Marvin sat near the stove smoking his pipe. Sleet brushed across the windows.

Doc and Marvin stayed all night. Toward morning, Doc came from the bedroom and stood for a time at a window.

Amos asked, "How is she, Doc?"

"Weak," he answered.

Marvin snored quietly in his chair by the stove. Doc turned.

"She ought to be in the hospital. She needs a transfusion."

"I'm ready any time, Doc."

"Yes, yes, but there's more to it than that." He went to the window again. "I hate to move her. Maybe later today." He walked across the kitchen and back. "Where's your phone?"

"At the other house, but it don't work."

"Line's down, I suppose." Doc went to Marvin and gently shook him. "I'm staying here, Marvin. You go home and call Lije Willis, or if your phone's out of order, go find him."

Marvin yawned. "He'll be working on the road somewhere."

"Yes, I know, but get hold of him and tell him he has to come in here with a truck load of sand. Then call Harry Remington and tell him to get up here with his ambulance when Lije has the road sanded. We've got to take this girl out of here today."

"Sure, Doc." Marvin was still sleepy, but he stood up. "Lije and Harry. I see." He moved to his coat hanging behind the stove. "That all?"

"Yes, if you've got it straight."

"I have."

Amos went out with Marvin to the woodshed and helped him take the blankets from the team. They hitched the horses to the sled. The sleet had changed to rain. Amos shivered as the damp air struck through his jacket. There was a streak of light in the east. Marvin drove down the road and Amos went back into the house.

## Chapter 36

Slowly the gray morning passed. Amos went to the barn and did the chores. He came back and made breakfast for himself and Doc, although he could scarcely force himself to eat the bacon and eggs. He was painfully aware of Joan in the bedroom and life seemed to have come to a stop in the little house.

Doc looked up from his coffee. "Take it easy, Amos. These things happen."

"Don't seem necessary." Amos got to his feet and stood in front of the stove. "What about the baby, Doc?"

"Harry and I'll tend to everything." He looked at the clock. "They ought to be here soon."

Amos went into the bedroom. Joan's face was pale, encircled by her brown hair. He did not know whether she slept or lay unconscious. He changed to his suit and waited in the kitchen.

At last he saw the town truck come along the road with Lije driving and Jake shoveling sand from the back. Harry Remington's ambulance-hearse followed, and Amos realized its last trip to Whichertown had been to bring Mort to the cemetery.

With Doc superintending, they moved Joan to a stretcher and carried her to the ambulance. She smiled wanly at him, but was too weak to say anything, and then she closed her eyes. Doc got in back with her.

"Amos, you ride with Harry."

"I think I ought to stay with Joan."

"Well, all right. Get in. Harry, take it easy now."

"Sure, Doc." Harry's lean face was sober.

Jake came to the door. "I'll fix it up with Marvin to do the chores, Amos."

"Thanks, Jake. Don't know when I can get back."

The door closed and Amos settled himself on the floor of the ambulance as Harry drove slowly down the road. He could look out the window over Joan's blanketed form to the slopes of Cobblestone where the clouds were beginning to lift. The house appeared small and deserted, vanishing behind the bare branches of the trees.

The ambulance rolled over the bridge across Carr Brook and began the slow descent of Footstep Hill. The chains ground into the sanded ice of the road, sliding a little while Amos caught his breath. He saw the beach wagon in a woods road where Lije and Jake must have put it. And then they were down the hill and after a time began to move faster on the main road. The chains blended their crunching into a steady hum. Joan did not move as Doc examined her and put back the blankets. He nodded at Amos, and said to Joan, "You're doing fine."

Amos dozed, sitting up, and felt a weariness through all his body while at the same time his mind projected itself toward Fallsburg and the hospital and Joan safe and well. He hardly noticed the familiar road but seemed to return to his senses as the ambulance turned into a drive past the brick building with the many windows, and stopped under a porch at the rear.

He opened the ambulance door and got out and waited beside Doc as white-coated orderlies came and slid out the stretcher and disappeared with it down the yellow corridor. Doc followed. A nurse walked toward him after stopping to speak to Doc. Amos saw that she was young and freckled.

"This way, please."

He followed her into a little room, uneasy that Joan had been taken away. The nurse smiled. "We'll just type your blood and see if you can be a helpful husband." After she had taken the sample, she went away and he was left alone in the room with the metal table and the yellow walls, sitting in a chair and looking at the floor. When the nurse came back, she led him down the corridor to an office. "You're not her type," she said in a joking tone. "But it's all right, there are other donors. Miss Wickham here will help you with the forms and there's a waiting room across the hall."

He answered the questions of the blond girl behind the desk and then went into the waiting room where he picked up a magazine and turned the pages for a while before he put it down and stepped to the window. He looked out at the wet snow and the gray sky over the buildings of Fallsburg. There was a white house beyond the hospital grounds. Two little boys were sliding down the backyard on a sled. He could see them laugh as they slipped on the ice and struggled back up the terrace. They looked excited and happy in their snowsuits. One had a red scarf around his neck. Finally they left the sled and went into the house.

The hill back of the new house in Whichertown would have been a good place to slide. He turned from the window and sat again in a chair.

The freckled nurse came into the waiting room.

"You can see her now," she said.

He followed the nurse to an elevator and they were lifted up two flights and the door opened on a corridor. They went past a nurse at a desk, past half-closed doors and another nurse walking quickly in her starched white uniform.

He entered a room where Joan lay in bed. Doc stood beside her and a strange young doctor was at the foot of the bed. He went to her and her eyes brightened. He put his hand on her arm, touching the coarse white bedgown.

She whispered, "My poor darling, you must be tired out."

"No. How are you feeling?"

"Fine. They say I'm almost as good as new." She smiled up at him.

He looked at Doc while a vast feeling of relief passed through him.

Doc said, "Just a question of time, Amos. She's getting along nicely." Then he went on slowly, "Well, I've got to go. This is Dr. Williamson, Amos. Are you going to stay here, or go back with Harry and me? Joan will be all right."

"I'll stay."

"Good enough. Of course you understand she'll be here quite a spell? She can't go back to Whichertown until she's strong."

"Yes."

The doctors went out with the nurse and he and Joan were left alone. He didn't know what to say, and could only sit in the chair near her and take her hand. He found that he could not think of his life or of the farm and Whichertown in any future sequence. He felt that he had been cut loose from all his past and from all the plans and dreams of living there with Joan. It was as though he had no foundation under him and he knew an empty loneliness which was beyond remedy. But Joan was well and that was all that mattered. He would not again subject her to life in Whichertown.

She said, "You'll have to get back to the farm, Amos."

"Marvin is looking after things."

"You can go, you know. I'm all right. They'll take care of me."

"I want to be here." He looked at her slim hand. "I don't think I'll be going back—not for good."

"What do you mean?"

"I'm through with Whichertown. I don't know what I'll do, but I'll find work somehow and take care of you. We won't go back to the farm to live. I've had enough of it, you have, we both have."

"But, Amos. . . ."

"No, don't talk about it."

She sighed. "I guess you must love me, Amos, but I don't see how you can."

"Well, I do."

She closed her eyes. "You better get a room at the hotel and have some rest. I'm afraid I'm going to go to sleep."

He bent over to kiss her and she fell asleep almost at once. He sat for a time beside her and then got wearily to his feet and went down the hall to tell the nurse he was leaving but would be back in the evening. He found his way to the front door and walked out to the street. He noticed that the wind had shifted to the west. In Whichertown the clouds would be breaking up and tomorrow there'd be sun glistening on the icy trees and wind rattling the branches while ice fell to the crusted snow. He turned down the street and tried to empty his mind and rearrange himself in accord with the city surroundings. He felt like a stranger, walking toward the center of Fallsburg.

## Chapter 37

Amos stayed for two weeks at the hotel. Afternoons and evenings he spent at the hospital with Joan. As her strength slowly returned, they talked about what to do and where to live. Amos had no interest in the future and he let Joan do most of the talking. With his decision made against returning to Whichertown, he seemed to have entered into a condition of suspension and stagnation, in which he was merely able to exist. When Joan suggested they find an apartment in Fallsburg, he agreed to look around.

Each day before he went to the hospital, he walked the streets of the city until he was familiar with it, from the shanties and tenements along the river to the tree-lined streets of big houses back on the hill. When he saw a sign, "Apartment to Rent," in the window of a house, he would go in and look at it, but the idea of living in two or three rooms of another man's house was so far beyond the grasp of his imagination that he could only shake his head to the owner and go back to the street. It was not until Joan had left the hospital, and he had taken her in a cab to see some of the apartments, that he began to realize he was actually going to live in Fallsburg.

Joan liked a three-room apartment on a quiet side street above the city. It was in a big house which had been built for a single family.

"Kitchen, bedroom, and living room," Joan said. "All we'll need, and there's lots of sunlight in the living room."

She glanced about at the high ceilings. "It may be hard to heat. Amos, you go down cellar and look at the furnace."

Amos followed the little gray man who owned the house. Because he'd never seen a furnace before, he had no way to tell what it could do.

"It's a good system," the little man said. "I never have complaints about the heat."

"The rooms aren't very warm now."

"No. You see I've shut off some of the radiators because nobody's living in it."

"Well, I guess it's all right."

The next day he took the morning train north and walked from the station across the covered bridge to Lije Willis' garage. He saw the Tarlton beach wagon.

Lije waved a greasy hand at it. "I brought her down here. Didn't seem she ought to be left out in the woods."

"Much obliged. Can I rent your truck?"

"Sure, Amos."

"We're moving to Fallsburg."

"No. For good?"

Amos nodded.

Lije wiped his hands on a rag. "Can't say I blame you. Whichertown's a poor place, to my mind."

It was so many other things to Amos that he did not reply.

Driving alone into the hills, he found that the old feeling of going home came back to him and he fought it off. He looked at the snowy fields and woods along the road and thought how well he knew them all, but he refused to let his mind dwell on them.

He stopped at the Hostetters'. When Mrs. Hostetter opened the door and he stepped into the warm kitchen with its smell of cooking and the faint underlying odors of woodsmoke and barn, he knew again the old sensation of security and familiar surroundings from which he had been gone for two long weeks. But again he dared not give himself up to it.

Marvin lifted his lean frame from a chair and knocked out his pipe in the stove. "Well, I suppose you're coming back to the farm. I've just been up doing the chores. How's Joan?"

"She's all right, but we're not coming back."

"What's that?"

"We've decided to move to Fallsburg."

Marvin asked slowly, "How about the farm?"

"Well, I've written Pa and we're going to sell off the stock. And Marvin, I'd like you to have Drum."

"Thank you, Amos. I can use a good fox hound." Marvin rubbed his pipe in his big hands and stared at the floor. "It don't seem right there won't be Jackmans in Whichertown."

"Maybe not, but there ain't going to be any."

Marvin sighed. "I suppose you have had a run of bad luck."

"Had enough, I guess. Can you come up and help me load the furniture?"

"I reckon."

"And, Marvin, there's some logs I cut, over in the pines beyond the sugar orchard. I don't like to think of them rotting in the woods. They're yours if you want to yard 'em out."

"I'll do that, Amos. Likely you'll have an auction next summer?"

"I shouldn't wonder."

The thought of all the things on the farm—tools and plows and furniture he had known and used since birth—the thought of their being sold at auction appalled him, but after the first shock of the idea, he felt anxious to get rid of them. He did not need them now. All he wanted was the furniture for the apartment in Fallsburg.

"Can you go now, Marvin?"

"Sure."

The road had been plowed after the snow which had fallen since the sleet storm, and the truck climbed steadily between white banks into Whichertown. After the stock was sold, Lije wouldn't plow the road, and the snow would drift in almost level and unbroken except for the tracks of rabbits and foxes. There would be nobody in Whichertown for whom to open the road. The Jackmans would be gone, except those in the cemetery, and they had no need of a road.

Amos steered past the walled cemetery and stopped by the barway to the new house.

They had to shovel out the snow to get the truck to the door.

He went inside. It had been cleaned and looked ready to live in.

Marvin said, "I brought Myra up and she fixed things a little."

"You done a lot for us, Marvin."

"Nothing much."

"We'll straighten it out when I sell the stock."

"Any time, Amos."

Loading the furniture did not take long. Amos packed dishes and clothes in boxes. When only the stove and sink were left, he went out and locked the door. It seemed like an empty gesture, for no one would be here in Whichertown to bother the place.

As they got into the cab of the truck, Marvin asked, "Anything you want down to the old house?"

"No, there's nothing I want."

"Take a look at the stock?"

"No, I'll be heading back to Fallsburg."

He started the engine. Without another glance at the little house or at the woods and mountains to the east, he let out the clutch and drove into the road and held his eyes straight ahead. He did not want to look back.

That afternoon, he and Joan moved from the hotel to the apartment. Joan was tired, and when he had set up the bed, she lay down.

She said, "I didn't get any food. I wasn't sure we'd be here today. I've been busy having the electricity turned on and buying an electric stove and refrigerator and getting the phone in. And now I've collapsed. I guess I'm not very rugged yet." She raised herself on one elbow and looked around the bedroom and past him toward the kitchen. "But isn't it nice to have all this?"

"Yes, sure," he answered. "I'll go out and buy something for supper."

"There's a store down on the corner. I'd like a steak. And Amos, I did get us a bottle. It's in the kitchen cupboard."

"I'll make you a drink."

He went into the kitchen and poured whiskey into a glass and then opened the new refrigerator. The little wooden one they'd had at the farm, for ice, was still on the truck parked in the drive. Tomorrow he'd sell it at the secondhand store outside Fallsburg on his way north to return the truck to Lije and get the beach wagon.

Holding open the door of the new refrigerator, he looked at the shelves and at the white enamel inside.

Joan called to him from the bedroom. "The ice is in trays above there. You pry out the cubes with the little gadget I left on the table."

He fixed the drink and when he had taken it to Joan he poured himself some and swallowed it straight.

He put on his coat and went outside. The street lights were on, throwing shadows across the snow as he went down the porch steps and along the sidewalk. He could feel grit under his feet and realized there was sand on the packed snow. He walked by houses with lighted windows and the people moving about inside. He was aware of the quiet hum of the city, of people close together in houses all around him. He heard a car horn down on Main Street.

At the store on the corner, he bought steak and potatoes and milk and bacon and eggs and coffee and sugar, and oranges for Joan. The money in his pocketbook would not last forever and neither would the money in the bank, Joan's money. While the clerk was putting the groceries in a bag, he thought of work. He had never worked for wages and he did not know how to look for a job. He supposed work was scarce. Everyone said times were hard.

He continued to think about it as he returned to the apartment and cooked the supper of fried potatoes and steak. With a drink on the kitchen table, he moved about the strange little kitchen alone and wondered where he could find work.

Joan came from the bedroom in her dressing gown, yawning. She wrinkled her nose. "Smells good, darling. It woke me up."

They ate at the table on dishes from the half-unpacked boxes.

"Amos, what's today?"

"Tuesday, I guess."

"I mean the date."

"I couldn't say."

Joan lit a cigarette. "I think Mother and Dad get into San Francisco tomorrow. I wrote them there, so probably they'll call us right off, all excited." She laughed. "I'm very fond of them."

"They've been away a long time."

"Doesn't it seem like a long while?" Joan pushed back her chair. "Now you go sit in the living room while I do the dishes. We've got to get a radio. That's one thing I did miss at the farm."

Early in the evening, Joan went to bed, but Amos sat up late, feeling a tired restlessness which stirred him like a caged animal. When he finally undressed and lay down beside Joan, he couldn't sleep. He was thinking of Whichertown, not of the recent times but of other years, and it was so vivid that he might be walking again across the fields or climbing from pool to pool on Carr Brook with a fish rod in his hand. The scenes came back to him against his will, for he knew that the Whichertown of his dreams was no more, that he should reject the earlier memories and recall what had happened to him there in the past months, what had happened to Joan and his family. Yet he could not shut the old scenes from his mind and at last gave himself up to them. He was hunting again through the familiar woods, or gathering sap in the sugar orchard, wading through the deep snow with the yoke on his shoulders weighted by the full buckets. He lived at the cabin on the pond, he worked about the farm. All the seasons and all the changing days came back to him.

They continued to haunt him every night. During the two weeks when he looked for work, walking from one mill office to another, applying at contractors as a carpenter, watching the newspaper while he became more and more discouraged, the memories came back to him at night and he found that he looked forward to them because they made his life bearable.

He arranged for the sale of the cattle and horses on the farm. He paid Marvin Hostetter. The return to Whichertown to do these things was a dead event, unconnected with the memories and dreams at night.

The Tarltons arrived from the West and stayed a few days, putting up at the hotel. Joan was pleased and gay, talking with them about the trip.

One evening her father remarked, "You kids better move to Boston. I can help you more there." He glanced about the little apartment. "This will do temporarily but you'll want something better. I can find a spot for Amos in the business and help out till he has a chance to learn the ropes. How about it?"

Joan looked doubtfully at Amos.

He said, "Thanks, Mr. Tarlton. I guess I better stay here."

"Any prospects?"

"No, but I'll find something. I'm grateful, and all, but I'd feel better on my own."

Joan nodded. "I think Amos is right. Thanks a lot, though, Dad."

Tarlton shrugged. "As you wish. Tell you what, before we leave for Florida, I'll take Amos over to the Fallsburg Machine and Tool Company. Used to know the superintendent in Boston."

The Monday after the Tarltons left to spend the rest of the winter in Florida, Amos started work on a drill press in the machine shop of the Fallsburg Machine and Tool Company. Rapidly days passed into weeks, and weeks into months while he drove himself to learn the machinist's trade. It did not come easy to him for he didn't have Mort's mechanical ability and at times the spindles of his drill press seemed like prison bars and he hated the noise and closed-in air and smell of oil. He was more tired in the evenings than from a day's work in the woods and he wanted only a drink or two and supper, and his dreams. Even after Joan was well again, he did not return to her completely at night for he longed to lie back and think of Whichertown.

One day in late spring, when the leaves of the trees along the streets had opened out and a warm breeze blew in the windows of the machine shop, Amos looked up from the casting he was clamping in a jig. His foreman stopped by the drill press and said in his abrupt way, "The super wants you in his office."

There had been talk of a layoff and Amos supposed he was the first to go, but because of the Tarltons the super thought he ought to break the news himself. He took off his apron and walked down the lines of drill presses and milling machines to the wash bowls against the wall where he washed his hands.

The super, heavy in his chair behind the blueprints and jigs on his desk, was talking to a tall man in flannels and a sport jacket.

"Amos, this is Mr. Shadworth. Amos Jackman."

Amos shook hands and waited for the older man to speak.

[ 279 ]

"Greg Tarlton—old friend of mine—suggested you might be interested in selling your farm. I went up there yesterday. Beautiful location."

"I guess it is." Amos realized he didn't know what to say about the farm. As long as it was Jackman property, he had been attached to it somehow and he couldn't quite set his mind to giving it up, even,if Pa was willing. "Roads poor," he said.

Mr. Shadworth smiled. "I know, but that's not too important. I'm just looking for a summer place."

"I see. There's some land and a cabin out on a pond."

"Greg told me. Does that go with the place?"

Amos nodded slowly. "Yes, I suppose it does."

"Would you be interested in selling?"

"We might. I'd have to find out what Pa thinks."

"All right," Mr. Shadworth said briskly. "Do that, will you? I'll call you in a few days." He took a memorandum book from his jacket pocket.

Amos gave him his address and phone number, shook hands and went back to his drill press, feeling weak and sad, but certain what he should do.

That evening he wrote Pa. A few days later the answer came.

Amos read the letter when he got back from work, putting his dinner pail on the table and opening the envelope with his jackknife.

Dear Son,

Go ahead and sell the place, if you've a mind to. I guess the Jackmans are done with it. . . .

There were more details, about selling the tools, about Gram's share, about himself and Rose. At last Amos put the letter on the table and sat down and stared at his hands. Joan came and picked up the letter and then leaned over and kissed him.

"My poor Amos. I'm so sorry. It doesn't seem fair when I like it so much here. Do you want to move back?"

"No," he said. "There's nothing in Whichertown for us."

"I'll go back with you."

"Sure you would." He stood up and kissed her. "But the old days are gone and we'll make out here. Well, when it's all settled, I ain't ever going back. I should hate to see the fields grown up to woods."

Two weeks later, Mr. Shadworth owned the farm. It was easy, Amos learned, to sell a place if someone wanted to buy it—easy to dispose of property which had been Jackman for almost two hundred years.

On Sunday he took Mr. Shadworth over the boundaries, along the walls he had mended and through the woods to the piled stones marking the corners on the slopes of Cobblestone. The woods had leafed out and there were ferns and flowers underfoot. In the afternoon he walked with Mr. Shadworth out to the pond and cabin, returning as the sun set and the shadows crept among the mountains. He drove back to Fallsburg alone.

That night he dreamed of Whichertown again, lying half asleep beside Joan while the night sounds of the city went on outside the house. But now in his mind the fields of the farm were grown to tall grass and hardhack and the pines were coming in, small green trees scattered from the edges of the woods, growing rapidly in the uncut fields. There were cars around the old house and guests in the new house which he had built with Mort and Whicher for Joan, and people in chairs under the maple, but none of them knew how it used to be—only he and Rose and Pa and Gram, and in time only he and Rose and then nobody would know.

Slowly he came wide awake and lay still for a moment before he got out of bed. By the faint glow from the street lights outside, he made his way to the kitchen. At last he felt free. He was aware that he had accepted the change of the farm and Whichertown from the present to the past. He thought of them with diminishing regret, for that's how things were, and he almost smiled to himself as he switched on the light. He went to the sink and filled a glass with water from the faucet. He remembered the old barrel and the ever-running water of the lead pipe in the farm kitchen. Someday he would tell his sons and daughters about them.

He heard Joan's voice from the bedroom. "Amos," she called. "Are you all right?"

"Yes, I'm fine." He put out the light.